Good Material

Those baby names included: Noah, Blue (?) and Zebedee.

Snob. Once said that she thought people who wear straw hats at the airport on the way to their summer holiday are 'regional'.

Lingered too long in museums at every artefact or painting and would have a go at me if I walked through the exhibition too quickly.

Once saw her nod respectfully at a TINY JADE SPOON in the British Museum.

Only saw her cry a handful of times in nearly four years together and it wasn't when we broke up.

One time was when we were watching a Joni Mitchell documentary.

Ruined my life.

Goes to therapy every week and has done since she was twenty-nine but would never tell me what they spoke about and I've never seen that she has anything wrong with her.

Was too connected to dogs and spoke to them as if they were people.

Her rude dad.

Her weird mum.

Comes from a family who go on long circular walks and play board games.

Annoyingly loquacious and was on a debating team at her school, which meant I didn't win an argument in nearly four years even when I was right about loads of them.

Always on at me about biting my nails, picking my feet, too much hair in my nostrils and bum hole etc., despite the fact she's always fiddling with her cuticles.

Talked at the cinema.

Pretended she's unsure about wanting children because she cares about the planet, but I think she just didn't want children with me.

Would never talk seriously about having children, despite knowing how much I want to be a dad, but would some-times say 'That's one of my baby names' to people in conversation.

but would never know why she'd be offered an OBE in this fantasy when I asked her.

Would definitely never reject an OBE if it were offered to her.

Would take an hour to go to bed, no matter what time she got in, because she'd do a seven-step skincare routine, browse shopping apps and listen to podcasts. And yet only left twenty minutes from her alarm going off to having to leave the flat in the morning.

Always late for me, never late for work.

Can't drive (childish).

Somehow managed to relate the plot of every film we watched back to her own life.

Her unbearable sister Miranda who carries nonsensical home-made signs at protests saying things like HISTORY IS WATCHING and who I know hates me because she always ranted about 'straight white guys' when she came round for dinner, no matter the topic. She used to say 'Sorry, Andy' but didn't by the end.

Her work friends: boring and cliquey and not fun *or* funny.

All talk about being some big adventurer but never followed through. Wanted to take a year off to travel because she never had a gap year ('next year'). Wanted to move to Paris ('not the right time'). Wanted to get an undercut ('work wouldn't like it'). Wanted to go to an outdoor sex-themed rave ('when my hay fever gets better').

Reasons Why It's Good I'm Not With Jen

Can't dance. Has no rhythm at all. Used to find it adorable until I saw people laughing at her and hate to say I was embarrassed.

Once overheard her say 'Let's grab a cappuccino some time and we'll talk' to my teenage cousin who wanted advice about his university applications.

Generally has quite nineties ideas about what is glamorous, like cocktails or spending twenty pounds on a plate of tagliatelle in a 'little place'.

Refuses to get to the airport a minute earlier than ninety minutes before a flight takes off.

Don't have to persuade her to like where we live any more.

When she would go for a run in the evening she would come into the living room, stretch in front of the TV and say 'What's this?' and make me explain the programme I was watching even though she knew what it was, just to make a point that she was exercising while I was watching *Help, I'm a Hoarder!*

Talked too much and too smugly about coming from a big family, as if it was her decision to have three siblings.

Always used to boast about how she'd reject an OBE if it were offered to her because of her apparent lefty republican values

Summer 2019

I expect you've seen the footage: elephants,
finding the bones of one of their own kind
dropped by the wayside, picked clean by scavengers
and the sun, then untidily left there,
decide to do something about it.

But what, exactly? They can't, of course,
reassemble the old elephant magnificence;
they can't even make a tidier heap. But they can
hook up bones with their trunks and chuck them
this way and that way. So they do.

And their scattering has an air
of deliberate ritual, ancient and necessary.
Their great size, too, makes them the very
embodiment of grief, while the play of their trunks
lends sprezzatura.

Elephants puzzling out
the anagram of their own anatomy,
elephants at their abstracted lamentations —
may their spirit guide me as I place
my own sad thoughts in new, hopeful arrangements.

— A Scattering, Christopher Reid

For Lauren Bensted, queen of my heart

FIG TREE

UK | USA | Canada | Ireland | Australia
India | New Zealand | South Africa

Fig Tree is part of the Penguin Random House group of companies
whose addresses can be found at global.penguinrandomhouse.com.

First published 2023
001

Set in 12/14.75pt Bembo Book MT Pro
Typeset by Jouve (UK), Milton Keynes
Printed and bound in Great Britain by Clays Ltd, Elcograf S.p.A.

The authorized representative in the EEA is Penguin Random House Ireland,
Morrison Chambers, 32 Nassau Street, Dublin D02 YH68

A CIP catalogue record for this book is available from the British Library

Hardback ISBN: 978–0–241–52366–7
Trade paperback ISBN: 978–0–241–52367–4

www.greenpenguin.co.uk

MIX
Paper | Supporting
responsible forestry
FSC® C018179

Penguin Random House is committed to a
sustainable future for our business, our readers
and our planet. This book is made from Forest
Stewardship Council® certified paper.

Good Material

DOLLY ALDERTON

FIG TREE
an imprint of
PENGUIN BOOKS

Friday 5th July 2019

There is a jumper and a shirt hanging on the washing line in my mum's garden that look like they're holding hands in the breeze. I stand at my bedroom window and watch their interplay change with the direction of the wind. I watch until exactly 7.03 p.m., when I pick up the phone to the woman I've loved for three years, ten months and twenty-nine days, who dumped me and smashed my heart like a sinewy piñata eight days and twenty-two hours ago.

We agreed I would call at seven but I wait until three minutes past to make a point that she doesn't get to call the shots any more. I scroll to her name in my phonebook: Jen (Hammersmith). We found it funny – my chosen life partner, reduced to a borough. It's not funny now it's lost all its irony. It's just a fact. I am about to call Jen (Hammersmith), a woman who I would probably never be friends with, who lives in a part of London I would never visit.

'Hello?'

'Hey,' I say, my voice breaking like a bagpipe. 'It's Andy.'

'I know.'

'Have you deleted my number already?'

'No? Why would I delete your number?'

'I don't know, just the way you picked up the phone and said "Hello?" like that, so formally, like you're answering the phone at a dental practice.'

'I didn't say "Hello?", I said "Hello!"'

'No you didn't, you said it like a question, like you were unsure of who was ringing.'

'I knew you were ringing. We agreed on the time.'

'I just thought because I was ringing later than we planned . . .'

'We said seven,' she says brightly. 'And I know your number anyway.'

'Why?'

'Because at the beginning I used to delete your number all the time, so I ended up accidentally memorizing it.'

I think back to the conversation we had a few months into our relationship, straight after we told each other we loved each other for the first time. She admitted she used to delete my number after every time I texted, so she didn't see my name on her phone and obsess over when I was going to message again. I don't understand how this is happening. I want to go back there. How do they time-travel in the films? I'll do anything. Fall from a great height. Electrocute myself. Go into a cupboard and spin around ten times. I suppress a sob and it sounds like a hiccup.

'Oh, Andy,' she says.

'I'm fine,' I say, honking like a bagpipe again. 'How's Miranda's?'

'It's okay. The spare room is where the baby sleeps now, so I'm in the living room on a blow-up mattress, but it's all right.'

'Are you surrounded by placards that say "History is Watching"?'

'No, I'm not,' she says. One of our favourite jokes, extinguished along with our relationship. We were only allowed to make it when we were in cahoots; when we were so close that her family felt like my family, even though they drove me mad. But she'd crossed over now. I'm not her family any more, we are no longer playing for the same team. I am just a man from the Midlands who she would probably never be friends with, being rude about her sister.

'How's your mum?' she asks.

'She's fine, she hates you, her Zumba class are plotting your death.' Another arctic pause. 'She's devastated, obviously.'

'Can I write her a letter? Then I won't contact her again, I promise. I just want to say goodbye.'

'She'd like that. She adores you.'

'I've never met a mum like your mum.'

'I adore you.' More silence. I take a cigarette out of my pocket and light it.

'Are you smoking?'

'Yeah.'

'Don't, Andy, you worked so hard to give up.'

'Don't care,' I snap, hoping I sound like a romantic outlaw. I inhale and feel the peculiar comfort of my lungs tightening.

'I've started again as well. I might have one if you're having one.' I hear her rummage around in her handbag. 'It's weird, being here. Sleeping on the floor. Smoking and drinking as much as I want. Not seeing anyone. It sort of feels like Christmas.'

'Like *Christmas*?'

'Yeah. Just, like, my world has stopped for a bit.' I stay silent. 'You know what I mean.'

'No I don't, actually. Because it feels like the opposite of Christmas to me.'

'What's the *opposite* of Christmas?'

'I don't know. Easter? The worst birthday ever? My own fucking funeral except I'm alive at it?'

'Andy – can we try to avoid the hysteria? I know this is awful for you, it's awful for me too. But people break up all the time.'

'Stop saying that! Stop referring to "people breaking up" like we're a YouGov poll or a vox pop.' My pride stops me from saying what I actually want to say, which is that 'people break up all the time' is a sentiment that only comforts the person ending the relationship. They're not in love any more and they don't want to feel guilty about it – I know because I've said it myself. I didn't realize what a useless statement it is to the person being dumped.

'My therapist suggested I do something this week that I found helpful, and I think you'd find it helpful too.'

'Your therapist suggested that I "write a letter to my ego", so I'm sorry if I'm not gagging to hear whatever she advised.'

'Do you want to hear it or not?'

'Go on.'

'She said that at the end of a relationship, it's useful to write a list of reasons of why it's good you're no longer together.'

'I can't write that list because I want us to be together.'

'I don't think you do.'

'I do, that's all I want.'

'Try writing this list. I think it will help you separate the fantasy of us from the reality of us, which I think you know deep down wasn't working.'

'I can't believe you're being so clinical,' I say. 'I've never heard you talk like this before.'

'I'm just trying to help us both move on.'

'Whatever. No point discussing it any further.' I can't find my footing in this conversation – I lurch from desperation to indifference. I want her to know how much I love her and I also want her to think that I don't care about our relationship any more. I don't know what the desired outcome is. I wish I hadn't had three beers. 'I don't think these phone calls are helping us,' I say.

'Neither do I.'

'Maybe we should agree to not speak for a while.'

'If that's what you want,' she says.

'It is what I want.'

'Okay,' she says, taking a deep drag of her cigarette. 'Have you told Avi yet?'

'No.'

'*Andy.*'

'I'll tell him when I'm ready. Please. I'd like to have a tiny bit of a say in this break-up.'

'Who are you talking to?'

'You're the only person I can talk to about this stuff,' I say, revolted by the baldness of my own love. 'Please make sure Jane doesn't tell him before I do.'

'She's sworn she won't, but she can't keep it up much longer,' she says. 'He's your best friend. He can help you process this.'

'We don't work like that, Jen, but thanks.' There is a pause that I wait for her to fill. She doesn't. 'So goodbye, then, I suppose,' I say with weary cheer. 'And we'll just text if we need to talk about flat stuff or whatever.'

'Yeah, sure,' she says softly. 'Look after yourself.'

'I love you, Jen.' I can hear her considering the risks of saying this back to me, her therapist on her shoulder saying things about codependency and boundaries.

'Lots of love,' she replies.

I hang up.

Mum comes in with two mugs and I throw my cigarette out of the window.

'I thought you only smoked when you drank,' she says, placing one mug on my bedside table and sitting on the edge of the bed cradling the other.

'I've had three drinks and it's not even eight.'

'That's all right, given the circumstances.'

I sit next to her and pick up a mug that has *I Support Aston Villa and This is the Only Cup I'll Be Getting This Year!* emblazoned on its front in burgundy Courier New.

'This tea tastes of marzipan.'

'I put some Disaronno in it,' she says.

I put my arm around her and she leans into me and smells my T-shirt.

'Do I stink of fags?'

'Yes,' she says, putting her face into my shoulder. 'God, it's good.'

'Jen wants to write you a letter. I've said she can. Hope that's okay.'

She nods. 'I love Jen.'

'More than me?'

She considers this. 'A *bit* more than you. She bought me lovely candles.'

'Fair enough.'

She gets up from the bed and walks over to the blue and silver CD player, its hardware scratched from decades of use. She picks up a case and takes the CD out.

'You can stay here for as long as you want, you know. I love having you here.'

'Thanks, Mum.' A tinkling sound and a surge of strings warm the room. 'What's this you've put on?'

'*In the Wee Small Hours*. The best break-up album of all time.' She returns to sit next to me. 'Listen to it every day until you feel better. I listened to it non-stop when your dad left.'

I imagine my mum feeling like this while I was a newborn baby, unable to make her tea or put my arm around her or play her albums. She pats me on the back and heaves herself up in that way she does since she turned sixty. I'm instantly comforted by Frank Sinatra's voice, the sound of every December. The kind of voice that lets you believe in an alternate world of luxury and elegance and romance and string orchestras.

'It feels like Christmas,' I say.

'Good!' she says cheerfully, closing the door behind her.

I walk to the window and stare out at the washing line. The sleeves take turns to reach out to each other as they dance in the air. Everything is a sign since she left. Everything is another clue to help me understand what's happening.

I think about our first kiss on her front doorstep.

I think about our first argument and our last argument and every argument in between.

I think about the first birthday presents we bought each other.

I think about her top lip and the mole on her side and the way her nose seems to change shape with every angle she turns it towards.

I think about the first night we spent in our flat together: lugging her across the threshold, empty rooms, Thai food, too much red wine, a drunk argument about the need for a magazine rack, a giggly fuck on the floor.

I think about the first six months we shared a bed and how she would fall asleep on my chest with my arms around her and we would wake up in exactly the same position.

I think about the shape we made in our sleep when we were comfortable. Backs to each other, bums touching.

I think about the first time I made her laugh and how that sound will always be the most satisfying noise in the world to me, even better than the laughter of an audience.

I think of the possibility that I will never hear her laugh again, never buy her a birthday present, never guess what she wants from the takeaway menu, never hear her secrets or kiss the petals of her eyelids.

I take a photo on my phone of the jumper and the shirt in case I forget what it feels like to be loved. I close the curtains and get into the bed I've been sleeping in since I was a little boy. And I cry and cry and cry and cry.

Monday 27th July 2015

Thirty-first birthday parties were better than the thirtieths. The thirtieths had too much symbolism. Symbolism is good for a story but bad for a party. But by thirty-one, we knew where we were. One hangover a week, merino knitwear, DIY, IPA – the early thirties.

It was Jane's birthday, the girlfriend of my best friend. They'd been together for two years, she was pregnant with their first baby and I'd finally got the official promotion to birthday drinks attendee. The pub was in a Zone One no-man's-land – the result of coordinating twenty-five people's locations and travel times and babysitters' costs. You end up with a place where nobody would ever normally socialize.

'ANDY!' Avi shouted as I walked into the pub, sparsely populated with people I didn't recognize. 'BRINGER OF VIBES, HAVER OF FAGS.'

'Y'alright, mate?' I said.

'Fags! Fags! Fags!' he chanted. I took a packet of Marlboro Lights out of my jacket pocket and noticed the woman to his right, silently amused by his specifically-five-pint looseness. 'MY BROTHER!' he bellowed in my ear, holding my face and kissing my cheek. 'What did I say? You can always rely on Andy for cigs.' He grabbed the packet and pulled one out.

'Do you mind?' the woman asked, reaching for the pack.

'Go ahead,' I smiled. She wore jeans and heels and hoop earrings. Her shoulder-length blonde hair was tucked behind her ears. I couldn't remember if jeans and heels and hoop earrings had always been my favourite combination on a woman, or whether it was only now my favourite combination because it was on her.

'Oh, sorry,' Avi said, his breath soured from beer. 'Jen, this is Andy, my best mate. Andy, this is Jen. Jen is Jane's best mate.'

'Ah, nice,' I said inconsequentially. 'How do you guys know each other?'

'We met at uni.'

'OXFORD!' Avi bellowed. 'Oxford twats!'

'I know this mood and this is a mood that peaks too early,' I said. 'You'll be in bed within an hour if you don't get a glass of water.'

Avi rolled his eyes. 'Andy's a comedian.'

Jen gave an expression of genuine interest. 'Oh reall–'

'Hey, what's even less funny than a comedian?' Avi continued.

I sighed. 'I don't know, what's less funny than a comedian?'

'A failed one!' he said, pointing at me and slapping my chest.

'Brilliant,' I deadpanned.

He walked towards the door with his cigarette and Jen got up to follow.

'Would you like a drink?' I asked her.

She looked at her nearly empty glass and hesitated. 'Er –'

'Go on,' I said.

'All right, vodka tonic, please. Thank you.'

As I was waiting for the drinks at the bar, Jane came over, arms outstretched.

'Hey, happy birthday!'

'Why can't Avi be this tall?' she said, nuzzling into my chest. 'It's so *fit*.'

'Because Avi is going to have a full head of hair forever. He can't have everything. He'd be even more annoying.'

'That's true,' she said, pulling away.

'He seems –'

'Oh, he's steaming. He'll be in bed with a doner before eleven. I've told him I'm not taking him home. How are you?'

'I'm good,' I replied, distracted. 'Your mate Jen.'

'Have you met her?'

'Yes.'

'She's the best.'

'Is she single?'

'Always. Forever single.'

'Really?!' I said. 'That surprises me.'

'Why?'

'She just seems lovely,' I said.

'You're so old-fashioned, aren't you?' she said with a smile.

Avi appeared through the doors, Jen following behind him.

'Av,' Jane snapped. He turned to her like a well-trained terrier. 'Come with me, I wanna introduce you to someone.'

'Who? I already know every boring cunt here,' he slurred, flapping his hand around the room. She gripped his arm and yanked him away. Jen took a seat next to me at the bar.

'Thanks,' she said, picking up her drink.

'Cheers,' I said, picking up my pint glass to clink hers, immediately regretting the formality of the gesture. The silence between the clink, taking our first sip and putting our drinks back down seemed to go on uncomfortably long.

'I've never met a comedian before.'

'Some of my reviewers would say you still haven't,' I replied.

'Go on then, tell me –'

'Don't say it.'

'Say what?'

'A joke. "Tell me a joke."'

'I wasn't going to say that!'

'Oh *really*? What were you going to say?'

'Tell me how you got into comedy,' she said.

I took in the finer details of her. Her enormous, sleepy blue eyes. A small scar in between her brows. The shades of golden blonde streaked through her hair. A nose that went from seeming small to prominent, straight to slightly curved, depending on the way in which she turned her head.

'How do you think I got into comedy?'

'Um,' she pondered, taking a sip of her drink. 'Always felt like an outsider growing up? Didn't know how to be yourself? Didn't know how to be friends with boys or make girls like you? Then one day you did a show-stealing performance in a nativity and made everyone laugh. And you thought: Yes! Aha! This is how I make people love me.'

'I really am that much of a cliché, aren't I?' I sighed. 'What do you do?'

'Guess.'

'Dancer.'

She let out a hoot of laughter. 'Pervert.'

'I know, I know, I'm sorry. Um. PR.' She shook her head. 'Publicist.' She shook it again. 'Handbag designer.'

'Jesus Christ, it's like a man from 1962 has been asked to come up with women's jobs. Catalogue model? Make-up counter girl?'

'It's because you're so –' I floundered as she raised her eyebrows at me – 'glam.'

'Fuck off.'

'Give me a clue.'

'Okay, the clue is . . .' She took a few seconds to think as she had another gulp of her drink. 'I'm overpaid.'

'Finance!'

She raised her glass with a false grin. 'Insurance.'

'Wow.'

'You don't have to say "wow",' she said.

'What do you insure?'

'Ships.'

I nodded slowly, taking this in. 'You a maritime sort of woman, then?'

'No.'

'Grow up by the sea?'

'Ealing,' she laughed. 'My dad did it, so I guess I got the interest from him.'

'Ah,' I said. 'Wanted to impress Dad.'

'*Everybody* wants to impress their dad,' she said. 'That's the thing that motivates all our decision-making. Or at least that's what my therapist says. Your job is much more interesting, anyway!' she added with renewed crispness, possibly sensing my probing thoughts about what she talked about in therapy.

'My job isn't really my job, though. I only do stand-up sets a couple of times a week.'

'What do you do for the rest of the time?'

I took a deep breath to prolong this brief moment in which she'd heard the word 'comedian' and thought I was successful.

'Lots of different things. I host corporate events. I do roleplay training in hospitals. I dress up as Jack the Ripper and do historic walking tours. Drama workshops in schools. Sell cheese on my friend's market stall. Club it altogether and it makes a surprisingly decent living.'

She scanned my face intently, looking for sarcasm or sadness.

'I don't know anyone like you,' she said.

The evening went on like this for a few hours. We took turns to buy each other drinks, never moving to half-pints or single measures. We pulled our stools closer and closer to each other. We found reasons to touch each other – she playfully hit my arm when I goaded her, I gently touched hers when she shared something personal. She ruffled my hair when I said I worried it was thinning; she leant into me when I said I liked her perfume and I smelt her neck (Armani She – she'd never bothered to try anything new after getting a bottle for her sixteenth birthday). We shifted from overfamiliarity to inquisitiveness from sentence to sentence; alternating from feeling like old friends to strangers. We gave too much information about ourselves, then we pulled back. We got a kick out of the novelty of each other, heightening ourselves for the other one's enjoyment (she, the fauxhemian corporate West London girl; me, the scruffy comedian who never had enough bog roll in the flat). We made too much comedy of our differences and placed too much meaning on our similarities. It was flirting to a Premiership standard. Any time someone came over to talk, it felt like our match had been disrupted. I was desperate to return all my focus to her and I could feel she wanted to do the same to me.

Avi, predictably, was in an Uber home by half ten with a kebab. Jen and I snuck out just before last orders to go find some terrible bar on our own. Ten-pound entry fee, stamp on the hand, drinks out of white plastic glasses, fake orchids in the toilets, underage girls dancing to Ja Rule, middle-aged men watching them.

We sat in a booth, the red pleather peeling off the seats.

'WHAT'S YOUR WEEK LOOKING LIKE NEXT WEEK?' she shouted over 'Mambo No. 5'.

'I'M GOING TO EDINBURGH TOMORROW,' I bellowed back. 'I'M TAKING A SHOW UP TO THE FRINGE FESTIVAL FOR ALL OF AUGUST.'

'WHAT'S THE SHOW?'

'IT'S CALLED *NO HEAVY PETTING*. IT'S ABOUT MY EXPERIENCES OF BEING A LEISURE CENTRE LIFEGUARD.'

'DID YOU ENJOY IT?'

'NOT REALLY, I ONLY DID IT FOR A FEW

MONTHS SO I WOULD HAVE SOMETHING TO WRITE ABOUT FOR EDINBURGH THIS YEAR.'

Her face was unable to hide its bemusement.

'HAVE YOU BEEN BEFORE?'

'EVERY SUMMER FOR TEN YEARS.'

'IS IT FUN?'

'NOT REALLY!' I shouted, sipping my vodka Coke and dancing in my seat to distract myself from my discomfort. 'I'M DOING THE FREE FRINGE THIS YEAR, WHICH MEANS THE VENUE COSTS ME NOTHING BUT IT ALSO MEANS THAT NO ONE HAS TO PAY TO WATCH ME. I HAVE TO WALK AROUND WITH A BUCKET AT THE END OF EVERY SHOW ASKING FOR DONATIONS.' She nodded, unsure of how to react. 'PRETTY EMBARRASSING FOR A MAN OF THIRTY-ONE.'

'WHY DO YOU KEEP DOING IT?'

I bopped my head from side to side, biting down on to the plastic straw as I contemplated the question.

'LOVE, I THINK,' I finally shouted, my voice breaking over the song-change to Nelly's 'Hot In Herre'. 'UNRE-QUITED LOVE.'

She looked at me with a soft expression that I couldn't read. Pity? Arousal? Admiration? Amusement? Disgust? All of the above?

'COME DANCE WITH ME,' she said, shuffling out of the booth.

She couldn't dance for shit and I loved it. If Jen had been a good dancer, she would have had too much on her side. Her self-possession was already enough; the bad dancing counteracted it adorably. The curves of her body and her stylish, laid-back clothes suggested she would have as much control of her limbs and hips as she did her smarts and wit, but she had absolutely no rhythm.

The moves that should have been languid were jolty, and when she should have been keeping in time with the beat, she looked like she was wading through molasses. I relished the fact that it's much easier to put the gear stick into neutral on the dance floor as a man, so shifted from foot to foot, moved my head and my shoulders like I was working out a knot, held my drink to my chest and tried very hard not to close my eyes or give a sensuous expression that would suggest I was capable of losing myself in the music.

The *Grease* medley and flickering overhead lights signified it was the end of the evening, and I hurried Jen out of the bar before she could see the puddles of sweat that had collected on my T-shirt, most worryingly around my stomach.

'Where's home?' I asked.

'Hammersmith.'

'Hammersmith? Random.'

'"Hammersmith, random,"' she said back to me. 'Observational, your work?'

'I didn't realize people lived there. I just thought it was a motorway and a theatre.'

'A real John Betjeman, you are.'

'Give me your number,' I said. I handed her my phone and she put her number in. I saved it as 'Jen (Hammersmith)'. 'How are you getting home?'

'Bus.'

'Do you want company?'

'Where do you live?'

'Tufnell Park.'

'That's miles away from me.'

'I know. I'm not angling for an invite into your flat, I swear,' I said. 'I just want to keep talking to you. If you fancy it.'

'Okay,' she said. 'Yes, I do.'

★

We sat on the top deck and spent the journey sharing stories from the places we passed. Pubs where I'd died at open mic nights, bars where she'd gone on bad dates. Every road offered another destination of a past bad date. I tried to seem unsurprised by the volume, but I was silently estimating how many dates per week this girl must have been on in the last decade. I wanted to know how and why she had been on her own for so long, but I didn't want to seem judgemental or boring. No matter how late it got or how much we drank, she stayed so certain and playful and articulate. I had to work hard to keep up and match her confidence. I cringed as I watched drunken thoughts tumble out of my mouth like Scrabble tiles and I tried to piece them together into clever observations.

We walked to her flat and stood on the steps outside. It was a grand Victorian building with bay windows and its own gate and hedge. Her flat occupied the first floor and was, she kept insisting, the smallest. We stood on her steps, speaking in hushed voices, and pretended not to be cold. After a few minutes, we fell into our first silence of the night.

'Is this the longest it's taken you to kiss a girl?' she asked.

'No, this is fast for me. I've spent years gearing up to make a move in the past.'

'Ah,' she said, nodding. 'Men never make the first move any more. What's happened to them?'

'It's not them, it's you.'

'Me?!'

'Yes, this is your fault for being so fucking hot and clever and funny – how is anyone meant to kiss you, it's like trying to kiss . . . Tom Selleck.' She raised her eyebrows. '*Young* Tom Selleck,' I corrected myself.

'Don't make me do it first.'

'I won't.'

'I don't want to have to make the first move,' she said.

'You won't have to,' I said.

She put her hands around the back of my neck, pulled me towards her and kissed me. I felt tiny and enormous; like I was her toy and her king.

'Too late,' she said, kissing me again.

I felt the euphoric relief when you've spent hours presenting your very best anecdotes and making your best jokes, smelling your pits and checking your nose hair every time you go to the toilet, and you realize it hasn't been for nothing. I would not be the punchline to the joke, not tonight. I hadn't messed up. She fancied me too.

'I wish you could stay over,' she said.

'I can stay over.'

'No you can't,' she said.

'Why?'

'Um –' Her face crinkled while she searched for a reason.

'You've got a boyfriend,' I said. 'Some enormous . . . rower hedge-fund manager. Called Tristan. He's up there asleep.'

'No,' she said.

'What is it?'

She sighed. 'I don't like spelling it out like this, Andy, but I'm desperate to fuck you.'

'But?'

'But I'm on my period.'

'So?!' I said. 'I don't care. I fancy everything about you.'

'You fancy my period.'

'I fancy your period,' I repeated. 'Cover me in it, I don't mind.'

'You're disgusting.'

'So I'm leaving for Edinburgh in seven hours. And I've got to wait a whole month to take my dream woman for a drink?'

'Yes,' she said. 'Until then we can text. I'm a great texter.'

'Must have a lot of time on your hands to text, keeping all those ships afloat.'

'You're a bell-end.'

'You're a *beauty*.'

'Beauty and the bell-end,' she said. 'What a fairy tale.' We kissed some more.

'*Desperate*, you said?'

'Goodnight,' she replied.

I held her head in my hands and took in her features: eyes swimming, skin reddened from too much vodka, top lip flaky and swollen from dehydration, black make-up dust collecting in the delicate lines under her eyes. Still so impossibly gorgeous at half three in the morning.

'*Tell me exactly how desperate*,' I whispered, tucking her hair tightly behind both ears. 'I think I need to hear it.'

'Goodnight,' she repeated, turning away and putting her key into the door.

I took two night buses home and got into bed at four a.m. The next day, I got the coach to Edinburgh for my month at The Fringe. The show was shit. I somehow lost money on a run that was meant to cost nothing. No one came to see it. Everyone who did see it saw right through its inauthentic and hollow premise. My comedian friends who came to see it would say 'Great, mate' as they looked into their pint glass when I saw them in the bar afterwards, and changed the subject. One of the reviews declared: 'This is the most spectacularly weak hour of comedy I have ever seen at The Fringe', which I shortened to: 'the most spectacular . . . hour of comedy I have ever seen' for the flyers.

Jen and I texted every day and spoke on the phone every night. It was the happiest August in Edinburgh I'd ever had.

Saturday 6th July 2019

Sobbing is a sedative. I wake up after a ten-hour dreamless sleep and it takes me a few seconds less than yesterday morning to adjust to my new reality. I'm in my mum's house, it's not Christmas, Jen's broken up with me, conveniently in the exact month of the break-clause in our rental contract. Her stuff is gone and is sitting in a storage unit in London. All my possessions are alone in our flat. The extent of my self-pity means I am starting to feel sorry for my toothbrush and my record collection and my trousers. All alone in NW5, none the wiser. Not knowing what's about to hit them.

I instinctively reach for my phone underneath the pillow to check if Jen has messaged or called. She hasn't. I open Instagram and the first circle that appears on my story updates is Jen. Of course it's Jen – this phone knows me better than anyone in the world. Never has there been a worse time for all of my algorithms to understand my interior life better than I do.

I stare at the circle for a few seconds and deliberate whether to watch it, doing the mental calculations of loss of dignity vs gains of new information. In the hope that the Instagram story is a block of text on a neon gradient explaining to her 467 followers exactly why she ended our relationship, I click on it, feeling a rush of masochistic euphoria. It is instead just a photo of a park near her sister's flat posted at 6.47 a.m., a time I know to be her morning run. I watch the story four times in succession, making the most of the fact that it's eight in the morning and I've already fucked it because she knows I woke up and looked at her Instagram page so I might as well luxuriate in my own patheticness. I hold my finger on the screen to pause the story and bring my face up to the picture, looking for evidence. Sunshine on the path, a blue sky, a brown-green pond. What can I glean from this? What signals are here for me to read? *Why did Jen fall out of love with me?*

I head into town with a list of bits that Mum needs buying. I think she's sick of me moping around the house.

As I walk through crowds of shoppers, I sense Jen next to me and my body reacts involuntarily. Head light, heart galloping, breath short. Armani She. God damn her for choosing such a widely used perfume. Why would she do this to me? Jen, so unbelievably fussy about every other tiny aesthetic and brand detail. Jen, who wouldn't so much as buy an airport panini on a foreign holiday because everything that passed our lips had to come highly recommended from *Condé Nast Traveller*. Jen, who filled our flat with ancient rugs and sandalwood diffusers and grapefruit-flavoured gin. The one thing she chose thoughtlessly was the one thing that would follow me around forever; that reminded me of her skin and hair and clothes and bed. I turn to my left, expecting her to be there, but instead see a stranger carrying shopping bags and speaking into her phone, completely unaware of me.

The first place I find to drink is a prosecco bar in Grand Central. I'd normally opt for some underground, low-lit dive with booths and stools and an old, beardy barman with a towel over his shoulder who imparts passing wisdom, but needs must. I sit at an up-lit circular champagne bar surrounded by mother–daughter dates and female friends meeting for a browse around the shops and a glass of fizz. I am told there is no house wine, so order a bottle of the cheapest red they have and plug back into a podcast about the AI apocalypse. Avi messages.

The third I've ignored in the last ten days.

I gulp down the first glass, which tastes astringent on my empty stomach, and then halfway down my second, tastes completely delicious. It is a familiar black magic that happens in the space of one sip. And then I feel myself shifting into this other realm of being, this other state of consciousness: I feel sort of okay about me and Jen ending! The more sips I take, the calmer I feel. I relax into the facts of it easily – Jen and I didn't make it. So what! We had a pretty good run of it! I finish my third glass and pour the fourth.

'Andy?' I turn around to see Debbie, one of my mum's friends. Her hair is changed – now a deep burgundy red and styled short into hedgehog spikes. 'It is you! Oh, love. Look at you. Mum's told me everything.'

'Hey, Deb,' I say, giving her a hug. 'How are you?'

'How are YOU?' she says, gripping my arm. 'Never mind me, how are *you*?'

'I'm fine. Bit of a weird time, you know, but fine. Getting through it.'

'It's good you're drinking, I'm glad to see you drinking. When Malcolm left me I had my first drink of the day at eleven. How are you sleeping, is your sleep disrupted?'

'It's okay actually –'

'Yeah, it will be up and down,' she says. 'Now listen. If there's one thing I'd say to you, it's this: you've got to WIPE her.' She did a vigorous wiping motion with her hand, like she was miming a rag on a car window. 'WIPE. That's the only way you'll move on. Wipe her from your life, wipe her from your memories.'

We chat for a while longer, but most of it is not sinking in because I've had an idea. By the time we say goodbye I really do think of Debbie as a very close friend and promise myself that

I'll spend more time with her one-on-one next time I come home.

Boots is flooded with strip lighting which makes my drunkness more obvious. I knock over a promotional display of fast-absorbing sun creams as I enter and, while bending over to pick them up, lose my footing and trip over a shopping basket. I head straight to the perfume section via the Meal Deal fridge and get the attention of a kindly-looking sales assistant.

'Excuse me,' I say. She turns around and smiles warmly. 'Do you have any Armani She?'

'I can check,' she replies brightly. 'Come with me.'

'Thank you –' I look at her name tag – 'Sally.'

'You're welcome. Let's have a look. Hmm.' She peers into the glass cabinet. 'Ah, yes, here we go. Armani She.' She hands over the cylindrical bottle.

'How many do you have?'

'In store?'

'Yes.'

'Let's see.' She bends down to open a drawer and counts. 'We've got four bottles here.'

'WRAP 'EM UP!' I say, slamming my hand down comically on the counter, making a noise that is louder than I had anticipated. Sally flinches in surprise.

'So you'd like them gift-wrapped?'

'No, sorry, just a bag, please.'

'Lovely,' she chirps, moving behind the counter and scanning the bottles. 'Are these presents you're buying today?'

'Yeah.'

'Lovely. Who for?'

'Girlfriend.'

'Four bottles! How generous.'

'It's the only perfume she wears.'

She scans through the prawn mayo sandwich. 'And you are aware these food and drink items are included in the –?'

'Meal deal, yes. Two meal deals, please.'

'Wow, four bottles of perfume AND a meal deal!' she says. 'Can I trade you for my husband?! I got thirty quid in an envelope for Christmas and a Thigh Master for Valentine's Day last year!'

I laugh along too. I laugh and laugh and laugh and laugh and pay £159.14 and wonder who is more depressed, me or Sally.

The canal is dirtier than I remember. I haven't been here since Avi and I used to come to smoke hash after school. I wait until the towpath is clear of people and tee up the right song for a proper sense of ceremony, but nothing quite hits the spot. 'I Will Survive' feels cinematic in theory, but too camp for this scene when I play the first few seconds. Eminem lends an adolescent nostalgia to the moment, but as I skip through every track of *The Marshall Mathers LP* all of it feels too angry. I inexplicably settle on 'Sultans of Swing' by Dire Straits, light a cigarette, take the first bottle out of the bag and throw it in the water. I close my eyes and turn my face to the sky, trying to force an epiphany or even just a metaphor about sending things out into the water to go on their own journey, but I draw a blank. I hear chatter from a distance and spot a pair of figures walking in my direction, so I quickly turn the plastic bag inside out and dump the three other perfume bottles in the canal. I search for a sense of triumph as I walk on. Four fewer potential opportunities for me to smell Jen. That was a fantastic idea.

Wednesday 10th July 2019

I never knew the Sun and Lion opened at ten a.m. I leave the house in search of a café with Wi-Fi when Mum goes to work as I can't spend another day lying on the sofa, one eye on my laptop, one eye on daytime TV. I walk past the pub and see its doors are open. WHY NOT COME IN FOR BREAKFAST? asks the sign on the door. Why not, I think. *Why bloody not.* This is exactly where I want to be – in the warm, cosy cocoon of nostalgia. Where I can be in the company of my teenage self and he can remind me of something about hope and youth and what it is to know you have things ahead of you that are new.

I refrain from the Full English and instead order fried eggs on toast with a side of sausage, bacon, beans and mushrooms. I open my laptop and finalize the details for the van that's picking up all my stuff from the flat at the weekend and the storage unit I've rented indefinitely. I open WhatsApp and look at the last message Avi sent me.

> Omg STOP airing me I can see you're online all the time bro

I ignore it and open up my thread with Jane.

> Hi Lil J

She immediately comes online and starts typing.

> Hey Big A, how you doing? Xxx

> In a pub for breakfast, I'll let that speak for itself. How are you?

I'm fine. Have you spoken to Avi? He's trying
to get hold of you.

No, not yet. Mate I have a favour to ask you.
And you can say no.

Go on?

I look up at the high panelled ceilings of the pub. If it wasn't
for the cricket playing on a flat screen and the old man at the bar
with a glass of indecipherable brown spirit in one hand and a
pint of Guinness in the other, this place could almost be mis-
taken for possessing grandeur. I screw my eyes up tightly and
take a deep breath.

Is there any way I can stay with you and Av for a bit?

Of course. You can stay as long as you like.

Thank you thank you thank you. And I can help
out with the boys, np.

Don't say that you'll regret it.

Ha. I love you Jane

love you too

I turn my phone screen over and clear my throat. Another
decision made for the funeral of my and Jen's relationship. Being
at Mum's meant I could put it off for a while, but I can't pretend
it isn't happening any longer. Van booked, storage unit booked,
temporary home found. I had organized the flowers, the hearse
and the burial in one morning.

A young blonde woman serves me at the bar.

'What can I get you?' she asks.

I think about the implications of moving my first drink of the day up to a time that can only be described as mid-morning.

'Go on, I'll have a pint of Guinness,' I reply.

'Pint of Guinness?' she says, completely unfazed.

'Yes.'

'Sure, coming up.' She gives me a smile that doesn't give away a trace of sympathy or concern. Her green eyes are bright and alert. She reminds me of someone but my mind won't let me flick through the files and find out who.

After the fourth pint, all my Spotify playlists have lost the meaning I found in them in my previous pints. I'm too unfocused to do any more work or admin. I go on to the open browser tabs on my phone, hoping to find a half-read *New Yorker* long read, but instead find only:

Jennifer Bennett Facebook
Jennifer Bennett LinkedIn
The UK's funniest comedians under 30 – ranked!
Jennifer Bennett Twitter
Cheapest storage facilities in London
This man ate only papaya for a month to stop his receding
    hairline. You'll be shocked when you see what happened

I open up the thread of Avi's messages from the last couple of weeks that have all gone unreplied. I type him a message in seconds and, before I have time to change my mind, I send it.

Love you man

I order a large glass of red wine to mark the passing of the day. My phone makes a sound – a new message from Avi.

wtf is wrong with you have you been
diagnosed with something terminal

                                                  no why?

You've ghosted me for weeks then the first thing
you say is you love me wtf

                    Sorry I'm drinking pints in the sun and lion
                        and it just made me thinkof us thats All

Why are you there?? Who with??

                                          Home to see mum

OK but who you at the pub with

                                                  On own

this is so random. How long you been there??

                                                  A bit

OK I don't get any of this but J says we're seeing
you at the weekend?

                                          Yes will be nice

I wait for him to type a reply but he goes offline. The barmaid
with the familiar features comes over to take my empty glass.
'Nicky!' I yelp. 'That's who you remind me of!'
She looks at me blankly. 'Who's Nicky?'
'Sorry, I've been trying to work it out all day. You have
almost exactly the same face as my first girlfriend, Nicky. She
was about your age when we were going out.'
'Ah, okay,' she says politely.
'I was your age too, obviously!' She laughs along. 'Actually,
I think she worked here? Yes, she did!' I say, now in a full

conversation with myself. 'She had a weekend and summer job here behind the bar! That's probably why you remind me of her.'

'I think I've just got one of those faces,' she offers with a smile. As I leave, the old man raises his glass to me.

Nicola was the only good break-up I've ever had. 2000–2002. Met in school, lost our virginities to each other, broke up before we both went to university, which was, thank God, the year O by Damien Rice was released, which I cried to for a full fortnight. By the measurement of time, it was my shortest relationship, but it still feels like triple the length of any relationship I've been in since.

I walk to nowhere and think about Nicky. It's strange to think that everything we know about romantic love and sex we first learnt from each other, and yet now we don't speak. I know she's moved back here, got married and had a baby. We like each other's photos on Instagram and wish each other a happy birthday when we can remember. As I look her up on Facebook to send her a message, my phone, drained of battery and exhausted from being my only companion all day, dies. I stand on the street thinking of ways to contact her and realize how depressingly impotent I am when I don't have a working smartphone.

I find a phone box, put in some change and dial Nicky's old landline.

'5901?' a female voice trills.

'Hello – Mrs Ainsley?'

'Speaking.'

'Hi, it's Andy.' I allow a pause to let the significance of this land.

'Andy . . . ?'

'Andy Dawson.' I wait for a sound of joyful recognition. Nothing.

'Sorry, you're going to have to help me out, this isn't ringing any bells,' she chuckles, although I don't see what's particularly funny. 'Andy *Dawson*,' she says, mulling over my name as if it's a crossword clue.

'I went out with your daughter Nicky. A while back. At school.' A few moments pass.

'Ah! Yes! Andy. Gosh, it must be, what, twenty years?'

'Seventeen, yes. How are you?'

'Very well, thank you. Is it Nicky you're trying to get hold of?'

'Yes! I'm back home for a bit and I wanted to know if she fancied a catch-up, but I don't think I have her most up-to-date number.'

'I'm sure she'd like that, shall I pass on a message?'

'Would you mind just asking her to give me a call? My number's the same as it was.'

'Of course.'

'Thanks so much, Mrs Ainsley.'

By the time I get to Avi's parents' house, I'm starting to get a day-drinking hangover that hits late afternoon and has become a recurring feature of the last two weeks. I really want to talk to Avi but I can't seem to talk to him so I figure having a cup of tea with his mum and dad, who still live two streets away from my mum, might give me what I'm craving. I just want to be cosy with people I've known my whole life. I want to hear about their holidays and his dad's lawnmower and lovingly laugh about all the ways Avi is useless.

I ring the doorbell and get nothing. I try again but there is still no response. I bang the door very loudly, remembering that his mum has gone partially deaf, but there is no reply. I scrawl a note to them in my notebook, tear it out and put it through their letter box.

★

When I get back to Mum's, I pour myself a gin only to find we have no tonic so instead I mix it with a fruits of the forest soft drink. I put my phone on charge in the lounge and turn on the TV just in time for a late-afternoon game show in which pet owners compete for a cash prize by guessing what their pet is thinking, confirmed or denied by an animal psychologist. My phone rings – I leap across the sofa and scramble along the carpet hoping to see Jen's name, but instead see an unknown number.

'Hello?'

'Andy,' a crisp female voice says. 'It's Nicky.'

'Hi, Nicky, hey! How are you?'

'I'm good, thanks. Mum said you were trying to get hold of me?'

'Er, yes.'

'How . . .' I can hear her searching for the most polite arrangement of the words *what the fuck do you want*. 'What's up?'

'Oh nothing, not an emergency or anything, sorry if it seemed that way.' I pause for a beat, waiting for Nicky to fill the gap with talk of what a lovely surprise it was to be reminded of me and funnily enough she was only just thinking of me the other day, but nothing comes. 'Sorry, I realize this must seem . . . very out of the blue. I'm staying at my mum's for the moment.'

'Ah, how is she?'

'She's well! Getting older, but aren't we all.' I laugh knowingly.

'Send her my best, if she even remembers me.'

'Of course she remembers you,' I say.

'So why was it you wanted to get hold of me?'

'I wanted to see if you wanted to hang out, but my mobile was dead. And I realized I remember your landline. From all those years ago. Isn't that mad?!'

'It's not my landline, it's my mum and dad's landline.'

'So where are you living now?' I ask, veering us into small talk.

'Not far from them. With my husband and my baby.'

'Yes, of course, sorry, I didn't think you were still living at home with your parents! Anyway,' I sing-song these three syllables, 'I'm here until Saturday and I was wondering whether you'd like to have lunch or a coffee or maybe even a glass of wine –'

'I can't, sadly, I have to book a sitter way in advance –'

'I could come to you,' I say, having visions of me and Nicky eating olives at a farmhouse-style kitchen table, me and her husband affectionately teasing her as we bond over having both been her boyfriend. 'It would be great to meet your husband!'

There is a fairly long pause.

'Andy, I don't want to seem rude – and I really have nothing but good feelings towards you and our time together – but I don't think it's necessary to meet up. We last saw each other half our lifetime ago. I'm not sure what we'd even talk about.'

'I just thought we could hear about what we're both up to now.'

'I think we probably get everything we need to know from social media.'

'We could talk about the old times –'

'I don't really think about that stuff any more. I have my own business now and a family, I don't really have time –'

'I understand. I'm sorry for bothering you.'

'I know you're a very . . . nostalgic person, but –'

'No, you're right, sorry, I'd had a few drinks. And I saw a girl at the Sun and Lion who looked like you, and she worked there like you used to, so think it all reminded me of you or something.'

'I worked at the Black Bull.'

'Oh, okay. Sorry, my brain is a bit muddled at the moment.'

There is a loaded pause.

'Is everything okay, Andy?'

'Sorry, yes. I'm going through a break-up, which has sent me a bit west.'

'I'm sorry. I remember you found ours very hard. I hope you're okay.'

'I'll be fine. Nice to speak.'

'And you. Bye, Andy.'

Saturday 13th July 2019

Bon Iver released a new single two days ago. I've been storing it up for my train journey back to London for maximum wallowing. I booked myself a window seat especially so I can listen to it on repeat while I stare out of the window, having flashbacks and realizations. I squeeze in next to a man making a Power-Point presentation on his laptop and eating a tuna baguette at half nine in the morning, plug into Bon Iver, stare out of the window and resent reality for taking away what really could have been a crucial turning point in processing the end of this relationship.

> *I know it's lonely in the dark*
> *And this year's a visitor*
> *And we have to know that faith declines*
> *I'm not all out of mine*

What is that thing they say? Poetry is the most reviled and redundant art form, everyone rolls their eyes at it and takes the piss out of it. But the second that something shit happens in our lives, it's the first recourse we have. Halfway through my second listen, I get what I want. My neighbour turns his body away from me and opens a packet of cheese and onion Hula Hoops, and I'm grateful for this respectful refusal to acknowledge my silent sobs.

When I get out at Euston, I stand on the street a while and hover by the entrance to the tube. I have a cigarette, then another one. I contemplate going to the pub opposite the station – anything to avoid going home – but eventually force myself underground and on to the train. I don't know what I'm expecting to find in my flat, but I don't want to see it. When I approach the entrance to our mansion block, I half expect to see police tape around the door.

The flat smells of lemon-scented cleaning products and has been stripped of nearly all its furniture. Jen didn't want to move into a furnished place because she has all sorts of opinions on pine wardrobes, but I didn't own much furniture and couldn't afford to buy any, so she brought bits and pieces and her parents gave us some. My clothes are folded up into neat piles on the floor, my books are stacked up by the wall. I can tell how much effort she must have put into taking away all her stuff and organizing mine for me. I wonder whether she invited her friends around to help her and if they all drank wine and held up each and every pair of my rubbish pants and had a right old laugh about it. Or maybe she hired professionals and they all had a laugh about it. I don't know why but I've just got the distinct feeling people have been laughing at my pants since I was last here.

Giraffe Storage Kentish Town is located underground with an entrance that looks like a car park. The front desk is manned by a man in his early twenties with blue hair that matches his uniform polo shirt.

'Hiya,' I say. He looks at me without expression, not even a nod. 'I've booked a unit under the name of Dawson, Andy Dawson.'

He turns to the desk, taps at the keyboard and clicks his mouse for a minute or so. 'I've got nothing here for an Andy Dawson,' he says.

'Andrew? Andrew Dawson?'

More tapping and clicking.

'Yeah, that's not coming up.'

'That's weird, look, I've got email confirmation of the booking.' I open up the email and show him. 'Is there any name it could possibly be under?'

He sighs and returns to the screen.

'Well, I've got here Andrew DawsonDawson –'

'Yes! That's it. I must have written the surname twice.'

'Well,' he says, laughing to himself, 'is that the name on the photo identification you've brought today to verify the booking?'

'No?'

'I didn't think so,' he says with a self-satisfied nod. 'So that's void now, that booking, we're going to have to start from the beginning.'

'Okay, I'm really, really in a rush so couldn't we just –'

'It's company policy.'

'It is my name, you can clearly see it's my name.'

'We've got two options here,' he says, raising his voice. 'We start again with a new booking. Or we sit here arguing about it, which for someone who's apparently in such a rush, seems like it doesn't quite make sense.' There is a silent stand-off until he draws his weapon – a clipboard and new customer form. I take it from him without breaking eye contact, then fill it in.

'Absolutely ridiculous,' I mutter to myself.

'What's that?' he barks.

I shake my head and refuse to answer. When I hand it back, he glances down, sighs theatrically and passes it back to me.

'You're going to have to do this again.'

'Why?'

'You've filled it in wrong. Here you've said you're storing all your belongings, but you've booked a sixteen-foot unit.'

'That's correct.'

'That will not hold all your belongings.'

'Yes it will,' I say.

'*All* your belongings? Your bed, your mattress, all your furniture –'

'I don't have any furniture.'

There is a pause as he tries to make sense of this.

'Right, okay, so have you been backpacking or –'

'No, I haven't been *backpacking*, I just don't have that much stuff. Why do you need to know any of this?'

'I'm just making sure that you're not a time-waster –'

'CAN I JUST BOOK THE SODDING UNIT.'

'RIGHT,' he shouts, holding up both his hands as if I posed a physical threat. The next few minutes pass in a circular row about whether 'sodding' is a swear word and therefore 'verbal abuse', until I finally apologize and the tiny, pathetic unit with enough space to house thirty-five years of my tiny, pathetic life is booked.

On the train out of London and into south-west suburbia, to Avi and Jane's, I message Jen.

> Hey, taken my stuff. About to drop keys off at estate agent. Thanks for nooking cleaner. Let me know how much I owe you x
>
> *booking

I stand outside their very grown-up semi-detached, conjoined to a row of other identical semi-detached houses. Avi opens the door and looks at me with a blank expression.

'Hello? Can I help you?'

'Hello, mate!' I say, going in for a hug. He recoils. Jackson, my nearly four-year-old godson with Jane's curly hair and Avi's brown eyes, runs to the door.

'UNCLE ANDY!!' he screeches. 'UNCLE ANDY!'

'No, Jackson, this isn't Uncle Andy. This is a stranger who I don't recognize.'

'Uncle Andy, why is your face so big and weird?'

I walk into the hallway and scoop Jackson up into my arms. 'Big AND weird, that's very descriptive. Where did you learn that word?'

'Bacteria,' he says slowly.

'What about it?'

'Seriously, mate,' Av says. 'Where've you been?'

'Oh, you know,' I mumble, putting Jackson down, who immediately runs off like a restless puppy. We walk into the kitchen, where Jane is poking a plastic spoon of orange mush into their two-year-old son's mouth.

'Hey!' she says, glancing up at me.

'Can you stay for a bit?' Avi asks, taking a beer out of the fridge and offering it to me. I catch Jane's eyes, which give away her concern.

'Yeah,' I say, taking it from Avi.

'Great.'

Jackson comes rushing back into the kitchen, so out of breath he can't speak.

'I – I – I –' he gasps.

'Whoa, honey, just calm down. Remember, we take a deep breath –' Jane says.

'I – I saw in the garden a worm,' he says in his little croaky voice, eyes bulging.

'Yeah?' Avi nods.

'And – and – he is all wriggly.'

'Okay,' Avi says slowly.

Jackson steadies himself on the chair and slows his words.

'He is prime minister,' he finally solemnly informs us.

'I tell you what!' Jane says with the sudden enthusiasm of a

43

children's TV presenter. 'How about you watch a movie this afternoon? Yeah? Anything you want.'

Jackson jumps up and down, wailing with delight. Jane and Avi clean up while I take the boys into their chaotic lounge, make my way through the plastic toys that carpet the floor and put *Brave* on.

'So why were you at your mum's?' Avi asks as I walk back into the kitchen, pointing at my suitcase on wheels. 'Have you just come straight from the station?'

'Yes.' Jane looks at me pleadingly. 'No,' I correct myself. 'I'm actually going to be staying with you guys for a bit.'

'Why?'

'I've already asked Jane.'

'What's going on?' He looks between Jane and me with incredulity.

'Jen and I broke up.'

'What? When?'

'A couple of weeks ago. When we came back from Paris.'

'You knew this?' Avi says, turning his head to Jane.

'He told me not to tell you.'

'Unbelievable,' he says.

'I'm fine by the way, mate.'

'So all those times you've been going round to Jen's and seeing Jen, it's to talk about the break-up?'

I immediately want to direct the conversation to exactly how many times Jane has seen Jen and what exactly Jen's told her, but I don't want to be too obvious about it.

'Yes, Avi. Obviously. She's my best friend.'

'Yeah,' I agree. 'They're best friends. They tell each other everything. Which is so nice, that you two can be that for each other. She's probably told you all about why she did it and how she's feeling about her decision now, hasn't she?'

'Andy, I love you,' Jane says. 'But I cannot and will not be an information-passer between you and Jen, so don't even try.'

'Fuck sake,' I say, shaking my head in outrage and taking a swig of beer.

'I'm in total shock,' Avi says. 'How did it happen?'

'Went to Paris for the weekend, everything was fine, had a nice time until she turned a bit quiet and off on the second day, but didn't think anything of it. Got the Eurostar home. Got on the tube back to ours. Put our bags down. She said she didn't want to be with me any more.'

Avi takes this in.

'Did she say *why*?'

'She said that recently she's wondered whether we're compatible.'

'What does that mean?'

'No idea, mate. And then she said the most fob-off thing I've ever heard in my life, which is that not only does she think we're incompatible, she's starting to wonder whether she wants to be in a long-term relationship at all.' There is a long pause while Avi contemplates this. 'Ever.'

'So she's met someone else.'

'AVI!' Jane thwacks him across the arm.

'Thanks, man, that's really helpful.'

'Sorry, sorry,' he says.

I nervously peel the label off the beer bottle.

'I mean, obviously she's met someone else,' I say. 'There's no other explanation.'

'Sorry, why is there no other explanation?' Jane asks.

'Because people don't break up with people who they've had absolutely no prior problems with just so they can be single. No one likes being single *that* much.'

'I'd like to be single,' Jane replies. 'I think most women would. It's men who don't know how to do it.'

'I hate today,' Avi says sulkily.

'Babe, I don't *want* to be single. I want to be with you and our boys. All I'm saying is, I could also see another life where I was on my own and quite happy.'

'Lies!' I say. 'You're only saying that as a hypothetical thing, you wouldn't actually be happy without him.'

'Thanks, man.'

'And that's what I don't get,' I say, ranting now, having written a collection of speeches in the last two weeks and had nowhere yet to recite them. 'Like, did I ever fantasize about being single? Sure I did! But the point is, relationships are challenging and boring and annoying, and that's unavoidable. You have to work through it, you can't just opt out of the whole thing.'

'You've never been single, though. Jen's been single most of her life until she met you,' Jane says.

'So?'

'So maybe she really does just want to be on her own, maybe there isn't a big lie.'

'Yes there is,' I say, bringing my beer down on to the table harder than I meant to. 'She fell out of love with me and I don't know why.'

'Break-ups can be a good thing,' Jane says. 'They can teach us about who we really are.'

'Yeah, maybe, like, break-up number one or two,' I sigh. 'But break-ups have depreciating gains. I'm thirty-five now. I know who I am. I am already sick of myself.'

She puts her hand over mine. 'It will only be shit for a bit,' she says. 'I promise.'

Avi looks at the table.

'Thanks for letting me stay.'

'Of course, mate,' he musters. 'And we're going to have a massive night out with the boys. You'll feel better soon.'

'Cheers, mate.'

'Do you want another beer?' Jane asks.

'I think we've finally run out,' Avi says. 'We bought all the beer in the Mitcham Morrisons.'

'That should be an album title,' I offer and Avi laughs generously, relieved to have moved off emotions. 'I'll nip out and get some more.'

'Go with him,' Jane says to Avi, making me feel like his hopeless little brother.

Avi and I don't talk explicitly about Jen again that day. We go to the supermarket and I buy groceries to say thank you for letting me stay. We stop at the pub on the way home and have two drinks. We lug a mattress up to the converted-but-not-yet-furnished attic where I'll sleep like Paddington Bear. We give the boys their tea. I drunkenly read bedtime stories to Jackson and make him laugh with hammy voices. I make prawn curry for us and we drink wine around the table and stay up talking. Whenever we reference the break-up we say 'because of what's happened'. I feel increasing dread as the clock hands move closer and closer to eleven, the time I've come to know as the latest parents with young children can stay up.

They tell me to leave the washing-up and they head upstairs, but I can't bear to go to bed with my thoughts. I plug myself into a podcast about whether trees can talk to each other and do the washing-up, staring back at my face in the reflection of the kitchen window.

I brush my teeth and get into bed and lie awake, gazing up at the skylight, thinking of all the times that Jen and I slept in the same house as Avi and Jane. The holidays, the weekends away. We'd all say goodnight and go to our separate beds and I liked knowing that they were probably talking about us in whispers just as we were talking about them. I'd never been in a relationship with another couple before and I loved it. I loved us. I loved that Jane and Jen knew things about each other that Avi and

I didn't know. I loved that Jen and Avi had 'their song' that, when played at Jane and Avi's wedding, made them rush across a dance floor to find each other. I loved that Jane took the piss out of me and I took the piss out of Jane. I loved that when I saw a film or a festival that looked like it would be fun, I'd send a link to our WhatsApp group and a question mark. I loved that we all knew each other's family members and our drinks orders and most embarrassing sex stories. I loved that Jen and I were god-parents to their first child. I loved that they FaceTimed us from the hospital bed an hour after their second was born.

Jen and Jane, Avi and Andy. It was perfectly synchronized. It was a group de foudre.

There are so many hidden miniature break-ups within a big break-up. There are so many ahead of me that I haven't even thought of yet. I've been so busy mourning Jen, I'd forgotten I'd have to mourn us four too. I open WhatsApp and scroll down to our group, named 'Js & As'. I read back through years of shared language and plans that turned into memories and photos as I scroll through the weeks. I scroll until my eyes ache and I put my phone under my pillow.

Sunday 14th July 2019

I am woken at 7.10 when Jackson rushes into my room and throws himself on to my bed, shouting something about a hamster policeman. Jane runs after him.

'JACKSON!' she yells. 'JACKSON, COME HERE.'

'Too late,' I shout back sleepily while Jackson burrows under the duvet like a hound.

'Jackson,' she says, summoning her Serious Parent voice. 'What did I say? I said Uncle Andy needs to sleep.'

'Uncle Andy is having a breakdown,' I say, ruffling his hair and reaching for the phone from under my pillow.

'I WANT A BIRTHDAY CAAAAAAAAKE!!!!!' he screams.

'Jackson!' Jane raises her finger to the air. 'We need to do our breathing exercises and slow down. Otherwise I won't let you have that cereal again, the sugar gets you too wound up.'

'Oh my God.'

'What?'

'Jen's messaged.'

Jane sits on the edge of the bed. 'What did she say?'

I hold up the phone screen to her in dismay.

    X

'What does that mean?' I ask.

'It's a kiss,' she says. 'She must have wanted to acknowledge your message about the flat and the keys.'

'But why a *kiss*? And why did she send it at —' I hold the

phone close to my face and look at the time stamp – 'one twenty-
seven a.m.?!'

'I love Aunty Jen,' Jackson declares.

'Maybe she was on a date and felt guilty that she forgot to
reply to my message so she just sent me that kiss,' I say.

'I love Aunty Jen.'

'The answer to these things is always the simplest,' Jane reasons. 'I know that's not what you want to hear, because you're
in your obsessing phase so you can keep thinking about her. But
the boring explanation is probably the right one.'

'Aunty Jen has yellow hair and she looks like a princess!' Jackson says, jumping up and down on the bed, narrowly missing
my shins.

'All right now, shush,' Jane says, scooping him into her arms.
'Let's leave Uncle Andy to it, I think. I'll make coffee.' She
ushers Jackson out of the room.

I think about the message all day, each hour giving it an entirely
new meaning. One kiss could be absolutely loaded with
subtext – it is a *kiss* after all. But then again, it could also be a
ruthless gesture. Just a kiss is the sort of rushed thing she'd send
to her assistant in response to a message about a meeting room
change.

We eat breakfast, we go to the playground, we have lunch at a
local pub. I fall into the routines of their life and, as always, am
staggered at how different it is in this other time zone of a young
family. Of course I know it's different – Jen and I had had
enough conversations over the years where we said as much over
and over again. But when you're living in it, rather than visiting
it, you realize it's *really* different; that new parents not only
aren't complaining too much, they're not complaining nearly
enough. My body feels different when I'm on Avi Family Time.

I've got the light-headed, unfocused, disorientated feeling of jet lag all day. I am starving for lunch at eleven, yawning and thinking of a nap at two. I watch Avi, otherwise so impatient and bad-tempered – the sort of man who complains in restaurants and mutters in queues – do it all with no grumbling. Not just that, with genuine joy. It's quite incredible.

'Hello, egg,' Rocco, the two-year-old, says, sitting on my shoulders as we walk through the park.

'What egg?' I ask. He rubs the patch of my hair that is very slightly thinning at the back. 'Egg,' he says with an affectionate pat. I look to Avi for outrage, but he's laughing. As is Jane.

'Thanks, Rocco,' I say.

Jackson is bent over in hysteria and laughing theatrically. 'Uncle Andy has an egg on his head!'

'All right, all right, that might be you one day, judging by your maternal grandpa,' Avi says.

'Uncle Andy is an ugly POO with fat cheeks, and he has a big egg on his head!'

'Ah – no,' Jane says suddenly. 'Jackson, that's rude. You take it too far.'

'You can be funny without being mean,' Avi says. We've all come to a standstill. 'Because otherwise you can hurt people's feelings.'

I don't want to disrupt their disciplining methods, so look to the ground like a child myself.

'Dippy egg,' Rocco mutters to himself, poking his head with his finger like it's a soldier looking for the yolk.

'Okay, that's enough now, say sorry to Andy,' Avi says.

I smile as they say sorry and try to ignore Rocco jabbing at my head curiously for the rest of the walk. When I get home I put on a baseball cap.

★

'Are you going to go on the apps again?' Avi asks as he prods at a stir-fry.

'Don't know. Can't think about that yet,' I reply. I hear faint shrieks and splashes from upstairs as Jane does bathtime.

'Can I be honest with you?'

'Yeah?'

'I think taking up a new hobby is your best bet at this time of life.'

'What sort of hobby?'

'I dunno like. Not *gardening*, but –'

'Definitely not gardening.'

'No, I said that, I said *not* gardening,' he says slightly impatiently. 'Climbing, maybe.'

'Yeah, maybe.'

'I just think, if you're being honest with yourself, the last time you were single, you could still run around after girls in Soho on a Saturday night. But you don't want to be doing that, not now.'

'Stop talking like I'm some elderly flasher in the park. I'm thirty-five.'

'Thirty-five is old.'

'Thirty-five is the youth of middle age,' I say. 'We're at the first stage of something new rather than being at the last stage of being young. I felt relieved when I turned thirty-five. It was like turning eighteen again.'

'Thirty-five is closer to fifty than twenty.' There is a pause and we say nothing. 'Anyway. You all right if I go ahead and organize this boys' night?'

'Yeah, go on.'

I go to the downstairs toilet, switch on the spotlights and take off my baseball cap. I hold my phone aloft on selfie mode and examine The Egg. The little fucker is right. There is more skin emerging. This is a disaster – my hair's been pulling back from the temples since school, but I've always been able to make my peace with that. But the back of the head is the most valuable real estate of a man's body. Every disappearing hair in that post-code renders a catastrophic loss on the overall asset.

Closer to fifty than twenty.

I take a photo and make a vow to do so daily, so I can keep track of its progress and somehow try to hold back the hands of time. I've been too busy being happy with Jen to really take notice of what's been going on. But it's wake-up time now. I take three photos and put them into a new album on my phone called 'BALD'.

When I return to the kitchen, the boys are in their pyjamas. Red-faced, wet-haired, smelling of soap.

'They wanted to come say goodnight to you,' Jane says. I bend down to give them both a hug, holding one in each arm.

'Don't hide the egg,' Jackson says softly, taking the cap off my head.

'Okay,' I say. I squeeze them both and Jane takes them upstairs. In one brief exchange, the entire, exhausting day that feels like it began a month ago is almost worth it.

After dinner, I go to bed early and browse for available flatshares and lodgings. My phone lights up with a message from Avi on the group chat of six men called Armadildos, an in-joke from our schooldays that's gone on far too long.

Avi
BOYS. Andy needs a night out. Him and Jen are over = pints. When's good for everyone?

It's all he can do and I love him for it – drinks, distraction, solutions. I open up Jen's message again and stare at the singular *X*, hoping it will bring new meaning. It doesn't. I see she's online and wonder who she's talking to. Jane? I open up a chat with Jane to see if she's online, but she's not. It's this sort of behaviour that makes me feel the most depressed – more than the morning drinking, more than the binge-eating, more than the post-break-up wanks when I try to think about anything other than her, but there she is, knocking at the door, like a celebrity guest on a nineties sitcom. I hate that I've become a private investigator for my own broken relationship.

Jon
Ah, bummer! I'm so sorry man, hope you're ok.
Weekends difficult for me atm because I'm filming on Saturdays.

I browse through double rooms in Kentish Town but find nothing under £750 a month. I go further out, but still find nothing. It's been years since I've had to do this. God, I had it easy with Jen.

Jay
Sorry Andy bro sending you love. I'm free every weekend (upside of having a baby) but can't be out too late (downside of having a baby).

Avi
Don't downside of having a baby me. This is an emergency.

Jay
Hmmm will suggest to Andrea but don't think she'll be happy

Rob

Whipped.

Jay

Cunts

Rob

I'm in! Altho don't have loads of time at weekends rn, seems to be the bday party of every member of wife's family. Hope you're OK dude.

Jay

Should we do a google doc might be easiest for working out days we're free

Rob

We can't do a google doc for a night out. that's so bum out

I check Jen's Instagram. No new stories.

Andy

Thanks guys, appreciate it. Altho agree with Rob not doing a Google doc for a night out

Avi

Andy, stay out of this, we're looking after you. Everyone else – no Google docs.

Matt

Hey all, Andy hope you're OK. big yes from me to this. Bit tricky with kid schedules, Sara's schedule etc, but here's what's looking free for me at a glance: 27th Jul, 15th Aug (only until 10 pm), 23rd Aug, Sept 12th.

Jon

I can do 15th Aug, but probs only AFTER 10 pm because of work

Avi

Suck a bag of dicks, the lot of you, Sept 12th ffs

Andy

Honestly it's fine I'll get a meal deal and stay in.

Jay

Lol

Jon

New Bon Iver SLAPS btw anyone want to go see him on tour next yr?? Here's a song for you . . . Faith by Bon Iver
https://open.spotify.com/album/6udb0IhmEdSQvWwjfnh6UA

Matt

Stay focused Jon

Yes! Double room in a five-man houseshare, Muswell Hill, £675 a month. I click on it to find an unfurnished single room with a note that I also have to provide my own bedroom door 'if wanted'.

Avi

OK I'm taking control of this shitshow. Our friend is a heartbroken, homeless melt with no regular income. We are taking him for a massive night out THIS sat (july 20th) and i don't want any excuses.

Andy

Going to bed night guys.

Something's changed since I was last single. When me and my last ex broke up, a mere handful of years ago, I remember it releasing a burst of energy in the group. Everyone was excited for me. There was a sense that I'd returned to the club, that my membership was going to be renewed. But I don't feel that now – I feel like my singleness may end up being a bit of an inconvenience for everyone.

Then I realize: half of them were single four and a half years ago. None of them are now.

Closer to fifty than twenty.

I close my laptop and turn off my light. As I go to bed I hear the landline ring and Avi having a whispered conversation with his mum. He asks a lot of worried questions and then reassures her that it's nothing to worry about and says goodnight. I hear Avi explaining to Jane what had happened – his parents came back from visiting family in India this evening to find a note on the doormat in their hallway. It was scrawled in red biro in handwriting they don't recognize, unsigned, and read: *I came to see you but you weren't here. I'm staying here a while and I'm coming back. I love you.*

He blames it on kids playing a prank and told his mum that she shouldn't bother reporting it.

I say nothing, admit nothing, and go to sleep.

Tuesday 16th July 2019

First gig after the break-up. I'm hoping it will make me feel better, but I've learnt that an audience is an unreliable girlfriend. I do an early shift on the cheese stall and get a train to Emery's place late afternoon. When I arrive, he's in double denim outside his flat inspecting something on the door of his VW Beetle. Rollie lodged in his mouth, sunglasses on, silver hoop glinting in his left ear, curly hair wild in the breeze. He sees me approaching and stands up straight.

'My boy, it's been a minute,' he says, walking towards me with his arms outstretched. I give him an awkward hug. 'Where have you been?'

'Taken a bit of time out. Went home to see my mum.'

'Coventry?' he ventures. 'Nottingham?'

'Birmingham.'

'Ah, of course. I've always found there to be a nobility to the Midlands. Its people and its landscape. Right. Shall we get going?'

I rearrange empty fag packets and sandwich boxes to make space on the passenger seat. Emery fiddles with his rear-view mirror then pulls out on to the road. He takes a tape out of the glove compartment with one hand and shoves it in the cassette player. A male voice growls out of the stereo.

'Warren Zevon,' he says. 'D'you know him?'

'A bit.'

'Beautiful man. You know he used to have comedians open for him on tour? Because he understood its power as an art form was on a par with rock 'n' roll. He respected us. He knew that a good comedian is a rock star and a good rock star is a comedian.'

I let him go on like this uninterrupted. He sings along tunelessly to lyrics about Russians and lawyers and hiding in Honduras and I roll down the window and smoke a cigarette. He is only a year younger than me and remains, infuriatingly, just about the most stunning man I've ever seen. His eyes are so transfixing and enormous, his jaw so strong, his cheekbones so high and his lips so full, it's almost as if he is consistently daring himself to see if he can ever make himself unattractive. He grew out his golden-blond hair to his shoulders and never seems to wash it, wears charity shop patterned shirts, rants about freedom of speech in his sets, lectures people snobbishly about culture, boozes to such extremities that he's permanently red in the face from drunkenness or a hangover. But he can't do it. He will still always be the most attractive man in any room. He irritates a lot of people in the industry because he calls his comedy 'his message', but I'm strangely fond of him.

'Jen and I broke up,' I announce out of nowhere, mainly to stop him from singing.

'NO!' he says, pushing his sunglasses on to his head and turning to glance at me. 'When?'

'A while back. Last month.'

'Who ended it, her?'

There is a pause.

'How did you know?'

He lets out one of his famously booming cackles, both mean and jolly.

'Sorry, my boy, just an educated guess. How are you doing?'

'Um. Honestly?'

'That's all we allow for in this car.'

'Like. Awful? The worst I've ever felt in my life. I spend ninety per cent of my waking hours thinking about her. I don't think I'll ever be happy again? That sort of thing.'

He nods slowly. 'You're in The Madness.'

'Yeah.'

'Terrible, terrible state for a man to be in. A few things can ease The Madness – can I give you my advice?'

'Please.'

'Okay, first and foremost: stop wanking about her.'

'How do you know I'm wanking about her?'

'Just a feeling I have. But you've got to stop.'

'Well, it's not, like, the start of *Street Fighter* where you choose your fighter. It's not like I select her as my subject. Sometimes she just pops into the room, you know? The mental room. It's the erotic equivalent of that adrenaline jolt you feel when you realize you're both in the same pub. Do you know what I mean?'

'Yes and it's pathetic,' he says, taking a piece of gum from the multipack in his glove compartment and shoving it in his mouth. 'As long as she's the subject of your masturbation, your body is still attached to her.'

'So you're telling me you NEVER have a nostalgiwank about your exes?'

'I mean, I feel like I've had a wank about everything at this point,' he says. 'But once a relationship is over, I don't allow myself to think about her in that way for at least a year. It's the only way I can move on.'

'Maybe I'll just stop wanking altogether.'

'No, you mustn't do that,' he says gravely. 'Samuel Johnson said: "Having a penis is being imprisoned with a mad man. But you must let the mad man speak."'

'Can you stop talking in riddles?' I sigh. 'You're not on a radio panel show now.'

'Why would you choose to fantasize about a woman who

doesn't want to be with you? That's not the function of fantasy. Tug yourself off to Cleopatra, for God's sake, go wild.'

'That's the point, her wanting to be with me *is* my wildest fantasy right now.'

'God, you really are in The Madness,' he says, shaking his head, turning the music back up and wailing along all the way to Colchester Comedy Club.

We're the last ones to arrive, but the hierarchy of backstage has already asserted itself. The most powerful of the group is Danny, the headliner – a circuit veteran with Eric Morecambe glasses and majority material about his former life as a geography teacher, but not many stories post-millennium. He's spent twenty years doing panel show appearances for money and literary festival interviewing for prestige, if not the arena sell-out tours he's always wanted. One rung below him is Emery, the compere of the night. Then there's Thalia – on first – an up-and-coming twenty-three-year-old with a ukulele and stories about her intrepid sexual past and the failings of the Tory government. And then there's me and Dean. The sagging middle. A couple of TV appearances between us, a tiny bit of radio, many friendships with recognizable comedians with large social media followings on which we're sometimes lucky enough to get a cameo. The forgettable filler to pad out the evening, with our boring T-shirts and our unchallenging observational bits about finding the perfect shower temperature.

Dean and I gravitate towards each other and make small talk about work and mutual friends. Thalia asks Emery and Danny for career advice as she tunes her ukulele. Emery drinks JD and Coke and revels in his role of guru to the wide-eyed ingénue, saying 'I must defer to Danny on this' just enough times to appear reverential. Danny is friendly but jaded, finishing nearly every story with 'the circuit's just not what it was any more'.

I watch Emery introduce himself to the audience and tell his story – orphaned aged twenty-one when his parents died within six months of each other, while clearing out their attic he found two rare mediaeval chess pieces, getting them valued for a million quid, blowing it all on cocaine, entering Narcotics Anonymous and finding salvation in stand-up. Every comedian I know is in agreement – if it didn't sound quite so shit, I'd be envious of him for getting such a good fifteen minutes out of it.

He gets the audience revved up, then they flatten slightly with Thalia's set in which she makes the early-days mistake of pointing out how nervous she is, only making the audience nervous too. Dean's on next with some stuff about what his cat would make of his relationship if it could speak – fairly experimental for him. Then I warm up for Danny with all the safe stuff, starting with how it's useful to have an accent that everyone underestimates and ending with my theory about how it's actually the garlic and herb dip that keeps us all in a life-long contract with Domino's Pizzas. It's not my most memorable work, but hearing a room of people laugh at my jokes is the best I've felt since the break-up. Danny does the same set I've heard him do for a decade and the audience love it. All in all, a good gig with no one's performance being so bad that we have to leave early to avoid talking to them when they come off stage.

When we say goodbye to everyone, I hear Thalia bemoaning her set to Danny and praising him for his.

'That's because there's nowhere for me to go,' I hear him say plainly as he drinks from a paper cup of tea. 'There's nothing for me to gain from the value of mistakes any more. You were the real triumph tonight because you've got everything ahead of you.' She laughs and playfully tells him that's not true. He puts his jacket on and chucks the empty paper cup in the bin.

Emery puts on a Bill Hicks tape for the drive back to London.

'Why didn't you talk about Jen tonight?' he asks.

'I don't do that kind of soul-baring stuff on stage,' I reply. 'That's not my sort of comedy.'

'Yeah, I know that, but I'm wondering whether this could be your chance to create your opus. Venture away from all that –' he puts on a miscellaneous Midlands accent – '"Have you noticed this funny thing about sausage rolls?" sort of vibe.'

'I don't do that vibe.'

'Didn't you make a joke about sausage rolls tonight? I thought you did.'

'I think what you're referring to is the bit about a *panini*, not a sausage roll. About how the tomato in it is always weirdly hotter than any other ingredient. That always gets the biggest laugh from the audience.'

'People really are morons.'

'Thanks.'

'Sorry, but they are. I despair.' We return to silence for a few minutes. 'I think you've been given a gift, you know,' he continues. 'Not just to grow as a man, but to grow as an artist. The voice of the heartbroken cuckold. Philosophical rigour on wanking. Mastery.'

'Hmm,' I say, unconvinced. 'Not hugely appealing, that.'

'This will be your dead dad show,' he says.

'I don't have a dead dad. You have a dead dad.'

'You could get a really great hour out of it,' he says excitedly. 'I'm jealous.'

'I don't know why,' I say.

'There are lots of good things about being single, you know.'

'No, I don't know. I've hardly ever been single. Tell me what I can look forward to.'

'Freedom. Fun. The wilderness of a weekend.'

'What's that?'

'You know . . . the unknown terrain of a Friday or Saturday

night. Not knowing where you'll ramble, who you'll meet, the mountains you'll climb, the lakes you'll swim in.'

'I'm no good in the wilderness, I don't think,' I sigh. 'I want a resort. A nice, comfortable, all-inclusive resort of a weekend.'

This makes Emery cackle.

'Lace up your walking boots and come join me, Andy! The weather's lovely out here!' He slaps my arm with his hand that isn't on the wheel, then turns the volume up on his Bill Hicks tape.

When I get back to Avi's it's gone one a.m. I give some cash to Emery for petrol and get out of the car.

'Andy!' he shouts from the window as he rolls it down. 'Remember: a broken heart is a jester's greatest prop.' I smile defeatedly. 'You've been handed a clown wig and collar. You could get some of your best work out of this.'

'Maybe.'

'We're on the same bill next Sunday, aren't we?'

'Hull,' I nod.

'See you in Hell!'

'*Hull*,' I correct him.

'That's what I meant!' he cackles and drives off.

When I get in, Avi is up uncharacteristically late, working on his laptop at the table.

'Hi, bro,' he says, barely looking up from his laptop. 'How was the gig? Good to be back on the horse?'

'Yeah. It felt good,' I say. 'Do you mind if I have a drink?'

'Help yourself,' he says. 'You must be knackered.'

I get a bottle of whisky and a glass from the cupboards.

'Want one?' I ask.

'Nah, got a pitch tomorrow morning.'

I pour myself a glass and sit at the table.

'Do you ever miss the wilderness of a weekend?'

'The what?'

'The feeling when you're young and single, when you don't know where any weekend could end up. What party you could go to and what person you might go home with, all that kind of stuff.'

Avi leans back in his chair and contemplates this. 'Nah.'

'Really?'

'In my experience, being single is a lot of awkwardness and insecurity. And bad nights out. And disappointments. And then you have, like, one incredible Saturday night once every three years that could only happen if you're single.'

'Like that night we met those two unbelievable girls in Edinburgh.'

'Outrageous,' he says.

'And we went up to Arthur's Seat at dawn and took pingers. And you got a handjob and I got a hug.'

'Exactly! *Exactly!*' he exclaims. 'And it's easy to look back and think that those sorts of experiences were what being single was. But for every night like that, there were thirty nights where you and I wandered around bars trying to find people who might like the look of us, and found no one, and ended up on a two-hour night bus home being moody with each other.'

'Yeah,' I say. 'I think you're right.'

'And the truth is, I was only ever going out to find some-one to stay in with.' He half laughs at his own sentimentality. 'I don't do well without responsibilities. I've accepted that I'm quite a boring bloke. I like having people to look after and feed.'

I'm taken aback by this rare moment of sincerity from him.

'I'm really glad you got what you always wanted, Avi,' I say. 'I would have done anything to have had a dad like you.'

He looks at me and says nothing for a while, his eyes fixed on my face. I feel nervous, worrying that he's going to cry.

'Fuck off,' he finally says. 'Stop taking the piss.'

'What!? I'm giving you a fucking compliment!'

'No you're not, you're being a fucking cock.'

'Oh my God, I was being fucking sincere, but fine.'

'Oh, okay,' he relents. 'Cheers, that's nice of you to say.'

'Jesus fucking Christ, I'm never trying that again.'

'Sorry.'

'I'm going to bed. Good luck with your pitch tomorrow.'

Saturday 20th July 2019

The big day has arrived. Avi wakes me up at eight a.m. with a mug of tea for me in one hand and Jackson's grubby palm in the other.

'Morning, buddy,' he says.

'Morning, mate.'

'Jackson – go on.'

'ALEXA????' he shrieks. 'PLAY "INSOMNIA" BY FAIFLESS.'

'Good boy!' Avi gives him a kiss.

'*Playing InsomniabyFaithless,*' the robotic voice replies. I rub my eyes as the haunting opening of my and Avi's favourite song to request at a club starts to play loudly from speakers around the house.

I get downstairs to find Jane in a similarly upbeat mood. She's going away this weekend, and Avi and I are dropping the boys off at his brother's house for a sleepover with their cousins so they can both have a night off.

'Where are you headed, Jane?'

'New Forest,' she replies, sipping coffee. 'Ardleigh House. Spa hotel.'

'Nice! With the girls?'

'Yep,' she says. I clock a look between her and Avi.

'So Jen's obviously going,' I say, trying and failing to sound as relaxed as possible.

'Yeah, she is – sorry, I can't lie to you, Andy,' Jane says. 'It's actually for her, the trip.'

'Why?'

'To help her with the break-up,' she says, as if it's obvious. 'To take her mind off things, cheer her up. Talk it through.'

I look at Avi indignantly. 'You hear that? She gets a whole weekend.'

'I've got a whole weekend planned.' He shrugs defensively.

'Oh yeah, like what?'

'Like . . . tomorrow. When we're hung-over. I've checked if the local KFC delivers on Uber Eats.'

'And?' I demand.

'They do.'

'We're doing a hammam and a forest walk,' Jane offers.

I try not to let it bother me, but it does. Why does Jen get a hotel spa weekend? *She* broke up with *me*. Is she sad? Does she need cheering up? Why was it so easy for five of Jen's friends who are all mothers or expectant mothers to drop everything and spend a weekend away at a hotel, yet I could barely get my best mates to come out for a few drinks? I want to get more information from Jane about the spa trip, but I am aware I only have a certain amount of questions I'm allowed to ask before she rightfully tells me I'm being inappropriate and shuts down all channels of data, so decide to save them up for tomorrow when the trip itself has happened and I can gather more intelligence.

We're the first to arrive at the pub. I'm pleasantly surprised when I discover that Avi has rung ahead and booked a table, which, translated into female terms, is the same as organizing a hammam treatment and a forest walk. Jay arrives first wearing too much aftershave and making murmurings that he can't be out past last orders because he's got to be up early with the baby. Then bounds in Rob, who's always been the communal energy source of a night out – every group needs one – and tonight is no exception. Matt comes shortly afterwards, looking tired but ready to chew over old jokes and affirm historic character dynamics – he brings the integrity and history of the group. Finally, Jon arrives from a day of shooting, in his cameraman uniform of a Patagonia T-shirt and cargo shorts, and we get a good seven minutes' worth of ribbing him about this.

And then: something extraordinary happens. For the next three hours, we sit around the table, we drink. And no one mentions my break-up. Not once. In fact, it's almost as if we're playing a game where we have to name as many random topics as possible to avoid talking about the one I thought we had all gathered in aid of. We talk about the most confident bald men we know, Matt's wife's keenness versus Matt's reticence to buy a Samoyed dog, the contents of Rob's benign cyst, the death of the iTunes voucher, the rumoured sex offence of our maths teacher from twenty years ago, China's one-child policy, we all do a bit of observational comedy on ill-fated experiences with self-service supermarket checkouts. And none of us mentions my big broken heart.

I go to the toilet and feel uncharacteristically livid at them all. I want to lash out with my pain to force them into acknowledging what I'm going through. I want to take my mangled break-up in my mouth and drop it in front of them like a cat bringing in a bloodied mouse from the garden.

I return to the bar and order six shots of tequila and take them over with six tiny wedges of lemon on a round silver tray. The sight of this provokes groans from the table rather than cheers – something that changed quite suddenly in our early thirties. We drink them in one, slam them on the table, suck our lemons, and then, through a wince, I blurt out:

'So. Jen and me. We're over.'

It is clumsy and strange and, understandably, they don't really know what I want from them. They ask me about how it happened, then they ask all the practical questions – when I moved out, where I'm planning to move to next, if I've heard from her since. They give me obvious pieces of advice and manage a few platitudes about 'better to be out of something now than wasting your time and it happening further down the line'. And then begins the great tradition of men sitting around complaining about women as a means of therapy. They all share break-up stories, they talk about their exes. I sit with my best listening face on, take none of it in, wondering why I thought this might make me feel better.

Jay tries to peel off at eleven, but we bully him into coming on to the next destination with us. The bar is a loud, busy chain trying to convince us it's not a chain with neon signs and velvet banquettes and gold geometric tables. We find a corner where we sit and huddle, and Rob, sensing a lull, goes to buy drinks and comes back with three jugs of an indistinguishable fruity red cocktail.

I go to the toilet to have a few quiet minutes to myself and, just drunk enough to ignore my better judgement, go on to the Ardleigh House Spa Hotel website. I look at the infinity pool with steam rising off it, the library with a roaring fire, the kitchen garden that 'we're proud to say provides 90 per cent of ingredients used in the fine-dining experience of The Orangery restaurant'. I imagine Jen and her best friends in fluffy white robes, lounging in a large suite, drinking wine, talking in that way I'd sometimes overhear Jen and her friends talking to each other when they came round to our flat. Each taking turns to present an emotion they've felt and all of them putting it under the microscope for inspection, as if it were a gem with a billion faces.

I return to the table and pour myself another glass of nameless cocktail.

'Time to talk to some birds,' Avi shouts in my ear, flinging his arm around my shoulder.

'No,' I say, shrugging off his embrace petulantly. 'I'm fine.'

'Come on!' shouts Jon.

'What about her!' Avi shouts and points at an attractive blonde ordering a drink at the bar. 'Go on!' I can't be bothered to protest so get up and approach her.

'Hiya,' I say half-heartedly.

'Hello!'

'You having a good night?'

'Yeah, I am, thanks. Are you?'

'Yeah, just here with my mates,' I say. 'How about you?'

'Same, here with mates.' The barman presents her with three drinks and she gives me a polite smile that suggests a full stop to the exchange.

'Would you like to come join us?' I ask.

'Ah, that's nice, but think I'm going to head back to my friends.'

'Sure,' I say. 'Have a good night.'

'You too.'

I have, in my slightly perkier moments in the wake of my and Jen's break-up, let myself believe that chatting women up might be fun; that, with age, I might have got better at it. For some reason, this assumption gets stronger with every break-up, despite not having done it for the years I've been in a relationship, and despite never being very good at it in the first place. And then I'm thrown into the world of flirting and I realize that sitting on the sofa with the same woman watching box sets has not made me more courageous and charismatic. In fact, it has done possibly the exact opposite. How could I have let myself believe, even for a second, that single thirty-something life would be an endless buffet of opportunities, when I know it is, at best, small plates.

★

The queue for the club is long, we're all drunk and starting to get sleepy. Jay is anxiously looking for escape routes, Jon's working overtime with strained statements of excitement about getting on the dance floor, and Avi's giving me the same advice over and over again.

'We go in there, we get a drink. Then you go find a girl to pull, you don't have to marry her,' he shouts, eyes swimming. 'You just need to get your dignity back.' He keeps saying this: that I need to find my dignity, that I've lost my dignity. That he'll always respect me, even if I don't have my dignity. These are the things my friends seem to prize above all else when at their most drunk, the words repeated ad infinitum: respect and dignity.

Jon's refused entry on account of his cargo shorts and Jay, spotting his exit, gallantly volunteers his trousers. They stumble around holding on to each other as they take off their trousers and swap them over, standing in their pants in front of the grumpy bouncers, sending a ripple of amusement along the queue. Jay vaults over the rope and practically sprints to break free from the group and find a taxi. Finally, we're in.

The tiki-themed club is made of a large circular dance floor, with a bar and seated areas wrapped around it, acting as a strange sort of viewing gallery. We head on to the dance floor, clutching our drinks in a bid to pep ourselves up. The music is, thankfully, mostly the music we listened to when we were growing up. I would venture a guess that this is because the tiki club is hosting a noughties nostalgia night. This is confirmed when I look around and see only people in their late teens and early twenties, singing along in a way that feels ironic rather than with genuine fondness. As I dance, I calculate whether a nineteen-year-old is closer to Jackson's age or my age and realize he's bang in the middle of us. All the boys are singing along to Eminem's 'Without Me', Avi giving a particularly rousing rendition.

'I REMEMBER WATCHING THIS WITH YOU ON *TOP OF THE POPS*,' I shout at him. He nods, smiling, but I'm sure he hasn't heard me.

Matt and Jon, who've briefly disappeared, return to the dance floor holding two shots for me. I do one after the other to make them go away quicker. 'Hit 'Em Up Style' by Blu Cantrell is playing.

'I REMEMBER WATCHING THIS ON *TOP OF THE POPS* TOO,' I bellow into the cavern of the circle we've formed.

'STOP TALKING ABOUT *TOP OF THE POPS*, YOU MUPPET,' Rob shouts.

'WE WERE TOO YOUNG FOR *TOP OF THE POPS*,' Matt joins in.

Maybe we were. Maybe I'm just saying it because I'm worried someone's going to look at me and say 'He looks like he watched this on *Top of the Pops*', so I'm saying it first. But I'm not that old. Am I? I don't know how old I am any more. I don't know where I want to be. I'm not technically too old to be in a club, but I don't want to be in a club. And I don't want to stay in either. I don't have anything you're meant to have to stay in – no girlfriend or baby or pet or flat of my own. I don't want to be on a night out and I don't want to be on a night in. Where do I want to be? I close my eyes as the opening for 'Blue (Da Ba Dee)' plays and I feel like I'm spinning on a merry-go-round. I want to be in my favourite pub with Jen. Then I want to go to the cheap Italian at the end of our road and eat too much bread and too much spaghetti, drink two bottles of Chianti. I want to go home and drink whisky with her and dance in our living room and sing along to our favourite songs until the neighbours complain and then I want to fall into bed and fuck and go to sleep at one a.m. with her in my arms, too drunk to take off her make-up or brush her teeth. That's what I want.

'I WANNA FAG,' Avi shouts.

'ME TOO,' I shout back.

I'm relieved to get outside. I'm soaked in sweat and shiver in the night breeze. Avi takes a fag out, closes one eye to focus and shoves it in my mouth, before doing the same with his.

'I miss Jane,' he slurs. 'And I miss those other cunts.'

'Who?'

'My kids. You know, they're all right actually, they can be a laugh. If they weren't my kids, I would be like, Jesus, don't want to sit next to them at a dinner party. Their stories are too long and sometimes they shit their pants. They're a solid four out of ten.'

'Yeah,' I say blankly.

'But because they're my kids, I just think they're a ten out of ten. I do! I can't help it.'

I don't know what does it — the effort of trying to follow Avi's train of thought, the mixing of drinks, the cigarette, the crisps-only dinner — but, out of nowhere, I bend over and flood the smoking area with pink vomit.

Avi summons the boys, almost triumphantly. There is a sense that this was always the unsaid intended end to the evening. They act as if they have led me on a shamanic ritual and now I am healed. The consensus is that we head back to Rob's. His wife's out too and he's got balloons left over from Glastonbury.

I barely speak in the cab, or when we get back to Rob's. I try hard to keep my balance. We all sit on the two sofas, Rob puts on a Britpop playlist and Matt fills the first balloon with a canister.

'Here we go, pal, this should sort you out,' Jon says, passing it to me. I hold the full balloon in my lips, close my eyes and start taking shallow breaths. The balloon works its magic and only my hearing is left in the room as I breathe in and out on it. I am transported. My body is suddenly in a marquee. I'm in Dorset, at a cosy country wedding. I know I'm only a few inhalations into the balloon, but I've been here for an hour already. There are fairy lights everywhere, Pulp is playing. Jen is wearing a long, sky-blue dress and she comes over to dance with me. We dance for another hour, then another, even though I know I'm on the same balloon. I breathe in, out, in, out. Jen and I are leading a conga line, laughing as we recruit elderly relatives and little nieces and nephews. Now Blur is playing. I don't know whose wedding this is but I love it and I love them.

'Bloody hell, mate,' I hear someone say in the distance.

'He's drawing on it like it's his pension!' Rob shouts and they all laugh. Then everything goes black.

And that's the last thing I remember.

Sunday 21st July 2019

I wake up in a bed I've never woken up in before. Avi's. He's not there, I'm alone. It's eleven a.m., I'm in his tracksuit bottoms, a pair of pants I don't recognize and nothing else. I clutch my head, finding relief from my hangover as I press my hand into various points of my skull. I go to the attic to find a T-shirt and head downstairs, where Avi is making tea.

'Hello, mate, good morning!' he says cheerily. 'How's the head?'

'Um. Awful? What the fuck happened last night?'

'How much do you remember?' he says.

'That's the worst reply to that question,' I say.

'Nah! All good, mate. But yeah, what's your last memory?'

'Doing that balloon at Rob's.'

'Right, so we did balloons, had a couple of bevs, got a cab home, all good.'

I look at Avi's wide smile, barely distracting from his sticky eyes.

'Something weird happened.'

'No it didn't!'

'Why did I wake up in your bed, then?'

'Oh, it's because we were so drunk when we got in, we thought it would be a laugh if I slept in your bed and you slept in my bed!'

I take this in.

'Why would that be a laugh? And whose Y-fronts am I wearing? Where are my clothes from last night?'

'Oh Christ, mate, I don't know. I was battered. We had a good time and that's all that matters, right?'

'Right,' I say, unconvinced. 'It was a great night, thanks for organizing it, man.'

'No worries, man. You ready for a Zinger Tower yet?'

'Definitely not.'

I search for a new podcast to keep me company in the shower. Everything in the top ten is hosted by a male comedian more successful than me and I cannot bear it, so I land on number 17, *Mum's the Word*, a weekly discussion about new motherhood hosted by two former *American Idol* contestants. I sit under the water for almost an hour, vomit twice, and have to use the showerhead and Jackson's pineapple-scented bubble bath to get it all down the plug hole, which is potentially the lowest moment of my adult life to date.

By the time I dry and change and get downstairs, I'm just about ready for a mug of tea, which leads to a nearly-thirty-five-quid KFC order while Avi and I lie on the sofa and watch *Harry Potter and the Deathly Hallows Part One* in silence. Jane arrives a couple of hours later with the boys and, thankfully, I still feel too ill to muster the energy to question her on the various spa activities of Ardleigh House Hotel. I summon the strength to make the long Sunday-night tube journey to Euston, where Emery stands at platform five, wearing a short-sleeved shirt with an eighties diamond pattern on it and holding a plastic bag clanking with gin-in-a-tins.

'This. Is. The problem,' he says in response to my whining about Jen, which begins in Kings Cross and ends just outside of Stevenage. 'Heterosexual men and women are not well-matched. There was a factory fault when God, whoever she is, made them with the hopes of compatibility.'

'What do you mean?' I ask as I chomp a meal deal sandwich.

'Reverse break-up schedules,' he explains. 'When men and

women break up, men hate everything about their ex-girlfriend for three months, and then they miss her, and then they think they love her, and that's when they text her. Meanwhile, she has spent three months loving him and then she *hates his guts forever*,' he says, leaning in for emphasis, his breath hot and tangy with gin. 'We were never meant to be with each other. Men and women are not compatible.'

I process what he's said. 'Hang on, this isn't relevant at all. What you're saying is I'm following the female pattern of behaviour in a break-up. And hopefully she's following the male. But we don't know that. Maybe she just went straight to hating me and stayed there.'

He sips from his tinnie.

'Oh yeah,' he says. 'Sorry, not helpful at all, my boy. I'll be honest – I've been drinking since midday.' He shudders at the memory.

One of the very few things that I dislike about Emery is that he can go on stage completely legless and it almost always works in his favour. Everything about his comedy lends itself to drunkenness. The ranting, the repetition, the expletives, the shouting about politics, the enormous generalizations made about women. The more red in the face and wild he gets, the more they seem to love him. He makes up a little sketch on the spot about how Mark Zuckerberg will be treated at the gates of hell – all of it meandering, none of it making much sense, but with enough shouting and spittle and pauses for gulps of beer, he seems like a tortured, anarchic genius. When really I know he's just in a state of drunken idiocy.

I am straight on after him and, as I walk on stage and mop up his excess charisma, I can sense that my set isn't going to work. The audience is all hopped up on him. They want more rock-star comedy and I have a feeling my gentle new material about how hard it is to get a bunch of thirty-somethings on a night out isn't going to work. As I feel it flop from beginning to end, I'm reminded once more that there are hundreds of different ways to feel good when a gig goes well. And only one way to feel bad when a gig goes badly.

We catch the nine-thirty back to London, with just enough time for me to get a second dinner from Subway.

'I'm thinking about getting a personal trainer,' I say, stuffing the foot-long into my mouth.

'Oh GOD,' Emery bellows dramatically and lowers his head on to his fold-out table in despair.

'I know it's a cliché but –'

'It's more than a cliché, it's BOURGEOIS, Andy.'

'Well, bourgeois or not, I've got to do something about this,' I say, gesturing at my middle.

'So, what, you're going to give yourself a makeover?'

'No. Maybe,' I say, taking a sip of Coke. 'I'm someone who lives in their head, I'd like to at least try to live in my body too.'

'Hmm,' he says sceptically.

'I don't just want an internal existence. All the self-obsession and the over-thinking. I feel like a brain in a jar with no limbs sometimes.'

'And you're not even that clever,' he offers.

'Cheers,' I say, shaking my head and picking up my phone. I open Instagram and look in the folder of message requests to see if anyone has posted about my set. I see a message request from a girl, @Tash_x_x_x_

Hello funny guy x

I go on to her profile and hold the screen close to my face to try and make out her profile photo. Late twenties? Long dark hair, thick eyebrows, brown, almond-shaped eyes. Relaxed smile. Very white teeth.

'Oh my God,' I say.

'What?' Emery replies, looking up from his book.

'Some absolute babe has DM'd me.'

'Show me,' he says.

I turn the phone screen round to him.

'Bot.'

'Not a bot, look.' I show him the few photos she's put on her grid. A little fluffy dog. An iced latte. A woman who looks like it could be her mum.

'Do you think she was there tonight?'

'Dunno.'

'Are you going to reply to her?'

'I don't know, should I?'

'YES,' he says.

I type:

Depends who you ask.

I hold it up to Emery.

'Good. Self-effacing. Succinct.'

I send it. Emery grips my arm and grins. 'This is the signal,' he says. 'You've sent the invisible flare up. It's happening.'

'What's that?' I ask.

'When a person becomes single, they transmit something out into the world without even trying and it's at a frequency that only other single people can hear. Suddenly every ex is in their in-box, strangers are trying it on –'

'Oh my God, she's seen it,' I say. 'She's typing. Oh my God, she's typing.'

I've watched you, you're funny. And fit.

My jaw opens. I show Emery the message.

80

'Definitely a bot,' he says, before sinking back into his chair and taking no further interest in the messages.

> I think you must be mistaking me for someone else.

She types.

> I saw you at Crouch End comedy club last year. You were soooo good

> That's very kind of you. What's your name?

> I'm Tash x

> I'm Andy

> Lol yes I know

> What do you do Tash?

> I'm a nanny

I pause and consider my response, cautious of my own enthusiasm.

> Cool.

> What you up to this fine sunday eve

> Got possibly the worst hangover of 2019 which was soothed no end by a gig in Hull. Now on the long train home.

> Lucky for you you've got me to keep you company.

Emery doesn't glance up from his book again for the rest of the journey. I spend it attached to my phone, DM'ing Tash.

The tenor of our messaging is how I remember conversations during my brief time on dating apps – flirty without ever feeling the flirting is aimed specifically at me. Friendly without friendship. Suggestive without ever really suggesting anything. I get home at half one at which point I've been on/off messaging Tash inanities for three hours. I brush my teeth, take a photo for BALD and go to bed.

> Goodnight Tash. Thank you for brightening up what would have otherwise been MAYBE the worst train journey of my life.

My pleasure. Goodnight gorgeous.

Wednesday 24th July 2019

'And finally, the nominees for most effective employer brand development are . . .'

I turn to the screen behind me as animated words appear: 'ABC Employer Brand Team.' There's a limp round of applause from the mass of darkness in front of me. 'Absolutely Management.' More applause. 'And —' I say expectantly, but no other words appear. 'Oh. Okay, just two nominations. Well. Fifty-fifty chance. And the winner is . . .' I open the card on the stand. 'Absolutely Management.' I hear one person whoop from a far-away table and I clap while a woman in an impossibly sparkly dress does the very long walk from her seat up to the stage. I hand her the award and we stand stiffly next to each other for a photograph.

'Well, that's the ceremony part of the evening done for the Recruitment and Headhunting Awards 2019, I've been Andy Dawson, you've been an absolute pleasure. I may not know what your jobs are, but I know you get paid a lot for them, so go buy some champagne and hit the d-floor. Thank you very much and goodnight.'

As I leave the function room and walk down the hotel corridor to get my jacket, a man approaches hurriedly. He wears a suit, blue shirt and tie and is bald but for a band of grey hair encircling the bottom of his head. He puts his hand out to shake mine and clasps it with the other one.

'I'm Bob,' he says. 'Good to meet you. I've gotta tell you, that was absolutely *fantastic*. Normally these events are dull as anything, but you really got it right.'

'Cheers,' I say. 'I'm glad you enjoyed it.'

'I'm from Birmingham too,' he says.

It takes all my will not to casually enquire into the origin story of his hair loss and whether it started at the front or the back.

'Oh yeah, do you live there now?'

'No, moved to London thirty years ago. I've actually been living on a canal boat the last few years.'

'No way!' I say. 'Not very corporate of you!'

'Yeah, yeah,' he laughs. 'I get that a lot.'

'How d'you end up there?'

'Divorce,' he says, leaning in conspiratorially. 'Nasty. I didn't know where I wanted to lay down roots next and an opportunity came up to buy a houseboat and I thought – why not. Shocked, my kids were. They were like: "Dad, we can't believe you're doing this." And I *did* do it.'

'Good on you!' I say. 'I'm going through something similar. Broke up with my girlfriend last month and just moved out. I'm living with my best mate and his wife for now, which can't go on forever. But the thought of becoming a roommate to strangers again at thirty-five is so weird.'

He looks at me with an intent gaze.

'Have you ever considered boat life?'

'No?'

'I think it could be exactly what you need right now,' he says. 'It's a perfect place for an artist, like yourself. The community on the water is unreal. And I tell you what, the ladies love it.' He leans in again as he says this and lets out a wheezy laugh. 'I'm looking for someone to rent it, actually, if you're interested.'

'Where are you going?'

'Met a nice lady. She's taken me back to dry land. But I'm not quite ready to sell her.' He takes a well-rehearsed pause. 'The boat that is!'

'Very good,' I say.

'Look – here's my number. Drop me a text if you want to talk more about it. I could do you a nice little deal.' He presses a business card into my hand, pats my back and walks away. Only then do I notice the very, very tiny plait that he has resourcefully formed, poking over the top of his blazer collar.

I pick up a Chinese takeaway on the way home and Avi, Jane and I watch Boris Johnson's first speech as prime minister.

'. . . *And so I am standing before you today to tell you, the British people, that those critics are wrong. The doubters, the doomsters, the gloomsters – they are going to get it wrong again . . .*'

'Hate him,' I say.

'Me too,' Avi chimes.

'Why do you hate him?'

'Tory cunt,' Avi says.

'Yeah, Tory cunt,' I agree.

'Of course he's a Tory cunt,' Jane says. 'He's the leader of the Conservative party. I don't like him either, but can you give me one reason other than that pathetic English habit of droning on about how much you hate Tories just to prove you're a good person.'

'Smug,' Avi says.

'Yeah, smug,' I agree.

'Big, posh, useless polar bear.'

'Exactly,' I say.

'. . . *with high hearts and growing confidence we will now accelerate the work of getting ready. And the ports will be ready and the banks will be ready and the factories will be ready and business will be ready. And the hospitals will be ready . . .*'

I don't admit that the reason I hate him quite as much as I do is that he's the first prime minister in my adult life who has more hair than me. No wonder he is so smug. I would be too. The lid on him is outrageous. There's so much of it he can't even be bothered to brush it.

'I've found a one-bed for five hundred quid a month. In East London,' I say.

'Five hundred?!' Jane asks.

'Yeah! Large studio.'

'That's brilliant, mate!' Avi says. 'Where exactly?'

'Hackney. It's on the canal.'

'Canal views!' Jane says. 'Ringadingding, sounds like a bachelor pad.'

'Because it floats on the canal,' I say. They both look at me, confused. 'It's a boat.'

'A *canal* boat?' Avi asks.

'Yes, obviously.'

'And you'd live on it full-time?'

'Yes.'

'*Why?*' he exclaims.

'Because I met a man today who offered me a great deal on one and it's the only way I can see myself being able to afford my own place in London. And it will be an adventure!'

'But . . .' Avi is uncharacteristically lost for words. 'Don't you get terrible sea sickness?'

'Yeah, like, on a pedalo in Corfu when we were nineteen after I'd had eleven cider blacks.'

'Don't you think you should spend more time on some boats before you decide to live on one?'

'Avi, mate, can you not just be pleased for me?'

'Sorry, sorry. I am. Good on you, mate. And all who sail in her.' He raises his can of Coke to me.

'Thank you,' I say sulkily. 'I'll move out this weekend. I've encroached on you guys long enough.'

'You haven't at all,' Jane says. 'We've been happy to have you. And it will be fun to come hang out on your boat!'

'Yeah,' Avi says unconvincingly.

I go upstairs and spend a good half-hour in front of the bathroom mirror twisting my arm and head in uncomfortable positions, trying to get the clearest photo I can for BALD. I lie in bed on top of the covers and flip back and forth between the last week's worth of BALD's contents to try to gauge any progression or regression. Tash messages.

> Hello you. How's your day been?
>
> > All good, other than the demolition of democracy stuff.
> > How're you?
>
> Same same.

Like many times in my recent messaging with Tash, I'm not quite sure how to respond. She seems to want to message all the time, but about almost nothing. She's resistant to giving me many details about her life. She doesn't want to go into depth on anything – interests, ideas, jokes. All we seem to message about are the happenings of our day, tinged with slight horniness. So I'm surprised when she writes:

> How are you tho?

Comparatively, this is real Frost/Nixon stuff for Tash. I write and rewrite a reply several times.

> > I'm feeling a bit blue, Tash
>
> Why?
>
> > Don't want to bring the mood down
>
> Go on, funny boy. Bring it right down.

My thumbs hover over the keypad.

> Going through a break-up

She types immediately.

> Break-ups are the worst

> Yes they are

> I'm sorry ur going thru that

> Part of life isn't it? Like taxes and experimental new flavours of Walkers that don't sell. Unavoidable

> Do you have ppl you can talk to

> Hmm. Not sure.

I feel like I want to cry, and I am not sure why. She types for a while and I'm nervous about what's going to appear in our chat. Finally, the grinning emoji with the handsy hug appears. And we're back in business.

> Where are you now

> In bed

> Naked?

There are many reasons I choose not to reply to this message with the lie that I am also naked and not in a pair of Batman boxers my mum bought me for Christmas. The most pressing being that Emery was screenshotted wanking on FaceTime to a girl who DM'd him two years ago and it went viral online and thank GOD he got a show out of it, but I'm not about to make the same mistake as him.

When can I see you?

Why?

If we're gonna be naked we should probably be naked together? Might be fun.

When was the last time you were naughty irl?

I pause and think of what to reply. I don't know whether to be honest. I'm not sure if honesty is what's required in this sort of exchange – it feels like so long since I've done this.

Not for a bit

R you gonna be naughty soon?

If you'd like to be, yes please.

Night Andy x

Night Tash xx

Friday 26th July 2019

The blue-haired man and I exchange precisely zero niceties when I return to the storage facility. He silently hands me the keys, I walk down the long corridor and wonder how many of the units are being used for the same reason I rented mine – wartime bunkers for our life's content to hide in. When I open the door's padlock and see my minimal possessions, I pretend I am a stranger and imagine what I would make of this person's life from his selection of objects. I don't make the mistake of hiring a van again having realized that all of it can fit in a large taxi.

Bob waits by the boat wearing a short-sleeved linen shirt, long shorts, sandals and a pair of wraparound sunglasses. He dangles the keys in front of me.

'She makes a fine home for a free man,' he declares.

'Cheers, Bob,' I say.

'Come aboard, I'll show you all her nooks and crannies.'

I make a decision in that moment to never, ever gender the boat.

We step along the deck and down into the boat and I try to hide my surprise at how small it is. I can feel the tips of my hair touch its roof.

'Riiiiight,' he says on an out-breath. 'I'll rattle through this as quickly as possible. Fire, fuel, leccy, bog. Those are your basics. Fire – can you start one?'

'Yes,' I lie.

'Fantastic, wood's over there. You'll need to nurse that through the night if it's cold. Fuel – it lasts a long time but there's no gauge to tell you when it's about to run out, you'll have to use the dipstick. I'd check it today, if I were you. Gas,' he says, walking over to the hob. 'That's wired from a camping bottle that you'll need to keep renewing. Electricity – keep an eye on your battery health. Shower – very basic, does the job. Toilet,' he says with a new tone of severity, leading me into the tiny bathroom. 'Now – this can be a little dicey. It's a porta-potty. That'll get full and need emptying about once a fortnight. To empty it, you remove the lower half and then find an Elsan point. Only trouble is – Elsan points are often overflowing or out-of-order or closed, so then you have to . . . think laterally, let's put it like that.' He laughs knowingly. I laugh too, but I don't know what he means. 'Bed!' he announces, striding through the boat. 'You're a pretty tall fella, how tall are you?'

'Six foot two.'

'Not a problem, then,' he says with a wide smile. 'So the bed's on the horizontal, as you can see, which is about six foot, so you'll just have to slightly curl up at night when you go to sleep so you can fit in it.'

There is a pause as I try to figure out whether he's joking.

'I mean, that sounds a bit like a problem, Bob.'

'Nah, not for a bohemian like yourself,' he says.

I am deeply mistrusting of wherever he's got this idea of me.

'Very narrow, isn't it,' I try to say in an offhand way.

'Well . . . yeah!' he laughs. 'It is a narrowboat! Don't worry, you'll get used to her. Right, so I think that's all I need to tell you. You've got my number. The only other thing to say is – you've got five more days before you have to move her along.'

'Along? Along to where?'

'Wherever you can find free space. Might be east, might be west, could be north. Could set sail on the river out to Oxford. Who knows! That's the fun of it.'

'Can't I just keep it here?' I ask.

He looks at me, aghast.

'Here?' he says, pointing at the boat's floor.

'Yeah.'

'God, no, this isn't a mooring! Do you know how much a mooring in Hackney would cost?!' I look at him blankly. 'About a grand a month, at least! Daylight robbery if you ask me.'

'So how much do I have to move it?'

'Every two weeks, otherwise you could be evicted,' he says matter-of-factly. 'RIGHT. I'll be off, then, captain!' He stands up straight and salutes me, before walking up to the deck and on to the towpath, leaving me alone on my new home.

I take a photo of the bare shell of its yellowy-white interior and send it to Tash.

I'M ON A MOTHERFUCKING BOAT!!

Good to keep it light. Nice talking point. I've been sensing her interest in me wane over the last few days. Her messages are becoming more and more spaced out and she's asking fewer and fewer questions. She refuses to elevate our relationship and make it more tangible – I've given her my number but she only DMs. She won't agree to a specific date to meet up. I worry that the boat message doesn't invite a response, so follow up a few minutes later.

Let's hang!

I put on a podcast series about a woman in America who scammed fourteen different men into donating various vital organs needlessly, and unpack my things. I unwrap my mugs and cutlery and bowls. I put my clothes away in the small wardrobe and two drawers under the bed. I put a duvet and pillows on the bed. I'm moved in in less than an hour and I'm not quite sure what to do next.

There's a café on the towpath where I sit and have a coffee. I wander away from the canal and buy some groceries and a couple of bottles of wine. I manage to tell everyone I encounter that I've just moved into a narrowboat and I am met with statements of jealousy or wonderment. It is the most interesting I have ever felt and I enjoy answering their questions on the practicalities of plumbing and post and electricity with the authority accrued from an hour spent on the boat.

I make my way back through the rain and on to the boat to find water collecting on the floor underneath the windows. I send a text to Bob.

> Hi Bob – think the rain is leaking through the windows?
> Has this happened before?

I fiddle around with the locks and open and close them a few times, which only invites more rain in. Bob replies.

> Yes! Quite normal. Don't worry. Use towels, T-shirts etc until it stops. Might be worth having a spare set or two of tea towels for this purpose.

I use my bath towel and a few T-shirts to absorb the water and make beans on toast for dinner. As the sky gets darker and the rain falls harder, I get into bed to warm up. I hotspot my phone for internet and watch a film on my laptop as I make my way through a bottle of wine.

I wonder what Tash is up to and, too embarrassed to send her another message, type her handle into Instagram to see if she's updated her stories. Her page doesn't come up. I backspace and type it again.

User not found

I go into the WhatsApp group formerly known as Armadil-dos, recently changed to Balloon Loons, the natural conclusion to any night out. I type a message into the group.

Andy

What does user not found mean on Instagram?

Matt types.

Matt

Profile deleted or she's blocked you

Andy

How do you know a she

Rob

Lol

Avi

As if you would care if it was a bloke

Jon

You been pied?

Andy

Can I find out if blocked or deleted???

Matt

What's her Insta handle

Andy

@Tash_x_x_x_

Matt

Not coming up for me either, she must have deleted her profile or changed her name

Jay
Did you send her a nude hahahahahaa

I turn my phone screen-side on to the bed, feeling disappointment and sadness that is wildly disproportionate to the relationship, if you can even call it that. I realize the last week has felt like I have been on a very brief but very real holiday from my mind. Away from Jen, away from the memories of our relationship. I had been allowed a few days of respite – a little sojourn to Tash Island with all its attractions and sunnier climes. And now it's over. I'm back to where I was a week ago, back on the mainland of my misery. I hear a loud noise and get out of bed to see that the force of the rain has slammed a window open. I close it and find another T-shirt to mop up the water.

And then, as I'm picking up soaking items of my own clothing and putting them into a plastic bag, I realize something else:

I don't think I like being on this boat. In fact, I think I hate it. I think the only thing I've enjoyed about the boat so far has been *leaving the boat and walking around telling everyone that I live on a boat.*

Could it be that the boat and Tash came into my life at the exact same time and I got my feelings all muddled? Did I confuse my enthusiasm for a potential new girlfriend with my enthusiasm for living on a canal boat? Did I conflate the two? Did I think that my new life on a boat went hand-in-hand with a new relationship with an outrageously attractive woman who thought I was hilarious?

I finish the bottle of wine and open another. The rain continues and the boat gets colder. I can't work out how to turn on the heating so instead have a scorching hot shower and only realize when I'm drip-drying naked that my towel is being used to stop the boat from flooding. I shiver as I get back into bed and look at my phone. No new messages.

95

I miss going to bed knowing other people are also asleep in the house. This is the first time I've slept somewhere on my own since the break-up. Was Jane right when she said that men don't know how to be single? Am I really so reliant on the ambient shapes and sounds and smell of another body?

I finish the last of the second bottle of wine and open up my and Jen's WhatsApp chat. This is a bad habit I've got into – going down into the cellar of our digital relationship and doing a search on words that take me back to different periods of our near-four-years' worth of talking. Sometimes I'm in a sentimental mood and the key search terms I choose take me to the most loved-up moments of our time together – *baby*, *darling*, *I love you*, *I miss you*. Other times, I want to return to the horniest phases of our relationship and I revisit all our historic sexts. Tonight, I'm afraid, it's the latter.

> Cock

I type into the search bar of our chat and press return. The word appears in our chat as a message. She immediately appears online.

> What???

she replies.

Oh Jesus.

Oh Jesus oh Jesus oh Jesus this hasn't happened. I haven't done this. She's typing. She's replying too fast for me to come up with a believable excuse. I have to think fast.

> I know you're hurting Andy but you can't speak to me like this. It's unacceptable. More than that – it's abusive.

My thumbs, numb from the cold and sluggish from booze, poke at the keypad.

I'm so sorry Jen I made a mistake this was meant for Avi

I stare at her online status. She types nothing.

Jen I'm so sorry genuine mistake.

OK.

I'm sorry that must have been so weird to get a random message from me saying cock

A bit, yeah

So soryr again. Hope you're well. X

X

Another one of those solitary kisses. I put my phone under the pillow, turn off the lights and pull the duvet up over my head. I close my eyes and try to summon Jen's face. As always, I can only see her one feature at a time. The nose that changed shape with every turn of her head. The heavy eyelids, her long, straight lashes. The five freckles that appeared across the bridge of her nose in the summer. There was something eternally unknowable about her face, her thoughts, her brain. I always felt there had been a part of her that I would never truly understand, a part that was only for her.

The rain continues for the hour it takes me to get to sleep. It's still raining when the light wakes me up through the bare windows at dawn.

Monday 29th July 2019

It takes longer to move out of the boat than it took to move into it. Bob messages to tell me to leave the keys in the code-locked box attached to the deck and it is clear from his tone that the simpatico relationship between us has disappeared. When I return to the storage facility for the third time in a month, the blue-haired man insists that I have to fill out an entirely new customer form even though I am to rent the exact same storage unit.

I think Jane's had a word with Avi and told him not to joke about the boat, because when I arrive at their place it's not mentioned at all. The mattress has been lugged back up to the attic, Rocco runs up to me and kisses me, Jackson has done a drawing of me holding Avi's hand. I get the sense that the entire household has been briefed on something.

I order yet another takeaway that night as a paltry offering of thanks. While we're opening cartons of pad thai and red curries, Avi says:

'Shall we tell him?'

'Yeah,' Jane replies.

'Tell me what?'

They look at each other knowingly.

'I'm pregnant,' Jane says proudly.

'What? *Again?* Haven't you just gone back to work at your agency? *Three?* What the hell? Av, can't you get the snip or something?'

'Mad, I know,' he shrugs. 'But we've always wanted three. I sort of wish we didn't, but we do.'

'I want a gang. I come from a gang. It's fun,' Jane says.

'I see,' I say, not seeing. 'Well, come here.' I stand up and envelop them both in a group hug. 'I love you guys. Any more humans made by you two can only be a good thing.' We all squeeze each other and I miss Jen so much it brings a sharp pain to the middle of my chest.

The baby news is enough to make me head straight up to bed after dinner, prop my laptop up on my stomach and refuse to go to sleep until I find somewhere to live. I put out embarrassing pleas on social media. Everything is out of my budget and, when I enquire into the few rooms I can afford, they've already been taken. After two hours of searching, I'm stopped by the sight of a comparatively low price in a comparatively good part of town. I read and reread it a few times.

LODGER WANTED HORNSEY
NO REMAIN VOTERS
£618 PM inc. bills

I am looking for a lodger in my two bed house in Hornsey I will live there my name is Morris i have no pets i am 78. There is a garden i do not accept rent in a bank account only cash or cheques. The room is a big room double bed furnished. NO to ALL practising religions and musical instruments. I have a television bath, shower. All genders ages welcome no under 25s. All nationalities welcome excl dutch. My number is 0208 341 9595 please call me if you would like it goodbye

'HELLO?' a male Northern voice shouts.
'Hello, is this Morris?' There is a pause.
'WHY?'

'My name is Andy, I saw your advert for the room online?' Another very long pause. 'Hello?'

'Yes?' he yelps.

'Is the room still available?'

'Yes?'

'Okay. Can I come see it?'

'How do you know my name?' he asks.

'It's written in the advert.'

'Oh. Yes, it's a two-bedroom house, quite big. Your room is big, with a bed and some other bits of furniture. Yes?'

'Yes, sounds great. Could I come see it tomorrow?'

Another pause.

'Do you work for the state?'

'The *state*? No, I'm a comedian.'

Another long pause.

'Okay, you can move in in two days' time,' he says briskly. 'Thirty-three, Montague Avenue, please do not ring the doorbell.'

'Say that again, thirty-three –'

He ends the call.

Wednesday 31st July 2019

When I walk into Giraffe Storage Kentish Town, the blue-haired man doesn't even look up as he pushes the key across the counter.

'Don't worry, this is the last time you'll ever see me,' I say.

He pretends he hasn't heard and stares at the computer screen.

I arrive at the address Morris gave me and knock on the door, avoiding the bell as instructed. No one comes. I knock a few times and still get nothing. I go to the front-room window, which has been left open a crack, and shout through.

'HELLO?' I shout. 'HELLO, MORRIS? I'M AT THE DOOR.'

I hear movement from within the house and, after a few moments, a small man with patchy wisps of white hair opens the door.

'What?' he asks. 'Who are you, what do you want?'

'I'm Andy,' I say. 'We spoke on the phone. I'm taking the room. I'm moving in today.'

He looks at me cautiously with enormous black-brown eyes, alert and vulnerable like a woodland creature.

'Where are all your belongings?' he asks, looking expectantly behind me.

'Here,' I say, pointing at the bags and boxes on the ground.

'That it?'

'Yes,' I reply.

'All of your things?'

'Yes.'

His gaze remains suspicious as he looks at my stuff then looks me up and down.

'Are you living off-grid? To avoid the taxman?'

'For fu– *no*,' I say exasperatedly. 'I just don't have that much stuff.'

He pauses another beat before finally beckoning me in.

'All right, come in.'

I follow him into the house. The hall is covered in old rugs and lined with plants in pots, and plants in baskets hang down the terracotta walls.

'Wow, a lot of foliage. Are they real?'

'Yes,' he says, picking up a plastic watering can and tending to a large spider plant. 'You mustn't touch them, please don't try to be helpful. I have a very strict routine.'

'Understood,' I say. 'Can I?' I gesture towards a door.

'Yes, look around,' he says.

I nod and walk into the living room, which isn't filled with as many plants because the walls are lined with neat, high columns of newspapers. I look at the top of the nearest pile – the *Evening Standard*, 1993.

'You mustn't touch those either,' he says.

I turn round to see him standing in the middle of the room, watching me.

'No problem. Quite a collection you've got here.'

'Important to have a record.'

'Yeah. If only there was a web of information and history that the whole world could access from their own homes!' I say jokingly. He looks at me blankly. 'Bad joke. About the internet.'

'I have Wi-Fi here. Broadband.'

'That's good.'

'I didn't have broadband for the past few years. Before that I had dial-up. Then before that I used to go to my friend Tim's house, he only lives on the other road, but then I started think-ing that I didn't want my information and my web searches logged on his computer. Not that I was doing anything I wanted to hide, but I don't know how all that data could be used, so I asked Tim to reset the computer, but of course I've since read there is no such thing as resetting anything these days, not once you've put in your name and your address and you've signed up to something, they're tracking you for the rest of your life, even when you delete your logins.' He's barely pausing for breath as he speaks, hurrying to the end of every sentence like he's wor-ried that he's going to interrupt himself. It goes on like this for a while and I make the right noises so he thinks I'm listening.

'Shall I see my room?' I ask when he takes a half-second pause and I spot my opportunity.

'Yes,' he says, immediately marching out into the hallway and up the stairs.

Upstairs is the same – plants, patterned wallpaper peeling slightly at the edges, piles of newspapers, lots of lamps – tired, lived-in decor, but clean and oddly cosy. On the landing I spot a vinyl rack with LPs of mostly Beatles albums.

'Beatles fan?' I ask.

'Yes,' he says.

'Me too,' I say.

'Just four lads from Liverpool,' he says, shaking his head. 'And they went on to change the world.'

'Yeah. Mad to think, isn't it.'

'This house has some Beatles history to it.'

'Really?!'

'Yes,' he says. 'I bought this house forty-nine years ago from a man named Terry McAllister.' He's already losing me. 'And he assured me that George Harrison's cousin was a friend of his who lodged with him for a while. And in 1963 George stayed over for the night in this house on the sofa.'

'Very cool,' I say.

'I'm trying to get a plaque put on the front of the building, but English Heritage will not reply to my letters or calls.'

'I can't imagine they've got much else going on.'

'Well, exactly!' Morris says indignantly. 'Maybe I could use your help as a lounge singer. Do you have much of a public profile?'

'I'm not a lounge singer,' I say. 'I'm a comedian.'

Morris's face resumes its suspicion. 'A comedian? You don't seem like one.'

'Well I'm not doing a set right now, Morris,' I say, slightly impatiently.

'I always liked Tommy Cooper. I went to see him once,' and he's off again, gasping for breath in an anecdote-telling competition with himself.

While he talks, I open the door to my bedroom. It's larger than I expected. I put down my bags and walk over to the sash windows which look out on the long, narrow, well-kept garden. I spot a mound at the end of the grass, up against the fence. I squint to try to make out what it is.

'. . . whereas nowadays, all comedy is about sarcasm and swear words and –'

'Morris,' I say, and he stops mid-flow.

'Yes?'

'What's that at the back of the garden?'

He joins me at the window. 'Anderson shelter.'

I look at his face to see if he's joking.

'Did it come with the –?'

'Built it myself,' he says.

'Impressive. Have you had any use for it?'

'Not yet, no. But it's all kitted out for when I need it. You'll be welcome to use it too, as part of your rent agreement.'

'Thanks.'

'Okay, I'll let you get settled in,' he says, walking to the door.

'Thanks, Morris. I'm pleased to be here,' I say, surprised that this isn't entirely a lie. He nods and turns away. I look out at the Anderson shelter's dome roof, part concealed with patches of grass.

'Andy?' I hear a few seconds later. Morris is back in the door frame with a strange look on his face.

'Yes?'

'I wouldn't mind, you know. I wouldn't tell anyone.'

'Tell anyone what?'

'If you were avoiding the taxman. If you were going off-grid. I'd understand.'

'Okay, cheers, Morris!' I say with too much enthusiasm, trying to break the eerie atmosphere. 'I'm not doing that right now, but I'll let you know if I am.'

'You are safe here,' he says haltingly. 'I wouldn't tell anyone.'

'Cheers,' I say again.

He nods once more and disappears with surprising speed.

I manage to round up three of the boys for the pub trip that night. I realize that the previous night out was their pastoral obligation satisfactorily fulfilled. No more is required of them. Every friendship entitles men to their one NHS pub session for a break-up, but that's the lot. I'm in BUPA territory now, which is why I buy the first round of drinks.

'He sounds mental,' Avi says, shaking his head. 'No wonder the rent is so cheap.'

'I like it,' Rob says. 'You being a lodger with an elderly man. It's like something from the 1970s.'

'He's definitely not dangerous,' I say. 'But he's . . . spooky. I wouldn't be surprised if it transpired that he wasn't a real man and was actually, like . . . a ghost.'

'I'd love it if Andy ended up lodging with a ghost,' Rob says merrily.

'Got dumped, moved on to a canal for two nights, moved in with a ghost,' Matt says with a huge grin on his face, putting his arm around me. 'There's no one else like him.'

'Glad you all find my life so funny,' I say into my pint glass.

'It *is* funny. Funnier than anything you've done on stage, mate!' Rob says, cock-a-hoop at his own joke.

'Are you gonna talk about this on stage?' Avi asks.

'Morris?' I ask.

'No,' Avi says. 'This whole thing, your whole breakdown.'

'Oh,' I say. 'No. Guys, was going to ask you, it's Jen's birthday next week, and I was wondering –'

'Whatever you're going to ask, the answer is no,' Avi says.

'Agreed,' Rob chimes.

'Agreed,' Matt repeats.

'You don't know what I'm going to ask.'

'No, you can't ring her,' Avi sighs. 'You can't write a song about her, you can't get her name spelt out in Labrador puppies and arranged on her road.'

'I literally was just going to send her a text.'

'No,' Rob says.

'No,' Matt says.

The immediacy of their unanimous response makes me suspect that they've spoken about this without me. I think of the WhatsApp breakout group they may have formed called something like: Managing Andy. I feel like I'm being *managed*.

'Why would you send her a text, mate?' Avi says. 'You've broken up.'

'To be polite,' I say.

'Bollocks,' Avi says.

'Bollocks,' Rob says.

'Yeah, sorry, mate, that's bollocks,' Matt says.

'You're just looking for a reason to get back in touch with her,' says Avi.

'Okay,' I say. 'You're right, I shouldn't say anything.'

'Distract yourself next week,' Avi says. 'You're starting with that personal trainer. Settle into your new pad.'

'Hang out with your ghost landlord,' Matt says.

'Don't think about her,' Avi says, before moving on to another topic.

I wish I could explain to him that I don't want to think about her any more, but thinking about her is not a choice; that – even though Jen is no longer in my physical life – the room inside my mind that has been occupied by her for the last four years still exists. I want to convert it into a home gym or a meditation room or get in a new tenant, but I can't. Sometimes I wake up and the first thing I think of is Jen, and I imagine the tiny version of her in a doll's house bedroom in my brain and I'm comforted by Imaginary Jen who wants to keep me company for a little bit longer.

When I get home, I can hear a programme about the moon landings playing very loudly from the living room.

'NO NEED TO SAY GOODNIGHT,' Morris's voice bellows from out of the half-closed door. I go upstairs, brush my teeth and familiarize myself with my new bathroom's lighting scheme for getting the most data-efficient photos for BALD.

Lying in bed with my laptop balanced on my stomach, I log into the local neighbourhood message board and browse the topics to see if I can find any furniture going cheap.

- **Squirrels eating rubbish again**
- **Hi, my name is Big Boy**
- **Squirrels eating used sanitary products from BINS**
- **Is someone feeding this cat??**

- **I came home to find faeces in my doorway**
- **Armchair going for free pick up today**
- **Stop whining, Nythia**
- **Recommendations for shoe repair??**
- **Hello, first time making a post here**
- **PLEASE NO MORE SQUIRREL POSTS**
- **I'm looking for a girlfriend**

I click on to the last one.

> Hello. I have been alone for a long time. I am looking for a girlfriend. Please help me. She may be in this local area or further away.

I scroll through the replies underneath.

> I'm so sorry you have lost your girlfriend. I assume the police have been alerted? Can you post a photo of her so we know what to look out for?

> Do you mean you can't find your gf?? Or that you are looking to meet someone?

> It's not appropriate to use this website as a matchmaking service. That's not what this is. This is for neighbourhood support, news, sharing resources and goods etc

> Leave him be, he's not hurting anyone

> Are you a squirrel hahaha

> If you find a girlfriend and she has a sister, let me know LOL

I open my iPhone notes and draft five different birthday messages for Jen.

Friday 2nd August 2019

'What do you want?' she asks. She stands in front of me in the gym in a crop top and workout shorts – hands on hips, long, dark hair in a high ponytail, stern expression, 'KELLY – DREAM BODY SCULPTOR' printed on her name badge.

'To get fit,' I say. 'To feel healthy.'

'Now, we both know that's not true.'

'Er, to feel strong,' I say, through short breaths.

She strolls round to the control panel on the step machine and presses the button a few times, pushing it up to its highest level.

'Why do you want to feel strong? Who's made you feel weak?' she demands. The machine's pace slows and the resistance gets harder. How can I be so out of breath and my legs ache so much when all I'm doing is slowly walking up a pretend staircase while 'When Love Takes Over' plays?

'My –' I gasp – 'my ex-girlfriend.'

'Aha. Now we're being real,' she says.

'Although,' I gasp some more, 'it's not her fault I feel weak. She just –' I grip the handles tighter – 'broke up with me. That's allowed.'

'Well listen, by the time I'm finished with you, she's gonna regret that decision. Boy, is she gonna regret it.'

I nod and hope she doesn't ask me any more questions.

We do incline walking, weights and stretches. She measures and weighs my fat and muscle. We set targets, she gives me a meal plan, I sign forms and hand over my credit card.

'Now, remember: fat is your friend,' she says. 'Carbs and sugar are an absolute no. But fat is an important part of the

Dream Body plan I've drawn up for you. And it greases the synapses, which is what you need right now, in your state. You need to be –' she slams one hand into her other palm like an axe, making a smacking noise – 'sharp.'

'Fat good,' I nod, not understanding how or why this could be the case. 'Got it.'

She softens her stance. 'What was her name?'

'Whose name?'

'Your ex.'

'Jen,' I say.

'Jen. That's good to know. You see, Andy, I like looking at things as a whole. I work whole-istically. I'm not just going to upgrade your body, I'm going to help you heal you.'

'Thanks, Kelly.'

'Because, truth be told, you and I are in the same boat. We're on the wrong side of thirty-five, we've both just been dumped by the love of our life. You – Jen. Me – Natalie.' I'm not sure how much this relates to my Dream Body plan, but I carry on nodding with a serious expression. 'And we've both got a point to prove and the point is this.' She reaches out with her hand and firmly holds my arm. 'World – I'm not done with you yet. I'm here, I'm fit, I'm energized. Give me all you got.'

I nod. 'Absol–'

'*Give me all you got*,' she says, leaning in for emphasis.

'Absolutely,' I accidentally shout, keen to express my enthusiasm.

I spend the day working on the cheese stall at an exhibition centre for a food and drink trade show. I hadn't thought of how bad a decision this would be for the first day of my new eating plan, and how tired and hungry I would be from my early-morning personal training session. All I think of all day is food. I wander past the stalls with my tray of samples and barely sell anything as the bright overhead lights glare on to platters. I list items in my head and put them into the categories of my new food plan. Bread – forbidden. Potatoes – only sweet. Alcohol must be clear in colour and occasional in consumption. Salmon – unlimited. Fat is your friend. Sugar is your enemy. Carbohydrates want to take away all your dreams of happiness and love. Potatoes and pasta are plotting against you. But it's time to fight back.

It's nice to obsess over something other than Jen.

Until exactly six o'clock, when I finish at the trade show, leave the exhibition centre, take out my phone and wait for an odd number of time (6.23 p.m.) to send Jen the casual birthday message I've been working on for days.

> Hi Jen. Happy birthday! 35 is gonna be great. I hope you have a birthday that's better than the time I took you out for a seafood tower and we got food poisoning. But maybe not quite as good as the time we celebrated by going to Fleetwood Back, the no. 1 Fleetwood Mac tribute experience. Because nothing could ever top that night (or those wigs). Anyway. Thinking of you and raising a glass to you. Loads of love, Andy x

I am relieved to press send. I've drafted and redrafted it so many times I could recite it off by heart. I'm pleased with the ground it covers in such a tight wordcount. It's nostalgic without being manipulative. It's friendly without being too casual. If I were reviewing this first-birthday-since-the-break-up text, I would call it 'bold and rigorous' and award it four stars. I see Jen appear online and immediately start typing.

> How could I forget those wigs? Thanks Andy. Appreciate it. Hope you're really well. X

I know we're in a precious, fleeting opportunity for back-and-forth messaging, so I think on my feet. I hadn't expected her to write back so quickly, so I haven't drafted a reply to her reply. I've got to keep the ball in the air but I don't know what to say. This is why I'm no good at improv.

> Wonder if the Mick Fleetwood impersonator is using that wig to moonlight in a Kiss tribute band??

I stare at her online status which remains unchanged for a few minutes. Finally, she starts typing.

> Haha X

And that's it. I fucked it. I know what 'Haha X' means, and it means please stop messaging me. Sure enough, she goes offline seconds later. I stare at her replies and read the words so many times that they start to look like squashed ants and lose all meaning.

Once I accept that Jen isn't going to reply to me again, I pick up dinner on the way to my gig. I walk straight past the BLT baguette and instead pick up a 'Pump Up the Protein Pack'. On her instruction, I send a photo of the package of three cold hard-boiled eggs wrapped in smoked salmon to Kelly, to help me 'take accountability' for my eating. She replies instantly.

> ROCK STAR!!!! Protein for strength, healthy fats for brain power. You GOT THIS, ANDY. See you on the flip for breakfast pix, iron man

As I eat a cold hard-boiled egg wrapped in smoked salmon on the top deck of the bus I realize that, since the day we broke up, I have been counting down to Jen's birthday. Hidden somewhere inside me, there was the belief that Jen's birthday would mark the beginning of our relationship again. That it was going to open up our channels of communication and that she would be so overwhelmed by the memories of past birthdays spent together, there would be no other option but to reunite. The opportunity for all this came and went in less than five minutes and I feel overwhelming disappointment in myself that I have screwed it up so badly. I make a mental list of all the other possible events in the coming year that might open the gateway for casual texting.

Christmas
My birthday
Planning a surprise birthday for Avi or Jane together (why
    would we do this for the first time now we're broken up?)
Nuclear disaster
Death of someone we both know (not hoping for this)
Terminal illness diagnosis for either of us (see above)

I go into my WhatsApp group and listen back to all the various funny voice notes I've sent on the boys' group chat over the last year. I observe with interest that it is never other people's voice notes I want to relisten to, and only my own, and decide the only telling thing about this is that I really must start a podcast next year. The bus passes a McDonald's and I imagine the order I would have right now: bacon double cheeseburger, chicken nuggets, chicken selects, apple pie, large fries. I am pathetic.

I am starving.

There is a myth that London in August is good for comedians, seeing that the majority of us are in Edinburgh for the festival during that month. When I first stopped going to Edinburgh a few summers ago, I hoped this was true – sadly, I quickly learnt that the rare gigs booked in London are either poorly attended mixed bills of middling acts, or weddings. The worst hour of your life if you're a stand-up.

Tonight is the former. I am fourth in line on a long mixed bill at a Soho pub that goes late into the night, including a woman who writes live sonnets about audience members and the headline act: a married man and woman who do a puppet show with their respective genitals. Backstage, I manage to avoid conversations with any of them and instead write lists on my iPhone notes of foods I am allowed to eat, and think of ways to put them together. Two tins of tuna and an avocado. A pot of Greek yoghurt and fifteen almonds. Feta cheese and ham. Blueberries and chicken breasts. My set is the poorest I've done this year – I am so light-headed and unfocused that halfway through I forget whether I've already told a story I told a matter of minutes ago.

When I get home, I eat an enormous wedge of Stilton from the cheese stall, neat, in less than twenty seconds, while standing up at the kitchen counter. I choose not to send a photo to Kelly.

Saturday 3rd August 2019

Unbelievable dream about Jen. The memories of it are so clear and I am unconvinced she didn't actually come join me in my subconscious last night. I wake up feeling truly happy for the first time since our break-up. I wish I'd known this *Inception* hack for heartbreak before now. You've just got to eat some really mouldy cheese really late at night and you get to have your dream reunion with your ex.

My good mood carries me through a day of admin and, very nearly, into the night, until I turn up for Saturday beers with all of the boys only to find that everyone has cancelled last minute other than Avi and Rob. I can't shake the feeling that these meet-ups and their diminishing attendees feel like a cause that no one believes in any more. The first post-break-up night out felt like a society — like a brotherhood with one shared goal: *Andy's going to be okay, we're going to make it right.* But as time moves on, I can feel their support for The Andy Society waning. Avi's yawning on his second pint and Rob keeps talking about getting up early the following morning to go to his in-laws'. I get the hint and suggest we call it a night before nine o'clock. They both can barely hide their relief.

When I arrive home I go to the kitchen for another enormous pre-bed wedge of Stilton and find Morris peeling potatoes and piling them up in a mound on the counter.

'Hey.'

'Evening,' he says, not looking up. 'How're you?'

'I'm fine. Tired. Just did a gig.'

'A *gig*?' he says, looking up inquisitively. 'In your jazz band?'

'No, I'm a comedian,' I say, pulling open the fridge door and reaching for the Stilton. 'I do stand-up comedy.'

'Oh,' he replies with a 'fair enough' nod.

'What you cooking?'

'Not cooking, just doing some . . . advanced planning, shall we say.'

'What for?'

'Winter,' he says.

'You're . . . ?'

'Freezing potatoes for winter.' He says it as if he's explaining the obvious punchline to a joke that I don't understand.

'Why can't you buy potatoes in winter?'

'Some things are going to happen next year,' he says wearily. 'Unexpected things. So I'm filling a freezer with food for if and when I need it.'

'What things?'

'Not clear yet,' he says.

'Did you do it last year?'

'Of course,' he says.

'Who told you this? About the upcoming year?'

'It's shared information. From some online website communities I am a part of.'

This is something I don't understand about Morris, how randomly he shifts from telling me far too much to telling me absolutely nothing. Yesterday he gave me a tour of each radiator in the house, giving instructions for use and their individual backstories as he went. But today he cannot explain why he's freezing potatoes for winter.

'Cool,' I say, giving up, eating the Stilton straight out of its paper.

'You shouldn't eat cheese so late at night,' Morris says. 'Not good for your innards.'

'Thanks, Morris, I'll be okay. Got a strong constitution.'

'I have a friend, a man called Ian, who lives in a place in Nottinghamshire called Cropwell Bishop –'

'Night, Morris!' I say loudly, throwing the cheese wrapper in the bin. He looks startled momentarily, then nods.

'Goodnight, hope that cheese doesn't disturb your sleep.'

In my final attempt to recreate the dreams of last night, I go into my camera roll, where my phone has considerately created a slideshow of my and Jen's relationship named 'Together Through the Years'. I press play and watch a cross-faded collection of photos of the two of us set to an ethereal electronic library track. I close my eyes to go meet her in my dreams.

Sunday 4th August 2019

Cheese thing didn't work. Had no dreams at all and woke up at three a.m., dehydrated and with stomach cramps. Was back and forth to the bathroom so many times that I ended up taking my pillow in there and sleeping on the floor. I am shaken awake by Morris a few hours later.

'ANDY? ANDY?' I jolt upright and open my eyes. 'ARE YOU DEAD?'

'Obviously I'm not dead,' I croak, rubbing my eyes.

'What are you doing on the bathroom floor?' he asks, his black-brown eyes staring at me intently.

'I'm sick.'

'Is it drugs?' he barks. 'Heroin?'

'No. I've got a bad stomach and I haven't really slept.'

'Oh,' he says, the concern leaving his face as he circumvents me to get to the sink. 'Oh, sorry to hear that.'

'Why did you think it was drugs?' I ask, heaving myself off the floor.

'Well, it's a well-trodden path for musicians, isn't it?' he says, squeezing toothpaste on to his toothbrush. I clutch my pillow to my stomach and drag my feet as I leave the bathroom. 'Do let me know if I can be of any help,' he adds.

'That's nice, thank you. Think I'm just going to try to sleep it off.'

'I did warn you not to eat that big block of blue cheese so late at night,' he shouts after me.

'It wasn't a block, it was a wedge.'

'Very big wedge,' he mutters.

★

I sleep until noon and, when I wake up feeling no better, cancel my evening gig. I go downstairs for more water and find Morris at the kitchen table writing a letter.

'How are you feeling?' he asks.

'Not so good.'

'There are some tins of soup in the cupboard you are welcome to, when you feel up to it,' he says. 'Plenty of tins.'

'Thanks, Morris. Always prepared, aren't you?' He nods. 'What are you doing today?'

'I've got to run a few errands. Go to the hardware shop. Then drop this to Belmarsh Prison,' he says, tapping the letter.

'Right,' I say, filling my water bottle up from the tap. 'You know someone in there?'

'Yes and no, shall we say,' he says. There is a long pause as he looks at me without blinking.

'If you don't want to tell me who, that's fine,' I say.

'It's Julian Assange.'

The words hang in the air for a few moments while I consider my response.

'He a friend of yours?'

'No, of course not,' he says impatiently. 'I write him letters to offer my support, emotionally and financially.'

'Financially?'

'Yes, just fifty pounds a week,' he says, opening his chequebook and picking up a biro.

'Does he ever cash them?'

'Not yet, no.'

I suddenly have a thought that solves so many of the mysteries of Morris. The absence of a wife and children. No mention of any girlfriend.

'Would you like to have a . . . private relationship with him?' I ask tentatively.

Morris's face flushes with colour and his eyes widen. 'Don't be so ridiculous,' he barks. 'Honestly, goodness me. What a suggestion.'

'Oh sorry, sorry. I just thought maybe –'

'Never have I heard anything so –'

'Sorry!' I say. 'Wrong end of the stick.'

'He is a fine, fine man,' Morris says in a slow, grave voice. 'He has my utmost respect and support. And he should have yours too.'

'Not sure he does to be honest, but –'

Morris stands up abruptly and tears the cheque away from the book.

'IF you'll excuse me,' he says. 'I have to deliver this by hand.'

'Can't you put it in the post box?'

Morris sighs as he puts the cheque into the envelope and seals it.

'No, I cannot,' he says. 'Higher risk of interception.'

I take my water upstairs and stand at the landing window as I watch Morris leave the house. He shifts his weight from one foot to the other, but walks quickly, his small frame and fast scurry resembling a vole.

I go back to bed and sleep all afternoon. When I wake up in the early evening, I can hear Morris clattering about downstairs, listening to a radio programme about 5G. Restless but depleted of energy, I open my laptop to find something to watch. I'm not sure if I'm feeling particularly self-pitying because I've spent the day in bed ill like a child, but I find that everything reminds me of Jen. Romantic films remind me of Jen for obvious reasons. Comedy reminds me of Jen because anything I find funny I imagine sharing with her. Films about family remind me of Jen, as she's the person I wanted to have a family with. Even a nature documentary about the sea reminds me of Jen because of her enthusiasm for coastal holidays and swimming.

I settle on a true crime drama but fall back asleep within minutes. When I wake up, I'm surprised to see I've slept through the whole evening. And I'm even more surprised to see a message from Jen.

Thursday 8th August 2019

'Let's talk motivation,' Kelly says, strolling around the mat while I heave myself up and down in my third set of burpees. 'We're heading into week two tomorrow. That fat-burning high might have plateaued. The endorphins might be harder to find when we're working out. So what's gonna motivate us? End of set, take a pause, breathe.' I lie flat on the floor, my red face pressed into the mat as I breathe heavily. 'Because when we're tired first thing in the morning and reaching for a cinnamon bun instead of hitting the weights, what are we gonna think of to keep us on track? Stand up, let's move into set four.' I haul myself up. 'Off we go. So, I'll give you an example. Me and Natalie used to go to Ibiza every year. Keep your core tight. I'm going in a few weeks. Now, we're not talking at the moment, but I'm pretty sure, from what I hear, that she's gonna be there too. Land on your heels. So do you know what I think every time I'm craving that Big Mac? I picture myself walking into the club, amazing woman on my arm, looking like my absolute best self, Natalie looking at me being like: *What have I done? Why have I let her go?* So we've got to find that thing for you, Andy. That image. That dream. Because sculpting a dream body is not for sissies. End of set, take a pause, breathe.' I lie on the mat, resting my sweaty face into the wet patch it's formed. 'Now, you don't look like you spend a lot of time in the club, am I right?' I nod silently. 'More of a –' She searches for her words. 'A Côte Brasserie man, yes?' I do not nod. 'So every time you want to stay in bed and miss training, you're gonna imagine yourself looking ripped as fuck, you've got a lovely lady on your arm, smart pair of loafers on, your favourite . . . sleeveless pullover.' I cannot hear one more word of how Kelly sees me. I already know too much. 'And you walk into that restaurant and there's Jen. She's looking up at you and she's thinking: *Why the hell did I throw that away?* Right, let's get up for that final set.'

I walk back home in the early-morning sun and reread Jen's message, a message so economical in its words, so meticulous in its content, that I know she would have sent it to Jane for feedback and approval.

> Hello. Hope you're good! Sorry, this is extremely boring, but I've been told today that we can't close our joint account without going into the bank together. It's not good for either of our credit ratings to have unused bank accounts sitting empty, so would it be ok to get that sorted asap? I can work around you. Thanks, Jen. X

After a few texts in this crisp and formal tone, it became clear that Jen was not going to work around me, but instead I had to very much work around her and meet her at a bank near her office, during her lunch hour, on the day that suited her. Which is today.

I lock my phone screen and see an image of Jen and me from last New Year's Eve. We rented a cottage by the sea with Avi and Jane, in a beautiful village in Ireland near where Jane grew up. On a drunken afternoon walk, Av took a photo of us kissing over a kissing gate. The whole trip is one of my happiest memories with her and I haven't been able to change the picture yet. I scroll through my camera roll to find something to replace it with so that it is Jen-proofed for our meeting later. But I can't find any photos since our break-up that aren't screenshots of things from the internet or photos of my own head.

When I get home, I take a few more photos for BALD and am pleasantly surprised to find that I seem to have gained hair in the last fortnight. I'm confused as to how this has happened and wonder if it could possibly be the change in my diet. Before I leave the house, I do one last Jen-proofing of myself. I don't know what I'm on the lookout for, other than I LOVE JEN written on items of my clothes.

I see her through the glass doors as I approach. She is uncharacteristically early, fiddling with her hair before picking up her phone, reading something on the screen and typing. My heartbeat quickens and I can already feel myself breaking into a sweat, despite walking purposefully slowly from the station to avoid this happening. I step to the side of the building to take a few deep breaths. It's just Jen. She's your friend. She's just a woman. She's just a person.

As I enter the bank, she looks up and spots me. She smiles and stands up. I walk towards her.

'Hey, Andy,' she says, opening her arms for a hug. She squeezes me tightly, pats my back and makes a noise as if she's stretching after a workout.

'Hey,' I say. There is silence for a few moments.

'Was it easy to get here?' she asks. The love of my life, asking me about my mode of transport to the bank because she has nothing else to say to me. She's gone from girlfriend to uncle-standing-in-the-hallway-as-I-arrive-for-Christmas in a matter of weeks.

'It was hard to navigate the tube map, but I made it in one piece.' She looks confused. 'Sorry. Bad joke. Bet you've missed those.'

'Oh,' she says, smiling. 'Got it. Where are you living at the moment?'

'Hornsey. I'm lodging.'

'Nice place?' she asks brightly, looking for me to alleviate her guilt about my living situation by saying: *Yeah, Zone One penthouse with its own private sauna, amazing what six hundred and fifty quid a month gets you in London now.*

'Yeah, it's nice.'

'Nice housemates?'

'Just the one,' I say. 'He's fine.'

She sits back down in the chair and I take a seat in the one next to her.

'Shouldn't be too much of a wait, they've said.'

'Great,' I say. More silence. 'Where are you living?'

'Still at my sister's,' she says. 'It's a little bit cramped with the baby. But there's still a month until the tenants move out of my place, so I'm lucky I've got somewhere to wait it out.'

'How is Miranda?'

She's opening her mouth to reply when a man in a bank uniform appears from behind a door.

'Jennifer Bennett?' he asks.

'Yes,' Jen replies, standing up quickly and picking up her handbag. We follow him into the room. I hold open the door and gesture to Jen that she should go first. She walks past me and our bodies are the closest they have been since we broke up. I feel like I'm in the presence of a celebrity. A couple of months ago, Jen was the woman whose pants I put in the washing machine with mine when I put a load on. Now, she is unfamiliar and untouchable; someone I have a one-way relationship with in photos and memories and in my imagination. I cannot believe she's real, here and standing next to me.

'Good afternoon, hi,' the man says. 'My name is Anthony, I'm going to be your advisor today.' We both nod and smile as he takes a seat behind the desk with a computer and we sit down on the other side. 'So, today we're looking to close a joint current account, is that right?'

'Yes,' Jen replies.

'Okay,' he says. 'And can I ask why?'

Yes, you can ask why, Anthony. Because I've already asked why, numerous times. It's your turn now. Please can you get an answer for why our relationship ended that is satisfactory.

'Yes,' Jen says. 'We have had a shared bank account for the last few years, mainly for bills and rent when we were living together. But we're not living together any more, so there is no need for us to have a joint account.'

'Okay, no problem,' Anthony says cheerily and starts clicking the mouse and tapping at the keyboard. Jen and I stare ahead saying nothing. I mentally chew through our interaction so far, trying to stay in the moment and not pre-emptively analyse. And then I have a sudden thought. A realization that taints every conversation I've had with Jen since our break-up. A realization so urgent that, as much as I try, I cannot keep to myself.

'When did you tell your tenants you were moving back into your flat?' I ask. Anthony looks up, concerned. He quickly realizes I am not directing the question to him and returns his focus to the computer. Jen looks at Anthony then looks at me.

'A month ago? Why?'

'And you said you're moving back in in a month?' I ask.

'Yes.'

I leave a pause so she has time to clock that she's been caught, backtrack on her story and invent an alibi. She says nothing and looks straight at me with her enormous glassy blue eyes. The nerve.

'Jen – that's impossible. Landlords have to give their tenants three months' notice. You told them you were moving back into that flat a month before we broke up.'

Anthony has the decency not to look up from his computer but shifts in his seat.

'It's two months,' she says. 'Legally, I only have to give two months. So I told them the week after we broke up.'

'That's not true!' I say, squawking slightly. 'Everyone knows it's three months.'

'Er, everyone knows it's two months, Andy,' she says, in a tone verging on sneering. 'So can we just get back to this?' She gestures towards Anthony, who is still valiantly pretending to be absorbed in the computer screen.

'Everyone like who? Like someone who has barely rented in their entire life? Or someone who has been renting since they were eighteen?'

'Oh, here we go,' she says, slouching back in her seat. 'My dad helped me buy a flat nearly ten years ago, therefore I'm not allowed to have an opinion on anything.'

'You're not allowed to tell me the fake rules of renting to cover up your lies.'

'I'M NOT LYING!' she shouts. Anthony relents and looks up.

'Yes you are. Of course you are. You just "suddenly" decided you didn't want to be with me and "maybe didn't even believe in love" while we were having a lovely weekend away?'

'Why can't you accept what I've told you?' she yelps, flinging her hands around as she speaks, something she only does when very drunk or very angry. 'You can make up as many stories as you like to make me the bad guy. But I've told you everything I can tell you from my side.'

'You knew you didn't want to be with me before we even went to Paris,' I say. 'You knew you were going to leave our flat, you knew you were going to leave me the minute we got back.'

Jen turns towards me in her chair. Her face has taken on an expression that I recognize from our worst drunken rows. A look that tells me she's about to say something vicious.

'Do you know what, Andy? You need to just get a girlfriend.

Jesus. Just get a new girlfriend and you'll forget about me and be fine.'

'"Get a girlfriend" – what the fuck is that supposed to mean?'

'Can we just get this done, some of us have to get back to the office,' she says.

'God, you love saying that to me, don't you? It rolls off the tongue so easily for you. You pretend like you support my work, like you think it's admirable to do something you love and earn no money for it. Like you wouldn't have preferred me to be some sell-out in the City. And then, the minute you need a weapon to beat me with, there it is.'

'What do we have to do to shut down this account, sorry?' Jen says, turning back to Anthony.

'Yeah, and while I'm here, can I please remove her as a contact on my online banking?' I add, unhelpfully.

'You can do that yourself through the app,' Anthony says. 'It's actually very easy –'

'Yes, good idea, I'd like to do the same,' Jen snaps. 'I don't like seeing your name every time I make a payment.'

'Great,' I say.

There is a brief pause in which I can feel the aftershock of our words. Anthony looks confused. He waits a beat before speaking.

'So, yeah, as I say, you just open up the app, go into the –'

'And don't worry about transferring me that two hundred quid,' Jen says.

'What two hundred quid?' I ask.

'The two hundred quid you owe me for the Eurostar to Paris.'

'I don't owe you that, I booked my own tickets.'

'Sure you did,' Jen says with a theatrical snort-laugh.

'LOOK,' I bark, getting my phone out from my back pocket. 'I think I even took a screenshot of the booking.' Jen leans in to look at my phone to examine the evidence and I go on to my camera roll. A zoomed-up photo of my bald patch appears. I quickly come out of it and huff. I side-glance at Jen to see if she clocked it but I can't make out her face. I scroll up through my photos and mutter to myself. 'It's here somewhere, what date was it –' There is agonizing silence as Anthony stares at the desk.

'Andy – I don't care about the two hundred –'

'Well, it seems like you do care, so –'

'I really don't,' she says. 'I just want to get this account closed. And then we can move on with our lives.'

'No,' I say. 'I'm not having this hanging over us.' I remember the chequebook I have in my jacket pocket to pay my rent to Morris. I take it out and write one out to her for £200, finishing with a cartoonishly large signature like I'm in a play. I stand up.

'Take it,' I say bitterly, ripping it out and throwing it at her. As the three of us watch it flutter slowly to the ground in front of me, I realize I've never seen anyone in a film throw a cheque before, probably for this reason. I bend down to pick it up and hand it to her in the conventional way. 'I'm leaving.'

'Good,' she says.

'I do just need to see some identification to close the account today,' Anthony says in a harried way. I take out my driver's licence from my wallet and put it on the desk. I refuse to sit back down. Jen takes her passport out of her bag and places it in front of him. Anthony looks at both, checks them against the screen, does some typing and clicking for a few minutes and then looks back at us with a smile. 'That's all done for you. Is there anything else I can help you with today?'

'No,' we say in unison.

'Thank you,' I add.

We walk through the bank purposefully, keeping our distance from each other. Jen gets outside before I do and she stands still, glaring at me.

'What?' I ask.

'I know it is not in the male vocabulary to discuss defeat, Andy,' she says. 'But I think you are going to have to find someone to talk to about us.'

'Is that how you see me in our break-up? Defeated?'

'No,' she sighs. 'I worded that wrong, what I mean is –'

'I really don't need any more little theories about me from your therapist, but thank you.' I can tell this embarrasses her, as her face reddens and she looks away. 'And by the way, that ISN'T true. I REVEL in defeat. I do so FREQUENTLY.'

'This is difficult for me too,' she says. 'I miss you, I'm always thinking about you. Lots of things remind me of you.'

'Like what? What *things*?' I demand. I don't know what I'm trying to get at. There is a pause. She says nothing. I wait. She still says nothing.

'This is too hard,' she says, waving her hands in a way that suggests she's given up. 'We can't talk without hurting each other. It doesn't work.'

'We can agree on that,' I say. 'Goodbye, Jen.' I walk away and, after a few paces, turn back. 'I can't even look at the sea any more because it reminds me of you.'

'If you can't look at the sea that's YOUR FAULT, ANDY,' she shouts. Passers-by look at her, surprised to see someone so well-put-together bellowing something so demented in the middle of the day. 'Not mine. YOURS. YOU need to go fix your relationship with the sea, NOT ME.' She turns and walks away.

'YOU'VE RUINED THE SEA,' I shout before I turn and walk the other way.

She always was melodramatic.

Saturday 10th August 2019

Avi and I meet at the pub to watch the football. No one else joins us despite the invitation on the group chat. The society has dwindled to just two members. I don't blame them. I wouldn't turn up for meetings any more if I wasn't me.

'Saw Jen,' I say, halfway down my first pint and a few minutes after kick-off. Avi looks ahead at the screen.

'Oh yeah,' he says, not looking up at me. 'How was that?'

'Shit.'

'Why did you meet up?'

'It was to close down our joint account at the bank,' I say. 'But we ended up having a massive fight.'

'Couldn't you have closed it over the phone?'

'No, apparently you have to do it in person and bring ID.'

Avi frowns. 'No, don't think that's true,' he says. 'I'm pretty sure you can do it over the phone.'

'Can I ask why that's the bit of the story that has interested you most?'

'Sorry,' he says, forcing his eyes away from the TV. 'Do you want to talk about it?'

'Nah,' I lie.

Avi's focus returns to the football. He puts his arm around my shoulder, pats it twice then removes it.

'Which Beatles break-up do you think Jen and I are most like?' I ask.

'Oooh, that's a good question, um . . .' He exhales pensively. 'Dunno.'

'Come on. Think.'

'Okay, er, maybe Pattie and George?'

'Why?'

'Fit posh blonde.'

'Can you think a bit harder?' I ask.

'Okay, um . . .' He closes his eyes to think of a satisfying answer. 'OH. I know! Heather and Paul.'

'Why Heather and Paul?'

'Fit blonde who's made you mental.'

'I was thinking maybe more like John and Yoko.'

'Did they even break up?'

'Yeah, they were apart for eighteen months. He went off and had his freedom, partied, made music. Yoko got the peace needed to make her art. Then they got back together. It was his lost weekend.'

'You think this is your lost weekend?' he says, a little too disbelievingly.

'No, *she's* John. I'm Yoko. Jen's having her lost weekend.'

Avi shrugs. 'If you say so,' he says.

'I do say so.'

Villa lose. We've known each other long enough and we've watched enough games together to know that all we want to do is go home and sulk on our own. We finish our drinks and walk to the station.

'Can I give you some advice?' he says.

'No,' I say. 'Go on.'

'You are locked in a prison of your own nostalgia. You need to let go of the past.'

'Bollocks. I don't think I am. Do you think I am?'

'Yeah,' he says. 'You're not allowing yourself to see things clearly.'

I sigh huffily. 'Sorry I compared us to John and Yoko, it was just a joke.'

'It's not just that,' he says. 'I can feel that you're all, like . . .' He stops walking to make his point. 'Bogged down. In the memories and unlived potentials of that relationship. It's going to drive you crazy.'

'I'm an artist, this is what we do. We overanalyse. We masticate our misery until it's pulverized enough to swallow.'

'I'm an artist and I don't do that,' he protests.

'You're a graphic designer.'

'Look – I used to be the same,' he says. 'I used to obsess over ex-girlfriends and women who rejected me. And then I got married and had kids. And I had to stop. There was no time for all the moping around.'

'Well, tell me how I do that,' I say. 'Without having a kid.'

'You've just got to try to stop thinking about her,' he says, in an exasperated tone that embarrasses me. 'It's like you're forcing yourself to watch the Jen and Andy Match of the Day highlights package on repeat. And then you wonder why you still feel so shit about it all.'

I say nothing. I feel so humiliated by Avi's insights into me, so ashamed by the thought of him discussing these observations with other people, that I just nod in agreement and change the subject and ask him questions so I don't have to talk until we get to the tube station and go on our separate trains home.

I can sense that Avi views his role in this break-up as the executor of a series of tasks and chores. Having me to stay, organizing a big night out, a few mid-week meet-ups, a couple of breezy check-in texts, the tough pep talk. With each one, he hopes that the job is closer to being completed and I'm therefore closer to being cured. And yet the further he gets down his Andy to-do list, the more infuriating I become. On the way home, I stop in at my local for one more pint, which turns into two more pints and four fags, and I think about how wrong Avi is about the prison of nostalgia thing and listen to *Imagine* in its entirety.

When I get home after last orders, Morris is hunched over the kitchen table with a lamp positioned over a shower radio.

'Hey,' I say, aware I am swaying in the doorway slightly. 'Fancy a beer?'

'No,' he says, absorbed in his task. 'But thank you.'

'No probs,' I say, opening a tin. 'Good night?'

'Yes. Been fixing some bits and bobs that need fixing.' There is a pause before he remembers he's meant to ask the same of me. 'And you?'

'All right, watched Spurs versus Villa. Villa lost. So been drowning the sorrows,' I say, holding up the clanking bag of tins. 'You a football fan?'

'Not really,' he says.

He wants me to leave him alone. I go to the fridge and put the remaining beers on the shelf.

'Which Beatle do I remind you of, Morris?' I ask.

He looks up briefly and narrows his eyes. 'The drummer who was asked to leave,' he says.

'Pete Best,' I say. Morris nods, looking back down. 'Night, Morris.' He nods again.

I throw myself on to my bed fully clothed, tinnie in hand, and stare at the ceiling. I've got to at least try to be a little less annoying. I've got to find a way to talk about the break-up economically. Use my Jen tokens more sparingly in conversation.

What I need is a system. A way of getting through this break-up without losing all my friends. I'm going to have to instigate a tracking technique of how much I'm talking about her. Give myself a limit of Jen tokens to spend – a maximum of ten per meet-up, let's say. And not every mention carries the same token value, this is where I've been going wrong. For example: mentioning Jen's name in passing, where relevant, would amount to two tokens. But anything that involves going over past memories of our relationship is more like four tokens. Doing a scene-by-scene retelling of our meet-up at the bank – along with light embellishments, impersonations, etc. – that would be six tokens. Asking Avi to compare my and Jen's break-up to a Beatles break-up uses eight tokens. And bringing up the old estate agent's listing of her flat on my phone and showing people the weird floor plan and inviting them to slag it off? Well. That would be the full ten tokens spent in one go.

My phone rings. A FaceTime from Emery. I answer the call and, as his face fills the screen, I can immediately tell that he is five-pints-pissed in a theatre courtyard bar. There is a delay as the noise catches up with the picture – a roar of talk and laughter and drunkenness and togetherness. I wish I was there.

'My boy,' he bellows. His mass of curly hair has expanded from sweat, his cheeks are flushed, his eyes pale and glassy. His face wears booze like it's a suit that's perfectly tailored to him. 'My fine, fine boy.'

'Hey, man,' I say. 'How are you?'

'I am very well. August in Edinburgh. Land of the battered Mars Bar and the battered man. "*Edina! Scotia's darling seat!*"' he shouts in a patchy Scottish accent. 'As the great Rabbie Burns once decreed.'

'How's it going?' I ask, in equal parts desperate to know the answer and desperate not to know the answer.

'Can I be honest with you?'

'Yes.'

'Crushing it.'

'Really?'

'I can't quite believe it. I've never done an Edinburgh like this. Full house every evening. Different woman every night. Have you read the reviews?'

'No,' I say flatly.

'Read the reviews,' he says, smiling knowingly.

'I absolutely won't, but I'm very happy for you all the same.'

'What's up, baby?!' he bellows. I see him jostled in the queue and a flash of another hideously patterned shirt under his acid-wash denim jacket. 'You seem down!'

'August in London is rubbish. All my friends are either in Edinburgh or at water parks with their kids,' I say sulkily.

'Come here!'

'Nah,' I say. 'Too depressing. I don't want to feel like the guy who's been made redundant going back to the office to have lunch with everyone who's still employed.'

'Andy, this city did not make you redundant,' he says, looking up above the screen. 'Three pints of lager, two vodka lime sodas, two glasses of white wine, three shots of tequila. Thanks.' He looks back at the screen. 'You made yourself redundant.'

'Why are you buying such an enormous round?' I ask.

'I'm out with the cast of *Dracula On a Bouncy Castle*. It's a really funny show, quite high-concept, almost performance art piece. Hang on, gotta pay.' He hands the phone over to someone. I hear him in the background bellowing at them to say 'hi' to his friend Andy. A pretty barmaid holds the phone up to her face.

'Hi, Andy,' she says with a shy giggle. I appease her with a forced smile. Emery shouts that she should go out for a drink with him. 'Should I go out for a drink with your friend?' She giggles some more.

'No,' I reply. A fleshy colour engulfs the screen as Emery grabs the phone back. When I see his face, his eyes are no longer engaged in our conversation and are fully distracted by the barmaid behind the phone.

'Listen, mate, got to go.'

'Bye, mate.'

'Love you, dude,' he says and hangs up.

I google Emery's 2019 Edinburgh reviews and open the first one in the search results. A broadsheet newspaper. Emery's poster, an image of him looking unfathomably attractive holding an inexplicable pineapple, tops the article. 'Face of a Movie Star, Mouth of the Devil, Mind of a Genius' reads the headline. It is awarded five stars. I'm pleased for him. He deserves it. I can't get past the fourth sentence.

Thursday 22nd August 2019

I'm woken up by a loud knock on my bedroom door.

'Are you decent?' Morris shouts.

'Yeah, come in,' I reply. I sit up in bed and pull the duvet up to cover myself. Morris looks embarrassed at the sight of my dishevelled hair and bare chest. He averts his eyes to the wardrobe.

'I'm sorry to wake you, but there's something rather important I need to talk to you about.'

'Go on,' I say.

'The *Highgate and Hornsey Express* has finally agreed to speak to me about the George Harrison plaque.'

'That's great news.'

'Yes, thank you, it is. And it would be extremely helpful to me if you could be there and mention that you're a croupier.'

'A comedian,' I say.

'Sorry, sorry,' Morris says. 'A comedian. That you're in showbusiness. I'm hoping it might make them take it all a bit more seriously.'

'Okay. What do you want me to say?'

'You can say whatever you like,' he says. 'But I think it would be good if you say it is a disgrace.'

'Right, okay,' I say. 'So those are the words you'd like me to use? "It's a disgrace"?'

'If you'd like to, yes,' he says.

'Fine. What time is the reporter going to be here?'

'One o'clock,' he says.

'Cool.'

'I wonder what he'd make of all this? George, that is.

Probably would find it embarrassing! He was that sort of a person,' he says, chuckling to himself. The happiest I've ever seen him. 'Funny to think they were just four lads from Liverpool. And they went on to change the world.'

'I've got to go meet my mum at two,' I say. 'So the latest I can leave here is twenty past.'

'That's okay, and feel free to say what you like about the situation,' he says.

'That it's a disgrace?'

'A disgrace, yes. Thank you, Andy,' he says, looking up at me briefly and giving a nod of gratitude before letting himself out.

I am finishing my HIIT workout YouTube video in my room when I hear the photographer and journalist arrive. I shower, change and consider leaving the house via my bedroom window, climbing down the drainpipe and jumping over the garden's back fence to avoid speaking to them. I walk downstairs and see Morris standing outside the front door, which is ajar. A male photographer about my age is crouching in slightly unnecessary waterproof trousers and clicking away. The journalist, a much younger guy in a shirt with too much of something I think they call *product* in his hair, watches on with a dictaphone in hand. I stand in the hallway and find my jacket in the coat cupboard.

'Morris, if we could just have you looking a little more fed up, that would be great,' the photographer says.

'Right, um –' Morris says, looking down at his own body, searching for ideas. He folds his arms and frowns, pinching his mouth in fury.

'That's really fantastic, thank you,' the photographer says, a series of quick snapping sounds following. I walk into the doorway tentatively.

'Andy!' Morris says, more enthusiastic to see me than he's ever been. 'Here you are.'

'Hiya,' I say, turning to the journalist. 'I'm Andy, I'm Morris's lodger.'

'Hi, Andy, nice to meet you,' the journalist says. 'Would you like to be included in the piece?'

'Yes, I would, I absolutely would,' I lie.

'Great, thank you. What do you think about English Heritage's treatment of Morris?'

Morris looks at me encouragingly.

'Well, I suppose all I think is that it's a disgrace,' I say, summoning as much outrage as I can. 'An absolute disgrace.'

'That's brilliant,' the journalist says. Morris smiles gratefully.

'Now, Morris,' I hear the photographer say as I walk down the road. 'Do you have any George Harrison T-shirts or memorabilia or anything like that?'

Mum waits for me outside the department store. Her small frame looks even smaller in the mass of central London shopping crowds. I have the patronizing thought I always have when I see her in London, which is that she looks lost and slightly out-of-context here. I wonder if she feels the same as I walk towards her.

'Hello, son,' she says. I crouch slightly to hug her and surprise myself at how relieved I am to see her. I hold on too long and too tight. 'Oooh, big hug, that bad, is it?' She links my arm and we walk through the glass doors of the shop.

I follow her around the cosmetics counters and we try to catch up as she loads samples on herself. She tries on so many perfumes she runs out of wrist space and resorts to the full length of her arms, fore AND upper. She streaks the back of her hands with an assortment of identical shimmery lipsticks and waves them around in a fist to try and catch the right light. After a while, I make a subtle point of leaning on the counters or slumping on the makeover swivel stools.

'You know you can order almost everything online?' I say.

'I know,' she says, drawing another stripe of lipstick on to the last bit of spare skin on her hand, holding it away from her and squinting. 'But I like seeing things in real life.' She turns to the female sales assistant. 'Do you have any of that eyebrow gel in stock that everyone's talking about?' The assistant nods and bends down to one of those secret drawers.

'Why would your eyebrows need a gel?' I ask. 'Can't you just get a hair gel and use it in a smaller amount?'

Mum laughs at the stupidity of this suggestion. 'It's a totally different thing! It's a different . . . a different . . .' She searches for the word.

'Formula,' the assistant says as her head pops up, clutching a tube of the gel.

'Exactly,' Mum says.

'Don't they both just hold bits of hair in place?'

Now she's got the sales assistant onside and they're laughing knowingly.

'What does it matter to you?' she says, pushing me away. 'Go entertain yourself. I'll see you back where we met in fifteen minutes.'

I wander off in search of a department that interests me and resort to going up and down the escalators. I don't like feeling like this – a heel-dragging ogre who doesn't understand the intricacies of femininity; the sort of guy who makes the women in his life look at sales assistants for camaraderie, and roll their eyes and say 'Men!' A bloke who could never understand why his girlfriend needed to get her eyelashes tinted or own eight pairs of identical jeans or sleep on a silk pillowcase. Why was she always so hellbent on acquiring more volume at the roots of her hair via video tutorials, when she had a perfectly normal amount as far I could see? Why was it so unacceptable, nay, revolting to her to use a combined shampoo and conditioner? Why did I once overhear her describe the colour navy as her 'religion' to a female friend? And why did the female friend not question her on that but instead nod in agreement?

I really resent being made to feel like this sort of bloke. My useless ex-boyfriend. My hopeless son. And yet, as I find the only part of the shop that can hold my attention (electronic fans), I have to admit that maybe they're right.

I take Mum for afternoon tea, something she loves, at a posh hotel near the department store. I eat around all the carbs and sugar and she has the good grace not to say anything, and instead makes a point of describing how each and every thing she eats is delicious, in between updates on every happening of every neighbour, friend and family member. Thank God we don't talk about uncomfortable things. I present her with her belated birthday gifts – a novel and a pair of earrings that she said she wanted, and a pair of home karaoke mics as a surprise.

'What on earth?' she says, unwrapping them. 'Why would I do karaoke at home?'

'You might be infirm and housebound one day, Mum. And then you'll be happy you can still belt out "I Wanna Dance With Somebody".'

The bill arrives, but she won't let me pay despite my protest that this is her birthday treat.

'Absolutely not,' she says, getting her card from her purse.

'Please, Mum, I'd love to.'

'No. You barely ate anything.'

'Can we go halves at least?' I ask.

She relents. 'All right.' I take my wallet out from my jacket pocket. 'SlimFast was what I did,' she says, pushing the flats of her fingertips on to her plate to pick up the last cake crumbs. 'When I was going through hell. But I wouldn't recommend it. Gave me the shits.' I smile. 'And crash diets don't work, of course. Otherwise there would be no diet industry. They just make you miserable. But you already know that.' I look into my cup to avoid her eyes and drain the last of the tea. 'And no one is going to be with you because of the label in your waistband.'

'It's not about that,' I say, more snappily than I had wanted.

'Fine, fine,' she says, holding up her hands in truce. 'I won't say any more, sorry.'

I put my arm around her shoulders briefly and give the lightest squeeze as an apology. I look at all the pastry and bread gathered in the corner of my small plate. Like the leftovers of a toddler.

'I've got something for you as well,' she says, reaching down for her handbag. 'But I don't want you to get stroppy when you see it.'

'Oh God, what is it?' I ask.

She hands me a thick, shiny book. On the cover, there is an illustration of an elephant balancing a broken heart at the end of its trunk. The title reads: *Why Elephants Cry: The Science of Heartbreak*.

'I saw it on display in a bookshop. Might not be useful, but I thought it could still be interesting.'

'Thanks, Mum,' I say. 'My first self-help book! What a milestone.'

'It's not self-help, it's science.'

'Ah,' I say unconvincingly.

'How are you feeling?' she asks.

I want to talk to her about how I feel, but it's not even interesting to me any more. And I don't know how to choose the right words to correctly represent all the thoughts and the feelings that are piling up inside me. Women think we don't want to talk to them about our emotions because we're embarrassed of being vulnerable. It's more that we're embarrassed of seeming stupid. Every time I hear Jane and Jen or Mum and one of her friends talk about something emotional, it's like listening to an orchestra perform. Often with no warm-up, they launch effortlessly into the chosen symphony of feelings for the day. And when I offer my thoughts I know I'm ruining it – hooting along tunelessly like a grade-one recorder player.

'I'm okay,' I say.

We wander around London in the late-afternoon sun. We walk past men with loosened ties standing outside Soho pubs drinking pints, and then down to Trafalgar Square, where teenagers perch on the edge of the fountains. We're walking to nowhere because I don't want the day to end yet and I don't have a home of my own where she can stay. I imagine a different kind of son she could have had. One who has a job she can be proud of, who pays for all the restaurant bills and has a spare bedroom where she can stay. A son who gives her expensive birthday gifts and nice holidays and a daughter-in-law and grandchildren.

'I'm sorry that you can't stay at my house. I'm not sure you'd want to, to be honest, what with Morris. He's pretty eccentric.'

'Don't worry about it.'

'I do. I'm a shit son,' I say.

'Oh be quiet, what's wrong with you,' she says, hitting my arm. 'You're a good son. My favourite son.'

'Your only son.'

'Exactly,' she says chirpily. 'So, the best one. The best one by far.'

'I love you,' I say, a sentiment we normally only reserve for extreme drunkenness or family funerals.

'Come here, silly boy,' she says, and pulls me down into her

144

arms. 'You're going to be okay, chick. Listen to that Sinatra album,' she says, patting my back. 'I mean it.'

'I will,' I say, squeezing her hand.

'And eat some bread,' she shouts as I walk off.

I walk the two hours home, tracking my step count as I go. Why is it that London always seems the most alive and full of possibility on the nights when you've got no plans? I don't even bother texting my mates to see if anyone is free to meet up. I can feel the summer ending, and it panics me. I don't think I've ever attached any big hopes to seasons before, but when you're newly single, summer seems to be your promised time. A few months of non-stop parties and casual sex. I don't really know what I've done with my summer. I try to recall the best days of July and August and can't find any memories of road trips in a convertible car or getting high around a campfire or dancing by a poolside or on a rooftop with girls in bikinis. Not one. And now I'm going to be just as miserable but wearing more layers.

I listen to *In the Wee Small Hours* from start to finish twice. I wonder if Jen would like it – whether she'd find it too depressing or whether she'd like its sentimentality. It's weird not being in our subculture of two any more. There was Jen's culture, her little habits and ways of doing things; the collection of stuff she'd already learnt she loved before we met me. Chorizo and Jonathan Franzen and long walks and the Eagles (her dad). Seeing the Christmas lights. Big dogs and Greek islands and poached eggs and tennis. Taylor Swift, frying pans in the dishwasher, the words *absolutely*, *arsewipe*, *heaven*. Tracy Chapman and prawn jalfrezi and Muriel Spark and HP Sauce in bacon sandwiches.

And then there was my culture. Steve Martin and Aston

Villa and New York and *E.T.* Chicken bhuna, strange-looking cats and always having squash or cans of soft drinks in the house. The Cure. Pink Floyd. Kanye West, fried eggs, ten hours' sleep, ketchup in bacon sandwiches. Never missing dental check-ups. Sister Sledge (my mum). Watching TV even if the weather is nice. Cadbury's Caramel. John and Paul and George and Ringo.

And then we met and fell in love and we introduced each other to all of it, like children showing each other their favourite toys. That instinct never goes – look at my fire engine, look at my vinyl collection. Look at all these things I've chosen to represent who I am. It was fun to find out about each other's self-made cultures and make our own hybrid in the years of eating, watching, reading, listening, sleeping and living together. Our culture was tea drunk from very large mugs. And looking forward to the Glastonbury ticket day and the new season of *Game of Thrones* and taking the piss out of ourselves for being just like everyone else. Our culture was over-tipping in restaurants because we both used to work in the service industry, salty popcorn at the cinema and afternoon naps. Side-by-side morning sex. Home-made Manhattans. Bar-made Manhattans (much better). Otis Redding's 'Cigarettes and Coffee' (our song). Discovering a new song we both loved and listening to it over and over again until we couldn't listen to it any more. Period dramas on a Sunday night. That one perfect vibrator that finished her off in seconds when we were in a rush. Gravy. David Hockney. Truffle crisps. Can you believe it? I still can't believe it. A smell indisputably reminiscent of bums. On a crisp. And yet we couldn't get enough of them together – stuffing them in our gobs, her head on my chest, me trying not to get crumbs in her hair as we watched *Sense and Sensibility* (1995).

But I'm not a member of that club any more. No one is. It's been disbanded, dissolved, the domain is no longer valid. So what do I do with all its stuff? Where do I put it all? Where do I take all my new discoveries now I'm no longer in a tribe of two? And if I start a new sub-genre of love with someone else, am I allowed to bring in all the things I loved from the last one? Or would that be weird?

Why do I find this so hard?

Saturday 24th August 2019

On the landing carpet outside my bedroom door lies a copy of the *Highgate and Hornsey Express*, open on page five. There is an eerily close-up shot of Morris taken from below. He fills the whole frame, his arms behind his back, face stern.

FURY AS HORNSEY PENSIONER IS 'WRITTEN OUT OF BEATLES HISTORY'

A 78-year-old long-time Hornsey resident has expressed his frustration at being 'ignored' by English Heritage in a bid to secure a plaque for his house that he claims is an 'essential part' of Beatles history.

Morris Foster, a former laboratory technician, claims that his house was the site of an overnight stay by George Harrison in 1963. 'After a concert one night, George chose to sleep on a friend's sofa rather than booking into a hotel.' For those wondering whether a one-off visit of a notable figure qualifies commemoration, Foster has 'thoroughly researched' the rules and says the event 'absolutely' makes the house 'eligible for a plaque'. Unfortunately, English Heritage has ignored his multiple emails and letters.

'I am being silenced and written out of Beatles history,' he says. 'It is important that we mark and preserve these places of cultural significance, otherwise they will just be forgotten.'

Andy Dawson, 41, a record producer originally from Staffordshire, lodges with the Hornsey pensioner and is equally as outraged at English Heritage's treatment of his landlord. 'It's a disgrace,' he says. 'An absolute disgrace.'

Foster hopes that public pressure on English Heritage will result in a plaque. Himself a Beatles fan, he says he feels 'honoured' to live in the same house where Harrison's head once rested. 'They were just four lads from Liverpool,' he says. 'And they went on to change the world.'

***

Morris sits in the kitchen eating toast and marmalade when I come downstairs. Another copy of the newspaper is on the table, open on page five.

'Big day,' I say, switching on the kettle.

'Yes,' he says.

'You pleased with it?'

'Yes, normally I am distrusting of the press, but they told the story as it should be told,' he says. I chuck a teabag in a mug and ask with a gesture to Morris if he'd like one. He shakes his head. 'What are your plans for today?' he asks.

'I've got a gig, I'm not looking forward to it.'

'And that's in the capacity of a . . . ?'

I wait for him to finish his thought, intrigued at where it will go this time. 'As a what, Morris?'

'An after-dinner speaker?'

The kettle boils. I sigh and fill my mug with water.

'Morris, I'm a comedian. I tell jokes on stage and people watch me. You must know what a comedian is.'

'Yes, of course I do, no need to be so bad-tempered about it,' he says, shaking his head. 'I'm sorry my memory isn't what it was. I'm sorry I can't remember every tiny detail of every conversation we have. And, to be honest, you don't really strike me as a comedian.'

'Why do you keep saying that? I've been doing it since I was a student! I won Best Newcomer at the Edinburgh Festival once!' He stares at me blankly. 'I've been on TV!'

His face twitches with sudden interest. A phenomenon I'm used to over the years of trying to get friends and family to understand my job.

'Any programmes I would know?'

'I dunno, like, a couple of comedy panel shows.'

'Would you ever consider presenting a late-night chat show where you interview celebrities?' he asks. 'On a big channel that everyone watches?'

'Well, yeah, but —'

'Well you should make yourself available next time they're looking for someone,' he says authoritatively. 'Put yourself forward. You could probably earn a lot of money.'

I don't even know where to begin.

'Would you like to watch one of my routines on YouTube?'

'No thank you,' he says. 'I am sure I would find it crass.'

'Okay, well, would you like to go to the pub with me?'

He blinks a few times, not knowing what to make of this suggestion.

'Will you do your comedy at me?' he asks.

'No, I mean, like, do you want to hang out as friends? Go for a pint together? We obviously don't know each other that well, and we live together, so it would be nice if we did.'

'Fine,' he says coolly. 'All right, then. Yes.'

'Good,' I say. I glance down at the large envelope and scissors on the chair next to him.

'You sending the article to someone?' I ask.

'Yes,' he says.

'Is it to —'

'Mr Assange, yes,' he says. 'I want to keep him updated on the authorities.'

I nod respectfully.

★

The wedding is in London at least. I don't have to get on a train for once, just sit on a bus until I get to the former music hall they've hired for the reception. I go through my notes for all my standard wedding stuff – that's always quite easy because the crowd is drunk and only able to tolerate very obvious gags featuring drunk uncles and brides changing their mind at the last minute. The harder bit is the stuff they really pay for – the personalized section. The problem is, when I asked the bride and groom to send me some details about themselves so I could write some bespoke jokes, they replied with: 'We have a dog called Tosca and we love travelling.'

I hate wedding gigs. Every time I do one I swear I'll never do one again.

There are a group of men outside the venue who wear matching morning suits and are smoking.

'Hey, hello!' I say. 'Sorry, this is sort of awkward – I'm the comedian, I'm here to do a set? Is there a coordinator or an organizer or someone I could speak to?'

A man with spectacularly white teeth and a walnut-brown tan turns to me.

'I'm Robbo,' he says. 'I'm the best man.'

'Rob . . . ?'

'Robbo,' he says, correcting me with confidence.

'Great – hi, Robbo, sorry to get in the way, I just didn't want to disturb the bride and groom.'

'Oh yeah, yeah, good idea, so what can I do you for?'

'I just wanted to know when I'm on, where I should get changed, if there's anywhere I could sit?'

'Erm,' he says, scratching the back of his head and looking around. 'There's the portaloos just over there. And in terms of timing, difficult to say, maybe a few hours?'

'Okay,' I say. 'I thought I was booked before the dinner?'

'No, no,' he says. 'We all decided: comedian on after the best man's speech. So you don't upstage me. Although that would be unlikely!'

'Okay,' I say. 'Okay, so I've got a lot of time between now and then.'

He nods enthusiastically. I hate him.

'Anything else I can help you with?'

'Yeah, actually. I'm trying to write some stuff that's specific to them, but I haven't got much to work off. Could you really quickly tell me a few things about Will and Annie so I have a jumping-off point?'

'Yeah, so Will is just a proper laugh, so funny. We've always said he should have been a comedian,' he says.

'Funny in what way?' I ask.

'Just like . . . amazing at impressions.'

'Okay. What kind of impressions?'

'Like . . . all the characters from *The Office*, Kermit the frog –'

'Okay, and what's his wife like?'

'Same, a real laugh. Really sound girl.'

'Could you give me any more specific stories? I know it's hard to remember them off the top of your head, but the more specific the better.'

'Er, do you know what, mate, I'll have a proper think and come back to you a bit later with a list.'

'Great,' I say before he walks off. That is the last time I will ever have a conversation with Robbo. I've said the phrase 'I'll have a proper think' enough times to my agent to know that it means he'll never think about it again.

I find a local pub and nurse two drinks over two hours, while I try to cobble together ten minutes of material about a couple based on three facts about them.

★

I return just in time to catch Robbo's speech – a twenty-five-minute ramble from the groom's antics on the school rugby pitch to various drunken blunders on their Erasmus year abroad. Then, he introduces me as 'The Comedian', a man with no name. I walk on to applause. After over a decade of doing this, I can almost always sense how the crowd is going to react by the exact sound of their drinks being placed on the table and their clapping as I walk on. This audience is confused.

While Robbo's anecdotes about the groom being sick on himself in Madrid were met with rapture, they start chatting as soon as I take the mic and I'm seen as a background pianist. I try to win back their attention by involving members of the crowd, but it doesn't work because they all know each other and therefore they're all showing off. From the minimal information I have about the couple, I make a joke about the dog being called Tosca and how the groom doesn't strike me as an opera buff. This is met with boos, which makes sense, as I am the intruder in the room – the one person who doesn't know them is the one making jokes about them. Someone shouts that Will is funnier than I am, so I take my cue.

'I tell you what, man of the hour, Will – come up here and show me how it's done!' I say, bringing the groom on stage to applause and cheers. 'I hear you do a phenomenal Kermit.' I hand the mic over to him and step to the side.

When he's finally finished, I thank him for showing me how it's done, congratulate the happy couple, encourage everyone to have a fantastic night, put the mic back on the stand, pick up my bag and leave. All in all, I'm on stage for exactly sixteen minutes, seven of them taken up with the groom's monologue, but everyone is so drunk I don't think they are going to ask for their money back.

★

I get a text from Emery on the way home. I look at the date on my phone screen and already know what it is. Sure enough, as I open our message thread I see it – a photo of him clutching the award for Best Comedy Show. I know at the very base of my feelings, there is pride for him. I know that's the feeling holding all the other feelings up. But all I can acknowledge right now are those immediate, fleeting top layers that make themselves aggressively known. Inadequacy, jealousy, resentment. I take a deep breath, put my phone back in my pocket and decide to text him my heart-felt congratulations in the morning.

When I get in, I flop on the bed and take *Why Elephants Cry* from my bedside table and open the first page.

Elephants grieve in a similar manner to humans. Unbelievable as it may sound, they perform rituals of mourning and they even cry. They inspect, scatter and bury the bones of their dead for reasons that are largely still a mystery to us. The fact that they interact with the remains of their fellow elephants cannot be explained with a simple evolutionary reason and suggests a depth of emotional life that is far more complex to analyse. Why do elephants have a relationship to the carcasses of their own kind? Why is this their chosen way of saying goodbye?

Autumn 2019

Friday 6th September 2019

'Andy?' a female voice says. I turn around and see her – Daisy. Unchanged. Brown hair, heavy fringe, upturned nose, brown eyes, cherry-red lipstick, resting expression of constant, adorable worry. My last relationship before Jen. I'd pursued her after we matched on a dating app, we were together happily for just over two years until we started making plans to live together and I knew, immediately and seemingly out of nowhere, that I wasn't in love with her. I kept it a secret for a month or two, I even looked around flats and pretended I had all good intentions to move into one with her. I managed to stall the break-up process by finding problems with each of the flats we found – no window in the bathroom, no corridor to divide the space. Finally, she called me out on it, questioning my sudden discerning taste in interiors (I was then living in a squalid two-man houseshare with Rob that had two deckchairs instead of a sofa). It all came spilling out over one evening and in the course of two hours we were over. I still feel bad about how it ended – I couldn't find the courage to initiate it myself, so she had to ask me to break up with her. This is the first time I've seen her since that night and, now that I'm in the same position I put her in all those years ago, I feel connected to her in a way I've never felt before. I hug her tightly.

'Daisy, oh my God,' I say. 'How are you?'

'I'm well!' she says.

A small traffic jam of commuters has built up behind us on the narrow cobbled street. I put my hand on Daisy's arm and gently move us to the side. 'How are you?' she asks. 'What are you doing in this part of town?'

'Oh. Casting. Audition for an energy drink advert.'

'How did it go?'

'Terribly. I had to sit on a stationary chair and pretend I was on a rollercoaster.' She laughs and it almost makes the failed audition and lost fee worth it.

'How's teaching?' I ask.

'It's great, moved schools last year. I'm head of department.'

The conversation continues in this way for a few minutes – taking turns to ask each other questions about our lives, replying with answers that don't encourage further chat. As she speaks, I read her face for clues of how she is feeling. I want to say: I'm so sorry you've bumped into me. I'm so sorry this must have ruined your day or maybe even your week. I now know how much time you've spent imagining this moment of us seeing each other for the first time. I know it's not how you hoped it would be – you're probably not wearing exactly what you'd wished you'd worn, you're not saying the things you're going to wish you said, you don't have the man on your arm to show me what I missed out on. I now understand what it is to want to be with someone who doesn't want to be with you any more. I know how painful it was and probably still is. And I'm so sorry I put you through it and that we're now here, talking like acquaintances.

But I don't. When we get to the end of our small-talk check-list, we hug once more and then we say goodbye. I'll probably never see her again.

Morris sits in the corner of a pub, three-quarters down his drink. It is odd to see him outside of the house. He looks ahead, one hand on his glass, his dark eyes wide and fixed on nothing. He sees me as I walk towards him and his face remains unchanged.

'Nice of you to show up, goodness me,' he says, shaking his head. 'Don't worry, I've got all evening.'

'I'm so sorry, Morris, the casting ran over and then I weirdly bumped into an ex-girlfriend who I haven't seen since we broke up years and years ago.' I point to his drink. 'Same again?'

He nods. 'Lager shandy,' he says.

I go to the bar to get him another and myself a pint of Guinness.

'So?' he asks expectantly when I return to the table. 'Are they going to hire you? For the advert?'

'No, I don't think so.'

'You should ask them to consider you,' he says.

'It doesn't work like that.'

'Why?'

'I don't think they thought I was right,' I say.

'Why? Not funny enough? Too old?' There's a pause.

'Morris, have I offended you in some way?'

'No?' he says. 'Why would you ask me that?'

'You just say these things sometimes and I wonder why you feel the need –'

'I didn't realize you were so sensitive about everything!' he yelps.

'Let's talk about something else,' I say.

'Yes. Let's. Did you have a conversation with her? The ex-girlfriend?'

'Er . . .' I take my first sip, pondering how much emotional honesty Morris can take, then put it down. 'It was strange because I broke up with her and I think I really hurt her. Which I have thought about, of course, and felt guilty about, quite a bit. But someone's recently just done the same to me and before now I never really knew what that feels like, you know, and how much you think about when you're finally going to see them and how it's going to go.' Morris's gaze has moved into the middle distance and I can see, behind his eyes, a screen has come down and he's watching a film. An epic. *Chariots of Fire* maybe. *Zulu*. I pick up speed. 'So, yeah, it was weird because I felt so much more understanding of how she must feel, which is probably not great. Anyway. A lot of bother, this relationship lark. You've got the right idea, Morris. Never get married!' I raise my pint at him and take a gulp.

'How do you know I've never been married?' he asks, his focus turning back to me. I put the glass down and swallow, trying not to splutter.

'You were married?!'

'You don't have to sound so shocked about it!'

'No. Sorry. I'm not, of course I'm not shocked,' I lie. 'So when were you married? And how long for?'

'My wedding day was –' he does some mental calculations – 'fifty-four years ago. And we were married for eight years.'

'What happened?'

'She left me,' he said. 'I came downstairs one day and she had her bags packed and the dog on its lead. She said goodbye and left.'

I cannot believe how much Morris is divulging, so willingly and matter-of-factly. One shandy down. If I didn't already know he has absolutely zero sense of humour, I would assume this was a joke.

'Did she say why?'

'Yes,' he says, taking another calm, measured sip.

'Why?' I ask.

'Didn't much like being married to me. I was always too busy with work. Wanted to marry someone else. So divorced me and married him instead.'

'Do you know *who*?'

'Yes.' I wait while he lifts his glass and takes another sip. 'My brother.'

'What!' My voice squeaks slightly in disbelief. 'Did you ever see them again?'

'Twice. At my mother's funeral, and then at my father's funeral.'

'Did you punch him?'

'It was perfectly polite. We didn't speak that much.'

'How did you feel when you saw them?'

'No different to how I've always felt since the day she left.'

'Which is?' I ask. Who knew there would ever be a day where I was hanging on to Morris's every word.

'Pleased to have realized early on in my life that you can trust nobody. Rely on nobody. When someone tells you something, don't believe them. When something is given to you as a fact, ask yourself whether it really is a fact. Everybody is out for themselves in this life. Everyone. And that's how it should be. I should be out for myself,' he says, pointing at himself, his voice low and hushed now. 'And you should be out for yourself.' He points to me. 'And we all should be out for ourselves.' He gestures around the pub.

'Wow,' I say, taking these words in. 'That's quite a lesson to learn.'

'Yes,' he says.

'Did you have any children?'

'No,' he says. 'And I'm very glad I didn't.'

'Why?'

'They're destroying the planet, they ruin your house. They cost too much money. They're ungrateful. They're loud, they've got sticky fingers. It's disgraceful that in this day and age people think they still want to have them, they don't even question whether it's a good decision.'

'That seems a bit –'

'A bit what?' he snaps.

'A bit harsh, maybe.'

'Do you want to have children?'

'Yeah, I'd love to. I can't wait to have kids.'

'Well, with all due respect, I think that is not a wise decision,' he says with a knowing laugh. 'What with the world going the way it is.'

'What exactly do you mean?' I ask.

'I'll leave that with you,' he says, holding his palm up to signify that he has reached the end of this conversation.

We manage another hour, not without some seriously hard work on my side, but I manage to keep him talking. When he gets to the end of his final rant (Richard Branson) and he's had enough, he finishes his drink and says he'll see me back at home. It may not be immediate brotherhood, but it's a start. I'm proud of us. We tried.

I order another drink and send a message out to the boys on our WhatsApp group.

> I'm out. Who's about?

I open up a new message to Daisy and scroll back through our message history; something I've never done until now. Unlike my break-up with Jen, I never felt the need to go back over everything that had happened in our relationship. I've never been here before, down in the cellar of the Daisy relationship, cracking open all the old vintages, swirling them around in a big wine glass, taking a deep sniff and having a drink for old times' sake.

Avi
With in-laws in Ireland sorry big boy.

> **Andy**
> Anyone else? Will come anywhere in London.

Avi
Lol. Someone have a drink with the poor cunt.

Unsatisfied with the dull pain that comes with reading loving messages from a past relationship, I put my earphones in and play all of the songs I associate with Daisy. I scroll right back to 2013 and read them all, hoping that it might give me some insight into my and Jen's break-up. I scroll and scroll, desperately searching for an epiphany.

Jon
I'm not I'm afraid buddy!

I draft a message to Daisy on my notes app but choose not to send it. I order drink after drink and get up and down from my seat to go smoke fag after fag as I watch our entire relationship in text build brick-by-brick, stand steady for a while and then disintegrate.

I miss Tash. What the hell happened to her? I still find myself waking up and fruitlessly searching for her on Instagram in the hope that we'll be digitally reunited. God, I could do with some of her banal messages right now, as vanilla and comforting as custard.

Jay
Me neither buddy, sorry

I keep drinking, holding out for someone to reply and say they're up for a drink and I can get off my phone and on a bus to go see them, but they don't. I'm the last one in the pub. No epiphanies arrive. Or if they did, I can't remember any of them.

Saturday 7th September 2019

Here's something I've learnt about telling a story from the time I've spent on stage: the details are what's important. The things that shock or entertain or horrify aren't the facts of what happened, they are the specifics of *how* they happened. There are lots of reasons why today will be a day I remember forever and only one of them relates to a plot twist.

The first, most crucial detail, is that I am so hung-over when I leave for work this morning, I snooze my alarm twice and reach for a pair of jeans and a T-shirt that says: LIAM & NOEL.

Another important detail is that the job is for a haircare and skincare brand in a central London shopping complex and that, on arrival, it becomes clear that I have been hired in a capacity not entirely known to me or the manager of the shop. As I chug a black coffee, orange juice and Diet Coke in succession and the manager reads back through the emails with my agent, I am told I have been hired to help 'draw attention' to a demonstration of products happening outside to attract passing shoppers.

You would think the important part of this story comes when, nearing the end of my first 'set', as I make pithy remarks about pores, I see Jen. She stands a few feet away from the demonstration, smiling. I wrap it up as quickly as I can, give the mic to the manager and walk towards her. It instantly feels so much easier than when we saw each other at the bank – we hug and I make a joke of my ridiculous job, and she laughs, and it feels so good to hear her laugh. But when I ask what she's doing in central London on a Saturday, she looks edgy and speaks in a slightly garbled way and keeps trying to shut down the conversation, which I assume is because she's in a rush to get somewhere, so I tell her that I'll let her get on with her day and give her a hug goodbye.

But that's not the inciting incident. Oh no. That happens when we pull apart and a man walks towards us with two coffees. He hands one to Jen and calls her 'sweetie' and says sorry for the wait, the queue was crazy. I stare at Jen and say nothing and she says, 'This is Seb,' like that. Nothing else. 'This is Seb.'

And the mere fact of Seb's existence is not the most alarming detail. What must be mentioned is not just how Seb looks, which is perfect, but how he smells, which is also perfect. Seb is rugged and expensive. His skin is just tanned enough to imply long-haul travel, his hair just flecked with enough grey to be distinguished. Men like Seb are the reason men like me asked for an *Esquire* subscription for Christmas when we were students with a part-time job at the Toby Carvery. I have known Seb for ten seconds and I already know that he has a signature dish and a weights routine and more than three roll-neck jumpers and knows the secret to female ejaculation.

Jen says, 'This is Andy,' and he says 'Ahh' in a warm way and smiles and I know he knows exactly who I am. I ask what they're up to today in a seemingly casual way and he says: 'I need to buy a new mattress.' He doesn't specifically say 'so we can fuck on it', but it still feels extremely showy and in poor taste.

Another important detail is that, seemingly out of nowhere, he points at me and says, 'Don't look back in anger,' which I take as a remark about me not being able to let go of my relationship with Jen. I am aghast and want to tell him to mind his own fucking business, but instead I awkwardly laugh and say, 'I'm trying, mate, I'm trying!' and then he says, 'No,' and points again and I realize he's not pointing at me, he's pointing at my T-shirt and making a reference to the Oasis song and I say, 'Oh, of course,' and he says, quite needlessly, 'Great song,' and I say, even more needlessly, 'Yeah, a classic,' and Jen looks like she's going to vomit.

(Believe it or not, it's only at this point that the story turns from a comedy into a horror.)

I ask how they know each other and before either of them has a chance to answer, the excitable sales assistant rushes over to me to tell me that she's been in the stockroom and it transpires that they *do* have the follicle-stimulating shampoo for hair loss that I'd seen on the display and asked about when I arrived.

And then we all say goodbye and a microphone is put into my hand and I muddle through another half-hour of low-grade jokes about serums. I give them the mic, go find my jacket and leave as quickly as I can.

I take my phone from its pocket and see I have two new message notifications. The first is from Daisy.

Hi Andy, it's taken me all day to know what to reply to your voicemail, which was quite a shock to wake up to, to be honest. It was a nice surprise to bump into you yesterday and I didn't think about it much afterwards, so I don't know why you think you saw 'pain in my eyes' because there wasn't any. We ended a long time ago and any mourning I've done for that relationship I did then. It feels like you may be projecting some of your feelings on to me and I would encourage you to address that before leaving inappropriate voicemails. You don't need to apologize for 'breaking my heart', it's fine, I've moved on and honestly so should you.

Best,
Daisy

The second is from Jen.

> Hey! I hope you're ok and that wasn't awkward. It was
> great to see you. Xx

I put my phone back in my pocket and I do not reply to either of them because I don't have anything to say and I can barely form the end of a thought without another one interrupting. I'm battling through central London crowds and walking to nowhere because I don't know where to go or what to do. I feel both wronged and proven right and like of course this was always meant to happen, of course Jen was meant to be with someone like him. And I look back on myself this morning, with my sweet ignorance, and I want to hug him because it's so cute that he really believed that someone like him would end up with someone like her.

A man at Oxford Circus shouts into a speaker-phone and tells me that I am full of sin and shame. He hands me a flyer. He tells me that it's not too late for me, that it is still in my power to find righteousness and redemption.

'When you get to hell, you won't be brave!' he shouts. 'When you get to hell, you won't be brave! WHEN YOU GET TO HELL, YOU WON'T BE BRAVE!'

Yes I will.

Yes I will yes I will yes I will.

Thursday 12th September 2019

A few things I have learnt about Seb over the last four days:

- He and Jen work at the same company, which is where they must have met. He moved there a year ago.
- He grew up in a small English town which is on the border of Wales.
- His mum is South African.
- He is forty-four years old.
- Between the years of 2011 and 2016 he was in a relationship with a woman named Kate. She is now married with a child and living in Queensland Australia, running a business called Froth Femina which sells customized soaps in the shape of breasts. I also found Froth Femina's turnover for the last tax year on Australian Business Registry Services, which isn't necessary to include here.
- He enjoys going to an assortment of Caribbean islands on holiday (very original, Seb).
- He believes that from cargo, to hull to liability, he can provide global insurance products to suit all his clients' needs in a bespoke manner. I don't know what that means, but I learnt it from a YouTube video where he's talking about his job in shipping insurance.
- He rows, plays rugby, cycles and climbs. He likes doing all of these things to various degrees of extremity to raise money for charities (imaginative!).
- In 2017, he went to see Kasabian play in Dublin.
- He went to Cambridge University (again, bit on the nose).

- He has always worked in insurance.
- He was liking Jen's photos on Instagram three months ago, but she didn't start liking his photos until a month ago.
- His dad died of prostate cancer, which is sad and I'm sorry that it happened to him, but it doesn't redeem him in my mind in any way.

The Jen Inquiry has officially been launched. The questions to which it seeks answers are as follows:

- Why did she break up with me?
- Did she break up with me because she met Seb?
- If she doesn't believe in relationships, why is she able to be in a relationship with Seb and not me?

On my way to Jane and Avi's, I come up with conversation strategies. Now, more than ever, the tokens system must be observed. Just because there are two of them there tonight, doesn't mean I get double the amount. And asking about Seb uses up all of my ten in one go, so I've got to time it well.

When Jane answers the door, Rocco wailing on the stairs, Jackson attached to her leg like a koala on a tree, I get the familiar feeling of visiting a friend with a young family that this was the worst moment possible to have shown up. Jane gets me a beer and we sit at the kitchen table. Jackson shouts because he doesn't like Rocco looking at him, while Jane tries to talk, Avi tries to cook and I try not to say: 'SO TELL ME ABOUT SEB.'

But it's no good, Jackson keeps pestering, pulling at his mum's sleeve.

'Mummay,' he whines. 'Mummay, Mummay.'

'Honey – what is it?' she says.

'Can we play dogs?' he asks.

'Mummy's tired, I think,' I say. 'She's been at work all day and she's got a baby in her tummy. Why don't I go in the other room with you and we can play dogs while they make grown-up dinner?'

'No, I want Mummy. I only want to play with Mummy.'

'All right,' she says with a sigh, standing up. 'Go on then, how does the game go?'

'So I am a dog,' Jackson explains sombrely and slowly. 'And Rocco is a dog and the baby in your tummy is a dog.'

'Right,' she says.

'And we are all your pets but I am the dog you love the most, your favouritest one. And you like playing with me and walking with me, and Rocco is not your favourite dog, not at all, you don't like him that much. And the baby is also not your favourite dog and you only really want me to be your pet dog.' Jackson finishes, blinking at us earnestly, thinking nothing of how he imparted the rules of the game. Jane looks at me with a despairing smile and we try not to laugh.

'Okay,' she says, scooping Rocco up on to her hip with one arm and taking Jackson's hand in the other. 'I think let's leave Daddy and Uncle Andy and we can go to the other room.' She raises her eyebrows at me and walks out with them, Jackson throwing himself on to his hands and knees and barking. Avi waits until they've left the room.

'Jackson's struggling with this idea of being replaced, I think,' he says in a hushed tone.

'No shit,' I reply. I have never felt a stronger affinity with my godson.

I put the boys to bed and read them a story. When I say goodnight to Jackson, I give him a hug and tell him that he's always going to be my favourite one. He laughs and tells me I am not his favourite one because of my big nose.

When I return to the table, Avi is loading up plates with

spaghetti bolognese. I haven't told him about the great carbo-hydrate exodus, for fear of being ribbed mercilessly. I make enthusiastic sounds of satiation as I eat while I discreetly pick the meat off the pasta. I have been careful not to spend this evening's tokens until now, to capitalize on their full attention.

'So. You're never going to guess what happened last week,' I say, putting down my fork.

'What?' Avi says, turning his eyes up to me, his head bowed towards the plate as he coaxes strands of spaghetti into his mouth.

'So I'm walking through a part of town I'm never in.'

'Where?' Avi asks.

'Bermondsey, Av – this isn't the most interesting part of the story.'

'Sorry,' he says.

'And guess who I see?' I leave a dramatic pause. 'Daisy.'

'NO,' Av says.

'Did you speak to her?' Jane asks.

'Yeah. She tapped me on the arm and we hugged and we had a very polite conversation. She looked exactly the same.'

'Was it awkward?' Avi asks.

'No. It wasn't awkward until I got drunk and left her a late-night voicemail I don't remember, apparently saying that I'm sorry that I broke her heart.' Jane holds her head in her hands. 'And I completely forgot about it until she sent me a quite pissed-off text the next day.'

'So she should've,' Jane says, laughing. 'Jesus Christ, what a thing to wake up to.'

'Twat,' Avi says, laughing too. This is good, I'm glad I buried the lead like this. Get them warmed up, get the juices flowing, then I can slip in the Jen and Seb stuff like it's just an afterthought.

'Oh and THEN,' I say, 'the next day I am booked to make jokes about skincare and haircare for a beauty brand.'

'I do not understand your job,' Avi says, loading another portion of spaghetti on to his plate.

'And I'm outside the shop making jokes into a mic and who do I bump into? Jen. Not only Jen,' I say, leaving an even more loaded pause, 'Jen and her new boyfriend. What are the chances of that? Two exes in two days. What's God trying to tell me?!' I wait for their collective shock.

'Yeah, she said,' Jane says, the smile replaced with an awkward grimace.

'Oh, so she told you?'

'Yeah, she says you were really cool about it all.'

'So that Seb guy, he is her boyfriend?'

'As far as I know he's just a guy from work who she's seeing,' Jane says. 'Honestly, that's all I know, Andy.'

'Sorry, man, that must have been weird,' Avi says. 'But you seem fine. Nothing you can do but move on.'

'Well, I'm not really fine,' I say, making it rain with tokens. 'I feel really confused and, like, questioning everything she said about the reasons we broke up.'

'Why does it make you question everything?' Avi asks wearily.

'She said she didn't want to be in a relationship. Well, then, why did she go straight into something else with someone else?'

'She didn't sign a break-up contract for you, though,' Avi says in an annoyingly reasonable tone. 'She's kind of free to do whatever she wants now.'

'I think this is all because of her therapist,' I say. 'I think her therapist made her break up with me. I think it's because of my job. I think she said: "You should be with someone more on your level, financially," and I think that's why she dumped me for Seb.' In minus zero tokens now.

'Why are you not eating your spaghetti?' Jane asks.

'I am!' I say, shovelling a forkful of bolognese in my mouth. 'It's delicious.'

'You're picking at a pile of meat,' she says, examining my plate. 'What's up with you?'

'I'm just eating carefully.'

'You're on a crash diet. I've tried doing Keto enough times to know what you're doing. You're going to make yourself ill.'

'I'm eating loads,' I say, in a more shrill way than I'd like. 'I'm just eating carefully and exercising a lot.'

'You look different,' she says.

'You look like a *Tekken* character in a fleece,' Avi says, loading a third and final mound of spaghetti on to his plate.

And that's it. That's all I get. I don't try to get any further information. Court adjourned for the Jen Inquiry, witnesses Avi and Jane to leave the stand. We talk about other things for the rest of the evening.

But I can't stop myself from fixating on the way Avi spoke to me: his reticence to speak in any detail; his upbeat passive-aggression; the gentlest of impatience I could sense from both of them – 'you seem fine', 'nothing you can do but move on'. I don't like that he knows all this stuff about how I'm feeling – it's humiliating. I'm beginning to feel a strange resentment towards him that I know is not his fault, but it makes me not want to hang out with him any more. I don't like that my break-up has arranged us into roles where I'm falling apart and he's always together. I know he's not always together, but he confides in his wife and not me. The more I talk about how sad I am, the more my dignity is compromised, the more of an imbalance appears that I'm sure, on some secret level, he must enjoy.

I can't talk to Avi any more. I've got to find someone else to burden with all this. I scroll through my iPhone contacts all the way home but can't find anyone.

Saturday 14th September 2019

Kelly's trip to Ibiza was a disaster. She tells me the multi-chaptered story during our early-morning training session. She didn't walk into the club with another woman on her arm as planned. She bumped into her ex while off her head on the dance floor, only to see her getting off with someone else, then they had a big row and were both thrown out.

No detail is spared in the retelling and I've fully tuned out by the time we've finished cardio and get on to weights. Kelly doesn't notice my absence, she just wants a blank, nodding face to receive her ranting. I give it to her willingly, knowing how much I'd appreciate the same thing right now. I wonder how many times a day she will repeat this tale to clients beat-for-beat. As she gets further into the story, getting more and more wound up, I make a mental list of all the things I would be willing to do – actually, realistically willing – to have Jen break up with Seb and be in love with me again. I play out each of the following scenarios in my head several times and this is what I conclude:

Give a man a handjob if I didn't have to look at his face for the
   duration
Lose a bit of hair at the front (not any more at the back)
Go to her parents' house every weekend for lunch for the rest
   of my life
Give up alcohol for two years
Never eat ham again
(This one isn't good) Have my only remaining grandparent die
   (peacefully)

Live in Hammersmith

Never buy another pair of sunglasses

Lose a finger or toe under general anaesthetic (limbs too far)
　　(could probably get a show out of it)

When I tune back in on my last set of biceps curls, Kelly is laughing quite demonically and saying: 'More fool her, you know? More. Fool. Her.'

Wednesday 18th September 2019

As far as I know, there is no precedent for what your fake therapy patient name should be, so the formula I land on is my maternal grandfather's name + childhood pet cat name. Clifford Beverley. Clifford Beverley is on his way to his first ever therapy session, with a woman who I found relatively easily online and emailed with a fake address. I had the idea while imagining all the things Jen's therapist might have said about me which possibly contributed to our break-up and I thought: instead of all this solo theorizing, why don't I find out what a therapist would say to someone like Jen going out with someone like me? I'll imagine what Jen said about me and ask the therapist for advice. Not an entirely normal thing to do, sure, but I have no one else left to talk to and all my tokens are spent anyway. And I still need answers. The Jen Inquiry is an ongoing case.

I ring the buzzer of the tall, red-brick townhouse. A woman in her forties with a dark bob answers the door with a serene smile.

'Clifford,' she says in a spa voice. 'Come in.'

'Thank you,' I say.

She walks me down the white corridor and shows me into a room on the left.

'Take a seat,' she says, gesturing at the grey sofa. I note the box of tissues on the side table. She sits opposite me on a grey armchair. She waits a few moments, her face still serene but her smile replaced with an expression of practised neutrality. 'Why don't you tell me why you're here,' she says.

'I suppose I'm here because I don't know whether to break up with my girlfriend or not.'

'Okay,' she says. 'Tell me a little about your relationship first.'

'We've been together for nearly four years,' I say, rattling off the story I pre-prepared in the gym this morning.

'And what's her name?'

'Alice,' I say.

'Alice, okay.'

'We live together. And I love her, but I worry that she's not on the same path as me.'

'And what path is that?' she asks.

'I earn a lot of money and work very hard in a corporate job and she dosses about doing lots of different random jobs to support her creative ambitions and she doesn't have any savings and can't go on holiday that much or go to expensive restaurants –'

'Okay, hang on, hang on, I'm going to stop you for a moment, Clifford,' she says. 'Tell me what this creative ambition is for Alice?'

'She's a burlesque dancer,' I say. 'And when we first started dating I found it really, you know, interesting. Because I hadn't met a burlesque dancer before. I'm a lawyer and I don't enjoy it – in fact, I hate it, it bores me. I'm only doing it because that's what my dad did and I felt a lot of pressure to impress him. So when I met Alice, I found her job quite . . . brave. I admired her for doing something so different and not being traditional. But now I just want her to just . . . fucking . . . grow up.' I say it with conviction that surprises even me.

She takes this in and pauses before she speaks.

'Something that strikes me immediately is that you seem quite judgemental of her choices – this chosen "path" as you describe it.'

'I am, yes.'

'I wonder – is this something you felt when you were growing up? From your dad?'

'No, I don't know if it's got anything to do with my dad,' I say, keen to keep us on track. 'I think I just want a new girlfriend, maybe someone a bit more mature who does a proper job, like, maybe another lawyer or a CEO.'

She nods and leaves another long pause.

'Clifford – sometimes we can disguise our real reasons for judgement with something we find easier to accept about ourselves. Are your negative feelings towards Alice's job really about the fact she's not earning enough money, or has it got anything to do with the fact that her job is, in a way, sexualized?'

'No, it's not that.'

'Let's go back a bit,' she says, rearranging her hands in her lap. 'You mention your dad was a lawyer. What was it your mum did for a living?'

'No, no,' I say, glancing at the clock on the wall, and aware of the minutes ticking by. I can't afford another fake therapy session – this is my only chance to get answers. 'Forget about the burlesque thing.'

'But can *you* forget about it? Because it seems very much at the forefront of your mind.'

'It's not. It's not even worth talking about.'

She pauses again as she gathers her thoughts.

'I can sense a lot of anger about this, Clifford. Anger that I think goes beyond frustrations to do with salary.'

'No, sorry, what I mean is, that was misleading of me. She actually only does burlesque a bit. Her main income is . . .' I'm reminded yet again of why I don't do improv. 'Juggling. And I just need to know whether you think I should be with a juggler, or whether you think I should break up with her and be with a lawyer? What would you, as a therapist, say to that?'

'What I think is interesting about what you just said is that you're asking me to judge you just like your father judged you – just as you now judge Alice. But, what if it's not always about the "right" or "wrong" way to do things, Clifford? What if it's not about "you should do this" or "you shouldn't do that"; what my role is as a therapist or Alice's role is as a juggler,' she says. 'Let's go back a bit to your home life as a child . . .'

I realize this is a waste of money but feel like I have to see the whole session through, so I give her the full story of Clifford's made-up family, inventing it as I go, trying to remember all the details. I keep trying to bring the conversation back to the question of our different jobs, but she keeps veering it back to Clifford's parents. I jump up from the sofa once the fifty-five minutes have passed and she says, with what I suspect is a sense of relief: 'We have to stop there.' She sees me out, I thank her for her time and she tells me she will be in touch. I can't believe Jen spends a hundred quid a week on this dross.

I open my online banking app and resentfully transfer the remaining fee for the session, and I notice I still haven't been paid for any of my gigs last month. I ring my agent and am greeted by her assistant who says, again, that she's in a meeting but he'll make sure she calls me back. I check the agency's Twitter page and scroll back through months of exciting career announcements for other comedians. They are 'thrilled to announce' something at least three times a day. A sitcom that someone's starring in, a panel show someone is hosting, a comedy drama that someone has written, new clients they are now representing.

We are thrilled to announce our client Emery PHILLIPS has won EDINBURGH SHOW OF THE YEAR. A huge congratulations to Emery!

I compose a tweet:

I am thrilled to announce I cannot get my agent to call me back.

I post it. It gets three likes. I delete it.

Saturday 28th September 2019

Emery walks into the dressing room wearing an actual backwards baseball cap.

'Mate!' I say, genuinely pleased to see him. He's been off the circuit since he won the award and gigs have been half as fun without him.

'*Mate*,' he replies, walking towards me with his arms outstretched. He hugs me tightly and kisses both my cheeks, before holding my face in his palms. 'Let me see this beautiful man.'

'Where have you been?' I ask.

'I know, I'm a shambles.' He takes the cap off and runs his hands through his ever-expanding hair. 'Been a bit non-stop.' We both take a seat by the mirrors and he puts his feet up on a vacant chair.

'Yeah?' I say.

He smiles. '*Oh* yeah.'

I'm desperate to ask him everything but also want to know nothing.

'Anything exciting?' I ask.

'Irons are a'burnin',' he says in an unnecessary Texan accent. 'In them flamin' hot fires.'

'Okay, like, what irons?'

'Projects, they're a'cookin'.'

'Can you stop talking in riddles, Emery?'

His normal voice resumes. 'No, but seriously, man, I can't really talk about it all yet. Not until it's been announced officially.'

'Oh, come on! Tell me! Who wants to work with you? Who's

been in touch? What's been green-lit? *What's your 2019/2020 tax bill going to look like?'*

His phone rings and I see it's our agent.

'Ah,' he says, holding his finger up to me to signify that he needs a minute. He turns away from me in his seat. 'Hey!' he says. 'Recovered from those langoustines yet? Because I haven't!' He laughs uproariously. I hear her laughing on the other end of the call too. He catches his breath. 'What's up? . . . Uh huh . . . mm hmmm . . . yeah, yeah.' I get my phone out and pretend to be engrossed in it. 'I think we say we want to keep the rights to the stage adaptation . . . yeah . . . let's fight for it . . . like, the chances of it going from being a movie to a West End musical are low, but if it does, I would like a' – the Texan accent returns – 'piece of that pie, ma'am.' More laughter. 'Okay . . . let me know what they say . . . you are an angel.' He ends the call and turns back towards me. 'Sorry about that.'

'Don't be,' I say. 'I remember when she used to return my calls.'

'You know what it's like, she's got too many people on her books, too many comedians to call. Don't take it personally. She hasn't got any time.'

'She's got time to go out and eat langoustines with you,' I say.

'To be fair to her, she wasn't taking me out. The head of Netflix was taking me out and she wanted to be there as my representative.'

Unbelievable. 'That makes me feel better, thank you,' I say.

'Andy, you don't want to become one of those comedians whose agent ghosts them because they're always calling. We all know those stories. You're dancing dangerously close to being that guy.'

'All she has to do is book my jobs and stay in touch with me. That's how she earns her fifteen per cent. I don't understand why she can't just spare a few minutes every couple of weeks for a call.'

'I'll have a word with her,' he says, spinning the dome of his baseball cap on his finger. 'Would you like that?'

'No, I would not like that,' I say petulantly. 'I want her to just call me back without pressure from her hottest client. She signed me years before you, for Christ's sake.'

'Hot this month, lukewarm next,' Emery says, putting his arm around me.

'No, no, I'd never wish that.' I reciprocate the gesture by putting my arm around his shoulder, then we remove them from each other with a friendly pat. 'Sorry, I don't mean to sound bitter. Ignore me. This has nothing to do with you.'

'The Madness?'

'Like you wouldn't believe.'

'Another man?'

'*Yes*,' I say indignantly. 'How did you know?'

'Talk to me,' he says, taking out tobacco and papers from his jeans pocket.

'I ran into both of them.'

'That's a roughie,' he says with a filter between his teeth.

'And I've just become obsessed with him.'

'Sexually,' Emery deems, removing the filter and licking one side of the paper.

'Obviously not sexually.'

'ANDY,' he suddenly shouts. 'WAKE UP.' He taps the temple of my head twice. 'Of course you're obsessed with him sexually. You think that because you have a *New York Times* subscription and occasionally remember to drink kombucha that you're above mammalian impulses? You're not above mammalian impulses. It's DISGUSTING. But it's who we are. Why do you think "Mr Brightside" is *the* anthem of our generation for men?'

'The guitar riff.'

'WRONG,' he shouts, putting the cigarette in his mouth. He stands up and walks outside as I follow him. '*Jealousy*,' he barks over his shoulder to me. '*Turning saints into the sea, swimming through sick lullabies*. That song hits on something we can never articulate, which is that romantic jealousy is a turn-on, in its own dark way.' He opens the stage door, steps out and lights his cigarette on the side road. 'Because that man fucking the woman you love – it was you, and now it's him, and, crucially,' he says, passing the wet end of the rollie to me, 'it may *never* be you again. So the only way you can stay connected to her sexually is to imagine this bloke.'

I inhale on the fag and pass it back to him. Before I get a chance to say anything, Tim arrives – long, thin, bespectacled, posh.

''Allo, 'allo,' he says, putting his hand out to Emery. 'Didn't think you'd be here, man of the moment. Thought you'd be above mixed bills now.'

'Good to keep my hand in,' he jokes.

Tim turns to me. 'Andy.'

'Hey, mate,' I say, giving him a nod of the head that I know will suffice. 'Good to see you.'

'And you,' he replies, before squeezing between us and walking into the building.

Shortly afterwards, Marcus appears. Five foot five, point-featured, with a mod haircut and a deadpan way of speaking, both off stage and on stage. He would tell you your mother died in the same tone as informing you the Chinese takeaway has arrived.

The bill is as follows: Marcus compering, Thalia up top, then me, then Emery, then Tim, then Frank. Frank is a sixty-something American, who was once in a sitcom in the nineties before he moved to the UK, but is still just recognizable enough to headline a London gig on a Saturday night. The fact of his appearances on late-night American talk shows, even if last in 1997, fills the dressing room with a sense of glamour. Thalia sits cross-legged and agog on a chair, asking him to regale her with stories, as he paces around the room telling them without a pause for breath. Tim, as nervous and awkward as ever, sips a pint of rhubarb beer and laughs too loudly at everything he says.

Marcus is the perfect MC. His unflappable, nonchalant style puts the crowd at ease and, even in the face of the most disruptive drunk audience member, he manages to calm him down and get him onside while still very gently teasing him. Thalia, having grown in confidence since her first Edinburgh run, tries out some bold new material. Her multi-versed folk song about pansexuality goes down surprisingly well with the lairy crowd, particularly when she divides them into a call-and-response singalong, a cheap but effective trick.

I phone it in with the same old stuff, so practised that I barely feel like I've been on stage – it's like I've hit Comedian Cruise Control and my mouth and body move of their own accord without any instruction from my brain. Despite (or maybe because of) my laziness, it goes down well and it feels great. Emery has now entered his famous comedian phase, where he is just about well-known enough from industry recognition and commercial success to make references to it in his set. He riffs on all his old themes: his obsession with women, his despair at the modern world, his inability to grow up – all his darkness, flood-lit with jokes. But now he seasons it with mentions of his emerging fame and his new wealth. He manages to not be detestable by ramping up the self-deprecation in direct proportion to these new subjects. It works. Everyone loves him.

And then Tim has a shocker. His shtick is that he's a statistician and his act is made up of weird and surprising facts and figures that say relatable things about humanity. It's funny and very finely tuned, but it's also super geeky and requires concentration. He's the wrong booking for an East London bar on a Saturday night. The audience's attention quickly drifts, then he acknowledges the fact he's losing them in a way that is meant to be jokingly caustic but appears defensive, then they turn on him with heckling. We watch a bit of it until it becomes too excruciating and we go back to the dressing room to finish our drinks and leave.

'Are you guys going?!' Thalia says, before inhaling deeply on what at first seems to be a black USB-stick.

'Yeah,' I say.

She blows a banana-scented plume in our faces. 'We can't miss Frank headlining!' she says. 'He's a living legend!'

'We've seen him loads,' I say. 'We can give you a really accurate impersonation.'

'Yeah, we need to go,' Emery says, with a rollie already in between his teeth, patting his jacket and back pockets to check that he's got everything.

'Shouldn't we wait for Tim?' Thalia asks.

'NO,' Emery and I say in unison.

'Terrible idea,' Emery says.

'If someone bombs, you leave before they get backstage,' I volunteer.

'Really?' Thalia says. 'That seems kind of mean.'

'No,' I reply. 'The last thing he wants to do right now is face us. And then we don't have to patronize him with consolations.'

'Or give him fake compliments,' Emery says, brushing a loose hair away from Thalia's face. 'It's the brotherly thing to do.'

Thalia, semi-molten from Emery's touch, smiles.

'Okay,' she says.

'Where are you heading now?' Emery asks, cocking his head, brushing her hair back over her shoulders.

'To a bar, I think,' she says. 'My two housemates are here tonight.'

'Onwards!' Emery says, placing a hand on my back and a hand on Thalia's. 'Into the wilderness we go!' he says, turning his face to me to wink.

I don't want to go out – I've gone out three nights in a row after gigs and I'm tired from an early-morning workout and a day handing out samples of Cambozola at a street food festival. But I can't pass on the opportunity of a Saturday night out. Every night feels like a possibility for moving my break-up on in some way. I've never been out so much in my life. Sometimes I worry I'm only going out with the hope of bumping into her.

The wilderness of a weekend is never nearly as intrepid or romantic as the committedly single describe, I now realize. The bar where we find ourselves in Dalston is overcrowded, over-discovered and too loud, with a price list for drinks that is not as bohemian as the red-lit speakeasy signage would suggest. Emery flattens his entire torso on to the bar as he leans in and shouts into the server's ear, while Thalia bops her head to the sound of sixties rock 'n' roll and occasionally bellows 'IT'S SO GOOD TO SEE YOU, ANDY, YOU KNOW, I AM SUCH A FAN OF YOURS, I'M ALWAYS SO PLEASED WHEN I SEE WE'RE ON A BILL TOGETHER' into my ear, repeatedly, like she's trying to convince herself.

A circular table with a bench and stools frees up and we take it. Emery is in the middle of a very long story about acquiring his new American agent, when a woman walks over to us – mid-twenties, with shoulder-length, jet-black hair, a ring through her septum. She wears tight black jeans and a black long-sleeved crop top that shows her taut, narrow tummy, so pale that it looks almost silver in the low light of the bar.

'Hey, bitch,' she says to Thalia. Two words, one note, her expressionless face giving nothing away.

'Oh hey, BITCH,' Thalia shouts back at her, before clambering up from the table and giving her a hug. 'Sophie, this is Emery and Andy. Guys, this is my housemate Sophie.' In an oddly old-fashioned move, I feel the urge to stand up when I give her a hug. I can tell she finds this amusing by the half-smile that betrays her nonchalance.

'Hey,' she says. 'Great set.'

'Mediocre set,' I correct her. 'But thanks. I'm going to get a drink, does anyone want one?' Thalia and Emery are whispering in each other's ears and cackling.

'I'll come with you,' Sophie says.

Under the industrial lights that hang over the bar, I can pick up the intricacies of her – the thin, dark choker necklace, her wide-set green eyes, her feathery eyebrows two shades lighter than her hair, her cheekbones so high and defined, they look carved into her pale face like marble. She only allows me occasional glances of eye contact; the rest of the time her gaze roams around the bar, without ever looking like she's looking for someone better. Motionlessly observing everyone and everything, like a cat perched at a windowsill. She never laughs at my jokes but twice says 'That's funny' in response to something I say. She likes saying 'that's' something. 'I'm from Birmingham': 'That's cool.' 'I support Aston Villa': 'That's cringe.' 'I've been doing comedy for ten years': 'That's a while.' 'I'm thirty-five': 'That's an exciting age.'

'Don't say that,' I reply.

'What?' she says.

'"That's an exciting age." It sounds like that line from *Peter*

Pan. "To die will be an awfully big adventure."' This nearly makes her laugh, but not quite. She purses her lips tightly as she smiles, keen not to satisfy me with a grin.

'It's true. I wish I was thirty-five.'

'Well, I wish I was twenty-three,' I say.

'Now that sounds like some typical male Peter Pan bullshit to me,' she says, biting down on to the plastic straw in her vodka lime soda.

'Whoa whoa whoa,' I laugh. 'Peter Pan bullshit?'

'Yeah, all middle-aged men are Peter Pans,' she shrugs.

'Firstly – I am not middle-aged. I am in the first year of early middle age, which basically makes me more of a teenager than you are, when you think about it.' She gives me another lips-shut-tight smile. 'And secondly – how do you know what middle-aged men are like?'

'Because I can't stop dating them.'

'Really?!' I say in dismay.

'Yeah, my ex was, like, way older than you.'

'Huh,' I say in response, while I silently take this as my permission to fancy her.

Another woman who looks about the same age walks into the bar and joins us. Sophie gives her a hug.

'This is Emma,' Sophie says. Emma has white-blonde hair cut into a short mullet. She wears shiny rubber leggings, battered trainers and a five-sizes-too-big hoodie. Her face is delicate and her features are all slight – little eyes, narrow nose, rosebud mouth. She looks like a sulky fairy.

'Hey,' she says flatly.

'She was at the gig too,' Sophie says.

'Oh, cool,' I say. Aware that if Emma didn't volunteer this information, I probably don't want to hear her feedback.

'Yeah, not really my thing,' she says.

'You not into comedy?'

'I am, but like, not cringe comedy, no offence,' she says, unzipping her hoodie to reveal a neon-pink mesh vest. 'Not, like, straight white men telling jokes. Thalia was cool.'

'Sick,' Sophie says in response to her outfit reveal. 'You still going to the party after?'

'Yeah,' she says.

'Emma's going to an orgy.'

'Orgy in the –' I venture nervously, keen not to sound like an old pervert –'traditional sense?'

'What other types of orgies are there?' Sophie asks.

'Yes,' Emma says, straight-faced, before turning to the barman. 'Can I get a Diet Coke?'

'Gotta keep a clear head for a gang bang,' I joke.

Emma crinkles her face in repulsion. 'I don't drink,' she says, as if it were something I should have already known.

'Good for you,' I say, immediately regretting my accidentally patronizing tone.

I try to earn Emma's indifference – affection would be to shoot for the moon – but everything I say only escalates her very apparent irritation at me. So instead I just ask her questions. They tell me they call their flat 'the het ket crack den'. Although, they assure me, they've never tried crack. And, Emma points out, Sophie's actually the only heterosexual one now. 'Cringe,' Sophie sighs in response to this. 'Hate that about myself.' Thalia's pansexual, Emma's bisexual and has recently entered into a polyamorous relationship with both the male and female members of a couple.

'Tell him about the cage!' Sophie says excitedly.

Emma turns to me with a new level of focus. 'So, the couple I'm seeing,' she says. 'She's a dom.'

'She's called Dom?' I shout over the music.

'SHE'S A DOM,' Sophie shouts back. 'A dominant.'

'Oh, gotcha,' I say, nodding.

'And he's a submissive. And they have this cage where she makes him sit, sometimes all night, and beg for things.'

'Not just sex. Like, food and water. Can you believe it!' Sophie says, the most animated I've seen her.

'Have you been in the cage?' I ask gingerly, like a documentarian trying to hide any trace of opinion on the matter.

'Yeah,' she shrugs. 'It was hot.'

'The thing about the cage thing is . . .' I say, my opinions loosened by alcohol.

'Go on,' she says.

'Well, now this is just me,' I say. 'But whenever I hear about these elaborate sexual games, I find them kind of hot, until I think about the planning that goes into them. Like – imagine a person, on their hands and knees with a flatpack and a set of instructions, in the middle of the afternoon, listening to a podcast, assembling a cage.' Sophie finally laughs. 'It's so embarrassing.'

'Cringe,' she yelps.

'But that applies to all sex stuff,' Emma says.

'Yeah,' I say. 'Any time a girlfriend has surprised me by wearing new underwear, the first thing I think about is her sitting in her pyjamas and glasses, buying it online – the white glare of the laptop on her face, frowning in concentration.' Sophie's laughing even more now.

'Ugh,' Emma says, picking up her drink. 'Who would be straight, Jesus.' She walks over to Emery and Thalia's table.

Sophie lets me buy her another drink, not without protestation. She has 'rules' about older men buying her drinks. When I ask her how that works when she's dating one, she tells me that, in every relationship she's been in, she hasn't allowed for 'any gifts or compliments' from them in the first six months.

'Why?' I ask.

'Because it would be too easy for them to get me to fall in love with them by buying me a load of stuff or saying a load of shit they don't mean.'

I look at her light-green eyes, so wide-set they're almost reptilian. I try to find any flicker of comic exaggeration, but there isn't any. She's being completely serious.

'You're very . . .' I look for the right word.

'What?' she asks.

'Impressive,' I say. 'I know this breaks your rule of older men giving you compliments. And I know it's not even a particularly good one, I sound like I'm interviewing you for a university place. But I do find you very impressive.'

'Why?' she asks, that tight-mouthed smile returning.

'You so clearly know what you want and what you don't want. And I think that's great,' I say. 'At twenty-three I had no rules for anything.' The barman places our drinks on the bar.

We get outside and I take a lighter out of my pocket and pass it to her.

'Are you going to swing by the orgy?' I ask. 'Show your face?'

She smiles, lights her cigarette and hands the lighter back to me.

'Nah,' she says, exhaling smoke. 'I'm pretty old-fashioned. I just like fucking one man at a time.'

Again, I examine her face to see evidence of sarcasm, but find none.

'Very old-fashioned,' I say, lighting my cigarette. 'Just like the black-and-white movies, real Bing Crosby and Grace Kelly stuff.'

'It is!' she says. 'Everyone fucks everyone these days.'

'Sounds stressful,' I say.

'Does it not appeal to you?' she says, leaning against the wall. 'Being open?'

'Not at all. Does it appeal to you?'

'Yeah,' she says. 'I like the idea of keeping a long relationship exciting with non-monogamy. Why cut yourself off from the experience of falling in love over and over and over again?'

'Why cut yourself off from the experience of falling more and more in love with one person?' I say, more impassioned than I intended. 'Sorry. I know I sound so ancient, and I think people should do whatever works for them, but, for me, the fun of a long relationship is getting closer and closer to someone and knowing everything about them, it's not newness.'

'I think you'd just be jealous,' she says. 'That's what all men say who are against open relationships, and really they just don't want the woman they love to fuck someone else.'

'Yeah, I don't, and I don't think there's anything wrong with that. There's this interview with John Lennon which I love −'

'Cringe,' she says.

'I know, I know. I'm sorry.'

'Go on,' she says, turning her body towards mine while keeping it glued to the wall, head leant to one side.

'Okay, so he's in bed with Yoko and the journalist is interviewing him about "Jealous Guy". She asks him if the future of relationships will move away from this idea of belonging to each other. And he says that, while you can intellectually believe in that, when you are actually in love with somebody, you want to possess each other.' She moves closer towards me, letting her cigarette burn in her fingers. 'That's how I feel, I think. Like, I'd like to be more progressive and detach monogamy from love. But I can't. I find mutual possession hot. I want someone to be mine and I hope they'd want me to be theirs.'

She leans in and kisses me. It takes me by surprise − not just the timing of it, but the kiss itself. Her lips are different to Jen's. And so is the way she kisses. Sophie's kisses are hungrier, faster; like she's trying to eat all of me before her plate is cleared away. I let the cigarette fall out of my fingers and hold her head with one hand and the bare skin of her stomach with the other to assure her I'm not going anywhere. We kiss for what feels like half an hour. I haven't kissed someone like this, continuously without sex, for years.

Finally, we stop. She pulls away from me.

'Never ever quote the Beatles at me again,' she whispers.

I laugh. 'I won't.'

'Here,' she says, taking a step back and stumbling slightly. She gets her phone out and passes it to me. 'Give me your number.'

I tap my number into the phone and save it as 'Andy (cringe)'. I hand it back to her.

'Shall we go back in?' I say.

'Yeah,' she says. 'Although they probably haven't noticed we've gone.'

We walk into the bar. As I open the door for her, I put my hand on the small of her back and remember how fun it is to have a brand-new secret with a total stranger. This continues when we return to the group and, under the cover of the table, hold hands. Then we stroke each other's hands, then knees, then thighs. The other three continue yammering at each other and don't notice that we're barely speaking. At one point, Sophie goes to the toilet and texts me.

Come here, boomer

I go to the toilets and am yanked into a cubicle by Sophie. We kiss some more, even more frantically, up against the cold, hard, graffitied wall of the bog. When we return to the table, the overhead lights start to flicker as a sign that we have to finish our drinks. Emma shrugs her enormous hoodie back on and zips it up.

'You're not going to the orgy now, are you?' Thalia asks.

'Yeah,' she sighs. 'It only really kicks off now.'

We walk out into the street and all order our Ubers. Emma gets into hers first, barely saying goodbye to us, her mind already in the orgy. Thalia and Emery alternate between kissing and bickering about whose flat they go back to – her bed's too small, he lives too far out. Sophie and I both have a cigarette and chat about our Sunday plans. I like this tacit agreement to keep our kissing secret. There's no reason for it – no one would care. But being in the company of people who pride themselves on having no sexual shame or secrecy at all makes the privacy of our kissing – just kissing – weirdly, erotically taboo.

Thalia wins the playfight with Emery, which means when Sophie's taxi arrives, the three of them all pile in. He gives me a sloppy drunken hug, professing his love for me. Thalia does the same. And then Sophie, composed and still, stands in front of me and says nothing for a few seconds.

'Goodnight, Andy,' she says.

'Goodnight, Sophie,' I reply.

She blinks slowly, turns her back on me and gets in the car.

When I get into my Uber a few minutes later, I see the time on my phone: 3.17 a.m. I look out of the window on to the dark streets dotted with drunks – shouting and crying and tripping over and calling people they shouldn't call and eating greasy food. Every good night out hinges on discontent. This is the theory I've come to. When I go out with Avi and the boys, I notice that they're all too satisfied with their lives at home to have anything to really propel them forward into the night. Their sofas are too comfy, their wives are too warm, their on-demand television subscriptions are too innumerable. They're not searching for anything, they don't need to distract themselves from themselves. This is why comedians make the best drinking companions. They will never have enough validation, enough success, enough love, enough good stories, enough material. They will always be looking for something else. A good time needs the fires of tragedy underneath it to keep it on a rolling boil.

I guess I've entered the next phase of my break-up. The last person I kissed is no longer my ex-girlfriend. I don't know how regular an occurrence this will be, or whether it will be with the same girl, but it definitely feels like tonight I've moved into new territory. The climate is already different here. I'm relieved, but I'm also sad. No sooner have I left than I feel myself missing the old place; longing for the sharper pain of those first three months out of the break-up. I can already see how retrospect is going to give that time a different atmosphere than was there in the actual living of it. The lone binge-drinking will become wild, being at home with Mum will become cosy, The Madness will become romantic.

It's like I was off sick from life for a while, and sometimes it's nice to be off sick. Sometimes it's nice to not be a thing, in the world, trying so desperately to be a person. Here's what I'm getting at: I don't know if I really want to move on, because the further away I get from the pain, the further away I get from her.

'This music okay?' the driver says, referencing the frenetic free jazz coming from the speakers.

'Yeah, it's nice,' I say. 'Vibey.'

'Vibey,' he repeats, laughing. 'That's me.' He taps the wheel in time with the music. He wears an extremely strong aftershave. I'd put him at about forty-eight. 'I love jazz,' he says, continuing to use the wheel as a drum. 'Listen to it when I drive.

I spend eight months of the year here working all the time so I can spend the rest of the year in Egypt, where I am from.'

'Oh, nice,' I say. 'You got any family out there?'

'All dead,' he says, swinging his head to the beat of the snare.

'Sorry to hear that.'

'Don't be.'

'Who do you spend time with when you're out there?' I ask.

'No one. Friends, they've all moved. My brother, he's married and living in Canada. I got no wife, no kids, no one,' he says. 'And I love it. I am free. Like James Bond. This is the life for me!' He laughs. 'I think this is also the life for you?'

I smile. 'What do you do when you're out there?'

'Sit by the pool. Have a cold drink. Sometimes go out to meet a nice lady. Listen to jazz.' He turns the volume up, swinging his head and tapping his hands with even more vigour.

I don't ask him any more questions because for some reason I don't want to know any more of the answers.

Friday 4th October 2019

On the walk to the pub, I run through, one final time, all the reasons why it's perfectly okay that I'm going on a date with a woman who is twelve years younger than me. I make a list of all the things that cross over our culture: yes, it is true that 'Starry Eyed Surprise' was in the charts when I was a fresher and she was seven, but we were both adults for the cultural phenomena of Daft Punk and Pharrell Williams's 'Get Lucky'. That's a communal adult experience. And the same goes for world events. She won't have any memories of the 96 Euros, or Brazilian footballers running through an airport for a Nike ad or anything first-hand about Princess Diana. But by the time Prince William got married, she would have been studying for her GCSEs. So we can talk about that, very comfortably, if it comes up. Easy breezy! No problem at all.

And what's all this about shared timelines of culture anyway? Why's that so important? She wasn't alive when my favourite album was released, but guess what? *Bridge Over Troubled Water* was released in 1970, so neither was I! What am I meant to do about that? Only date women aged fifty-five and over so we can both talk about the origins of the rhythm recording on 'Cecilia'? That doesn't make any sense!

And what about all the other men? Why are you not coming after them, Andy? Why are you only having a go at me? She's been with men older than you. She likes us, we're her type. Why we're her type is not really any of your business, so just accept and enjoy it! If you questioned the reasons why every woman wanted to sleep with you and found satisfactory answers before you agreed to it, you'd still be a virgin.

And the other thing – the most important thing. Her self-possession. All her rules and her wisdom and her progressive ideas about sex and her terrifyingly clear communication skills. That goes some distance to re-addressing the power imbalance of our age gap and the fact I'm a man. And I know I have power in the world just by being a man, I know that, but I also don't *really* have any – I'm a balding, failed comedian with no savings who lodges with a seventy-eight-year-old tinned soup collector. So all in all, when you tot it up – add a few years for my thirty-something maleness, shave off a few years for her advanced emotional maturity, plus a few points for 'Get Lucky', minus a few for Princess Diana, to the power of her past older boyfriends, divide it by something – we're about even. If anything, I worry about myself in all this!

(There's also the fact that it's been nearly four months since I last had sex which is the longest I've gone without it in my adult life, but that's just a footnote to all of the above and was not a factor in considering the morality of me going on this date.)

She's already there when I arrive – leant over the table engrossed in something. Her black hair falls in front of her eyes in a glossy curtain. As I approach, I see that she's looking at black-and-white photographs. She senses me coming towards her and looks up. She smiles and stands. We hug, briefly and casually, like friends. She's already bought me a drink and one for herself, keen to implement her rules from the get-go.

She shows me the small stack of photographs she's examining. They're ones she's taken with her film camera and has just developed herself. I sit down and she lets me flip through them – hazy, low-fi photos of Emma and Thalia reclining in London parks with cans of beer and on sofas with bed-hair and mugs of tea. Close-ups of daisy petals in upturned palms and chip shop remains in a polystyrene box and cupcakes with cigarettes stubbed out in them. And then, Sophie standing naked. Hair pulled off her face, staring at the camera. Her dark nipples look-ing at me like they're waiting for an answer to a question.

'Oh yeah,' she says casually, taking the straw in her mouth and sipping her vodka tonic. 'They're self-portraits I did with a timer and tripod. You can look at them, don't worry. I'm a very naked person.'

I do, not unwillingly, but it is so strange to see the entire bare body of a woman I'm on a date with in black and white, flat, held in my hands, before I see it in real life. I also don't know what the right level of appreciation is in this context. Too much praise is surely lecherous, whereas not enough might seem rude. The photos go on and on, first at a distance and then in abstract close-ups – so close up it sometimes takes a while to work out what you're looking at. The drumstick of Sophie's collarbone, the dip and rise of Sophie's waist and hips. Sophie's little square toes. The cowrie shell of Sophie's navel. I can feel her looking at me looking at her body. I don't know what to say. I have noth-ing to say, I only want to touch her.

'Lovely motifs,' I finally say, shuffling the stack of photos in my hand like a newsreader packing away their notes. This makes her laugh and it feels good. I really would do or say anything to make a woman laugh.

She tells me about her job as a photographer's assistant – how lucky she felt when she was first given the opportunity to work with a big-name male fashion photographer; how frustrated she feels now, working with such a difficult, entitled, unreasonable and demanding man. But she says that it's worth it; that she's learning about what kind of photographer she wants to be one day, working so closely with someone who exemplifies every-thing she doesn't. She shows me photos on her phone of all her favourite shoots she's assisted on. She shows me a lot on her phone, in fact. Her phone never leaves the table, it is like a ready-to-go PowerPoint to illustrate all her anecdotes. When she had an undercut, when she went on holiday to Bulgaria, when she and Thalia went to a racoon petting zoo for the day.

We take turns buying each other drinks and she keeps an attentive score to make sure she doesn't fall behind on her rounds. She orders chips. She asks me why I won't eat them. For some reason I feel comfortable enough to tell her – that, for the first time in my life, I'm going to the gym four to five times a week. That I don't eat carbohydrates any more. That often the calories of alcohol replace what I would have had for dinner. That I think about food and protein macros all the time. That I sometimes wake up in the middle of the night because I've had a nightmare that I went to McDonald's and ate everything on the menu including the side of pineapple sticks, and the euphoric relief I feel when I realize that I didn't.

And she doesn't tell me that crash diets don't work or that this lifestyle is unsustainable or that it sounds like an unhealthy obsession. She doesn't even tell me that she's sure I looked great before I started losing weight. She just shrugs and says: 'Fair.'

She asks me about how I got into comedy and I tell her about my first terrible attempts at open mic nights as a student, then my first trip to Edinburgh as a punter, then my first summer there as a working stand-up. She tells me that Thalia had mentioned that I won Best Show at The Fringe when I was just starting out. I correct her and tell her I was Best Newcomer.

'What's the difference?' she asks.

'The difference is I was only competing against the other newcomers. When you win Best Newcomer, you're basically being awarded for being the best out of a load of people who don't know anything about how to do stand-up. Most people then go on to prove that they're not only the best of the newcomers, but the best in their industry. Like Emery, for instance.'

'But not you,' she says.

'Not me,' I say.

'That's very pessimistic.'

'I know,' I reply. 'This is my right as a thirty-five-year-old.' This leads us nicely into some flirty teasing about our respective ages.

We go outside to smoke and, when we go back to the bar together, I put my arm around her waist. She pretends to be unbothered by this and continues to chat to me about whose photo she'd most like to take, but her face betrays her indifference with a small smile which she tries to suppress, making her nose wrinkle in an extremely adorable way. We take our seats at our table again and she holds my hand.

Her phone lights up with a notification from a dating app and she shows me the profile of a man she's been speaking to. She shows me the profiles of all the men she's currently speaking to, and their messages, without embarrassment. She asks me if I'm talking to anyone on an app right now and I tell her about Tash, the disappearing virtual dream girl of the summer. She asks me what about her I found so attractive, and I'm honest when I answer. I like this easy conversation about our own desires, spoken about as if it's something different to the date we're currently on. We talk uninhibitedly – there's no feelings of jealousy and everything is said and received with good will. The fact of our respective attraction to other people is separate to the fact of our attraction to each other. It's so new to me. I've always thought the thing to do on a first date is reassure women that they're the first person you've ever fancied while also giving off the casual impression that thousands upon thousands of people have fancied you.

As we sit closer together and she occasionally looks into her drink as she speaks, I notice the colour of her eyelids.

'It's a new eyeshadow I'm trying to look more like Kate Bush on *The Hounds of Love* album cover,' she says effortlessly in one breath. 'Look.' She closes her eyes to show me two perfect almonds of shimmery, garish purple. I take this as an opportunity to kiss her.

'Was that a chat-up line?' she asks with amused disdain. 'I've heard of those.'

The bell rings for last orders and she asks me if I want to go back to her place.

'On one condition,' she says.

'A rule?' I say. 'You surprise me.'

'I don't do sleepovers,' she says. 'You can't stay. You have to go home tonight.'

'Really?'

'Yes,' she says. 'I want you out by two a.m.'

I laugh at her brazen efficiency.

'What?'

'Nothing,' I say. 'Out by two, I can sign off on that, yes.'

Her flat, on the very edge of South London, is dark and silent when she opens the front door. She tells me that Thalia is at a gig and Emma is at a rave with her boyfriend and girlfriend. She leads me into the kitchen and turns on the overhead strip lighting. It is a room that feels so familiar: two singed tea towels, four chairs – one with a missing seat. A counter littered with a container of table salt, an upside-down bottle of ketchup and a half-empty uncorked bottle of red wine, relegated to 'cooking wine' that will never be used. It looks like the kitchens I shared with Avi and Rob when we lived together. In moments like these I wonder whether women are just as disgusting as we are.

She gets two tins of Red Stripe from the fridge and shows me her room. I stand in the dark while she walks to her bedside and switches the small lamp on. Her room looks like the bedrooms of the first girls I kissed in the early noughties, which is both confusing and comforting. There's an inflatable clear armchair in the corner. On her desk there's a lava lamp. A pink polaroid camera sits on her windowsill. Her walls are papered with old music magazine covers that have been ripped off and tacked up: *i-D*,

Dazed & Confused, *Sleazenation*, *The Face*. Courtney Love, Kurt Cobain, Damon Albarn, Robbie Williams — a gallery of faces from my childhood watching over us.

I walk over to a cover featuring a young, grinning Kate Moss wearing feathers in her hair.

'I think I remember this cover,' I say, snapping open my beer.

She closes the curtains at her window.

'It was 1990, so you definitely don't.'

'Oh,' I say. 'You're right, I don't. I wasn't so familiar with her oeuvre aged five.'

She walks over to the bed and hops on to it, leaning back on her elbows and looking at me. 'You're not as old as you think you are,' she says. The low light casts shadows across her face that somehow fall perfectly under her cheekbones.

'I love when you talk filth,' I say, crawling on to the bed with her. She pulls me towards her by the fabric of my T-shirt and wraps her arms around the back of my neck. We kneel on the duvet kissing for a while until she pulls away.

'Can I take this off?' she whispers, pulling at my T-shirt.

'Yes,' I say.

She yanks it up over my head and runs her hands along my bare arms as she kisses me, more hungrily this time, digging her nails into my shoulders and making little noises of satisfaction.

'Can I take these off?' she asks, taking my trousers by the belt.

I hold her face in my hands. 'Sophie, you can do anything you want to me,' I say.

'Okay,' she whispers, smiling. We kiss as she unbuckles my belt.

'Including arse stuff,' I say. 'As long as it's not a surprise.'

'Don't you dare try and make me laugh right now,' she says.

'Okay, sorry.'

'Although — same rule for me,' she says.

'Good to know,' I reply, and we both laugh.

I pull her top up over her head to find that she's braless, her skin luminously pale, her nipples hard and small. I hold her by her bare stomach – taut and cool and covered in goosebumps. I push my fingers over them, trying to read her body like Braille. She puts her hand into my boxers and grips my cock. I gasp and unbutton her jeans, putting my hand under the lace of her underwear and feeling the softest, wettest part of her. Her moans get louder and longer as she breathes heavily into my ear. As is tradition for many of my first-time sexual encounters, it is at this point that my perspective leaves my head and pulls up a seat in front of us to get the best view as an audience member. An unexpected yet highly anticipated collaboration: *Andy and Sophie's First Fuck*. I wonder how it will play out. I'm struck by how adolescent we both look, kneeling on a perfectly made bed, one hand in each other's pants, jeans still on, kissing like it's an activity we've only recently discovered. If my finger wasn't on her clit, it could be 2001 again.

She grabs my hand out of her jeans, pulls it up to her mouth and puts her lips around my fingers. She looks at me with her purple-hooded eyes, her pupils glistening and wide in the low light.

'You're so fucking sexy,' I say without thinking, immediately regretting the drunken plainness of my words. Immediately worrying that *you're so fucking sexy* is the sort of thing a local MP DMs to one of his constituents before losing his job. But she doesn't laugh.

'Don't fall in love with me, Andy,' she says.

'I'll try,' I reply.

And then – *we are thrilled to announce* – I discover three things.

- Sex doesn't remind me of my ex-girlfriend
- I can make a woman other than my ex-girlfriend come
- My dick still works

Monday 7th October 2019

I go over to Sophie's flat on Saturday night after a gig. Then Sunday night after a gig. Every time, we do the same thing. We hang around her bedroom chatting, then we find a new way in which our bodies fit together and we both make each other come with a mutual diligence normally only reserved for relationships. Then we order food or have a drink together. Then I kiss her goodbye and make the very long journey home.

Tonight, we've just shared a joint watching an episode of TV on her laptop, when I'm jolted out of my mellow half-snooze.

'Andy,' she says into my ear, shaking me by the arm. 'Don't fall asleep.'

I open my eyes and slowly sit upright in her bed. She lies with her head on the pillow facing me.

'You're not going to make me leave now, are you?' I ask. 'It's a Monday night AND it's raining. My house is an hour and a half away.'

She shrugs. 'Those are the rules,' she says.

I groan, kiss the end of her nose and get out of bed.

'You're infuriating,' I say, putting on my jeans.

'I know,' she says. 'But isn't that more interesting? Wouldn't you prefer that to a girl who says "yes" to everything and makes your life easy?'

'I'd prefer a girl who lets me stay over so I don't have to get three trains home.'

'Really?' she says, sitting suddenly upright in bed like a cat alerted to a new noise. 'You don't like the chase?'

'No, I've never understood that,' I say, crouching and

peering under the bed to find my missing sock. 'I know some people are into it, but one of the most attractive things to me is knowing someone wants me. So I don't really get the appeal of someone being hard to get. Ah-ha!' I say, reaching for my sock, which somehow managed to make its way on to the lava lamp in our frenzy of undressing. Sophie continues to observe me curiously and says nothing. I sit on the edge of the bed and put my socks on. 'One of the lesser-reported tragedies of the London property crisis is that it is now possible for two people dating to live twenty miles apart from each other.'

'We're not dating, Andy,' she says, approaching me from behind and putting her arms around me. 'I know that must be hard for you, what with all your unspent boyfriend energy.'

I turn to look at her indignantly. '*My . . . ?*'

'You want to be someone's boyfriend.'

'What makes you say that?' I ask.

'You reek of monogamy,' she says. 'When was your last relationship?'

I wondered when this conversation was going to happen. I had congratulated myself for having spent five whole evenings with Sophie and not mentioned the break-up.

'A few months ago,' I say.

'And how long were you together?'

'A few years.'

She shuffles round and sits next to me on the edge of the bed.

'Sure,' she says, in a *knew-it* way. There is an uncharacteristically awkward silence between us. 'And you're still obsessed with her?' I try to laugh and instead make a weird, nervous sound. 'It's okay, you can talk about her. I don't care.'

'Really?'

'Yeah,' she says, taking a band from her wrist and tying her hair up into a ponytail. 'Tell me about her.'

'Um. She broke up with me in June. It was really unexpected.

I still don't really know why. She's got a new boyfriend called Seb.'

'And you know everything about their relationship because you stalk them both on Instagram?' she says, standing up and sitting cross-legged on the inflatable chair.

'I don't *stalk* them,' I say.

'Whatever,' she says. 'You need to block them both.' She leans over to her desk and the chair squeaks as she retrieves a bottle of grey nail varnish.

'I can't do that.'

'Why not?'

'Because Jen will see and it will freak her out. She'll think I'm hiding something from her.'

Sophie rolls her eyes and shakes the bottle of polish. 'Everyone knows the only reason someone blocks you is because they're going on your profile too much.' She opens the bottle and splays her hand flat on her leg. She slowly and carefully paints each nail, not looking up as she speaks. 'It's not an insult. If anything, it's a compliment.'

I take this in, unconvinced. 'Really?'

'Yes,' she says, holding her hand away from her to examine her work. 'Trust me. I'm the queen of heartbreak. You've got to block.'

'Okay,' I say, walking over to her. She stands up and kisses me. 'Thank you. And also, I don't believe you are the queen of heartbreak. I don't think anyone could ever break your heart.'

'Cringe,' she says, batting me away.

I walk along Sophie's street, a street I didn't know last week and which I now know pretty well. I am not sure what this feeling is. It's so different to any other feeling I've had when I first start seeing someone. I feel close to her, but distant from her. I feel excited but unsatisfied, caring but detached, invested and indifferent. It's like we've taken all the activities of coupledom and put them in a framework of two strangers who owe each other nothing; who have no past or future. It's confusing. Not confusing enough to stop, obviously, but it is confusing.

When I get home, I can hear Morris watching TV in the living room. I walk in to find him lying on his back on the floor underneath a Christmas tree.

'Hi,' I say.

'Could you come and hold this for me?' he asks.

'Sure,' I say, putting my keys on the side table and going over to the tree.

'If you just hold it upright,' he says.

I hold the tree by its middle. Morris fiddles with the screws in the tree stand.

'So, is there any reason –' I don't even have to finish the sentence before he's launched into the story of why he buys a Christmas tree every year in the first week of October. I must admit my concentration dips at points, but here's broadly what I understand: an old colleague of his now owns a Christmas tree forest in Hertfordshire, he wants to support this man's business but doesn't support Christmas as a religious festival or holiday of any sort, his friend therefore offers him a heavily discounted tree out-of-season which he enjoys until the last week of November and then disposes of himself because the council refuse to take discarded Christmas trees outside of January, which is the subject of one of his many online petitions, but it needs a further 9,982 signatures before it is eligible for a parliamentary response.

'. . . and, honestly, all these idiots paying a premium to buy a tree shipped over from goodness knows where –' He takes a brief breath and I see my opportunity.

'So what do you do on Christmas Day?' I ask suddenly.

He looks up at me with his frightened ferret eyes. He slides back on his elbows with visible struggle then turns on to his side. He slowly heaves himself up, refusing the offer of my hand for help. He stands upright and dusts the pine needles from his jumper.

'I wash all the curtains,' he says. 'It's a job that only needs to be done once a year, and I always remember to do it on the 25th of December.'

'Anything else?' I ask pleadingly.

'I eat a fish pie,' he says. 'And watch *Creature from the Black Lagoon*.' He looks almost bewildered that I am asking him this; that I would assume he did anything else but wash the curtains, eat a fish pie and watch *Creature from the Black Lagoon*.

'Right, I'm off to bed,' I say. 'Unless you need any help clearing up the needles?'

'No, no, that's fine,' he says. 'How are you, by the way?' This is something I'd noticed Morris had started trying since our attempt at a pub session. Not willingly or naturally, but he still gives it a go.

'I'm fine, Morris.'

'All your funny bits and bobs going well?'

'They're fine,' I say. 'Goodnight.'

I lie on my bed fully clothed for a further hour while I have one last deep inhalation on the glue bag of Jen and Seb's Instagram pages. I go back to the beginning of Seb's seventy-eight grid posts and examine each and every one of them. I look at every photo that Jen posted while we were together, taking particular interest in my comments of support or little in-jokes underneath, zooming in and using the keypad with precision so as not to leave my footprints on her notifications.

I put it off until it's past three a.m. Every time I go to press the button, I find myself needing one final big, deep sniff.

And then I do it – as quickly as I can. I block him. Then I block her. No posts available. Nothing to see. It really is that simple.

I wait to feel something, but no feeling arrives.

Friday 11th October 2019

I do not expect the UK Independent Pharmacists' Annual Autumn Party to be the best gig of my life, but do you know what? It wasn't the worst. Was there a sense of excitement when the chairman introduced a comedian, saying they might recognize him from some of his TV appearances? Yes. Was there an audible sense of disappointment when I walked on and they realized 'TV appearances' can refer to a handful of forgettable panel shows in the early 2010s? Also yes. But were they mean, these pharmacists? No. Did they punish me for their boss not having deep enough pockets to book someone famous? No. Did they throw bread rolls at me like the accountants did at the Greater London Accountancy Awards? They did not! Did they laugh at my pretty sub-par jokes about Big Pharma in the UK referring to industrial-sized containers of lavender-scented talc? They certainly did! So, as far as these sorts of gigs go, it was fine. The gig wasn't the problem.

The problem arises when, on the bus home, I make the decision to go on to the corporate booking website where I'm featured with hundreds of other comedians, speakers, sports stars and celebrities. I go looking for trouble. It's just a premonition I have and I want it confirmed, which it is.

A few years ago, Emery, who you can also book through their website, showed me the discreet pricing system. Next to each speaker is a teeny-tiny letter ranging from A to F. A means the person would cost between £30,000 and £50,000 to book to speak at your event; F means they'd cost you between £250 and £500. Emery and I had always felt a strange pride in being Es, not for its monetary value (between £1,000 and £2,000 a booking), but the reassurance that while we were undeniably at the bottom of the heap, we weren't at the *very* bottom at least.

But there, next to my name, is a terrible thing. One line of the letter lopped off, along with all my remaining dignity.

F

I message Emery.

> I've dropped down to an F. I can't help but feel this is a metaphor for my life

He immediately starts typing.

> It sucks man, I know

> You don't know, you've been upgraded. You're a D now, I've just checked

> I meant it sucks for you

I ring my agent but her assistant tells me she's out at a lunch meeting. I ask if she can call me back and he says yes, but suggests that an email would probably be better. Sick of having imaginary arguments with my agent every morning in the shower, I compose and redraft an email on the notes app, dialling back the fury with every edit until I finally reach something I would realistically send:

Hey –

I'm struggling to get hold of you and I'm not sure of the best way to move forward. I don't think it should be this hard to get you on the phone for a matter of minutes, especially having worked together for so long. There are a couple of things I would like to chat to you about, like why I've been demoted as a corporate booking. It's the only way I make any real money doing this, and I only get booked a few times a year, so I'm not feeling great about it.

I'm sorry to be that client, but I really do just need a few minutes of your time.

Let me know when's best to chat.

A.

Feeling the need for a quick dopamine hit of support and encouragement, I send Kelly a photo of the lunch I ate earlier today – two boiled eggs, a seared tuna fillet and a packet of bagged salad. I send it with a biceps emoji. She replies instantly.

> **Fully fuelled and ready to ROCK 'N' ROLL big guy!! Send me some progress pix!!!**

I send her the photo I took in the gym changing room this morning. BALD has been replaced by identical daily topless photos of myself and I don't know which is more embarrassing. She replies again.

> **HOT STUFF. Bet you're TEARIN up the dating scene right now!!! Let's get a session in fella, been a while since I've seen u and I wanna see this FINE FORM IRL**

I don't know what I'd do without her.

Avi and Jane send me their order before I get to the chippy. Haddock and chips for Avi, haddock and mushy peas for me, scampi and chips, pickled gherkin, pickled onion, pickled egg for Jane (her pregnancy is giving her vinegar cravings). By the time I get to their place, the boys are in their pyjamas and there's just enough time for me to read them a quick bedtime story before they go to sleep.

If I were feeling ungenerous, it would be easy for me to moan about the fact that the only time I ever really see Avi and Jane is at their house, with their kids; that there is rarely any effort to suggest a plan other than me slotting into their lives. But the truth is that I love their lives. I love this house and its colours and its clutter and its smells – warm laundry, kids' bubble bath, just-cooked lasagne. I want a home like this one. I hope they never stop asking me over.

Jane comes up to tuck the boys in and I go down to the kitchen where Avi is sitting at the table, gleefully opening up the packages of fish and chips and lining up a row of condiments.

'Listen, mate,' I say in a hushed voice, taking a seat opposite him. 'Can you do me a favour and not mention Sophie in front of Jane? I just don't want it getting back to Jen that I'm seeing someone.'

Avi is too engrossed by his array of sauces and seasonings to look up at me.

'Yeah, yeah,' he says, flipping open the cap of the malt vinegar and dousing his portion of chips. 'How's that going by the way?'

The delicious fumes of hot vinegar rise, stinging my eyes. I'm so hungry I can barely form a thought. 'Er good, yeah, good.' I reach over and take one of Avi's fat, glistening chips. I bite through its crispy skin. I'd almost forgotten what starch tastes like. Fluffy, soft, blankety, buttery? Did chips taste like butter before? I hold it in my mouth, trying to savour it. This is your one chip of the night, Andy, so you'd better enjoy every second of it. But it's too hot to hold on my tongue. My lips form a circle and I blow air out of my mouth.

'Hot?' Avi asks.

'Yeah,' I say. 'Can I have another one?'

'Sure.' He pushes his mountain of chips towards me. I have one. Then another, then another. I eat them quickly, hoping that the quicker I eat them the less of an impact they will make on my calorific intake for the day. If I basically swallow them whole, surely they will barely register in my body? I'd forgotten food could make you feel this good. I open up my package of fried fish and, having planned to eat around the batter, immediately go to the crispiest end, lop it off with my knife, spear it with my fork, dunk it in ketchup and shove it in my gob. I don't know what decides it – whether it's the power of the deep-fryer, the famous dieting plateau or the fact I'm dating someone so I can give myself permission to relax a bit. But for whatever reason, I can't find my willpower.

Jane walks into the kitchen, rubbing her bump as she lowers herself on to a chair.

'So,' she says, opening up her scampi and chips. 'How's the teenager?'

I put down my knife and fork and look at Avi.

'You are unbelievable,' I say.

'You didn't tell me not to tell her until just now!' he says indignantly through a mouthful of chips. He finishes chewing, wipes his mouth with a napkin and swallows. 'You know I tell her everything. You told Jen everything. If you'd said to me, "Av mate, I'm banging a twenty-three-year-old and, by the way, don't tell your wife,"' then obviously I wouldn't have told her. But you didn't.' He reaches over for the ketchup bottle. 'Probably because you were too pleased with yourself, to be fair.'

'I did not say I was *banging a twenty-three-year-old*,' I say insistently, looking directly at Jane.

'I really never thought you'd be that guy, y'know,' she says.

'See? This is exactly why I didn't want you to tell her,' I say to Avi.

'Go on then, spill,' she says, opening her can of Coke and looking at me expectantly.

'No,' I say.

'Come on,' she says. 'I was only teasing.'

'Okay,' I say, taking another chip from Avi. 'I WILL tell you. But only if you absolutely swear to me that you won't tell Jen.'

Jane holds up both hands in surrender. 'I swear. I absolutely swear,' she says. I look at her face for any signs of deceit and she narrows her eyes at me mischievously. 'Show me a photo of her.'

I take out my phone and open Instagram, trying to stall them with talk of how we met while I find one of her posts that's going to yield the least piss-taking. I have spent the last week trying to understand Sophie's Instagram page and I'm still lost. The photos are all weirdly low-fi, out of focus, dull, flat, unflattering, at odd angles. The images are strangely abstract – a pair of knickers on a chair, a roll of sellotape by a sink, two rose petals on a plate, Sophie pretending to smoke a pencil. And then there are the captions. None of the captions make any sense against the images. Underneath a photo of a burger reads: 'Mommy says don't put sugar in your tea, kids'. Under a selfie of her sticking her tongue out are the words: 'Buy low, sell high'. Looking at Sophie's Instagram posts and stories makes me feel unnerved; self-conscious, even. They make me feel like I should understand the in-joke and stupid that I don't. I click on to one of her sitting on a park bench wearing a bucket hat. The caption says: 'The Great Fire of London was in 1666'.

I hand the phone over to Avi. He stares at it for a while.

'I don't get it,' he finally says.

'I know, I know, I don't think there's anything to get,' I say.

'What does she mean by that caption?' he asks.

'I'm not entirely sure, I think it's just like a generalized surrealism that is a part of her online persona.'

Jane grabs my phone. 'Let me have a look at her,' she says. Avi passes the phone to her and she zooms in on the photo. 'She's very pretty.'

'I don't get that generation,' Avi says. 'All the kids in my office are the same, they post this absolutely absolute shite, thinking it makes them arty or something. What's that about? We never posted all that bollocks when we were their age.'

'No, we posted way more embarrassing stuff, like, seventy-nine photos from a digital camera of a completely average night out when we were students.' I look nervously at Jane, whose brow is furrowed as she does a deep dive into Sophie's profile. 'Here's my theory: Gen Z saw how we used social media, as the first young people who used it, which was way too earnestly and with too much personal sharing, and they found it extremely cringe –'

'Well, I find THEM cringe,' Avi bellows.

'But of course they still want attention because they're young and stupid like we were, but they do it in this style where they give less of themselves. They're showing off and trying to be funny and asking everyone to fancy them, but in this sort of enigmatic way.'

'Why has she posted a photo of a hand dryer with a war poem as the caption?' Jane asks.

My hands fidget as I try not to snatch the phone back. Sophie likes sending me naked photos, a lot of them, unprompted, and I'm worried one is going to land just as my phone is in Jane's hands.

'I don't know,' I sigh while Jane continues examining her profile. 'She's not like that in real life. Can I have my phone back, please?'

'What do you guys talk about?' she asks, turning the phone screen to us, showing an Instagram post of Sophie topless, her nipples concealed with two emojis – a wizard and a teddy bear.

The caption reads: 'Still life 3'. Avi laughs, which makes Jane laugh.

'All right, all right,' I say, reaching for the phone. Jane relents and passes it to me.

'So what's the deal, are you two hanging out a lot or what?' she says.

'Yeah, quite a lot,' I say.

'You've got to be careful there,' she says, brandishing an amphibian-skinned gherkin at me.

'You wouldn't say that if you met her,' I say.

'How does she feel about you?' Jane persists.

'She's not interested in anything other than casual sex. She doesn't want anything from me,' I say.

'That's something twenty-three-year-old girls say to older men so they don't get hurt,' she says.

'That doesn't make any sense,' I say.

'Yeah, well you haven't read the shit they tell us to do in magazines and books to keep you twats interested in us,' Jane says, taking a swig of Coke.

'She told me not to fall in love with her. She doesn't let me sleep over. I think I might even annoy her,' I say.

'Textbook,' she says. 'If you ever want to find a woman her age who's desperate for a boyfriend, find the girl on Twitter saying things like "kill all straight men".'

I let this sit and look at Avi for support. He shrugs and stays out of the conversation.

'She's testing you,' Jane says.

'No she's not. What happened to giving young women their autonomy? This isn't very feminist of you, Jane.'

She wipes her hands on a napkin, holds her tongue in the side of her mouth and stares at me, saying nothing.

'Now you've gone and done it,' Avi mutters.

'Okay, maybe I'm wrong,' she says. 'But I've been a twenty-three-year-old girl, you haven't.'

'I love you, but you are wrong about this,' I say. 'It's all under control.'

After I've left, slightly rattled by Jane's words, I send Sophie a text.

Hey! Hope you've had a good day! Everything cool?

She types for a while. In response comes a photo of her bum in a black thong.

Simp

I can't believe I get a stream of these photos. I don't know what I've done to deserve them. It's a relief – no more dark nights of the soul battling with myself about whether it's okay to wank over Jen's soft-core latter-relationship nudes of her trying on a bra in a changing room. I reread Sophie's message and smile, relieved to be proven right. Sophie doesn't need anyone worrying about her.

I do my nightly digital ablutions of checking Jen and Seb's Instagram pages, before clearing my internet history so I'm not tempted to check again until the same time the following evening. I can't do this through the app, because I've blocked them, but I quickly worked out that I can do it on the web browser on my phone because I'm not logged in.

Jen's remains unchanged; Seb has posted a new photo to his grid. My heart quickens as I click on to it. And then – I can't believe what I see.

A packet of truffle crisps.

The type that Jen and I bought together as a joke when we saw them at the till of the wine shop, then, against all our better judgement, discovered were completely addictive. The type we ate every time we watched a period drama together on a Sunday night.

I examine the rest of the photo for evidence. I recognize Jen's old flat by the sofa and bookcases. Two glasses of red wine sit on the coffee table with a bottle. I notice something familiar in the background and zoom in like I'm in a procedural drama. As my fingers splay and the pixels blur, I can't believe what I'm seeing. The undeniable image of Kate Winslet and her red curls, sitting at the pianoforte mournfully singing 'Weep You No More Sad Fountains' to a longing Colonel Brandon.

They're watching *Sense and Sensibility*. They're watching one of our films we used to watch together. Eating the snack we discovered together. I look at Seb's caption and feel smug that the person *I'm* seeing would have written something imaginative bordering on indecipherable under this image and instead Seb's written:

Thanks for introducing me to these! @jbennet85

Jen's written a comment underneath.

Prepare to be addicted x

Well. She's clearly a psychopath who is a danger to others and maybe even also to herself. She's lifted something directly out of our relationship and put it straight into her new one with no remorse. There is something about this insight into their relationship and the way they are with each other that feels like even more of a betrayal than the fact of their relationship itself. Is there any possibility they've realized I blocked them? Is this their retaliation, their way of dropping a bomb over Instagram, specifically targeted at me?

Well. I didn't realize this was allowed. Two can play at that game.

Tuesday 15th October 2019

Sophie and I meet in Chinatown for dinner. She whinges about her terrible day assisting on a magazine cover shoot; I whinge about my recent degradation via the corporate speaker bookings pricing system. Then she grumbles a little more widely about how is she ever going to make enough money to live on her own in London, and I join in the same grumble, which is perhaps inappropriate given our age difference. Our conversation occasionally veers into personally historic or philosophical dimensions, the way that is normal when you're first dating someone and trying to get a very quick glimpse into their soul. But we don't stay there for too long, and I'm glad we don't. It's nice to have someone to complain with over a shared crispy duck and it's all I can manage right now. The beginning of my relationship with Jen was full of the sort of mutual interviewing and confessions that made me feel more known to myself than I'd ever been before. And I'm fine not to know myself too well at the moment, I'm not sure I'd like what I discovered. I'm happy just to be on nodding terms with Andy for the time being.

When we wander around Soho to find a bar after we finish dinner, I do my best to pretend like I've just had an idea.

'I know!' I say, stopping and pointing at the karaoke chain I have been to many times before. 'Karaoke!'

'Cringe,' she says as she carries on walking.

'Oh, come on!' I say, too enthusiastically, reaching out and grabbing her hand. 'It's only cringe if you're in a big group. It's so, so fun if you're in a pair.'

'Why would we do that?'

'Because I can't sing both parts of "Islands in the Stream",' I say. She rolls her eyes. 'Come on. You can hire a booth for an hour. I'll get it.'

She relents and lets me lead her down into the basement bar.

I buy us two vodka sodas and two shots of tequila and we take them into our booth. With a practised hand, I get the mic to the perfect level of volume and reverb and open the song catalogue on the screen.

'Right, who's going first?' I ask.

Sophie sits with her phone in one hand and her drink in the other.

'You,' she says, not looking up from her screen.

'I was hoping you'd say that,' I say. At this point, I have no idea what Sophie will or won't find cringe, so I decide not to second-guess my go-to karaoke song choice. The list of what she deems to be cringe about me is becoming so unpredictable I have given up trying to find the logic that joins it all. My boxers, two of my T-shirts, the fact she once saw me drink a reduced sugar Lipton's Iced Tea, any time I cough, my love of the Beatles, my yawn, the subject of my university degree, my lifelong support of Aston Villa, whenever I say 'how are you'.

The synthetic backing music starts playing. I raise the shot of tequila to her, she does the same and we both down them in one. Sophie puts her phone down and sits back in her seat, observing me in her silent, feline way.

'*THERE'S DANCING!*' I sing into the mic. '*Behind movie scenes, behind the movie scenes. Sadi Rani.*' Sophie stares at me, unblinking. This look continues as I rattle effortlessly through the first verse, as word perfect as I was in the 1999 school talent show where Avi and I performed it together. At the chorus, I put the mic under Sophie's still-expressionless face for her to join in. She doesn't sing anything. I turn the mic back around to me. '*Well, it's a brimful of Asha on the* —' I put the mic in front of her again. 'Come on!'

'I don't know this song.' Her voice reverberates around the booth.

'Oh, sorry,' I say, but of course cannot help but complete the six further verses and three choruses.

When I get to the end, slightly out of breath from rapping, but with no commendation for the fastidious flow I kept from start to finish, I hand the mic to Sophie. She declines, saying she prefers watching. I buy her another drink and convince her into a series of duets, promising that I'll take the lead. We have a microphone each and choose 'Ain't No Mountain High Enough' followed by 'Total Eclipse of the Heart'. She relaxes slightly with every song, but I can feel myself forcing fun that isn't there. After 'Don't You Want Me', I suggest she sings some Kate Bush, sensing that the duets have given her just enough of a taste for it.

'Okay,' she says sulkily.

I take a seat as the whimsical piano introduction to 'Wuthering Heights' begins and Sophie stares at the screen, refusing to look at me, despite the fact I'm sure she knows every word off by heart. She talk-sings the lyrics, exerting as little effort as possible, her body still and stiff, her feet fixed to the floor. I keep an encouraging smile on my face so she isn't put off by me, and I think of my favourite early-days date with Jen. We went out for dim sum down the road, at one of those places where there's a photo of every single dumpling on the menu and the menu is as thick as a book and all of them look so good you order enough food for ten people. We drank beer and told each other long stories using loud voices and we fed each other dumplings and we kissed at the table and were the couple you would never want to sit next to at a restaurant. Drunk on beer and MSG and the newness of each other, we fell out of the restaurant and into this karaoke bar. We hired a booth for two, something we'd both never done before, having only ever done karaoke in big groups for birthdays or stag and hen dos. We sang together and we sang separately and we danced and I even attempted to lift her over my head at the end of '(I've Had) the Time of My Life'. We rapped and we sang power ballads and she did her show-stopper ('Think Twice') and I did mine ('Brimful of Asha') and we worked out what ours was together ('We Got Tonight' by Kenny Rogers and Sheena Easton).

Finally, when we were kicked out at two in the morning, we got a taxi back to her place. Then we had sex and talked and had sex and talked – we did this until the sun appeared in the small gap of her bedroom curtains. But I couldn't fall asleep because I had this feeling I hadn't had since childhood, the one you get on the night of Christmas Day when you can't wait to wake up and play with all your new presents on Boxing Day morning. She was better than any new present I could remember – she was my Game Boy and Tracy Island and Magna Doodle combined. And every day spent with her was something to come down from and every day that would be spent with her was something worth losing sleep over. I eventually fell asleep spooning her, my chest pressed into the valley of her shoulder blades, my face buried in her matted smoke-and-perfume-scented hair.

'Can we go now?' Sophie asks over the never-ending electric guitar instrumental that closes 'Wuthering Heights'.

When we get up into the night air, I feel cold and sober and mired in the failure of the evening. We walk to the tube station and I know the only thing that would feel lonelier than sleeping alone tonight would be sleeping next to a woman who isn't Jen.

'I might have to head back to mine,' I say as casually as possible.

'Oh,' she says. 'Are you sure?'

'Yeah, I've got a really early shift tomorrow so probably shouldn't be back too late.'

'You can stay if you like,' she says, looking away from me.

'That's sweet of you, but I haven't got any of my stuff.' We reach the tube stop and walk down to the ticket barriers. 'Sorry to be boring. I'll see you really soon?'

'Okay,' she says. 'Thanks. That was fun, I enjoyed it.'

'Liar,' I say and kiss her.

'No, I did, I swear,' she says, somewhat earnestly.

I kiss her again. We say goodbye, go through the ticket barriers and get on our separate trains.

Friday 18th October 2019

I think Emery's hair's getting bigger in accordance with his success. Every time I've seen him since Edinburgh it seems to have expanded an inch upwards and sideways. I arrive backstage and see him lying on the dressing table, engrossed in his phone, his former glam-rock mop looking decidedly muppet-like. He sees me enter but doesn't divert his attention from his phone. He holds out his hand.

'Hang on . . . hang on . . . hang on . . .' I stand gormlessly in the empty room. Finally, he slams his phone down and sits upright, fixing his pale-blue, bloodshot eyes on me with wild intensity. 'TALK TO ME,' he growls.

'A lot going on?' I ask without interest.

'Yeah,' he says, swinging his legs under the table like a little boy. 'Haven't *massively* been to bed to be honest with you. How are you? You're looking very gaunt. Are you okay?' He hops up from the table and walks towards me, massaging my shoulders in a way that is physically relaxing but socially uncomfortable. I pat his hand to indicate that I want him to stop and I take a seat in front of one of the mirrors.

'Is Thalia here?' I ask in a quiet voice.

'No, why?'

'Okay, fine. I'm feeling weird about Sophie. I don't really understand what our . . . thing is,' I say.

Emery removes a hip flask from his pocket and takes a swig. He offers me some and I decline.

'What's confusing you?' he asks, his breath hot from whisky.

'I dunno, man, it's just weird, I don't really know how I'm

meant to behave. It feels too intimate to be just a sex thing, but it doesn't feel like I'm dating someone either. We see each other constantly but I don't know to what end. I think maybe I'm using it as this weird methadone while I detox from Jen.'

'Oh, we all use each other for that, get over it,' he slurs. 'Romantic love is methadone to get us off our mum and dad.' He tries to steady his gaze on me, but struggles.

'How can you speak in riddles on no sleep?' I ask.

'Andy – is the sex good?'

'Yeah,' I say.

'Are you having fun?'

'Yeah.'

He shrugs. 'Then I think you have your answer,' he says, taking another swig of the whisky. 'You should enjoy this time. See what it brings up for you, creatively. It's like Samuel Johnson said: "The clearest your mind will ever be is the five seconds after orgasm."'

'Samuel Johnson didn't say that,' I say.

'Yes he did.'

'No he didn't. You can't just keep saying all these banal things about wanking and shagging and attributing them to Samuel Johnson.'

The dressing-room door flings open and in walks Archie, a twenty-five-year-old character comedian who is new to the circuit but has the confidence of a headliner thanks to his ever-growing online following. Emery and I have had many private conversations about how these sorts of comedians cheat the system by gathering an audience from well-edited videos intended to go viral, made from the comfort of their own bedroom. But everyone online loves Archie at the moment, and everyone in the industry loves Emery at the moment, and the pair of them know they have that in common without explicitly saying it, so they act like old friends.

Then comes Michelle, the compere for the evening. She's a safe and solid booking because her material always gets the crowd onside, no matter where she is. She's an Australian feminist in her late thirties, who met and fell in love with a geeky-but-cool English music journalist ten years ago who she has since married and had a kid with. Her insights on the British make every audience feel teased but loved, her stories about motherhood make women feel understood and her observations on men make us feel known and nervous enough to applaud very loudly at everything she says.

The last to arrive is Nick, a man in his late fifties who has an energy so recognizable in failed older comedians that Emery and I have given it a name: the Dark Sixth-former. He wasn't made head boy, his top-choice universities have rejected him and his A-level predictions aren't looking good. He infects every dressing room with his bitterness and he asserts his seniority over the younger pupils for a kick. Tonight he's absorbed in his phone, turned away from all of us and facing the wall while he sips on an energy drink.

Michelle introduces Archie, who's on first, with his character of the posh boy who pretends that he isn't posh. It's funny, but it's archetypal. You can see the jokes coming, with overblown details and predictable punchlines. But the audience love him, because half of them follow him online.

Michelle takes the mic from him and does a very funny bit about what it was like to date British men for the first time. She talks about our mannered awkwardness, our inability to make a date plan, our anecdotes that are so long they deserve a dedication, epigraph and acknowledgement. 'Faster and funnier,' she says. 'That's what these men need to be told. Say it with me: faster and funnier. FASTER AND FUNNIER.' She leads a chant and the audience follows. 'If your husband gets home from the supermarket and he starts telling you a boring story about what he found in the discounted fridge? What do you overly polite cunts learn how to say?'

'Faster and funnier!' they respond ecstatically.

Emery swaps with me in the running order because he's so drunk he's on the verge of losing his ability to communicate verbally. He stumbles on with a guitar he's found backstage. He's well-known enough now that the audience believe that catching him this drunk and disorganized is some sort of treat, like seeing Bob Dylan do a surprise set at the Roundhouse in the sixties. He plays the bassline of 'Seven Nation Army' and does some improv'd political songs that just about rhyme but don't make much sense.

'*Our future's gone up in flames but, hey hey hey,*' he croons into the mic. '*The person who we have to thank is —*' He encourages the audience to finish the line.

'THERESA MAY!!!' a drunk woman at the front stands up and bellows, delighted with herself. Everyone cheers and applauds like they've collectively written the lyrics for a protest song.

Michelle introduces me and as I walk on stage I can tell by the clap that it's going to be a flop. I fall back on all the old faithfuls: my impression of the least-worn T-shirts in the drawer bitching about you when you don't choose to wear them; my bit about people who choose daring pizza toppings to prove a point; some stuff about how long you can leave a kitchen bin before taking it out.

'Faster and funnier!' the drunk woman at the front shouts. Everyone laughs.

'Right. We don't weaponize the comedians' lines against each other,' I say with jokey authority, thinking this sort of meta-commentary on how the night is going might get them back onside.

'FASTER AND FUNNIER!' she shouts again and this

time the rest of the crowd joins her. They chant it together. I try to talk over them and carry on with my solid-gold stuff about paninis, but the chanting gets louder.

'What about a song?' I plead in an attempt at comic desperation. 'Why don't I sing you a song instead?' The chanting stops and instead the drunken woman shouts simply 'NOT FUNNY!' and everyone laughs. That's the biggest laugh of my set. Michelle comes on to the stage and takes the mic off me.

'OI!' she shouts. 'OI!' She motions to try to get them to quieten down. 'This guy is one of the good ones. His stories are quality. Let's give him a chance. Andy, mate – finish your set.' She passes the mic back to me. The audience are listening, but they're pissed off. Michelle meant well by trying to defend me, but it has only irritated them further. Not only are they bored of my jokes, they're annoyed they've been told off for being bored of my jokes. I cut my losses and rush through the last five minutes with some ropey material about how people walk weirdly through airport security machines.

'Sorry, mate,' Michelle says when we pass each other as I leave the stage.

'It's fine,' I say. 'Honestly, it's fine.' I walk past Nick, who sits on a stool in the wings and doesn't look up from his phone.

When I get to the dressing room, everyone's left.

Monday 21st October 2019

It begins before I even wake up. I sleep through the beginning of the earthquake.

I open my eyes at 7.42, take my phone out from under the pillow next to me and see a text from a comedian I barely know.

> Hey mate, saw what's happening online.
> Hope you're ok.

I have no idea what he's talking about, but there is no scenario in which this text is not one of the worst texts you can wake up to other than being informed of a death.

My heart races and my breath shortens. I open up the Twitter app and refresh my notifications – nothing abnormal. I go on to the newsfeed and don't see anything that concerns or involves me.

I type my full name into Google and click on the news tab. And there it all is. It's like I've leant too hard on a shelf in a library and realized it's a jib door that opens to a secret chamber. A whole wing of people, mingling with drinks at a party, talking only about you.

At the top is a link to an article for an online culture magazine. RIP STAND-UP COMEDY reads the headline. I click on it. There is no journalist credited.

> Last week, I witnessed the death of stand-up comedy as we know it. RIP, goodbye, we had some laughs except, honestly, no we didn't.

The worst of the offenders was a man called Andy Dawson. 'Man' may be too generous a word to describe him – imagine if your worst school geography teacher and a past-its-sell-by-date Cornish pasty had a son, put it in a plaid flannel shirt bought at Superdry in 2007, and then you might come close to getting a visual picture of the 'comedian' known as Andy Dawson.

I flick down the article to see how much there is. Paragraph after paragraph after paragraph. I scroll back to my place and read it all in one until I get to the final full stop. I don't know if it's my state of panic or my mind trying to protect me, but my eyes skip through the sentences, only able to retain certain phrases.

Tedious jokes about food, household items and thirty-something life with punchlines that are signposted for five miles like a motorway service station.

His comedic style resembles the paninis which he got a three-minute sequence out of – dry, bland, fake and insubstantial.

To call this sort of thoughtless drivel 'observational comedy' is to hugely underplay what the art of humans observing human behaviour can and should be. 'Observational comedy' as we know it must die today along with Andy Dawson's career.

As if the torture of sitting through his fifteen minutes wasn't enough, for some reason I found myself watching his old routines on YouTube and trawling through his jokes on social media. I can't quite believe I'm typing this, but it turns out I saw the very best of his work live. Three minutes on paninis is his Da Vinci's *Last Supper*.

It strikes me that this is where this type of traditional comedy has been leading – to this very nadir. Surely we have given enough stage space and airtime to balding men ambling around in bad jeans making remarks that have been said by another balding man in bad jeans before them? Surely it's time to try something else? Comedy that says something new, does something useful or simply just, I don't know, makes us laugh?

We therefore commit this stand-up career to the ground, earth to earth, ashes to ashes, dust to dust; in sure and certain hope of the Resurrection to eternal silence. Only then, in its place, can something take life that is new, imaginative and, please dear God, at least a bit funny.

I scroll down to read the comments – 789 of them. It's only been up for a few hours.

This article is vv gd

Never heard of this comedian but he doesn't look like he'd make me laugh tbf

FINALLY. SOMEONE'S SAID IT.

Just googled Andy Dawson, didn't know who he was, but now can't get it out of my head that he looks like the sort of guy who takes the biggest piece of lasagne without serving anyone else

Whoever wrote this is a genius

Ugh, saw this guy live once, she's right, he is dogshit

I sit upright in my bed and read all of them. I go on to the magazine's Instagram page and see a post about the article, with its own separate 456 comments. I read all of them too. As new people enter this party in the hidden wing, I follow them in, listening to every word they say and watching who they interact with.

Well-written article but who even cares??? About this man??? I've never even heard of him??????

This idiot is a disgrace to birmingham

HAHAHHAA. SOMEONE GIVE THE WRITER OF THIS THEIR OWN STANDUP COMEDY SHOW.

This is SAVAGE (and true).

I'm a woman just breaking into standup comedy and reading this piece about Andy Dawson is funny, but also depressing. A keen reminder that this is an industry where averagely talented men thrive.

I was at school with this mug. He was a bell-end then, unsurprised to see he's a bell-end now.

I click on the Instagram profile of the person who wrote the last comment – a man whose name and face I don't recognize. I look him up on Facebook and see we have no friends in common. On LinkedIn, I see we did go to the same school, but six years apart. Was I really a bell-end at school? I try to think back on all the times I might have behaved badly in the late nineties and early noughties. I was all right, wasn't I? A bit loud, a bit thick. But I basically kept myself to myself. Didn't I? I want to text Avi just to check that I haven't forgotten any crucial memories of this time. In fact, I want to text everyone in my phonebook whose number I still have from school and confirm that there's no animosity between us. I read the man's words again and notice that a carpet company in Sussex has liked this comment. What did I do at school that was so bad that a carpet company in Sussex seems to know what he's referring to?

I don't know who to call. Who do you call in this situation? I can't call my mum, because I don't want her worrying about me.

My pride won't let me call Avi, who already thinks my job is a waste of my time. I don't want to speak to Emery, because I can't bear to be the object of his pity. I don't want anyone whose opinion I care about to read these things about me, so I can't talk about it to anyone whose opinion I care about. There's only one person I want to talk to. The only person who could reassure me and put it in perspective and go to the pub with me and make me turn my phone off and maybe even help me see the funny side.

And she's the person I want to know about this the least. I would do anything to keep this article from her. If this were in a paper, I would go to Hammersmith and buy every copy in her local newsagent. But I can't control it. I keep seeing the article comments pile up, the Instagram comments, the retweets, the likes – it's like a fire I can't stop.

It is Jen who I think about all day – not the article, not its author, not my industry, not my agent, not Sophie, not even the Sussex carpet company. I only think about the words in relation to Jen. When I go to the gym, I think about her reading that I'm tedious and stupid and not funny. When I go to work on the cheese stand, I think about her telling Seb about the review – him laughing and her defending me very briefly by saying something like 'I know how hard he would have taken this', but then having a guilty laugh as he reads extracts aloud.

When I get into bed to try to watch a film and take my mind off it, I think about Jen reading everything that's been written in response to the article, each one confirming that the statements about me in it are correct, and in turn confirming her decision that it was right to end our relationship.

My phone rings. I am surprisingly relieved to see it's Emery. I hit the space bar on my laptop and pause the film.

'I see that today's your turn,' he says with paternal authority. 'I'm sorry, my boy.'

'Thanks for calling,' I say. 'You're the only comedy friend who has acknowledged it. I feel like everyone is trying not to look at me because they're so embarrassed.'

'It's not that – everyone is trying not to make this any worse for you,' he says.

'Yeah, I suppose so,' I say. 'I feel so ashamed.'

'Don't. Everyone has one of these days. They're part of our job. Sadly, today is yours.'

'What do I do?' I ask.

'You have to find a way to be fine with it.'

'You don't think I should post something funny and self-aware? So I look like I'm in on the joke or something?'

'No,' he says. 'You're not in on the joke. You have to say nothing. Anything funny will seem defensive. And anything serious will make you seem whiney. This is just one of those shit things you have to accept.'

'You're right,' I sigh.

'Do you want me to do anything? Do you want me to say something in your defence?' he asks.

That's all I want. I want someone to say: I know this person, this person is an okay person. He may not be the funniest or the best-looking or the most talented, but he doesn't deserve this. I want Emery to become my proof that I can't be all bad, I can't be so embarrassing and irredeemable because otherwise why would someone like him be friends with me?

But I also know that if he had wanted to publicly come to my defence, he already would have done. In social media terms, I'm deadly for the reputation right now. I'm toxic waste. I'm asbestos. Everyone should stay well clear. And, if I'm being really honest with myself, if I were in his position I wouldn't have tweeted in defence of me today either. I've seen this happen to other people, time and time again, and I've done nothing but sit and watch it all unfold and feel bad for the person who's going through it and relieved it isn't me.

'It's okay, man,' I say. 'Thanks for offering.'

I close my laptop and take a seat at my desk. I open a blank page of my notebook and stare at it for a while. All I want, this very instant, is to write new material; become new material. I want to throw out everything I've ever written and start again. But I can't find anything in my brain that I feel confident enough to even try out on paper. I can't think of any story or joke and not see it through the lens of every adjective I've read about myself today.

I try to sleep but I can't. I turn on to every surface of my body, hoping that each movement will shake the memory of today out of me, but it only makes me more restless. All my thoughts are muddled, everything has got mixed up. Jen and the strangers online have become the same person – the pain is living in the same place in my body in a weird, tangled ball. Jen couldn't be with me because of everything I read about myself today. And the reason they wrote those things about me is why some-one like Jen could never be expected to love someone like me.

Monday 28th October 2019

It turns out that all my agent needed to ring me back was to read a viral article about one of her clients murdering all of comedy with a fifteen-minute set. She rings in the late afternoon, while I'm out dumping a large bin bag of all my plaid flannel shirts at the charity shop.

'Andy?!' she yelps.

'Hey,' I say.

'So good to finally catch you!' she says with enthusiasm so convincing I momentarily forget she has ignored me for the best part of three months. 'How are you?'

'I'm okay, I haven't had a great week to be honest.'

'Yeah, yeah,' she says. 'I did see that. Oh, poor you. Rotten luck.'

'Is that why you're calling?' I ask, feeling unusually calm at the prospect of being dropped by my agent.

'Er – no, not just that. Just wanted to have a general catch-up really,' she says. 'But yes, mainly that. I wanted to check if you were planning on saying anything about the article?'

'Everyone's told me not to so I don't think I'm going to.'

'Good,' she says. 'Good. Yes. That's the right decision. Having been in this position with clients before, the best thing is just to keep your head down, all right? You know – you're fabulous, we all think you're fabulous, everything's going to be fabulous, you just have to, you know, take a deep breath and get on with it.'

I can't believe I used to take this shit seriously. Unsubstantiated claims of my genius, flimsy platitudes of reassurance, unevidenced statements of support – all spoken with this careful, pandering tone as if I am a baby monarch being paraded around my kingdom on a velvet baby throne. It's so embarrassing.

'Okay, well, I'd really like to talk to you about that. I want to take a show up to Edinburgh next summer. And I want to tour it. I want to write something completely unexpected, something I haven't done before. I don't really know what that is yet, which I know doesn't sound that encouraging, but I feel so ready to –'

'Andy, this all sounds brilliant,' she says. 'I reckon the best course of action is for you to have a proper think –'

'I'll have a proper think,' I say flatly, knowing that my allotted time with her is up and there's no point pushing for more.

'And drop me an email when you're ready to talk about the next steps, okay?' she says.

'Great.'

'Great,' she says.

Sophie arrives just before seven o'clock. Since the review, I haven't wanted to see anyone. But I relented when she suggested she come to my place for the first time – a sure sign that she really must be desperate to see me. We haven't hung out since the ill-fated karaoke night, but she's texted me a few times trying to instigate a meet-up. I don't know why I keep finding excuses not to.

I open the door to her and hug her swiftly, keen to get her upstairs before she has a chance to meet Morris. I hurry her into my bedroom and close the door. She swings her bag off her shoulder and dumps it on the bed. She shrugs off her coat and carries it in her arm as she walks around my room, inspecting it with cautious curiosity.

'So,' I say, sitting on the end of the bed and opening my laptop. 'Do you want to watch a film?'

She continues to examine everything she can find – picking up hair wax from the top of the chest of drawers and reading its instructions, sliding out random paperbacks from the shelf and inspecting their covers.

'Yeah,' she says absently. She picks up a framed photo of Avi and me when we were in our early twenties. 'Who's this?'

'Avi,' I say. 'My best mate.'

'Sweet,' she says, putting it down. 'How long have you guys known each other?'

'Since we were kids.'

'Would he like me?' she asks, picking up another photo frame.

'Um, I'm not sure he even likes me to be honest,' I say, newly fearful of anything complimentary I say being a promise of commitment.

'Is this your mum?' she asks, holding up a photo of Mum with her eighties mullet, holding me, her eighties toddler, wearing a tiny shellsuit.

'Yes,' I say.

She holds the photo closer to her face and narrows her eyes. 'You were a cute kid.'

'I wasn't, but thank you,' I say, browsing the films that Netflix has especially picked out for me and my viewing habits, which has often felt like the most constant act of romance in my life. 'Right. How about this insanely long new Scorsese thing with Robert De Niro?'

'Sure,' she says, putting the photo down. 'Do you have a photo of your dad?'

'I don't know my dad,' I say, taking a pillow and propping the laptop up on it as a makeshift TV stand.

'As in . . . you don't spend time with him or you don't know anything about him?' she asks.

'Both, I guess. Never met him and don't know that much about him.'

'That's really sad,' she says, coming to sit on the bed next to me. 'I'm sorry.'

'Don't be. A lot of boys I grew up with don't know their dads. I don't think of it as some big tragedy.'

Sophie does something she's never done before – she puts her arms around me, rests her head on my shoulder and gives me a hug.

'Hey, don't you worry!' I say, giving her a squeeze and pulling away. 'I turned out okay dadless, didn't I?'

She nods. 'It's still sad,' she says.

It is never explicitly mentioned that we aren't going to have sex, but this seems to be an understanding as soon as she takes off her trainers and asks for Diet Coke rather than a beer. She puts her head on my chest and we lie on my bed in mostly silence for the duration of the three-and-a-half-hour film. As the credits roll, I ask her what her plans are for the rest of the week and do some yawny stretching. She takes this as her cue to leave and starts to gather her things.

'Can I get you a cab to the station?' I say.

'Nah,' she replies, sitting on the edge of the bed and putting on her shoes. 'Did I have a scarf?'

'Um, not sure, let me think,' I say, unable to summon any thought other than how much I want to be on my own.

'I'm sure I had it,' she says, standing up and wandering around the room. Am I imagining this or is she moving slower than she's ever moved? She looks under each pillow, the duvet, the bed, the chest of drawers, in her bag, under the desk. 'I swear I was wearing it.'

'Well, don't worry, if it's here I'll find it,' I say.

'Yeah, I know, it's just so cold at the moment.'

'I can post it to you,' I say hurriedly. *I can post it to you.* Why couldn't I have found anything else to say? Something less administrative, less cold. Less obviously a plea to get the hell out of my house.

'Okay, sure,' she says and puts on her coat.

'Borrow mine,' I say, opening the wardrobe door and yanking it out so fast, a pile of T-shirts fall out on to the floor.

I walk her to the door and ask her to text or call me when she's home. She kisses me, says goodbye and leaves. As I shut the door, I rest my head on it, close my eyes and realize how shallow my breathing has become.

'If your lady friend plans on staying . . .' Morris's voice comes from behind me.

'She's gone, Morris,' I say, keeping my head against the door.

'Well, if on another occasion she plans on staying,' he continues, 'I'm sure you'll agree it would only be proper if she contributed towards the utility bills.'

'How much would this be?' I ask, turning round to face him. 'Hypothetically? I'm just curious.'

'Every stay?' He does some mental calculations. 'Off the top of my head, I would guess about three pounds.'

'No,' I say.

'And seventy pence.'

'Absolutely not,' I continue. 'I'm not charging women three pounds seventy to stay overnight here like it's a seaside bed and breakfast from the 1970s. No. I'll just pay it myself.'

'Suit yourself,' he says, wandering back into the living room.

I sit at my desk and open my notebook and look at the jumble of ideas I've written in the last few days to try to identify a theme for a show. I have become obsessed with themes. I'm convinced a theme will fix everything. I need to renew, improve, try something different. I can't just tell jokes any more, I need to tell a story of some sort. Once I have a theme, I will be the sort of comedian who is invited on literary podcasts to talk about my favourite books and asked to host radio documentaries about the Culture Wars. I will straddle the commercial/cult divide. I will be known as a great thinker, a public intellectual. When people write reviews pooh-poohing my work, it will be because it is so challenging and confrontational and a bit inaccessible to the masses, not because I look like a pasty in a flannel shirt. The theme will protect me. I turn to the most recent page of thoughts to see if I landed on anything.

> *Chiropractors – bollocks?*
> *Only visited two continents – is this funny?*
> *The whole concept of baths – weird*
> *Something about me balding*
> *Do dolphins know how much we pay to swim with them*
> *Pretend conversation with a dolphin*

Sophie texts me to let me know she's got home and I reply to say goodnight, with three kisses because I still feel so bad about saying that I'll *post her scarf*. I have a really terrible feeling that what I am experiencing is The Flip. That a change in power has occurred and neither of us realized what was happening until it was done. In my experience, it happens in every single relationship that fails. It happened the other way around with me and Jen, which now feels almost unimaginable. Jen was the one who wouldn't leave me alone in the very beginning. Then about three and a half months in, something shifted. I became the person who was more interested, who was pushing for more time together. She became the manager of Us – I would ask for things and she would grant them to me. She was the one with all the power. Because the person who is in charge in a relationship is the one who loves the least.

This case of The Flip is a disaster. I don't want Sophie to be more into me than I am into her. I can't be the manager, I'm already managing too much. It is weird to think that this must have been how Jen felt about me at some point, that she had to go through all this without telling me – realizing that I saw a future and she didn't, trying to find ways of leaving. It must have felt really bad. For the first time since our break-up, I feel sorry for her.

Saturday 2nd November 2019

I walk to a park to make the call. I can't risk Morris overhearing the conversation and, for some reason, I feel like if I'm in a public place there is less of a chance of being shouted at from the other end of the line. Two break-ups in the space of four months. How did I get into this situation?

I find a bench and take a deep breath. *It's fine, you've done nothing wrong. You never promised her anything. You've only been dating a month. You're probably imagining these feelings you think she has for you.*

'Hey,' she says.

'Hi. How are you?'

'I'm okay, how are you?'

'I'm good, all good and well,' I say, choosing and presenting my words carefully to her, like a baker giving a customer a little cake with a pair of tongs. 'Just . . . hanging about.'

'Cool?'

'Sophie, I'm ringing because I just . . . I just wanted to talk about us.'

'Yeah?'

'Just, like, wanted to temperature-check the vibe, check in with where we're both at kind of vibe.'

I hear her lighting a cigarette.

'Why are you talking to me like this?' she says. 'Can you just get to the bit where you dump me?'

'No, no, no,' I say through forced laughter. 'That's not what this is. Well, that's what I'm trying to clear up, really. Because to dump someone, we'd have to be seeing each other. And I've always been under the impression that we're not . . . seeing each other? In a formal way? But lately I feel like . . . maybe we are?'

'Okay, let's start seeing each other,' she says, exhaling. 'Let's go out. Fine.'

'No, no,' I say, leaning forward and putting my head in my hands. 'That's not exactly what I'm saying.'

'What are you saying?' she says, more impatiently.

'I guess I'm saying that I just need to be in something casual. I can't be in a relationship right now, I'm still all messed up from my break-up.'

'So you're saying you want to go back in time to a few weeks ago when we were just fucking?'

'I mean . . . yeah. Sort of.'

She laughs. 'You're the worst,' she says.

'How am I the worst?! I wanted to ring you to clear this up! I didn't want to let this fizzle out. I wanted to have a conversation with you!'

'What, do you want a round of applause for not ghosting me?' she asks.

'No, that's not what I was say–'

'The only reason you can't ghost me is because you're friends with my housemate. If you didn't know her, there's no way you would have called me.'

There is silence while I try not to interrogate whether this is true, and instead come up with any sort of response that could redeem me.

'Look, Sophie, I really like you. You're beautiful and smart and talented. If the timing was different, then maybe –'

'Yeah, sure,' she says, her voice cracking.

'Please don't get upset,' I say. 'I hate that I've upset you.'

'I'll give Thalia your scarf,' she says.

'No, let's meet up, it doesn't have to be like this.'

'It does,' she says. All the emotion and softness in her voice has gone. The Sophie I first met has returned: cool, closed-off and ruthlessly rule-enforcing. 'Don't call me or text me again, please.'

'Sophie –'

'Bye.' She ends the call.

Friday 15th November 2019

Miraculously, all the boys were free to meet up tonight. Jon, Jay, Rob, Avi and Matt – the full apostle set. Even rarer is that the night was instigated and organized by Jon, the most unreliable of the group. My instinct is that he's got something to announce – possibly that he and his very long-term girlfriend are getting married. He mentioned that he was thinking of proposing last year. I bet tonight will be the official allocation of best man, ushers and, the most annoying job which always falls on me, MC. The MC can't get drunk until after the dinner, is responsible for the pace of the entire evening and basically has to do stand-up for free. Sure, their interest in my comedy career waned by the time we were in our mid-twenties and they realized being friends with me would not provide secondary access to free drugs and girls off the television. But the minute they need someone to say, 'Ladies and gentlemen, the coffees are about to be served,' I'm suddenly the funniest guy they know.

I check in on Jen and Seb via my web browser. Both of them have been eerily quiet over the last week. I don't know whether this is a positive or negative sign – whether they have broken up or eloped. Sophie, meanwhile, has never been more active on Instagram. I wonder whether this is for my benefit – whether every photo of her having fun, being busy at work and generally looking obscenely fit is a message to me. A way of communicating indirectly that she is extremely out of my league and I was very lucky to have been with her and it is absurd that I was the one who ended things. She would be entirely correct, of course. I want to reply to every single one of them saying: 'Point very well made.'

I'm the last to arrive at the pub and everyone's already one drink down. There's a lot of talk about how different I look; not any clear compliments, but I think that's as close to praise for my physical appearance as I'll get from them and it goes some way to making the great starvation of the last few months worth it.

Everyone's taking their turn to complain about something. I can't remember what we used to talk about before we started the complaining portion of life. Rob's complaining about the builders doing his kitchen ('charlatans'), Matt's complaining about his oldest kid ('prick'), Avi's complaining about the young employees in his office ('melts'), Jay's complaining about estate agents ('Machiavellian') and I'm complaining about Sophie. Jon's staying strangely quiet.

At some point a couple of hours in, there's a lull in conversation and I lean across the table to speak to him, having to shout over the top of Rob and Avi's heated conversation about the election.

'How's things with you?' I ask.

'Er –' He takes a gulp of his pale ale and puts it down. 'Bit weird, actually. That's why I wanted to see all you guys.' Everyone gets wind of this and turns their attention to Jon.

'Yeah, Chrissy and I broke up,' he says, before giving a 'there we go' shrug and looking into his pint glass. 'Happened a few days ago. She's moving all her stuff out tomorrow.'

'Oh, lad,' Rob says with genuine tenderness. 'I'm sorry.'

'Yeah, I'm so sorry, I can't believe it,' I say. 'How do you feel?'

'I don't think I've really processed it yet,' he says. 'I feel like I'm in a dream or something.' He shakes his body slightly, as if he can get rid of his feelings like raindrops on a coat. And all I want to do is say: Yes, I know. You poor, poor fucker, I am four and a half months ahead of you on this expedition into hell and I'm so sorry you're at the beginning of it. I don't envy you. Talk to me, cry to me, scream at the sky, curl up like a baby. Let me help you and console you and tell you all the ways I've gone completely fucking mad since Jen left. Let me reveal every ugly, humiliating, childlike thought and feeling I've kept from all of you. I know what you're feeling and, while I don't know yet that it gets better, I do know you're not alone. I promise, you're not alone.

Instead it is agreed that the next logical step is to order a round of shots called a cement mixer.

And then the same thing happens that happened the night they were all gathered together to counsel me over my break-up. I watch the night repeat itself and I make no attempt to stop it. We all ask about the logistics of his break-up, enjoying coming up with our proposed solutions; revelling in our offers of sofas to crash on and the names of reliable removal companies. Then we all take turns to say bland, impersonal platitudes about how he's still young and he'll meet someone else and it's better to be out of a relationship and on your own rather than in the wrong one. None of us really ask him any questions about how he's coping. We don't offer any sort of emotional support, other than saying that we're all here for him, despite not having all been in a room together since the last time one of us had a break-up, four months ago.

Jay's the first to leave, mid-evening, to get home to help with the baby. Matt leaves shortly afterwards because of kid-related stuff. Rob goes with him. Avi, Jon and I move on to another location and I hope it's the last one. I've got a gig in Carlisle tomorrow and I don't know if I have the energy to stay out until three a.m. and go somewhere that requires a stamp to be put on my hand. When we get to the next pub, I go to the toilet and have a word with myself. I need to break this cycle. I return to our table with a round of drinks and Avi gets up to go for a piss. It's just me and Jon now. We're not quite drunk enough for proclamations of eternal brotherhood, but we're less awkward, looser-tongued. This is my chance.

'You know, Jon, it's been, like, rough since Jen and I broke up.'

'I know,' he says.

'And I just want to say: I really am here for you. If you want to talk or whatever. I hope you know that you can talk to me.'

'I know,' he says, thumping my arm affectionately. 'There's just not much to talk about, you know? Other than saying I'm really sad.'

And I want to say: We can just talk about being sad, if you like. You don't have to make the sad thing funny for me. There will be no conversational tokens system in place here. Because I am starting to think that talking about the sadness might be the same thing as processing the sadness. And if we're not doing that, then we only have our thoughts for company, and our thoughts are unreliable and they invent things and they lie to us and give bad advice. Not talking about the sadness is what leads us into The Madness.

But I don't know how to say any of this without sounding like an advert for online therapy, and I don't want to embarrass myself or him with my emotional illiteracy.

Just as I am about to launch into it all as succinctly as I can, Avi returns to the table and asks at what point in the 2010s did pub condom machines become so 'rarefied', with knock-off Viagra and chewable toothbrushes, which then takes the conversation off into a completely different direction. When we get to the bottom of our glasses, we've shared all of our vending-machine-related anecdotes and theories. Avi offers to get another round in and Jon says he thinks he might call it a night. With relief that I hope is not too obvious, Avi and I put on our coats

252

and we're all outside in the cold seconds later, eagerly walking to the tube station.

'So I'll see you at Jackson's birthday tomorrow,' Avi says to me as we all stand by the ticket barriers.

'Yeah,' I say. 'Do you know if –'

'Yes, Jen will be there,' he says.

'And do you know if –'

'No, I don't know if he's coming,' he says.

'Cool,' I say.

Avi turns to Jon and opens his arms for a hug.

'Chin up, fella,' he says. 'You'll be okay.'

'Thanks, Av.'

Avi walks away and down the escalator. Jon looks tired.

'Sure you don't want another drink somewhere?' I say.

'Nah, you're all right,' he replies. 'I'm up at five to shoot a toilet roll advert tomorrow.'

'That should be an album title,' I say. He laughs weakly. 'Okay. Well. You know where I am if you need a drinking buddy. I've been practising on my own, I've gotten really good at it.'

'Thanks, man,' he says.

I give him a hug, then we go our separate ways. I think about him all the way home. I hope he's all right.

Saturday 16th November 2019

Jen's there when I arrive. I see her as I walk through the front door. I take my coat off and hang it on a hook, glance down the hallway and see her perfectly framed by the kitchen door. She's at the end of the table, picking at her cuticles absent-mindedly as she talks to a woman sitting on the chair next to her. Avi brings me through the living room, which is swarming with screaming four-year-olds. They cover every surface – boys with their tops off jumping on the sofa, little girls in tutus sitting on the carpet, pairs of them chasing each other around the coffee table and wrestling behind the curtains.

'ALEXA!' one red-faced little boy screams into the middle of the room, eyes shut, fists balled up by his sides. 'PLAY CRAZY FROG.'

'Ah, Sam,' Avi says, gently putting his hand on his shoulder. 'Remember what we said? Only the grown-ups control the Alexa. Okay?'

Sam nods and runs off.

'All these entitled little pricks,' Avi hisses out of the side of his mouth. 'Know how to use everything in my house better than I do.'

'Where are all their parents?'

'Yeah, good question. It turns out fourth birthdays are the official age where birthday parties are seen as free babysitting. Only a handful of them have stayed.' He leads me into the kitchen and I can sense Jen watching as Avi introduces me to the dads, all leaning against the kitchen counters holding beers. He brings me over to the table where Jen, Jane and two other women sit. Jen stands up and we hug.

'And you remember Jen?!' he says, a joke I know he's been looking forward to cracking all day.

'Twat,' Jane says, heaving herself up from her chair.

'No, don't get up,' I say, bending down to give her a kiss on the cheek. 'Where's Jackson?'

'Is he not next door?' she asks.

'No,' I say.

'God almighty, he must be upstairs again, doing the grand tour,' she sighs.

'I'll get him,' I say.

I go upstairs and find Jackson with a group of children in his parents' bedroom, opening a drawer and showing them where his mum keeps her pants. I stand in the door frame and watch him. He tells them what they can and can't use in the room – they can touch the curtains but not the lamps, they can sit on the bed but not under the covers, and no one can try on his dad's shoes. When he sees me, he walks over determinedly and takes me by the hand into the centre of the room. He introduces me in a way that is oddly boastful, as if I am also an item that belongs to the house. I crouch down to hug him.

'Did you bring a present?' he whispers in my ear.

'Yes,' I whisper back. He grins and flings his arms around me. Then holds me at arm's length and looks at me intently, a frown forming on his little face.

'Aunty Jen is here, Uncle Andy,' he says, stroking the top of my head like a hamster. 'She is in this house, all right?'

'All right,' I say, then lead all the kids back downstairs.

When I return to the kitchen, I sit down at the table where Jen, Jane and two of the mums sit. Jane wearily tells us that they've hired an exotic pet handler who's coming in an hour with lizards, snakes and spiders. The other two mums complain about the expense of birthdays with every year their children get older. One of the mums asks Jen if she has any kids, and when Jen says she doesn't, they all make jokes about how she's the one with the right idea. I try not to observe Jen too closely, but I am fascinated by how she, nearly a stranger to me now, interacts with other strangers.

'When are you due?' one of the women asks Jane.

'Twentieth of March,' she says.

'Are you dreading mat leave? Are you already thinking about going back to work?' the other woman asks, tipping the empty bottle of prosecco into her glass and shaking it.

'Are you kidding?' Jane says. 'I can't wait. I've finally learnt how to have a good maternity leave on my third go. No NCT friends, no sitting at home on that sofa all day reading message boards on my phone convincing me I'm a terrible mother. No. None of that. The boys are in nursery. This is my last maternity leave. It's going to be long lunches and pub sessions with the pram every day.'

'I'm in,' Jen says. Jane raises her mug of tea to her.

Avi returns from the shop ten minutes later, a plastic bag in each hand clanking with bottles. He puts the bags on the table and makes a big show of taking the six bottles of prosecco out. He looks to Jane for acknowledgement, but she's rifling through party bags and taking out their contents.

'Avi,' she snaps. 'What the hell are these?'

'Oh babe, don't, they're the best I could do,' he says.

'What did I say to you?' she asks.

'Jane –'

'*What* did I say? What were the two specific things I said no to?'

Jen and I catch each other's eye and smirk to suppress laughter the way we always did when they used to bicker. Avi sighs.

'No sweets, no plastic,' he recites.

'So what are these?' she says, holding up packets of fizzy cola bottles. 'Hm? And these?' She holds up a neon chattering teeth toy. 'I said I wanted packets of flower seeds and wooden beads to make a key ring.'

'I couldn't find that in the shops!' he exclaims.

'Okay, well, do you know who's going to be the talk of the mum WhatsApp groups tonight? Do you know who's going to get slagged off for being a plastic sugar parent?' she asks, faintly demonically, as she opens a pack of the party bag sweets and starts chomping at them. 'It ain't you, Avi. It never is.'

'I know!' I say cheerily, standing up and clapping my hands together. 'I think it's time for Uncle Andy's surprise.'

I take my bag into the downstairs toilet and change into my camo clothes and face paint. Holding a Nerf gun in each hand, I charge into the living room full of kids and all of them scream. Jackson is so excited he holds his head in his hands and throws himself on to his knees in hysterical giggles. I tell him that the two Nerf guns are his present and hand one to him, then Jane gets out the packs of goggles I bought in preparation and sent ahead to the house. Once all the kids have strapped them on, Jackson and I charge around the room shooting at each other, dramatically rolling under and over furniture to avoid each other's bullets. The kids are beside themselves, screaming instructions at us to avoid the gunfire. I (quite reluctantly) give the gun to a child to try and they all take their turn in warfare against Jackson. Avi stands at the sidelines, flinching every time someone shoots. Jane and Jen laugh as I shout orders at Jackson like a marine general. Finally, when all the children are breath-less and purple-faced, I call time on the game in a military command and all the grown-ups applaud. I go to the bathroom, take off the camo make-up and costume and, while the kids eat

Party Rings and vegetable sticks, I quietly walk out of the front of the house for a cigarette.

As I reach for the fag packet in my coat pocket, the front door opens and Jen appears. She steps out and stands next to me.

'Can I have a cigarette, please, Uncle Andy?' she asks. I take one out of the packet and give it to her with the lighter. 'Thank you.' She lights up and hands it back to me. I light my cigarette and for a moment or two we smoke in silence. 'You look so different,' she says.

'Good or bad different?' I ask.

'I don't know,' she says. 'You don't look like you.'

'That's probably good, I think,' I say. 'I was pretty sick of that guy.'

She makes a sound through her nose that sounds a bit like a laugh.

'But seriously, what have you done?'

'I have not knowingly eaten a carbohydrate,' I say. 'For a long time.'

'And have you been working out?' she says, looking at my middle.

I try to suppress a grin of glee. 'You did not just say that to me,' I say.

'I know, I only heard how it sounded as I was saying it.'

'Is Seb coming?' I ask out of nowhere, nearly adding 'It will be nice to see him', but decide this is an embellishment too far.

'No,' she says. 'We're not actually –' she hesitates and searches for a word –'dating.'

'Oh?'

'Yeah, not any more. I just realized it was too soon, you know,' she says, wanting me to end her thought, but I don't. I wait for the rest of the sentence. 'You know. After us. I'm not ready to be thinking about that at all, not even casually.'

'Yeah,' I say. 'I kind of had the same realization recently.'

'In what way?' she asks, her big, kitten eyes widening as she brings the cigarette to her mouth.

'I called something off with someone,' I say as evasively as possible. 'For the same reasons. I don't feel normal enough to date anyone yet.'

'It's a fucker, isn't it?' she says.

'Yeah,' I say, enjoying this unfamiliar new kinship between Jen and me, having a fag together and bitching about our failed relationship like it's a difficult boss we both don't like.

At this exact moment, a van with WIZARD LIZARDS written on its side pulls up and parks outside the house. We stand in silence as we watch a grumpy-looking man with grey hair get out of the van, stomp around to the passenger seat and take a very large headdress in the shape of a spider out from the footwell.

'So when do you think the exotic pet guy is coming?' I ask. She laughs. We stub out our cigarettes and go back inside.

While the kids handle the various reptiles, overseen by the grumpy man in the tarantula hat, Jen and I help Avi and Jane clean up the mess the kids have left. We quickly and comfortably fall back into our old jokes and roles as a group as if we'd never been apart, and yet there is still an air of a school reunion about it all – that however much we enjoy today, it exists only for a few hours. When the last children have left with their party bags, Avi puts a film on for Jackson and Rocco and we sit at the table with the last bottle of prosecco and pour it out into four glasses. We toast the success of the party, the Nerf guns, wizard lizards, the new baby, living in the suburbs, pebble-dash semi-detacheds. We toast everything unremarkable because the length of time we've all known each other makes the simple laws of time so very remarkable.

★

Jen and I say goodbye to the boys, then Jane and Avi say good-bye to us both at the door. Jane and Jen talk about when they're next going to see each other and Avi takes his opportunity to communicate with me as discreetly as he is capable of.

'You okay there, lad?' he says, eyebrows raised as he opens his arms for a hug.

'Yep, all good, perfectly normal, totally fine,' I say.

He holds on to me for longer than he normally would and pats my back.

'You're a really good mate, you know that?' he says, still locking me in an embrace.

'Thanks, Avi,' I say.

'I mean it,' he says as we pull apart and he holds me by the shoulders. 'Thank you for being so good with the kids today.'

'Is this you . . . asking me to marry you?'

'Fuck off,' he says, pushing me away. 'Prick.'

The door closes and Jen and I look at each other, unsure of what to do. We've left our best friends' house like we always did, the same people as we always were, but with a completely different relationship to each other. We walk to the station and, at first, it feels like nothing has changed since the last time we left their house together. We discuss Avi and Jane and the kids, we pick over everyone at the party, who we liked and didn't like – no one spared, not even the kids. And then we talk like we haven't talked before. We update each other on our jobs and our families as if we're former best friends who fell out of touch.

'It's so weird,' she says as we walk off the train and along the platform. 'Isn't it?'

'What is?' I ask.

'Us, speaking like this to each other.'

'I know,' I sigh. 'I don't think I'll ever get used to it. There are so many things I want to tell you.'

'Me too,' she says.

We tap our phones on the ticket barrier sensors and naturally come to a standstill under the train departures board.

'I feel like I've been hoarding all this stuff in a box labelled "Andy". All these stories that I want to take out one by one and do a big show-and-tell to you.'

'I feel exactly the same!' I say, perhaps too excitedly.

There is a pause as she looks around, searching for nothing, but considering something.

'What are you doing now?' she asks.

'Nothing,' I say. 'Do you want to get something to eat?'

'I really want to,' she says. 'Even though I know we probably shouldn't.'

'I know we shouldn't,' I say. 'But I also think we should? I think we should break the rules for just one night. What do you think? We can tell each other everything.'

'We can have just this one night,' she says.

'You sound like Kenny Rogers,' I say.

'I listened to that song for weeks after we broke up,' she says. 'There we go, that's the first thing I want to tell you.'

'So did I!' I yelp, instinctively grabbing her by her arms.

'And I thought: Kenny Rogers is going to die one day and I'll be so sad. But at least I'd have an excuse to call Andy and sing "We've Got Tonight" together on the phone.'

'You can always do that,' I say, realizing I'm still holding on to her and letting go of her arms. 'So what are you thinking?'

She wrinkles her nose as she ponders this. 'Tapas?'

'*Yes*,' I say. 'Chorizo. Manchego. Beer. Yes. That's exactly what I want.'

'Big things of –' she says, miming a huge jug because she can't find the word 'sangria'.

'Yes,' I say.

★

We get the tube to Brixton and the first thing I tell her about is the houseboat. The story of the boat is one of those anecdotes of such colossal comic failure that, when we were together, I would have looked forward to getting home to tell her every detail of it, minute by minute. The only silver lining of an experience like the boat experience would have been turning it into comedy for Jen. So I tell her about Bob, sparing no detail of his man-in-later-mid-life-freefall appearance, the chilling prophecy he offered of who I could turn into one day. I tell her about the endless back-and-forth to the storage unit, the new forms, the wrong bookings, the ongoing feud with the blue-haired man behind the counter. Every twist and turn of the tale makes her laugh more, so much so that I find myself furnishing it with slightly made-up details, all of which add to the hopelessness of the story.

We walk to the restaurant and she talks about the nightmare of living with Miranda and her partner and the baby in the weeks after our break-up. She tells me of the post-partum gong bath hosted by Miranda for other new mums and babies in the living room. She tells me of the baby who never slept, whose cries kept her up all night in between the sound of Miranda and her partner snapping at each other. She tells me of the early morning when, in a headachey fog, she swallowed two of Miranda's encapsulated placenta rather than two paracetamol.

We get a table and order two beers and some olives and I tell her about Kelly and her brutal training and eating regime. She teases me about all the unused gym memberships I burnt through when we were together – the monthly direct debits in exchange for nothing but being able to say 'Oh yeah? That's my gym too' in conversation.

We order a jug of sangria and a ceramic dish of chorizo and we talk about the day I bumped into her and Seb. She tells me she'd had a premonition that morning that she was going to run into me, even though it was a part of London that neither of us normally hangs out in, and that she very nearly didn't accompany Seb on his mattress-buying trip that day because of it. She says that, when she saw me, she didn't feel surprised. And when Jane asked her why she didn't do the sensible thing of running away, her answer was: she couldn't. How could she run away from the person who knew her better than anyone? Why would she run away from her family?

I tell her about how well Emery's career is going and how hard I'm finding it not to use it as proof that mine is over. I say this was only further confirmed with 'the review' and she asks, with genuine bewilderment, 'What review?' and I think on my feet and say that I'm referring to all the raves Emery's show has been getting.

I really start to give the sangrias a hammering at this point and we order more chorizo and some patatas bravas and calamari and tomato salad, and she asks me, with the caveat that the question comes from a place of curiosity rather than accusation, why I blocked her on Instagram. I explain that the temptation to look at her profile had become a compulsion; that I had started checking her Instagram page more than I would check my email or the weather app or the *Guardian* homepage; in fact, I don't think the *Guardian* has had a single visit on my phone or laptop browser since our break-up, God love it. I told her that the girl I was seeing had told me that the reason you block someone is not because you're hiding things from them, but because you're going on their profile too much. I hoped that Jen knew of this rule, and if she clocked it, that she wouldn't take it personally.

'*Girl?*' she says, tracing her finger around the rim of the wine glass. 'Why do you say "girl"? How old was she?'

'Twenty-three,' I answer.

She scoffs and knocks back the last of her sangria.

'Men are so predictable,' she says. 'Even the good ones.'

And this comment really winds me up, and time was I would

have picked her up on it. But this is exactly the sort of exchange, at exactly this time of night on a Saturday, after exactly this amount of alcohol, that used to lead to the nuclear rows when we were a couple. I can see how it would go: I'd deny that being with a woman so much younger than me is any sort of expression of misogyny, she'd tell me that's bullshit, I'd tell her that I find her broad theorizing on men to be outdated and shortsighted and patronizing, she'd tell me that she's allowed to theorize about men, as negatively and as insensitively as she likes. *Why are you allowed to do that and I'm not allowed to make generalizations about women?* I'd bellow. *WHY?* And then I would be met with a convoluted barrage about the pay gap and illegal abortions and FGM and the biological clock and childcare systems and the fact that every three days in this country a woman is killed by a man. And I'd say that's all well and good but how has that got anything to do with me? And she'd say it has *EVERYTHING TO DO WITH YOU*, while slamming down her wine so hard that it would spill all over the table. Then people would start to look at us while I'd say, in an accidentally boastful way: *I never killed ANY woman! I never banned abortions! I never passed any legislation about maternity leave!* And she'd say that she can't talk to me when I'm being this literal and that if I won't acknowledge that my people have always made life terrible for her people, even though I haven't done so personally, *then she doesn't know if she can be with me any more.*

So instead I say nothing and we order two sherries and I ask her how her family reacted to our break-up and, with great satisfaction, I listen to her tell me how surprisingly devastated they all were. All three siblings, her weird mum, her horrible dad. They all, it turns out, quite liked me once they knew I was gone for good. And only now that we've broken up does her dad finally call me Andy and not Steve.

★

We split the bill and we go to a bar down the road. She gets a gin and tonic and I get a beer and I tell her about Morris. I do my best Morris impression, with his balls-of-black-plasticine eyes and his long, meandering stories. I tell her about the shadowy history of the wife who left him for his brother and how she has been replaced with a conspiracy about everything and everyone, other than Julian Assange who he finds to be a perfect being.

She does my favourite Jen laugh. Jen's got a lot of good laughs, a whole orchestra of them, and the one I held out for most was the big 'HA!' she only imparts on very special occasions. So loud it always makes people look. I hold her face in my hands and tell her I've missed her. She tells me she's missed me too. I ask her if she's glad that she broke up with me and she says that she doesn't know yet.

'When will you know?' I ask.

'I don't think I'll ever know,' she says, her big blue eyes wet and glassy from booze.

She asks if I want to go back to hers for a drink because it's getting so loud and I say yes. I go to the toilet and think of all the reasons why we would go back to hers other than sleeping together.

She drapes her legs across me in the taxi, the way she used to when we watched TV on our sofa. I put my hand on her thigh and try not to say *Can you believe this is happening? Can you believe we're going to do this? Did you think this was going to happen?* Instead, I keep my expression as nonplussed as possible as she tells a story about her boss who keeps saying 'all intensive purposes' in meetings, and she doesn't know whether she should correct him.

I'm flooded with such intense nostalgia as we walk through the communal hallway and up the stairs to Jen's old flat that even the sound of her door creaking open and shut feels like a track from a long-forgotten, once-favourite album. Everything looks the same as the first night we spent together. In the darkness of her hallway, she asks what I would like to drink and, hastened by the warm, comfortable ease of being back in this flat, I pull her into me and kiss her. She kisses me back, pushing me against the wall, and the picture frames clatter.

'This really is a bad idea, isn't it?' I say.

'Yes,' she says, leading me down the hallway.

She pulls me on to the bed and kisses me. We undress ourselves, just as we did in our relationship. There's something comfortable about it – romantic in its efficiency, honest in its lack of pageantry. There's something comfortable about all of this. The bedroom feels so familiar, she feels so familiar. The shape and smell of this room and the shape and smell of her feel like returning home. The brand of hand cream by her bed, the perfume on her neck, the amount of pillows on each side (three – too many!), that perfectly placed mole between the round of her left breast and the hollow of her armpit.

'I'm wearing my boring pants,' she says in between kisses as she pulls down her tights.

'I love your boring pants,' I say, laying her flat on the bed, yanking her tights down her legs and off her ankles. I kiss the space between her belly button and her waistband, the bit I know sends her mad, and pull her pants off with my teeth, which makes her laugh. 'I'm the only one who gets to see your boring pants. They're my favourite pants.'

Jen and I always had good sex. It never got boring. Even when it was predictable, it was the kind of predictable that made you feel grateful that you knew exactly what you liked. Jen and I had a good sex repertoire – it was a perfect balance of intimate and filthy. It was always comfortable and chatty. We'd try things out and mix things up, but had our fail-safes to fall back on. Tonight, our bodies instinctively know we want the Jen-and-Andy classic – the kind of sex we so often returned to. The kind of sex where we use our bodies and our words effortlessly and unimaginatively to get and give the maximum pleasure. A dance we know the routine of instantly, even when we haven't done the steps in a while. I have the obvious realization that this is all I've really been looking for the last four months – this was the solution. This was the only thing that would solve the problem of my broken heart and, of course, nothing else worked. The answer always was, and always will be, her.

I go to the bathroom, peel off the condom and tie it in a knot. The only evidence that the sex we just had was not relationship sex. I wrap it in tissue and put it in the bathroom bin. When I return to her bedroom, she's lying under the covers, on her side. I try not to get distracted by thoughts of what will happen tomorrow. I try to stop my mind from doing magical mental maths – we were together for just under four years, apart for just over four months, the symmetry is there, we're getting back together. I climb into the bed next to her and we make the shape we always made – her head on the right side of my chest, my arms wrapped around her, her toes entwined with mine. We lie saying nothing for a while.

'I saw this new film at the cinema last week,' she says sleepily, her consonants mushed up from her face being pressed into my skin. 'About a couple going through a divorce.'

'Who did you go see it with?'

'I went on my own,' she says. 'No one wanted to come with me because they all read the reviews and were too scared it would make them want to break up with their partners.'

'What happens in it?'

'It opens with them writing a list of everything they love about each other because their divorce mediator told them to do it as part of their separation. To help them remember why they ever got married when things get really messy.'

'Did it make you want to do it about me?' I ask, only half joking.

'I did do it about you,' she says, surprised at her own admission. 'On the train home I wrote a list of everything I loved about you.'

'Read it aloud!' I say, too enthusiastically.

'No,' she says, laughing. 'God, you're so needy.'

'Go on,' I say, tickling her waist.

'No,' she says, gently kicking my shin. 'It's embarrassing.' She cranes her neck and looks at the radio alarm clock next to her bed. 'It's so late,' she says.

'Remember when we used to do this all the time? Every date ended at four in the morning.'

'We were younger then.'

'Only a few years younger,' I say. 'Still in our thirties.'

'There's a million miles between thirty-one and thirty-five,' she says through a yawn.

'Is there? I don't think there is.'

Her eyes are closed and I can hear her breathing begin to slow.

Sunday 17th November 2019

The room is cold when I wake up. Jen is lying on her side, facing away from me, but I can already tell that she's awake.

'Morning,' I say. We kiss. She makes a point of how hung-over she is, going on about how there are chunks of the night that she can't remember, which is her way of reminding me that she doesn't want to be held accountable for things she may have said or done.

She asks me if I want a tea and I say yes and she says she'll go make us some. I want to stay in bed – to lie together and fuck and talk and recreate the magic of last night, but I can feel that it's disappeared. When she puts the radio on and clatters about in the kitchen, it is a sound that makes me suspect she has started her day without me, rather than inviting me to start it with her. She brings two mugs of tea into the bedroom and perches on the end of the bed where I still lie undressed and bleary-eyed, feeling like her teenage son who she's waiting to get up for the school run.

She has a shower and, when she comes back into the room to get changed, she turns away from me. She asks if I want a shower and I say no, and instead get dressed. As I get out of bed and collect my clothes from around the room, she doesn't try to stop me or ask me if I'd like to go for breakfast; instead, she asks what my plans are 'for the week'. I still can't quite figure out if this means I'll see Jen again – if we're going to do this again next weekend – or whether she's making me think about how I'm spending my time after I leave her flat as a statement that our time together has officially come to an end.

I pat my jeans pocket and can't feel my keys. She leaves the bedroom to check if they fell out on the stairs or in the hallway. I check under all the furniture in the bedroom and can't find them. She reappears and tells me that they're nowhere to be found. She says I probably left them in the bar – but I tell her I remember feeling them in my jacket pocket while we were out. The Uber, then, she suggests. I tell her that I think I remember having them in the Uber. She wonders if I misplaced them when we got out of the cab. She runs like she has suddenly had an idea – I hear the jangle of keys and the front door slam. I check under the furniture again. She returns, flushed and out of breath, and tells me she couldn't find them on the street. They must be in the Uber.

'Okay,' I say. 'I'll ring the driver.'

'Good idea,' she says.

'My housemate can let me in. He's always in.'

'Great,' she says.

'Can you keep an eye out for them here?'

'Absolutely,' she says, nodding. 'And I can always post them to you.'

I feel like my heart has stopped.

'What?' she says, reading my expression.

'Nothing,' I reply.

She walks me out of her flat, down the stairs and into the communal entrance. She opens the door and stands in the frame while I stand on the step. I go to say something, then don't. Then she looks like she's about to say something, but doesn't. Neither of us says anything. I eventually break the silence.

'Do you remember when we were on holiday on that Greek island?' I ask. 'And there was an open-air cinema and I made us go watch that John Lennon documentary?'

'Yes,' she says.

270

'Do you remember any of it?'

'Some of it,' she says. 'Why?'

'Our break-up,' I say. 'The last few months – this isn't your lost weekend, is it?'

She hesitates, then looks at the floor.

'No,' she says quietly.

I nod and pause to think about whether I want to know the answer to my next question.

'I was your lost weekend, wasn't I?' Her eyes are fixed to the ground as I wait for her reply. She screws up her face as she drags her foot along the carpet, back and forth, back and forth, making a line in its pile with her toe. She looks like a child in trouble, unable to meet my gaze. '*Jen*,' I plead. I wait some more. Finally, she looks up, her eyes full of tears.

'Yes,' she says. A tear spills out and runs down her cheek. I look at her face and I understand something I haven't been able to understand until this very second.

'Bye,' I say.

'Bye.'

I turn and walk away, hearing the door close behind me.

Reasons Why It's Good I'm Not With Jen

She didn't want to be with me.

Winter 2019/2020

Saturday 7th December 2019

The sun sets before five o'clock. The fact of this still surprises me every year. I always forget how long this season feels, how little light or colour there is. I stare out of my bedroom window at Mum's, watching dusk turn into night. I don't think there's a bleaker landscape than a garden of a suburban terraced house in England in the middle of winter. The Siberian desert has nothing on this: next-door neighbour's garden gnome entangled in cobwebs; bare, spindly branches outstretched into the flat, grey sky; empty washing lines; abandoned patio furniture; jars once used as ashtrays in the summer now filled with black rainwater and fag butts.

A knock on the door.

'Come in,' I say.

Mum enters, holding a mug of tea.

'How're you doing?' she asks, placing it down on a coaster on my bedside table and standing in the door frame.

'Okay,' I say. 'Honestly, Mum, you don't need to bring me tea. It's very kind, but you don't have to.'

'I know I don't,' she says. 'But you only come home when it's Christmas or you're heartbroken. I don't get many chances to make you tea.'

'That's not true.'

'It bloody is.'

'Is it? Have I always come home when I have a break-up?' She nods. 'I'm sorry,' I say.

'Don't be sorry! Just know you can stay when you're not heartbroken too. You can stay any time.'

'I know,' I say.

'Right,' she says. 'Are you in tonight? Or got a gig?'

'In,' I say. 'I'll make dinner.'

I pick up the mug and resume my position at the window. Maybe I should be here more. Maybe I should be here permanently. It's a thought that's crossed my mind more than once since I arrived for a short stay with my rucksack of pants and still-unread Great American Novels. I could afford to rent a one-bed flat, I could spend more time with Mum and get back in touch with my friends who stayed up here after we left school. Buy a car. Never bump into Jen. Never again schedule a drink with a friend for four months in advance because 'things are crazy'. Perhaps London is the problem.

I can feel its pull – my own life that I'm avoiding like a depressing friend. But I'm also not sure how much London is feeling my absence. I haven't heard from Morris since the day I told him I was going to stay at my mum's for a bit. I haven't heard from Jen. I've had a few check-in calls from Avi. The only person who I've heard from regularly is Kelly, whose messages I've started to ignore, which only seems to make her want me to send progress photos more. Never has a woman been so interested in topless photos of me, and not only is she a lesbian, I'm paying her.

But whatever magic fuel it was that allowed me to feel constantly hungry and still go to the gym five times a week has disappeared. The supply has run out. I haven't lifted a weight or gone for a run since I got here. I have, on a few occasions, woken up and managed to find my former will to eat raw vegetables and a surplus of dry, unmarinated proteins, but then Mum gets home from work and opens a bottle of wine and a large bag of chilli peanuts and, lo and behold, suddenly I'm dunking a Scotch egg (full-size, not miniature) into a tub of hummus (pine-nut-topped, not low-fat), and I feel strangely guilt-free about the whole sorry business.

I make chilli con carne and we eat dinner in front of the news. The latest opinion polls predict a Conservative majority and Mum huffs and grates more cheese on top of her chilli. I tell her that opinion polls aren't always right and she sighs.

'Labour governments have to be smuggled in,' she says, still grating, the mound of Cheddar getting higher with every huff and sigh. 'And he's not willing to be smuggled.' She points at Jeremy Corbyn on the screen.

We change channels and watch a surprisingly absorbing programme about a family who sold all their possessions to open a hotel in the Costa del Sol. We do the washing-up together and we talk about whether we have ever wanted to open a hotel in the Costa del Sol.

'I'd always be worried about what I might find in the bedsheets,' she whispers as I pass her forks to dry and put in the drawer.

Why do I have to go back to London? Couldn't I just be happy like this? Mince-based dinners in front of the news; a commitment to terrestrial TV programmes following families who start new lives abroad. Why can't I live with my mum until she dies and then live in her house on my own until I die, like I'm a closeted man in the 1960s? Surely I can make some decisions that reduce the risk of heartbreak and disappointment?

I put on my coat and go outside to smoke in the cold. As I light up, I hear the back door open behind me. Mum stands in her coat, arms folded, face stern.

'I'm going to let myself have one,' she says. 'Just one.'

'Why? You haven't had a cigarette in over ten years.'

'The election,' she says, putting her hand out and making a beckoning motion.

'Are you sure?' I say, slowly removing the cigarette packet from my pocket.

'Yes, I really am very upset about it,' she says, grabbing the packet from me. 'And in all honesty I have had a few fags since I gave up, I just didn't want you to worry about me.'

When we go back inside she tells me that cigarettes always give her a taste for a drink and suggests we have one. Sure, I say. Wine? No, it's brandy, she's after. *Hard stuff*, she says with relish. I go find the bottle of brandy and pour us two glasses. She sits down at the kitchen table. I can feel she's gearing up for something. I have that stomach churn I get when I know that someone is going to instigate a conversation about feelings.

'I want to tell you something, Andy,' she says. Here we go.

'Okay,' I say. 'What is it?'

'Getting dumped is never really about getting dumped.'

'What is it about, then?' I ask.

'It's about every rejection you've ever experienced in your entire life. It's about the kids at school who called you names. And the parent who never came back. And the girls who wouldn't dance with you at the disco. And the school girlfriend who wanted to be single when she went to uni. And any criticism at work. When someone says they don't want to be with you, you feel the pain of every single one of those times in life where you felt like you weren't good enough. You live through all of it again.'

'I don't know how to get over it, Mum,' I say. 'At this point I'm so tired of myself. I don't know how to let go of her.'

'You don't let go once. That's your first mistake. You say goodbye over a lifetime. You might not have thought about her for ten years, then you'll hear a song or you'll walk past somewhere you once went together – something will come to the surface that you'd totally forgotten about. And you say another goodbye. You have to be prepared to let go and let go and let go a thousand times.'

'Does it get easier?'

'Much,' she says.

I look into my glass and swirl the brandy around.

'I'm sorry, Mum,' I say. 'That you went through that when you were so young. On your own.'

'I wasn't on my own, I had you,' she says.

I remain fixated on the swirling brandy, worried that if I look at her face I will cry and ruin the moment.

'Right,' she says, necking the last of her drink. 'I'm off to bed.' Her committed avoidance of the awkward will always be my favourite thing about her. She puts both her hands on the table and pulls herself up from the chair. 'Put your earplugs in tonight, my brandy snoring carries through the walls.'

I pour myself one more drink and go outside for one more cigarette. I wonder where she is now – I imagine her doing her long night-time skincare routine or getting a taxi home or doing an impassioned rant in a pub somewhere with her third glass of wine in her hand. And then I say goodbye to her. I wash up the glasses and remember the ongoing dispute we had about how to stack things on the drying rack. I say goodbye. I go upstairs to bed and I remember when she first came to stay here, how strange it was to wake up next to her in my childhood bedroom. I say goodbye. And it feels okay. I say all my goodbyes, ready to no doubt meet her again tomorrow to say goodbye all over again.

Saturday 14th December 2019

I break up with Kelly on the train back to London. I send her a long text apologizing for my lapse in communication and use phrases that I know she'll respond well to, like 'soul-searching' and 'taking a moment to reflect'. I explain that I need to do some work on my insides rather than my outsides, so I'll be hitting pause on the Dream Body Plan™.

Instead, it's a ham-and-cheese sandwich for dinner. Picked it up at the station before I got on the train. I managed to resist getting a couple of beers for the journey. I've managed to resist all of this week, which must be the longest I've gone without a drink since the break-up. I might as well try it for a while. Carbs in, booze out. Who knows? Maybe that will fix me.

My phone sounds. A new message notification.

> Champ – I get it. This love stuff is one hell of a ride. Natalie and I are back together, but we're taking things slow. I wish you well on this journey we call life, Andy. If you ever want to throw some dumb-bells around, you know where I'm at. Heal well, my friend x x x

> Unfortunately you will be charged for membership until the end of January tho because you notified after the 1st of the month x

When I open the front door, I can hear the familiar sound of Morris being busy in a room somewhere.

'It's me, Morris,' I shout and put my bag down, checking

through my unopened post on the side. There are more sounds of miscellaneous tinkering, then he appears out of the living-room door. 'Hi,' I say.

'Hello,' he says, his arms behind his back. 'How have you been?'

'I'm okay, thanks,' I say. There is a pause while I try to think of something else to say, out of practice in the fairly niche discipline of conversation with Morris. 'Rubbish news about the election, obviously.'

'Yes, Giles at the Crouch End Anarchist Society is holding an emergency meeting tomorrow,' he says.

'I didn't realize there were anarchists called Giles.'

'I'm sure that is some sort of insult from your comedy routine, but luckily I am in a good mood, so I don't mind.'

I look at Morris and notice something different about him.

'*Morris?* Good mood?' I say. 'What's going on?'

'Well. I have had a pretty fantastic week,' he says, disappearing into the living room and returning with a piece of paper. 'You will not believe this. Look,' he says, waving the paper in front of me. 'Look at this!' I hold it and he points at two swirling initials at the top of the headed paper: *J.A.*

'What's J.A.?'

'Read it,' he says, grinning.

Dearest Morris,

I wanted to write to you to say thank you. I have read all your letters over recent years with great interest. I was particularly pleased to see that your efforts to acknowledge the Beatles history of your house have been rightly noted by the press. This can only be an encouraging step forward. I also appreciate your thoughts on my case and I have taken a lot of your advice on board. Thank you also for offering monetary support – these donations are not needed at this time, but I am grateful for your generosity.

Morris – I also wanted to write to you to tell you this: you are an important and invaluable member of our society. Without people like you, the corruption of this world would remain hidden in plain sight. Your mission to shine a light on falsehoods is something I very much understand and respect. You may well be met with cynicism or even ridicule, but you are on the right side of history. One day, many years from now, people will look back on citizens like you – those who held people in power to account – and they will know you were one of the ones to whom we should have listened. There is an Australian saying that you may be aware of: to be 'all sizzle and no steak'. A man can speak many words, can sizzle with the best of them. But action is what matters and, for this, you will always have my admiration.

Regards,
Julian

'Oh my God,' I say in disbelief. 'So – he's been reading your letters? He knows who you are?'

'It seems that, yes, he does,' he says gleefully, taking the letter back from me and looking at it with a similar amount of disbelief.

'I can't . . .' I struggle to find the right words. 'Can't get my head around this.'

'Well,' he says, carefully folding the letter up. 'There we are.' He is so full of energy that he slightly bounces up and down on the spot as he speaks. He glances down at my bag. 'Are you staying? Or on your travels again?'

'I'm staying,' I say. 'For good. I just needed a bit of time away. This break-up I think I mentioned to you. I just had a bad moment with it all. But I'm feeling better now.'

Morris stops bouncing and gives me one of his nods.

'Good,' he says. 'Would you like a glass of water or a cup of tea?'

'I'm okay,' I say. 'Thanks.'

'I'm actually just about to listen to a radio programme –'

'Yes, that's fine, I'm going upstairs. I did have something I'd like to ask you, Morris. And I really won't be offended if the answer is no.'

His face twitches. 'All right,' he says slowly.

'I wanted to know if you'd like to come to my mum's for Christmas. She'd like to meet you, and there's a room you can stay in, if you'd like to stay. Or you can just come for the day if you'd prefer that. My aunties will be there and a couple of cousins, but it's not too crowded. And it's just standard Christmas stuff. Booze, food. *The Snowman*.'

He frowns and narrows his eyes as I wait for his reply.

'Well, I'd have to wash the curtains next week, then.'

'Okay,' I say. 'I can help take them down, if you like.'

'Good,' he says, contemplating the proposition some more. 'Yes. All right, then.'

'Good,' I say.

I pick up my rucksack and reach for the banister to go upstairs. He walks back into the living room.

'If I had a son –' he suddenly says.

I turn to look at him, hands behind his back again, anxious eyes staring into nowhere.

'If he asked me for any advice about . . . personal matters – personal relationships – I wouldn't have a whole lot to say, because I don't know a whole lot about it. But I would say that –' He stops himself and makes a sound of a half-formed word, then stops himself again. He takes a breath and speaks in an uncharacteristically unhurried way. 'Life is a bit more difficult for women. More difficult than it is for us, I mean. And you don't need to ask them to explain why or understand it all. You just need to be nice to them.' He looks up at me nervously. 'Do you understand what I'm saying?'

'I think I do, yes,' I say.

He walks into the other room and turns on the radio.

I switch on the bedside light in my room and chuck my bag on my bed. I unpack my clothes, tidy up, message the boys to tell them I'm around, message Mum to tell her I got home okay and to set an extra place at the table for Morris at Christmas. I message Emery and ask him if he's free to meet up this week because I want his advice on an idea for a new show. Then I sit at my desk, open my laptop and write.

Dear Jon,

A real Dear Jon letter, how perfect is that?! Who knew you'd get dumped twice in the same amount of months. See, I'm one paragraph in and I've already fucked this.

I'm writing this because I can't say any of this to you face-to-face. I've spent the last few months questioning a lot of my friendships and wondering what their purpose is, if not to work through big emotional things together. But I now realize: I don't want that. And I know you've all been there for me in other ways. Maybe not in the literal sense, but I know you all would have done anything to fix me other than listening to me talk and allowing me to be sad without solutions. And now I am writing this letter rather than picking up the phone and talking to you because, despite everything I know, I just don't want to, and I don't think you want me to either.

I lost my mind when Jen broke up with me. I'm pretty sure it's been the subject of a few of your WhatsApp conversations and more power to you, because I would need to vent about me if I'd been friends with me for the last six months. I don't want it to have been in vain, and I wanted to tell you what I've learnt.

If you do a high-fat, high-protein, low-carb diet and join a gym, it will be a good distraction for a while and you will lose fat and gain muscle, but you will run out of steam and eat normally again and put all the weight back on. So maybe don't bother. Drunkenness is another idea. I was in blackout for most of the first two months and I think that's fine, it got me through the evenings (and the occasional afternoon). You'll have to do a lot of it on your own, though, because no one is free to meet up any more. I think that's fine for a bit. It was for me until someone walked past me drinking from a whisky miniature while I waited for a night bus, put five quid in my hand and told me to keep warm. You're the only person I've ever told this story.

None of your mates will be excited that you're single again. I'm probably your only single mate and even I'm not that excited. Generally the experience of being single at thirty-five will feel different to any other time you've been single and that's no bad thing.

When your ex moves on, you might become obsessed with the bloke in a way that is almost sexual. Don't worry, you don't want to fuck him, even though it will feel a bit like you do sometimes.

If you open up to me or one of the other boys, it will feel good in the moment and then you'll get an emotional hangover the next day. You'll wish you could take it all back. You may even feel like we've enjoyed seeing you so low. Or that we feel smug because we're winning at something and you're losing. Remember that none of us feel that.

You may become obsessed with working out why exactly she broke up with you and you are likely to go fully, fully nuts in your bid to find a satisfying answer. I can save you a lot of time by letting you know that you may well never work it out. And even if you did work it out, what's the purpose of it? Soon enough, some girl is going to be crazy about you for some undefinable reason and you're not going to be interested in her for some undefinable reason. It's all so random and unfair – the people we want to be with don't want to be with us and the people who want to be with us are not the people we want to be with.

Really, the thing that's going to hurt a lot is the fact that someone doesn't want to be with you any more. Feeling the absence of someone's company and the absence of their love are two different things. I wish I'd known that earlier. I wish I'd known that it isn't anybody's job to stay in a relationship they don't want to be in just so someone else doesn't feel bad about themselves.

Anyway. That's all. You're going to be okay, mate.

Andy

PS I've enclosed a book called 'Why Elephants Cry'. Crucially, it is not a self-help book. It is a science book. It's not that useful for getting over a break-up, but it's nice to always have something on you to read because your phone is going to be drained of battery for the next few weeks from stalking your ex or using dating apps.

PPS We never have to discuss or even mention this letter, in fact probably best if we don't.

Dear Jen

I am never sending this to you. I don't know what I'll do with it afterwards. I probably shouldn't keep it. Avi thinks my main life problem is that I'm locked in a prison of my own nostalgia. I thought this was bollocks and then after he pointed it out I walked past an Ikea lamp in my GP 's reception that I realized I had once owned and I felt a strange longing that could only be described as a deep psychological problem.

I'll write this list you suggested and then I'll throw it away, which seems a bit pointless, but I'm willing to try anything now. Any mad therapy exercise, any ritual, any poignant sequence stolen from a film about divorce.

Reasons Why I Loved Being With Jen

I love what a good friend you are. You're really engaged with the lives of the people you love. You organize lovely experiences for them. You make an effort with them, you're patient with them, even when they're sidetracked by their children and can't prioritize you in the way you prioritize them.

You've got a generous heart and it extends to people you've never even met, whereas I think that everyone is out to get me. I used to say you were naive, but really I was jealous that you always thought the best of people. I wish I was someone who could leave bags on display in a car without thinking they're going to get nicked and could make genuinely enthusiastic conversation with a door-to-door charity worker without thinking they're going to come back and burgle my house.

You are a bit too anxious about being seen to be a good person and you definitely go a bit overboard with your left-wing politics to prove a point to everyone. But I know you really do care. I know you'd sign petitions and help people in need and volunteer at the homeless shelter at Christmas even if no one knew about it. And that's more than can be said for a lot of us.

I love how quickly you read books and how absorbed you get in a good story. I love watching you lie on the sofa reading one from cover-to-cover. It's like I'm in the room with you but you're in a whole other galaxy.

I love that you're always trying to improve yourself. Whether it's running marathons or setting yourself challenges on an app to learn French or the fact you go to therapy every week. You work hard to become a better version of yourself. I think I probably didn't make my admiration for this known and instead it came off as irritation, which I don't really feel at all.

I love how dedicated you are to your family, even when they're annoying you. Your loyalty to them wound me up sometimes, but it's only because I wish I came from a big family.

I love that you always know what to say in conversation. You ask the right questions and you know exactly when to talk and when to listen. Everyone loves talking to you because you make everyone feel important.

I love your style. I know you think I probably never noticed what you were wearing or how you did your hair, but I loved seeing how you get ready, sitting cross-legged in front of the full-length mirror in our bedroom while you did your make-up, even though there was a mirror on the dressing table.

I love that you're mad enough to swim in the English sea in November and that you'd pick up spiders in the bath with your bare hands. You're brave in a way that I'm not.

I love how free you are. You're a very free person, and I never gave you the satisfaction of saying it, which I should have done. No one knows it about you because of your boring, high-pressure job and your stuffy upbringing, but I know what an adventurer you are underneath all that.

I love that you had an ecstasy pill in your pocket on our third date, and that you got drunk at Jackson's christening and you always wanted to have one more drink at the pub and you never complained about getting up early to go to work with a hang-over. Other than Avi, you are the person I've had the most fun with in my life.

And even though I gave you a hard time for always trying to impress your dad, I actually found it very adorable because it made me see the child in you and the teenager in you, and if I could time-travel to anywhere in history, I swear, Jen, the only place I'd want to go is to the house where you grew up and hug you and tell you how beautiful and clever and funny you are. That you are spectacular even without all your sports trophies and music certificates and incredible grades and Oxford acceptance.

I'm sorry that I loved you so much more than I liked myself, that must have been a lot to carry. I'm sorry I didn't take care of you the way you took care of me. And I'm sorry I didn't take care of myself, either. I need to work on it. I'm pleased that our break-up taught me that. I'm sorry I went so mental.

I love you. I always will. I'm glad we met.

Andy

Friday 31st January 2020

I check myself in the mirror one last time. It's six p.m. In exactly ninety minutes' time I'll be on stage with my new show. The newsreader on the radio tells me that we have five more hours of being in the European Union. Surely I can find a good gag about that? I know Brexit jokes were over before the referendum even happened, but I'm not in the market for a breakfast pun. There must be some sort of sophisticated parallel I can draw between breaking up with the EU and Jen breaking up with me.

When I go downstairs, Morris is kneeling by the doormat. He has a pair of rubber gloves on and he appears to be disinfecting the post with a bottle of antibacterial spray. I don't even bother asking why any more.

'Break a leg tonight, Andy,' he says.

'Thank you, Morris,' I say, stepping over him.

'I'm still hoping to make it to tomorrow's performance, but it depends where we are with cases.'

'Okay, Morris,' I say, again, totally at peace with not understanding what he's talking about. 'Let's see how we go.'

When I get to the venue, I do a soundcheck and then go over my notes one last time in the wings. I watch people file in, but can't yet see Jen. I check my phone again to see if she replied to my last text, but she hasn't. At 7.25, I prop my phone on a stool, open voice memos and press record so I can listen back to the show tomorrow.

At 7.30, the music starts. I do one final scan of the audience and I see her. Third row back – sleepy blue eyes, that nose that changes shape with every turn of her head. She looks up and ahead at the stage. I try to read her face but it's expressionless. The lights fade for my cue.

Reasons Why It's Good I'm Not With Andy

He over-orders food and eats to a point where he's so full he's uncomfortable, then complains about it for an hour.

Complains too much.

Has never and will never go to therapy, so he's stuck in the same behaviour patterns while leaving his issues unaddressed and I would always have to bear the brunt of that.

Not only would he never go to therapy, he looks down on it and sees it as self-indulgent, so he never appreciated the work I try to do on myself or our relationship.

He thinks being ambitious means wanting to get accolades and praise for something, rather than wanting to get better at something.

Moody when his comedian friends succeeded.

No interest in going anywhere new and would use my passion for travel as an example of our class divide, which may well be true but it was often said in a passive-aggressive manner.

Would cry at the stupidest stuff like when we saw The National at Glastonbury, or when we visited a stone circle in Cumbria, or when Freddie Mercury sings the line about taking his bows in 'We Are the Champions'. And he could never explain why this kind of thing set him off, even though it was obvious he couldn't cry or even talk about what he really wanted to cry and talk about, which is that he never knew his dad.

Self-pitying. Has a distorted view of how everyone else sees him because of his low self-esteem but also because he likes wallowing.

Moaned and moaned and moaned about how jealous he was that every podcast in the top-ten chart is hosted by a comedian, to the point where he couldn't even listen to any of them, and yet refused to come up with any ideas for his own podcast.

Too nostalgic. Couldn't live in the present. Will always think that yesterday was better than right now. He genuinely believes the peak of his life was when he was in his early twenties and doesn't understand that he has the power to make the best moment of his life the moment he's living in.

Used to say 'That should be an album title!' when he wasn't really listening to people and didn't know what to say.

He would never admit it, but he is obsessed with being famous. Whenever he posted something online, he would refresh the app every minute for at least three hours.

His music obsessions seemed romantic at first, but became boring, completionist and nerdy.

Tendency to be dramatic, especially in arguments, e.g. the time he shouted 'WE CANNOT LIVE OUR LIVES LIKE THIS' in a row about me being twenty minutes late for him.

Talks about women's issues in a chin-strokey, armchair-academic way which he thinks makes him a feminist ally but actually is quite tone deaf.

Insecure.

Needy.

Codependent.

Finds my family annoying, which I do as well, but it's his job as my partner to at least pretend he doesn't hate them, and he stopped pretending after about a year.

His mood was too altered by the wins and losses of Aston Villa.

Losing his hair at the back. This isn't a problem in itself but his years of obsessing over it would kill me.

Dysfunctional friendships. Those boys are nice, but they don't really talk to each other or support each other. They just get drunk and take the piss out of each other. Sometimes I felt like I was the only way he could access his emotions, which was too much pressure on me.

He will always consider his job to be more important than my job because he thinks that his has artistic integrity and mine is corporate and meaningless.

Lacks curiosity. This really hit home when we went to the British Museum together and I realized he was only interested in the things he already knew about, eager to give me extra facts at each display that he recognized, but rushing past the ones that he didn't.

On more than one occasion I watched him go to the gym then come back and eat a whole plain loaf of bread.

Made our break-up as difficult for me as possible.

Friday 31st January 2020

My mum has this story about me that she loves to tell. Every Saturday between the ages of seven and eight, I would wake up and say it was my wedding day. My parents and my brothers and sister had to call me The Bride all day. If we went anywhere – the shop, the park, a family friend's house – I insisted on wearing an old white lace curtain on my head and my white Holy Communion dress. At some point in the day I would have to take the artificial flowers that were in the vase in the conservatory and throw them behind me for someone to catch. Then I'd do the whole thing again the following week.

I've thought about this story a lot. I've wondered where that instinct came from, so strongly. Was it Ariel and Eric's wedding that did it? Prince Charming and Cinderella's? Was it the photos of my parents on their wedding day – Mum in her high-necked, bishop-sleeved 1970s dress, cascade bouquet of lilies falling down her skirt? And I've wondered why the desire left me, so suddenly, never to return.

I come from a long line of monogamists. Both sets of grandparents were married for seventy years. My great-grandparents were the same. My mum and dad met at university and married a few years later. I don't know if it's a Catholic thing or a conformist thing, but everyone in my family gets married, has a big wedding, has a big family and never divorces. Growing up, it was always assumed that's what was going to happen to me and my three siblings. Well, two siblings. My little brothers were destined for it. I was destined for it. Miranda, the eldest, was not, because Miranda came out as gay on her eighteenth birthday. From that moment on, my parents never referred to Miranda's future partner or Miranda's future children. Instead, I was burdened with two daughters'-worth of marital expectations. 'Jen's wedding' was often discussed in our family as an event as inevitable as death. Would Jen have Granny's engagement ring? Would Jen hold the reception at Chiswick House Gardens? (Ironically, it is Miranda who got married and had kids before any of us. She jokes that she only did it as a favour, to take some of the heat off me.)

The propaganda within our family and our family's social circles was that my mum and dad had a very successful marriage. They supported each other's ambitions, they made each other laugh, they were a great parenting team. This was my perception of their relationship until one day when I was thirteen and was sent home from school with a bad tummy. My mum was away on holiday with her sister and the school couldn't get hold of my dad. So I took the bus home like I always did and turned the key in the door expecting an empty house. When I went to the kitchen, a woman was leaning on the counter, drinking from a mug. She was wearing my mother's peach silk dressing gown. I stood in the kitchen, my heavy school bag still over my shoulder.

'Who are you?' I asked.

Dad rushed into the kitchen, looking exactly as he always looked when he came home from work, except his hair was wet because he'd just got out of the shower.

'Why are you home early?' he asked.

I didn't take my eyes off the woman, who put down the mug and wrapped her arms around herself in a gesture of either modesty or defensiveness.

'I was sick at school, they sent me home,' I said. 'Who are you?' I asked again.

'This is a colleague,' he said. 'We work together when I'm in

China. We're on our way to a meeting and I said she could come here to freshen up as she's just got off a long flight.'

I looked from her to Dad, then back to her again, unable to detect the exact lie but sure that there was one.

Later, he sat on the edge of my bed and suggested that I didn't tell Mum about this. When I asked why, he said that she'd worry that he was working too hard – entertaining clients and brokers around the clock as well as doing his job. And I knew this didn't make any sense but he used grown-up words that made me feel like I was safe, like there were missing pieces of information that I didn't understand but made this fine. Clients and brokers. Entertaining.

From that point onwards, I noticed details about my parents' marriage that I never noticed before. I realized that my mum and dad had met at university, had both obtained degrees, and yet my mum had not had a job since she married my dad. I noticed that Dad would tell stories and Mum would laugh loudly or say 'Isn't your father clever?' and this is what Dad would call 'sharing a sense of humour', which he credited for their successful marriage. And I realized that their concept of teamwork in parenting was that my mum was left for weeks at a time to raise us as if she were a single mother while she boasted that her husband was working in 'the Far East'.

Dad and I never spoke about the woman again, but she appeared as an unseen, unnamed cameo in our relationship for years afterwards. There were the few times I saw a number saved as a single letter ringing him. Or the presents he would bring me back from China, each trinket feeling like hush money.

I decided I had to do everything in my power to make my dad stay. I had to get eleven A★s in my GCSE exams to make my dad so proud of me that he never wanted to leave. So I did. I had to become captain of the netball team and captain of the hockey team and get a place at Oxford just like him, at the college that he went to, to study Philosophy, Politics and Economics just like he did. Every time he told me how proud of me he was, I felt like I'd bought a little more time.

I didn't take a gap year and, when I graduated from Oxford, I had planned on taking a year out to move back home, save some money and spend six months travelling through South America. But Dad encouraged me to apply for graduate placements at insurance firms 'for practice' and I was offered a job. I took it, worried that it was a fluke, and shelved South America for another year. My work didn't stimulate me, but the fear and stress and competition that came with it did. I saved and planned for a travel sabbatical, but every time I felt it was the moment to do it, I would be offered a new role or head-hunted for a new job at another company. It was like my career was my bad boyfriend – it sensed every time I was going to leave it and, at that exact moment, would promise me all sorts of things to make me stay.

My twenties in London filled up with everything other than serious relationships – going out with friends, staying in with friends, flatshares, sex, raves, runs, spin classes, weddings, promotions, reading the books that magazines told me to read, watching the films that newspaper supplements told me to watch, using all my holiday days as cleverly as possible to make time for wild weeks with the girls and long weekends with the family. People didn't really notice that I was always single because I had so many other things going on and they always wanted to hear about them.

But when I turned thirty, it all changed. My lack of long-term relationship could no longer be seen as an accident and instead became a problem. Everyone wanted to talk to me about my 'attachment style', each of them asking if I'd read the book or done the quiz like they were the first person to suggest it. 'I just don't understand it,' my mum would say, every time she said goodbye to me. 'You're such a fabulous girl – so clever, so attractive. I don't understand why they're not lining up.'

I don't know what made me decide I wanted to be in a relationship. I don't know whether it was something I actually wanted, or whether it was something I got frustrated with myself for not wanting. Did I get bored of myself? Did I become too familiar with the rhythms of single life? Did I start to believe what everyone was telling me? That I was going to run out of time and get left behind? Or was it that I thought that being in a relationship might prove something? That I wasn't unfeminine or unlovable or incapable of being a grown-up? That I was, in fact, perfectly normal like everyone else.

For my thirty-first birthday, I hired a cabin in the middle of the woods for the weekend, taking Jane and a few other close female friends. We went for long walks in the day and spent the evenings getting stoned around our poorly made fires. Every night the conversation would turn to all of their partners and I listened to these women I love talk about the men they love with despair and adoration and amusement and frustration. And I realized that this was something I wanted to try – not just being in love, but being in this club. I wanted to fling up the bonnet of a relationship and work on it and tinker with it and talk to all my friends about what I found and ask for their advice. I wanted to try this thing that had absorbed most of my friends for years: being someone's girlfriend and everything that comes with it.

'I think I'm ready to meet someone this year,' I said at the end of a drunken night in the birthday cabin. They all seemed excited, like I had announced my intention to move to the same neighbourhood as them. Which, in a way, I had.

I was naive to think that finding a boyfriend would be as easy as deciding I wanted a boyfriend. I asked everyone I knew to set me up with someone.

'You're in a bad cycle of the thirties to be single,' Jane said. 'The divorces haven't happened yet. Thirty-five will be the age when all your options open up again.' But everyone around me was telling me that I shouldn't wait until I was thirty-five. Being single and thirty-five seemed to be the thing that every woman I knew wanted to avoid at all costs. I had no reason to be terrorized by the thought of being on my own in four years' time, and yet I couldn't stop myself from registering everyone's fear on my behalf.

I dated all the men I was supposed to date – doctors, lawyers, men in finance. Men called Tom and James and Charlie. We never made it past date three. Either the conversation was flat or the attraction was missing and there was a polite, unspoken agreement that we wouldn't be seeing each other again. Or I was interested in meeting again and they weren't – always for the same reason of not looking for a relationship. 'I'm not ready for something serious and I don't think I will be for a while,' said a long-time single, never-married and childless man, aged forty-one, without a hint of doubt. He was clearly unaware of the expiration date marked 'thirty-five' that so many women think is slapped on them like a discounted chicken on display in a supermarket. *Good for him*, I thought.

Jane had told me about Avi's friend, Andy, before her birthday party. 'Great for a fuck, but nothing more,' had been her first words. He was charming, she said. And funny and sweet. But he was shambolic – a gorgeous, overgrown schoolboy who needed someone to take care of him. He'd been single for a few months, the first time he'd been on his own since he was a teenager.

I was attracted to Andy from the moment I met him – attracted in a way I haven't been attracted to a man before. I was addicted to his company. He introduced me to new culture and new ideas. He made me laugh. He was so fun and free of the worries that constricted every other thirty-something I knew. I loved how unbothered he was by convention. I loved that he didn't care that he was in his early thirties and had no savings and was living in a houseshare, because he was pursuing his passion. I respected his work ethic, the odd jobs he would take to pay his rent, the distances he would travel on a weeknight for a ten-minute comedy slot in front of a bunch of pissed students. I loved that he didn't really care about all the stupid stuff I'd been brought up to believe mattered. He only cared about comedy and music, his mum and his friends, and having a good time. He was like nobody I'd ever met before.

I liked him so much that I tried something I'd never done with a man before – I held off having sex. I wanted to take it slowly, having been told that friendship makes the best foundation for a relationship. I pretended to be on my period the first night we met and I pretended like that would stop me from inviting him to stay over. He went to Edinburgh the next day for a month and we got to know each other over the phone before we had our first proper date. I was determined to get this right.

For all his insecurities that I later discovered, he presented as a hugely self-assured person and it was a confidence that was infectious. I'd never before had first-time sex that didn't involve a carefully designed lamp scheme and draping myself on the bed in a way that is flattering but looks spontaneous to the male eye. But I didn't need to bother with any of that with Andy – the more myself I was, the more turned on he was. He was an intimacy junkie and he wanted to be as close to me as possible. I'd never felt so physically comfortable with anyone before. The first morning we woke up together, he buried his face in my armpit and kissed it.

There was something about my attraction to him that was beyond the grasp of my own understanding. He was the absolute opposite of what I'd been told to look for in a partner. He drank and smoked too much, he had no money, he had the neuroses of a beta male and the know-it-all confidence of an alpha male. He was self-reflective when it suited him, but not when it didn't. He was not husband material. And yet everything in my body was telling me to grab this man and hold on to him and love him with everything I had. I remember how good he smelt. Every time I inhaled him, my body would tell my brain that this was someone to make time for, introduce my friends to, do a weekly shop with, stand still with, hold hands with on the tube, invite into my home, lie next to in my bed.

I remained very happy for a while. It was my first serious relationship and I'd chosen a pro – I felt like Andy was teaching me how to do long-term monogamy. None of the changing phases of it bothered him. He didn't get freaked out when we went for a fortnight without sex, our first big row didn't make him think we were going to break up. When we stopped going out on drunken all-night dates and instead ordered food in and went to bed early, he didn't worry that the fun had gone. I followed his lead. The light-headed, dizzying feeling of our first year left me and something brand new came in its place. Contentment is probably the closest word for it. My favourite sound became the turn of Andy's key in the front door when he let himself into my flat after he came back from a gig late.

I soon realized that inevitability of every relationship: the things which initially draw you to each other become the exact things that irritate you the most. I'd loved Andy's nonconformity, which became irritation at the lack of structure in his life. He'd loved my independence, which became an annoyance at my remoteness. In the early days, he explained away my lateness with my free-spiritedness. After a while he thought it was selfishness. I used to love that he wanted to make everyone laugh because I thought it was a sign of his generosity. At some point

I saw it for what it really was – neediness. I realized he saw every social interaction as a miniature gig and therefore an opportunity for acceptance or rejection. His mood was so dependent on how he felt these conversational performances went and I hated being wise to it.

But the good far outweighed the bad. And I almost enjoyed those initial difficulties between us – it was new to me. I was finally under the hood of a relationship, torch in hand, fiddling with the engine. At last, I had something to offer to my friends when the conversation of boyfriends came up. Being unsatisfied was a part of the relationship experience, and the relationship experience was exactly what I wanted.

We moved in together after eighteen months. Andy was spending all his time at my flat so it made sense for him to stop paying rent for a room he didn't live in. What would have made the most sense would have been for Andy to move into my flat and for us to split the mortgage, but I was told this was not an option. He felt it was important that our first home together was completely equal – a leap we were taking together, with equal amounts of risk and faith. But it was illogical. Andy's budget for his portion of the rent would not get us what we were after if I matched it, so I ended up paying two-thirds of it and renting out my flat to cover my mortgage.

The conversation about children started coming up a lot at around the two-year mark. Andy had always told me he wanted a family; I'd always told him I wasn't sure. Seeing as he was the one who wouldn't have to carry a baby, or birth or nurse a baby, we agreed we would revisit the subject every year or so but otherwise try to stay present in our relationship and not talk too much about the future. This became impossible when our world was overrun with babies. There was a baby overpopulation crisis between 2017 and 2019 – there were suddenly more babies than friends. As thirty-five approached, nearly every woman I know got pregnant, keen to hand in their homework to mother nature before the famous deadline. We had fewer and fewer people to hang out with, swallowed up by the sinking sand of parenthood.

My godchildren multiplied. My social life was scheduled by the nap times and feeding schedules of babies. I held newborns on L-shaped sofas and pushed prams in the park and entertained toddlers in the pub while trying to have a conversation with their exhausted parents about anything other than babies and children. I waited for the moment when I would realize this was something I wanted and it never arrived. Andy kept telling me that no one is ever ready to have a baby and that it will always feel terrifying. The more he said this, the more resentful I became. The risk felt so much higher for me and it wasn't something he would ever truly acknowledge. This baby's life would rely on my maternity leave, my savings, my body, my career. I would have to make all the sacrifice while Andy's life could continue mostly as normal. He disingenuously offered to give up comedy and be a stay-at-home dad. We both knew that would never happen.

And then I began to get this feeling. A worry that I could sometimes block out but never fully shake off. I started to feel doubt. Doubt that extended far beyond the question of whether I wanted to be a mother. Did I want any of it? Did I want to be someone's girlfriend? Was it something I could do? In my years of being single, I had said as much to friends, which was always taken as an expression of insecurity or fear. 'You just haven't met the right person,' they'd assure me. But, there I was, with the right person. He wasn't perfect, but I was in love with him and he was in love with me. And yet I could never really understand whether I was in a good relationship or not. I couldn't measure what the reality of long-term love was; what was settling for something when I should be asking for more. For every chatty Friday-night dinner, there was a meal where it felt like we had nothing to say to each other. For every fun pub session, there was a drunken argument. For every night we had sex, there were five nights where we lay in bed on our phones not speaking.

During a flare-up of these thoughts, Andy and I went out for brunch on a Sunday. We'd woken up in two moods that didn't match. We kept missing each other's meaning – everything we said annoyed each other. We ordered eggs and pancakes and said nothing for a while. I had spent the previous evening at the hospital visiting my grandmother, who was very ill and in and out of consciousness. As we waited for our drinks to arrive, I told him of how I sat by her bedside, held her hand and spoke to her even though I didn't know whether she could hear me. I wondered whether this is something we should do for the dying – whether it's an act of companionship or really whether it's an act of indulgence. If she could hear me, was it frustrating for her that she couldn't speak back to me? Was I being selfish? Would the generous act in her last days be to allow for silence, even if it made me feel uncomfortable? To let her lie in the stillness that comes at the very end of a life? He didn't answer. I noticed that his unblinking eyes were stuck in the middle distance and I realized he hadn't been listening.

'Check. Your. Poo,' he said slowly. I didn't understand what he was talking about. I turned around and saw a double-decker bus drive past with a governmental health warning for bowel cancer on the side of it and that as its slogan.

Was this a relationship? Was this what being in love was? Is this what all my friends had accepted as their happy-ever-after?

It was around this time that Miranda and her wife began the process of conceiving a baby with Miranda's egg and a sperm donor. One day, I got a call from Miranda, who told me she needed to see me. I went to her flat, expecting her to tell me that she was pregnant. Instead, she said that the doctor had checked her egg supply and found she had a rapidly diminishing amount. He told her he estimated that she had about six months left to get pregnant using her eggs. She told me it could be hereditary and urged me to get a check-up. I put it to the back of my mind. I had other, more pressing things to prepare for.

I'd been put up for a promotion to become a senior partner at the company. If I got it, it would be the biggest jump in my career so far and would mean running a bigger team, dealing with huge clients and getting a substantial pay rise. I had a month to prepare for my presentation and interview. I knew five male colleagues who were also being considered for the role, and that was only the people they were interviewing in-house, let alone the people they were head-hunting. I'd never been under so much professional pressure.

Also at this exact same time, Andy got his first TV job. He was asked to present a brand-new comedy game show called *Ask or Task*. The premise sounded truly terrible from the off, a weak spin on truth or dare, made competitive for a cash prize. It had a small budget, was on a comedy channel, had a short episode run as a trial period and almost no preparation time, which strongly suggested that Andy was a last-resort casting option. But he didn't mind – *Ask or Task* meant Andy would have a hosting credit and a showreel, and there was talk of it being syndicated in other countries, which could bring him work abroad.

My possible promotion was discussed once. He asked a maximum of three questions about the new role I was applying for, then didn't ask me anything more. During that month, Andy and I lived separate lives as I prepared for the interview and presentation, and he filmed *Ask or Task*. I made him dinner when he came home. I'd run his lines with him before bed.

As the weeks went by and I tried to keep thoughts of fertility and babies out of my mind, I became increasingly resentful that this was not something Andy had to think about. We were both in a potentially life-changing moment of our careers, and he could completely focus on the challenge, whereas I was distracted. Our respective absorption in our own worries made us, for the first time, incompatible as flatmates. I didn't feel like we were teammates any more.

And then, over a period of nine months, a number of things happened. Each individual incident was not enough for me to end my relationship but, collectively, they were.

My granny died.

My granny who'd met my grandfather aged fourteen and who'd never been with another man. My granny who'd had five children and dedicated her life to being a mother. A woman who once told me that all she'd ever wanted was to be a ballet dancer, but her 'good years' were taken up with having babies and then the moment passed her by. A woman who was so dependent on her husband that when he died she had to 'ring a man' and pay him to change a light bulb for her.

In her last weeks, she had moments of lucidity, and I cherished them when I was around to talk to her. One of these conversations happened when it was just me and her in the hospital room.

'I suspect you will never have a husband,' she said, looking at me intently from her bed.

'Would you be upset if that happened?' I asked.

'Your mother would be,' she said, then lowered her voice. 'But I think you would be wise not to.' This surprised me as I had always thought that she and my grandfather had been very happy together.

'Why do you say that?' I asked.

Her hand, spotted in soft-brown splodges, the rails of her bones protruding, flapped gently at me to take it. I cupped it in both of mine.

'You have a home that is yours,' she said. 'And your own money. Don't you?'

'I have a bit of money, yes.'

'And you have your education. And you have your career.' I nodded. 'Then you have everything,' she said.

Mum came back into the room, gabbling about the queue for the coffee machine. Granny gazed at me dreamily. I leant across to kiss her cheek, which was pale and soft as a lily. I left the hospital and thought all afternoon about what she had meant. I got a call early the next morning to say she had died during the night.

A few weeks later, I watched a Joni Mitchell documentary.

I didn't really know her work. Andy was the one who wanted to watch it when we saw it was on TV one night. I enjoyed learning about her and her music, but the part of her story that left the biggest impression on me was when she talked about her long-term boyfriend Graham Nash. He asked her to marry him and, while initially she said yes, she then had a change of heart. She described both her grandmothers, one who was a frustrated poet and musician, so frustrated that she 'kicked the kitchen door off the hinges'. She talked about her other grandmother, who cried for the last time in her life as a teenager because she wanted a piano and was told she would never get one. She felt like she had 'the gene' to live in a way both her grandmothers couldn't. Joni, then a woman in her fifties, said: 'As much as I loved and cared for Graham, I just thought, I'm gonna end up like my grandmother, kicking the door off the hinges, you know what I mean? It's like, I better not. And it broke my heart.'

I cry so rarely, Andy couldn't understand what had moved me so much. I wasn't sure yet either.

My friend Sarah got pregnant.

Well, all my friends got pregnant. Jane was the first, then everyone else followed. But Sarah was different. This was a woman I'd met in my late twenties at a mutual friend's birthday party and we instantly hit it off. She was the first close friend who I felt like I'd really chosen. We weren't in each other's lives because of any obligation to the past or convenience of the present. We had no shared history and we had no reason to spend all our time together. But we did. Our friendship intensified as all our friends had children – she, like me, was unconvinced about having kids. And she, like me, found herself in a relationship in her early thirties where they weren't specifically working towards starting a family.

By the time I was thirty-four, Sarah was my only good friend who hadn't had a baby. Every time there was another pregnancy announcement from a friend, I'd just text the words 'And another one!' and she'd know what I meant.

She became the person I spent most of my free time with other than Andy, because she was the only friend who had any free time. She could meet me for a drink without planning it a month in advance. Our friendship made me feel liberated as well as safe. I looked at her life choices with no sympathy or concern for her. If I could admire her decision to remain child-free, I felt encouraged to admire my own. She made me feel normal. As long as I had our friendship, I wasn't alone and I had reason to believe I was on the right track.

We arranged to meet for dinner in Soho after work on a Friday. The waiter took our drinks order and I asked for our usual – two Dirty Vodka Martinis.

'Er, not for me,' she said. 'A sparkling water, thank you.' I was ready to make a joke about her uncharacteristic abstinence, which she sensed, so as soon as the waiter left she said: 'I'm pregnant.'

I didn't know what to say. I can't imagine the expression on my face was particularly enthusiastic, but I couldn't help it – I was shocked and felt an unwarranted but intense sense of betrayal. In a delayed reaction, I stood up and went to her side of the table to hug her, unable to find words of congratulations. I asked what had made her change her mind and she spoke in vagaries about it 'just being the right time' and wouldn't elaborate any further and give me an answer. And I needed an answer. I needed an answer more than anything that night. I needed to know whether she'd had a realization that I hadn't and, if so, I wanted to know how to get it.

When I woke up the next day, I realized the feeling I was experiencing was not anger or jealousy or bitterness – it was grief. I had no one left. They'd all gone. Of course, they hadn't really gone, they were still my friends and I still loved them. But huge parts of them had disappeared and there was nothing they could do to change that. Unless I joined them in their spaces, on their schedules, with their families, I would barely see them.

And I started dreaming of another life, one completely removed from all of it. No more children's birthday parties, no more christenings, no more barbecues in the suburbs. A life I hadn't ever seriously contemplated before. I started dreaming of what it would be like to start all over again. Because as long as I was here in the only London I knew – middle-class London, corporate London, mid-thirties London, married London – I was in their world. And I knew there was a whole other world out there.

Andy gave my mum a pair of karaoke mics for her birthday.

He knows she's never done karaoke in her life and in fact the most modern song she's ever sung is Handel's 'Messiah' in the church choir. And as I saw her open the gift, trying to think of something polite to say, I thought about how Andy always does whatever Andy wants to do. I thought back on all the presents I'd bought for his mum over the years and how much time I'd put into each of them – how I'd listened every time she said she liked a piece of jewellery I wore or mentioned a book she wanted to read and mentally noted it for her birthday and Christmas. Andy kept laughing to me afterwards about how baffled my mum had looked when she opened the present. And I realized he'd chosen not to be thoughtful but to be funny instead. To no one but himself.

I started to feel single.

This can be divided into three subcategories.

A) I was sick and he didn't look after me. Strep throat. It was agony. I was prescribed antibiotics for the first time since I was a kid and I took my first ever sick day from work. My boss told me to take a week. Every time I spoke to a colleague or a friend, they said, 'Is Andy looking after you?' and my pride wouldn't let me tell them that, no, Andy was not looking after me. He did a gig every night that week, never asked me if I needed anything picking up and, I think, made me one cup of tea.

B) *Ask or Task* rated poorly and was switched to a graveyard time slot so even fewer people watched it. Then he got the news that it wouldn't be recommissioned, but he didn't tell me.

His mum did.

C) I got the promotion and I didn't tell him.

See above.

And I thought: if I feel single, wouldn't it be easier to be single? And then I wouldn't have to worry about disappointing someone or someone disappointing me? When I'm single, I know where I am. I am alone when I'm ill, but I'm not abandoned. I get a promotion and I celebrate with friends, rather than worrying that my good news might make my partner feel insecure. I can navigate the difficulties of being on my own, but I don't think I can navigate the difficulties of this.

Wouldn't it be easier to be single?

I had a fertility check.

Just as my sister had warned, I discovered that I also had an unusually low egg supply. The results were given to me by an IVF doctor who, after she told me the news, asked if I was in a relationship. I answered yes and she wiped her brow in a comedy gesture of relief. 'Okay, phew!' she said. She told me to start trying for a baby immediately. I said I didn't want to try for a baby immediately. She then advised that I freeze my eggs or, better yet, embryos with Andy's sperm. I told her I didn't have time at the moment to go through a cycle of injecting hormones into myself every night and possibly going crazy because of it. I couldn't take time off work for the procedure under general anaesthetic to have my eggs retrieved. And she said that if I didn't have time to freeze my eggs, how on earth did I think I'd have time to have a baby? Wasn't it time I prioritized this? Because if I didn't prioritize this after the facts she'd just given me, when would I?

And I watched her go on like this, with her anguished expression and her tone of judgement and her statistics that were meant to terrify me into handing over all my bank details and filling out a form. And I felt rage like I'd never felt before.

'Don't talk to me like that,' I said.

Her eyes widened in surprise.

'Excuse me?' she said, holding her hand to her chest over her white coat. 'You have paid for a service that gives you all the information you need about your fertility, and that's what I'm doing. I am empowering you by giving you all the facts.'

'No you're not,' I said, standing up and putting on my coat.

'You're trying to frighten me. This isn't about empowerment, this is about shame. I can't believe you think it's okay to speak to me like this.' I picked up my handbag.

'It seems you already know everything, but is there anything else you'd like to ask?' she said icily.

'No thank you,' I said, leaving her office.

I didn't want to know all these words, charged with urgency and crisis. I didn't feel like they related to me. Hadn't I just turned twenty-one? Hadn't I just left university? Hadn't my life only just begun? I couldn't fathom how I had got here so quickly and how I could be expected to make such enormous decisions while I still felt so young. How had this happened?

I didn't know who to call but Jane, who told me to come round to her house. She made me dinner and banished Avi to childcare duties, so I could talk freely without worrying that he would overhear and tell Andy, who I still hadn't told about any of this.

'I think fertility doctors are like hairdressers,' she said. 'They act like everything's a disaster, because all they do is think about hair all day. But really – split ends are not a disaster. And they don't actually believe that anyone is going to do a leave-in conditioning treatment once a week, do they? No one's going to do that. No one has the time, and yet everyone's hair is fine.'

'Are you saying that freezing my eggs is like a leave-in conditioning treatment?' I asked.

'I suppose I am,' she shrugged. 'You'll find a way to make your hair work without it.'

On the way home, I got an email from the clinic advising that I freeze my eggs, with all the different options and payment plans attached. I replied, telling them to take my address off their mailing list and never email me again.

My parents asked Andy how his TV show went.

And not only did he say, 'Really well,' when they asked him if there would be a second series he said, 'It's looking likely.' I wasn't angry at him for lying, I was just so sad that he felt like he needed to. I realized quite how uncomfortable he must be in himself and how rubbish my family must make him feel. And I hated it.

Jane started saying 'Welcome to being in a relationship' to me over and over again.

I'd tell her about all the compromises I was making and how much Andy's self-absorption could irritate me and how I'd noticed that he'd stopped finding me sexy and started finding me sweet – that he used to grab my bum and kiss me, and now he kissed me on the head and pulled the zipper of my jacket up and down in a cutesy way. 'Wait till he stops finding you sweet,' she said. 'That's a whole other phase.'

I told her about how much time was spent comforting him and buoying him up and getting him out of low moods. How his emotions were always more important than mine – that when we had arguments, his feelings were discussed as facts and mine were interrogated as fabrications. 'Jen,' she said matter-of-factly, 'do you even want a boyfriend?'

I asked her if this was all stuff she put up with and she nodded. 'Welcome to being in a relationship,' she said.

And I thought: *I don't want to be welcome here. I don't want to get comfortable here.*

I challenged a political view of Andy's, which led to an argument, and he said: 'I would love you no matter what your opinions were.'

And I know he was telling the truth. He would have loved me unquestioningly and stubbornly forever. And I don't know if I want to be loved like that.

★

I told my therapist that being in my first long-term relationship made me realize my life had been just as great before, just a different kind of great.

And she told me that this was not something I should ignore.

We went away with Jane, Avi and their kids for New Year's Eve.

We booked a long weekend in Ireland. It should have been lovely – we'd rented a gorgeous cottage, we were right by the sea. Andy's best friend and my best friend were married, we loved them, we loved their boys. It was a cosy and convenient set-up and we were lucky that life had worked out so neatly for all of us. And yet I couldn't shake the feeling all weekend that Andy and I were playing the part of a couple. Avi and Andy would talk about football and jokingly complain about how we, their female partners, 'say one thing but always mean another!' Jane and I would stand in the kitchen drinking wine, talking about how our boyfriends always got too much hair cut off when they went to the barber. The whole time, I felt like we were two couples rather than four people, and I missed feeling like a singular entity with my friends. I felt like I was losing myself.

I saw my sister repetitively drop a phone on her head.

Andy and I had gone round for lunch with her, her wife and their newborn baby daughter. At one point, Miranda had slipped off with the baby so she could feed her and put her down for a nap. An hour or so later, I went to the loo and walked past Miranda, who was in her bedroom, perched on the end of her bed, crying, dropping her mobile phone on her head again and again.

'Miranda, what are you doing?' I said, going into her room and sitting next to her. There was a red mark on her forehead.

'I dropped a phone on her head,' she said, in between gasps for air.

'Whose head?'

'The baby's!' she wailed. 'I was feeding her and checking my phone with one hand and I accidentally dropped it on her head.'

'Okay, don't worry,' I said, putting my arm around her. 'These things happen.'

'I shouldn't have been checking my phone!' she cried.

'Miranda – it's okay.'

'I'm trying to work out if I hurt her, I want to know how much pain she felt,' she said, picking up her phone to drop it on herself again. I grabbed it out of her hand and placed it on the floor.

'Come here,' I said, pulling my big sister into my arms. I held her and rocked her gently and she wept and wept and wept.

And I was reminded that you should really want to have a baby if you're going to have a baby.

Andy's friend Jon and his girlfriend went travelling for a month and we agreed to look after their cat, called Doris.

I changed Doris's litter, I fed her, I gave her her medicine, I played with her when she yowled. Andy did nothing but stroke her when she sat next to him on the sofa.

My sister took me to a psychic for my Christmas present.

It was sort of a joke present. She knows I don't believe in all that stuff and this was further confirmed when the psychic spent the first ten minutes speaking in generalizations that could apply to almost anyone: 'you're at a crossroads', 'big changes ahead', 'you're often pulled between your head and your heart'. And then she told me a spirit was coming through. My grandmother.

'She's here with us,' she said, closing her eyes.

'What is she saying?' I asked.

'She's not saying anything,' she said, nodding gently, her hands aloft in concentration. 'But I'm seeing her kicking a door.

Does this mean anything to you? She's kicking a door right off its hinges.'

And I went to the loo and threw up.

I went to Paris with Andy and we had a row on the Eurostar before we even got there.

He was in a foul mood because his agent had rung him that morning to talk about his future. She'd said that Andy needed to come up with new material, that he had been relying on the same safe stuff in his routine for years. She suggested he devise a brand-new show, one with a theme and a story rather than just jokes, and that he take it to Edinburgh and tour it. Andy was ranting about how his agent was supposed to support him, and I gently said that I thought this was his agent supporting him by pushing him into the next stage of his career. He snapped at me and said I wasn't being supportive either. We drank the Marks & Spencer champagne we'd bought at Kings Cross in silence until we got to Gare du Nord.

The next day, as we stood in front of the Venus de Milo in the Louvre, I looked over his shoulder and saw that he was googling himself.

Specifically, he was googling 'Did *Ask or Task* air in France?'

I know why he was doing it: it was because he was feeling sore about the conversation with his agent and he needed reassurance that he wasn't wasting his life, that his work had had some impact on the world. He wanted to know if there was even the tiniest possibility that as he walked around the cobbled streets of Paris, a French person might spot him and say, 'Isn't that Andy Dawson? From that unknown subtitled English game show that only ran for eight episodes?', despite the fact he'd never been recognized in his home country. He needed to have hope that this could happen, more than he needed to take in the beauty and history of the famous ancient Greek sculpture that was right in front of him. More than he needed to hold the hand of the woman he was in love with, who was standing right next to him.

And let's say Andy had been recognized, in England and Paris and all over the world. Let's say the best-case scenario happened – that he fronted beloved comedy game shows and wrote award-winning sitcoms and did sell-out tours and made lots of money and gained the following and credibility he longed for. Let's say that happened. Would it make our life any easier? Would Andy's insecurities disappear? Would he stop thinking about himself? Would he put all his energy into being content with what he had, rather than yearning for the past and longing for something else in the future?

Or would it actually get worse?

And it was there, in front of the Venus de Milo, that I realized: I don't think I'm cut out to support a male artist. And I'm certainly not cut out to have a family with one. That, irrespective of where Andy's career might go, I would spend my life with a man who was so in need of affirmation from strangers that he stood on stage every night, even when he wasn't being paid, even when he was needed at home, because he wanted them to find him funny. Because he wanted them to love him.

There was nothing wrong with Andy and there was nothing wrong with the choices he'd made. He could make a woman very, very happy. But I knew then that she wasn't me.

He'd noticed I hadn't been myself over the last few weeks and he'd kept asking me what was wrong. It was torture because he was my best friend and I told him everything. But I couldn't tell him this, because the minute I said it out loud I knew we couldn't come back from it. *I don't know if we're right for each other, I don't want your children, I don't want anyone's children, I don't know if I want to be someone's girlfriend.* That would be it. The End.

So I'd lied and I told him I was stressed out with work, which was also true. Every time we went out I drank too much to silence all my inner turmoil and make the evening pass quicker. Every time we had sex I wanted to cry afterwards because I wondered whether it would be the last time and I hated that he had no idea I was having these thoughts. Every time we had sex I was reminded of how well this person knew me, how comfortable I felt with him and how purely and straightforwardly he loved me.

By the time we got to Paris, I felt like our break-up was always on the tip of my tongue. I was nervous to get drunk or have sex or have any conversation about anything, worrying that I would blurt it out. I couldn't break up with him in Paris. I couldn't tarnish that city for both of us with the memory of our break-up. I just had to get through the trip and then I'd talk to him about it when we got home. I'd practised the break-up with my therapist. We'd talked about it for months. She never told me to break up with him, but when she asked me why I would stay with him, I said, 'I'm worried about being alone and missing him,' and she told me that it wasn't a good idea to stay with someone for reasons of fear.

We stepped into our flat when we got back and I put the kettle on while Andy unpacked his bag. I thought about unpacking mine – taking all the items out and putting them away, as if I wasn't thinking about when I was going to pack them up again. I couldn't pretend any more. I couldn't do pretend unpacking and pretend tea drinking. I let the kettle boil and walked into our bedroom and told Andy I wanted to talk.

I understand now that I handled it badly. By the time I broke up with Andy, I'd been planning it for months without even realizing it. My subconscious had put him on a probation period, collecting reasons to end his contract without my knowledge. Incidents that were insignificant to him were weighty to me.

When I tried to explain why I had doubts about whether we should be together, he felt like he hadn't been given a fair chance to prove himself. I told him he shouldn't have to prove himself in a relationship, he should be allowed to just be himself. He asked why him being himself was not enough. I didn't have an answer for him, because I didn't know.

He grew frustrated with me, then angry, then despairing. We both cried, we held each other. We shouted at each other. It was the worst night of my life, but I was relieved to have finally let him in on the truth. I didn't have to lie to someone I loved any more. I left with my bag and went to my sister's. I couldn't go to Avi and Jane's because they were too involved in our relationship, and I wanted Andy to have someone to go talk to about the break-up without worrying I would be there. My sister said I could stay indefinitely.

My family were surprisingly upset by the news. It turned out that, in my mum's eyes, a skint comedian who she didn't like was a better prospect for a nearly thirty-five-year-old woman than no boyfriend at all. My dad said he was 'a nice man, for all his faults'. My brothers said they thought he was 'a laugh'. My sister unleashed all her long-held theories about the dysfunctionality of our relationship.

'It was *trauma bonding*, Jen,' she said exasperatedly in those first few weeks whenever she had the chance. 'He had a missing dad, we had a missing dad. You were trying to heal together. That cannot be the basis of a relationship.'

Once Andy had told Avi about the break-up, he moved in with them while he looked for a new place. Which meant I couldn't escape to their place whenever it became too much at Miranda's. I appreciated her putting me up while I waited for the tenants in my place to vacate, but being around a baby and two new parents in a small flat was not the best way to process a break-up. In a truly sisterly move, Jane promised that she would tell me everything I needed to know about Andy. I told her only to pass on the big headlines – if he was in trouble, if he had a new girlfriend, when he had moved out and where he was going. Otherwise, she didn't need to tell me anything.

With Andy's permission, I wrote a letter to his mum telling her how much I had enjoyed getting to know her and that I wished her all the best. She rang me to thank me for it and said she'd loved getting to know me too. She asked me what my plans were and I told her I wasn't really sure. I told her that I'd never thought I'd have to plan for being alone at thirty-five.

'I love my son,' she said. 'And I don't say this as his mum, I say it as a woman who's got twenty-six years on you. Everything you want to do in your life, you can do without a man, Jen.'

'What about children?' I asked.

There was a long pause.

'I could never regret having my son. His existence in the world is the best thing I will leave in it when it's my time to go.'

'I know,' I assured her.

Another long pause.

'But do I ever think about what my life would have been like had I been brave enough to not become a mother? Had I been brave enough to even imagine what that life could have been like?'

'Do you?' I asked, checking she was still on the line.

'I think about it all the time,' she said.

We said goodbye, knowing that was most likely the last time we would ever speak to each other.

I missed him and our life together, while also knowing it was right that we'd ended. I felt guilty for how it had ended. I worried about him, checked up on his social media accounts obsessively and asked Jane how he was, even when I knew she was sick of feeling like a go-between. I texted Avi and asked him to keep an eye on Andy, because I knew he would never have asked any of his friends for help. I developed insomnia and, luckily, many of my friends were breastfeeding and were also up late at night so would text me. My sister gave me an unhelpful book about the record number of women refusing to get married in Japan.

I tried to remember what I thought my life was going to be like without him. I'd had no idea what this was going to feel like, and it turned out to be just as bad as being in the wrong relationship.

I went back to the psychic without telling anyone, and spent the entire hour asking about Andy. I wanted to know if he'd find love and have children. I wanted to know if any of his dead relatives wanted to speak to me. I asked her if he was going to be okay and she took a pendulum out of a velvet pouch, held it in front of her, closed her eyes and asked someone unnamed if Andy was going to be okay. The pendulum moved very slightly in no distinguishable direction.

'Ah,' she said. 'He will be. But not for a while.' She put the pendulum back in its pouch, satisfied with this answer. At the end of the reading, she said that perhaps the best way to get in touch with my ex was not via the spirits of his grandparents but by picking up the phone. When a psychic is giving you this advice, you know you've really lost it.

All of this is an explanation and not an excuse for why I chose to catfish Andy in that first month after we ended. I know it is inexcusable and I still can't believe I did it. No one can ever find out that one Sunday afternoon I set up an email address and then an Instagram account for a woman called Tash; that I sourced all her Instagram posts from strangers' social media profiles which I posted over the course of a week to make it seem like a believable account. I followed a few celebrities who I believed Tash would admire, plus a few randomly selected strangers with open

327

profiles who I chose as her friends and colleagues. I followed Andy but didn't message him – always on the brink of deleting the profile out of shame. Until I went away with Jane and some other friends for a spa weekend.

They'd planned it to cheer me up and, because Jane organized childcare for the boys, Avi thought he'd make the most of a free weekend and take Andy for a big night out. It was strange to think of the two of us going through this rite of passage together, our friends rallying around us and acknowledging the break-up with a kind of ceremony, like a reverse hen and stag do. The girls gave me a limitless amount of time to talk about Andy, and I was reminded of how lucky I am to have them. I talked then they talked – they offered their insights and advice and stories of comparison. The more we talked, the better I felt. In the same way our group of friends dealt with every crisis, I was going to talk my way back to sanity with them. Sleepy from all the wine and talking and lounging around, we went to bed early after dinner. I was sharing a room with Jane, which we hadn't done in years, and as we giggled our way to sleep in the dark delirium of lights-out, I was reassured to know that the cosy sleepover feeling of this kind of friendship never disappears. Not even when one of you is a mother-of-two advertising executive and the other is a senior partner of an insurance company.

We were woken up at four in the morning. It was Avi ringing Jane's mobile. As she got out of bed to answer it, she muttered to herself:

'If that motherfucker is waking me up for no reason when I can have my first fucking lie-in for three-and-a-half fucking years –' She picked up the phone. 'WHAT?'

I rubbed my eyes as they acclimatized to the shapes of the room in the dark.

'Okay . . . okay . . . Did you put him in the shower? . . .

'Okay . . . And have you given him water? . . . Fine . . . sleep in the bed with him . . . Oh Avi, grow up . . . No . . . no, he's not going to die . . . Put a bucket by the bed . . . Don't call me again until the morning, okay? Okay. Goodnight.' She sighed and put the phone down.

'What's happened?' I croaked.

'Andy drank too much and Avi's also off his head and panicking.'

'What?' I sat upright in bed. 'Is he okay? Do you think you should drive us back?'

'No, Jen, he's not your boyfriend any more,' Jane said, getting back into bed.

'But what if something happens to him?' I asked, feeling somehow responsible for the state that he'd got himself in.

'Nothing's going to happen to him,' she said. 'He'll be fine.'

The next morning I crept out of the room early so Jane could sleep in and I rang Avi. I paced around the gardens of the hotel in my pyjamas, smoking a cigarette while Avi told me he'd stayed in the same bed as Andy to make sure he was okay. He said that he wasn't going to tell him what had happened.

'Why wouldn't you tell him?' I asked.

'Because it would embarrass him, it will make it worse,' he said.

'Don't you think it could be a wake-up call?' I pleaded. 'Help him realize he's not dealing with this very well?'

'No, Jen,' he said firmly. 'He won't have any memory of it and the kind thing to do is to pretend it never happened. It's not a big deal.'

'I'm going to call him,' I said.

'I don't think that's a good idea,' he said. 'He needs to move on.'

So that's when Tash decided to message him. I don't know what the desired outcome was. Initially, I just wanted to find out if he was okay. Like the psychic, it was another way of checking up on him without making myself known. I wanted Tash to be his friend, while his real friends were failing to support him in the way I hoped they would. I had to keep on top of my Tash voice, making her bland enough to be unidentifiable, while engaging enough that he'd want to keep talking to her. I enjoyed how he flirted with Tash – there was so little fun at the end of our relationship, I'd forgotten how charming Andy could be and how lovely it was to have his attention on you. But as comforting as it was to have Andy back in my life in a once-removed way, I was soon overwhelmed with guilt about my deceit. I started to wind our communication down when I could sense how eager he was to meet up with Tash. I established that he was fine and getting on with his life, albeit inexplicably living on a canal boat. I deleted her account.

My thirty-fifth birthday came round and I didn't want to celebrate. I was still living out of a suitcase and sleeping on a blow-up bed at Miranda's and I didn't feel like my normal self. Jane and my sister tried to organize a casual week-day dinner to mark the occasion, but Miranda was still nursing and couldn't be away from the baby and Jane was pregnant and permanently exhausted. I was happy to pick up a takeaway on the way home and watch a film.

I was presented with a birthday cake at work and, as I cut the cake and handed out slices on napkins to people in the company who I spoke to twice a year, Seb asked me how I was going to celebrate. He'd arrived about a year before, sending gossip and excitement around the office with his good looks that gave him the air of a retired underwear model. I liked him, always chatting with him when we found ourselves in the same lift or meeting room. I told him that I was lying low this year and didn't have any plans, and he asked if he could take me for a drink at the pub around the corner after work.

I once heard a theory about the first relationship that occurs after a big relationship ends. It's called the 90/10 rule. The theory goes: whatever the crucial 10 per cent is that was missing from your partner who was otherwise totally right for you is the thing you look for in the following person. That missing 10 per cent becomes such a fixation that, when you do find someone who has it, you ignore the fact they don't have the other 90 per cent that the previous partner had.

I think that's what happened with me and Seb.

As he sat opposite me in the pub, assertive and confident, telling me about his career and his past relationships and all the travelling he'd done, I thought: *This is an adult.* This is what was missing with Andy. I wanted an adult. Someone self-assured and self-reliant. Someone who didn't need me. We drank until last orders, then I went back to his extremely grown-up house with a wine fridge and underfloor heating in the bathroom. And I woke up there the next morning.

When Andy texted me the next day, on my actual birthday, with a message so overwrought and eager to please, I felt like I'd cheated on him. This feeling continued every time I saw Seb. When we had sex, I could only think of Andy. When we went out together, I only chose places where I knew we wouldn't bump into him. It was too soon for me to move on to someone else, but my relationship muscles were warmed up and, as we continued to see each other with a regularity that could be nothing else but 'dating', it felt strangely easy. I was in the habit of thinking of someone else.

When I saw Andy at the bank, I could feel how nervous he was to see me, which made me feel even more guilty. When he accused me of lying to him, I lashed out, because I hated being villainized and because I knew I was the villain. Then the call came from Jane that he was seeing someone. I had no right to feel hurt by this, particularly when Andy had had to go through the excruciating ordeal of bumping into me and Seb and had been so gracious about it. I asked Jane for her full name and she dutifully gave it to me, having already done some sniffing around on my behalf. When I went to look on her Instagram page, I saw that she'd blocked me. How did she even know who I was?

'She was obviously going on your page too much,' Jane advised. 'Take it as a weird sort of compliment.' A few days later, Andy blocked me too.

It was what I deserved, but I still couldn't stop myself from trying to find out more information about them. Which is how I ended up on Andy's Spotify page, discovering that he'd made a Spotify playlist titled 'S' and that one of the songs on that playlist was 'Cigarettes and Coffee' by Otis Redding. A song that soundtracked nearly four years of our relationship, repurposed for a twenty-three-year-old who he'd met a handful of weeks ago. That was when I really started going mad. I couldn't stop imagining how they were together: whether he made her weekly mixes like he did for me at the beginning; whether he kissed her armpit the first morning he woke up with her. Was the way Andy loved me actually nothing to do with me, and instead just the Andy Experience a woman gets when he chooses her?

Jane suggested I do 'a digital detox'.

I ended things with Seb shortly after that. The 10 per cent had made a strong case, but it wasn't enough to sustain anything beyond the short-term. And I clearly hadn't let go of the 90 per cent of Andy that I'd fallen in love with. I made a decision to avoid men for a while. Seb was understanding and told me he suspected that it was too soon for me to start seeing someone. He promised not to make it awkward in the office – a grown-up to the very end.

★

When I saw Andy at Jackson's birthday, all I could be was myself. I had no energy for anything else. I didn't have any information to find out, any secrets to keep from him, any residual resentment from those last months of our relationship. It just felt so good to see my friend.

He looked very different. Jane had warned me he'd lost a lot of weight, but I was still surprised to see how jacked-up and hollowed-out he was. I preferred how he looked before. Everyone I knew had said the same.

I never thought we'd end up having the night we did and I should have done more to stop it. I followed all my instincts and all of them felt so good, right up until the point when we turned off the light to fall asleep next to each other. Until that moment, each question I had could be answered. What if we get drunk? We kiss. What if we kiss? We go home together. What if we go home together? We have sex. What if we have sex?

I didn't know. Everything had felt so natural and right. And then the lights were out, I was lying next to a man I loved but couldn't be with, and I was back in the same place I'd got to six months ago. I'd reached the same dead end.

I pretended to sleep but I lay awake all night, thinking of all the different ways Andy and I could try to make it work while knowing that the same problems would return. I couldn't trap myself back in a relationship that was so painful to leave. When we woke up together, I could do nothing to hide my confusion and guilt and sadness, and I wanted him to leave for no other reason than how desperately I needed to be alone. I closed the door on him and went back up to my flat. I couldn't get further than the hallway before I sank to my knees, lay on my side and sobbed like I hadn't sobbed since I was a child.

Jane told me that Andy had gone back to his mum's for a bit. I didn't try to contact him. I spent a lot of time at Avi and Jane's and they were kind enough to let me stay over whenever I went round for dinner. We pretended it was because the journey back to my flat was too far to go late at night, but really we all knew it was because I didn't want to be alone. I thought a lot about being alone. On one of those nights, after the boys were in bed, Jane and I stayed up late talking at the kitchen table and I asked her if she was worried I would end up by myself.

'Jen,' she said, taking my hand in both of hers. 'You've always been alone, my darling. That's one of the things that makes you so unique. You were alone when I met you, you're alone in a crowd of people, you were alone when you were with Andy.'

I hugged her and buried my face in her dark hair like a comfort blanket, feeling so grateful that I have this person in my life who sees me more clearly than I can see myself.

'Jesus fucking Christ, don't have a kid or get married because you're worried about being alone,' she said, rubbing my back. I sat upright in my chair and she held me by my shoulders. 'Be alone, Jen. You know how to be alone without being lonely. Do you know how rare that is? Do you know how much I wish I could do that? It's a wonderful thing you've got going on there.'

Avi came into the kitchen and put the kettle on. He rubbed his eyes and put a herbal teabag in a mug.

'Knackered, I am,' he said.

'Have you been working?' Jane asked.

'I've been at my computer all night doing a favour for that ex-boyfriend of yours.'

'What favour?' I asked.

'He's writing some fake letter for that weird old landlord. Apparently he'll be made up about it. But he needed the headed paper logo to be perfect so the fella wouldn't suspect anything.'

'That sounds like a very nice thing for him to do,' I said.

'Yeah,' Avi sighed, pouring water into the mug. 'Well. He's a nice guy.'

We exchanged a smile and he went upstairs to bed.

I handed in my notice on Monday 6th January, the first day back at work after Christmas. They offered me more money, more responsibility and more benefits to stay. I said no. I booked a single ticket to Cartagena for Monday 30th March, exactly twelve weeks from that date. I put my flat on the market for a year-long rental. I'd start in South America and see where I ended up.

Andy rang me in the middle of January. We hadn't spoken since the morning he left my flat and I was surprised to see his name appear on my phone. His voice was careful and reverent, which immediately made me nervous. He told me that he'd written a show about our break-up that he wanted to take to Edinburgh and then tour next year.

'No,' I said instantly. 'No way.'

'Jen – it's not about you, it's about me. It's about how crazy I went in our break-up. All the jokes are on me, not on you.'

'If it's about our break-up then it's about me,' I said. 'No, I'm sorry.'

He went on to tell me that he knew this would be the thing to kick-start his career again; that it was the best writing he'd ever done. His tone took on a slightly threatening edge, implying that if I stood in the way of this show then I would be standing in the way of his success. All the frustration I felt in our relationship came rushing back to me and I was angry that the responsibility for his happiness had once again fallen on to me; that I was supposed to shelve my feelings to support him. I said something embarrassing about 'hearing from my lawyer' and ended the call, only realizing when I hung up that I had just given him another funny story for the show.

I went round to Avi and Jane's to try to rally their support, but I was shocked to find they were on his side. They pointed out that he was finally doing what I'd always wanted him to do when we were together. He was pushing himself. He was being brave.

'What are you worried about?' Jane asked.

'That he's going to talk about our sex life on stage,' I said. 'Or that he's going to make me out to be the bad guy, or say nasty things about my family.'

'Does that sound like something Andy would do?' she asked.

I thought about this.

'No,' I said.

'Go to the show,' she said. 'He's said he won't keep anything in that upsets you. I'll come with you.'

There's a fold-out board by the door. ANDY DAWSON WORK IN PROGRESS reads the headline. 'Why Elephants Cry' is the title, 'One man's journey into The Madness' in smaller lettering underneath. I haven't been here before – it's a theatre space above a pub that I often heard Andy talk about. I only recognize a few people – some of his comedy friends and his agent – but I keep my head down anyway. I've worn a roll-neck jumper specifically so I can sink my face into it if needs be. Jane and I take a seat third row from the front. I haven't told him I will be here, in case he censored the script for me. I want to see what everyone else is going to see.

'You okay?' Jane whispers. I nod. 'It's going to be fine.'

'Okay,' I whisper back, unconvinced.

'And if it's not, apparently the world's going to end before anyone gets to see it anyway,' she says, pointing at the front page of her copy of the *Evening Standard* that says, with the comic certainty of a disaster movie: KILLER VIRUS NOW 'SPREADING FAST'. We laugh and she squeezes my hand.

'Love Will Tear Us Apart' by Joy Division plays. Andy walks on stage to applause. He looks like himself again – soft around the edges, accidentally handsome.

'Europe has left me and so has my girlfriend,' he announces. 'Terrible.' He shakes his head. 'Absolutely terrible. Please don't leave just yet. This is a work in progress and,' he adopts an exaggerated therapy voice, 'as I've learnt in the last six months, so am I.'

He talks about the trip to Paris and how he hadn't seen our break-up coming. He reads aloud a list he made of all the reasons why he thinks I might have broken up with him, including the fact he's balding at the back and he leaves his wet washing in the machine for too long. He describes going home to his mum's house and the strange month that followed – befriending local drunks in eleven a.m. pub sessions, ringing his first girlfriend and trying to organize a meet-up, buying every bottle of my perfume in the local Boots and throwing them in the canal so there were a few less chances of being reminded of me (surely this story was made up or at least exaggerated?).

He talks about bumping into me and Seb, 'a truly preposterous-looking man', and how it made him even more hell-bent on working out why I broke up with him. He talks about setting up a fake email address and pretending to be a man named Clifford and having a therapy session where he imagines what I may have said about him to my therapist when we were together, in the hope of understanding why we ended (again, I can't believe this isn't exaggerated for comic effect, but I hope it's true because it makes me feel better about the whole Tash thing).

Throughout the hour, he reads passages from a book his mum gave him about the science of heartbreak and relates it back to examples of how he processed our break-up. The last section he reads is about how elephants grieve.

'If this were a previous show of mine, it's at this point I would say that elephants and I have more in common than just a large trunk, but I won't,' he says as he gets a laugh. 'I won't say that. Because I'm trying something different, ladies and gentlemen.' He puts the book down. 'I think, if I try to make sense of the madness of the last six months, I could say that I've been doing what the elephants do. I've been scattering the bones of us and who we were together. Reading all our old messages, throwing bottles of discounted Armani She into a canal, trying to recreate our memories, standing on stage and talking to you. It's a weird kind of mourning and a weird kind of celebration, to examine the skeleton of something that was once so magnificent, before you scatter all the fragments of it out into the world to say goodbye.'

He finishes with a long and delicately worded email he received from the therapist in which she says she isn't sure whether she can be of any help to Clifford. She suggests that he is fixated on his girlfriend's career because he is feeling lost in his own, and gives him a number for a career coach.

'I can see your side of the story as well as Alice's,' she concludes. 'And I wish you both all the best.' He uses it as an example of the perfect way to break up with someone. It is an unexpected ending, undercutting the sincerity of the penultimate section perfectly. When he takes his bow, the whole audience is on its feet, cheering and clapping. Our eyes meet, very briefly.

I order a vodka tonic for myself and a pint of Andy's favourite IPA. Andy walks out into the bar and is greeted by a few cheers from his friends. He comes straight over to me. Jane immediately envelops him in a hug and congratulates him. She tells him how excited Avi is to see it tomorrow night and apologizes for rushing off, but says she has an early start in the morning. She leaves and I pass Andy his drink. He takes a deep breath.

'What did you think?' he asks.

'I thought it was really great, Andy,' I say.

He drops his head on to the bar and gently bangs his fist.

'Really?' he says, standing up straight and looking at me pleadingly. 'Because you're the only person whose opinion I care about with this.'

'I loved it,' I say. 'I really didn't think I would, but I did.'

'Any notes?'

'Yes,' I say. 'But nothing to do with me. Just a few thoughts I have on the show generally.'

'What kind of stuff? Timing?'

'Yes,' I say. 'You spend too long on some bits and not long enough on others.'

'Could you send them to me?'

'Of course,' I say.

'I miss your notes,' he says.

'I don't remember you being too receptive to them when we were together,' I say.

'I know. I regret that. I regret a lot of things, as you've probably gathered from the last hour.'

'Some people write a letter,' I say.

'Why waste good material?' he says.

Emery approaches, his mass of hair stuffed under a backwards cap.

'My boy,' he says, putting his arm around Andy. 'And the muse!' he shouts, going in to kiss me on the cheek. 'She's here!'

'Hey, Emery,' I say as plainly as possible. I've always had such a big crush on him.

'You,' he says, holding Andy by the arms and shaking him. 'You. Are a genius. I knew you had this in you.'

'Yeah?' Andy asks shyly, clearly delighted to have his approval.

'It was –' he exhales, trying to find the right words – 'painful. Truthful. Unbearable at points. Fucking funny. You should be

339

so proud of yourself. And YOU,' he says, turning to me. 'Thank you for ruining his life. What a gift this woman gave you, Andy.'

'All right, all right,' Andy says, laughing, wriggling out of his grasp. 'Are you staying for a drink?'

'Yes, of course, I'll be over there,' he says. He takes Andy's face in his hand and kisses his forehead. 'Clever boy.' He walks off, lifting his cap and running his hand through his curly mane as he goes.

'One day that guy's going to come out of his shell,' Andy sighs. I laugh. 'So you really liked it?'

'*Like* is the wrong word,' I say. 'I hated hearing parts of it. But I think it will be a truly brilliant piece of work. It's the best thing you've ever done.'

'I'm glad you think so.'

I make small circles with my glass, watching the ice cubes clink, avoiding Andy's eyes.

'I went mad too, you know,' I say, looking up at him.

'Did you?'

'Oh yeah.'

'You should tell me about it,' he says. 'Not now,' he corrects himself. 'But one day.'

'One day,' I repeat, and we both smile. 'One day when we're ready to be friends or something.'

'Yes,' he says. 'Or something.'

'Good,' I say.

There's a pause.

'I can't *wait* for that day,' he says.

We smile again, understanding something that only the two of us will ever understand. His agent comes over and we're forced to break eye contact.

'Andy,' she says. 'Rock star. Absolute fucking rock star.'

I look back into my drink to stop myself from laughing, knowing how much he hates it when she calls him this.

'I couldn't believe what I was watching,' she goes on. 'It's so unexpected! Edinburgh is just the beginning for this. We've got a real hit on our hands. I've got promoters here who want to meet you, I've got a couple of people from the big Edinburgh venues. I've got a director here and he wants to talk to you about working together –' She looks at me apologetically. 'Do you mind if I steal him?'

'You steal him,' I say.

'Give me one minute,' he says.

She pats him on the arm. '*Rock star*,' she hisses excitedly.

Andy turns back to me and rolls his eyes.

'I should let you go,' I say.

'Jane told me you've quit your job,' he says. 'And that you're going travelling.'

'Yes,' I say.

'How long for?'

'A year, to begin with,' I say. 'My savings will run out before that. And then I'll work it out from there. Maybe try to get a job abroad. I don't have a plan. For the first time ever.'

His eyes flicker across my face, like he's reading something on it.

'You really did want to be on your own,' he says.

'I wasn't lying.'

'No,' he says. 'I understand that now.'

He opens his arms and we hug. I wish him luck for all the shows in the run-up to Edinburgh and we say that we'll keep in touch, even though we know that we won't. We hold each other for a while, then we say goodbye. As I leave the pub, I look back to see him sitting down to talk to everyone who wanted to talk to him. I turn on to a street I don't know and make my way home alone.

Acknowledgements

Thank you to my editors, Juliet Annan and Helen Garnons-Williams. This book took a leap of faith from both of you and I'm grateful that you trusted me and encouraged me to challenge myself. Thank you for your instincts, clarity and precision. Thank you for working so hard to make this story the best version it could be. I'm sorry about all those awful titles I suggested.

My life changed when I met Clare Conville ten years ago and told her about a truly terrible non-fiction book I was writing called How To Survive Your Twenties (I was 25 at the time). Thank you for reading it and telling me it wouldn't get published but that you thought I should write fiction one day. Thank you for your professional guidance and constant friendship.

Thank you to my team at Penguin who edit, design, sell and represent my books with such talent, thought and care. Emma Ewbank, Jon Gray, Natalie Wall, Ella Harold, Sara Granger, Karen Whitlock, Poppy North, Jane Gentle, Georgia Taylor, Annie Moore, Autumn Evans, Samantha Fanaken, Kyla Dean, Ruth Johnstone, Eleanor Rhodes-Davies, Meredith Benson, Laura Ricchetti and Alison Pearse.

Jenny Jackson, Anna Stein, Mary Gaule, Jonathan Burnham, Sarah New, Reagan Arthur, Amy Hagedown, Bhavna Chauhan, Amy Black, Kristin Cochrane, Val Gow, Kaitlin Smith and Maria Golikova – thank you for being my cheerleaders the other side of the Atlantic.

Nora Ephron wrote the greatest film and the most believable male character of all time because she interviewed her friend and director Rob Reiner for research. I always knew I would copy her when I attempted to inhabit the voice of a male narrator. So, the most sincere gratitude to my own Rob Reiners for the twenty hours of conversations in research for forming Andy: Tom Bird, Ed Cripps, Joel Golby, Gavin Day, Ivo Graham, Sami El-Hadi, Ross Montgomery, David Nicholls, Max Lintott, Ed Cumming, Nick Lowe, Jack Spencer Ashworth and Simon Maloney. Thank you for your honesty and trust. You'd all be too embarrassed to hear me say this to your face: I couldn't have written Andy, or his friends, or this book, without you.

Thank you to Ivo Graham for replying to my texts in the dead of night with all those questions about Colchester's comedy scene. I'm so glad that your work is in the world, and I'm even more glad that we're friends.

Thank you to Joel Golby, my first reader, whose notes were in equal parts supportive and instructive. I'm grateful for all your feedback over the years and only the mildest of piss-taking while doing so. I know that must be hard for you.

Phil Dunlop – thanks for letting me steal that joke. It's on page 75, it's the best one in the book.

Sienna and Zadie – I would not be able to write children or children's dialogue if it were not for you two. You are too young to read this book, but I want to thank you anyway. For the brilliant and weird things you say and do – for helping me remember how young minds work. I love you, and I love your mums for bringing you into my life. You can borrow all of my handbags.

Thank you to Elizabeth Day for giving me life advice that I can directly repurpose into a speech for a script or a novel and which inevitably becomes everyone's favourite bit.

Thank you to those who provided information as part of my research – Peach Everard, Millie Jones, Sofie Dodgson, Ailah Ahmed, Chris Floyd, Jon Watson and Surian Fletcher-Jones.

I spend most of my life texting three writers in an all-day back-and-forth about names, jokes, sex scenes, characters and titles – Caroline O'Donoghue, Monica Heisey and Lauren Bensted. This job would be far lonelier without you. Thank you Lauren for helping me with that scene I couldn't fix the night before my deadline. Thank you Monica for staying up until four a.m. to read it from cover to cover and sending me photos of your favourite pages. Thank you Caroline for coming up with the title (I'm sorry I didn't change Andy's name to Michael and call it *Open Michael* as per your suggestion). Thank you, all three of you, for treating your friends' writing projects like they're new lovers, and always being so genuinely excited to meet them.

Thank you to Lena Dunham and Richard E. Grant for their early enthusiasm and support for this book – a sentence I can't believe I'm lucky enough to write.

I lived with my mum and dad for a few months when I was writing *Good Material*. Like Andy's mum, they are the best of people and the kindest of parents. Thank you for looking after me when I was on a deadline; for giving me space and love and too much tea.

Thank you always to my brother Ben, a boy I'll never understand and always love. I hope this book makes you laugh.

Finally: the big one. The thanks for which a surplus of adjectives (uncharacteristically) fails me. My best female friends – thank you for always giving me my very best material. Thank you for all the talking and all the listening. But mostly, thank you for the times you have guided me through heartbreak. When I've been lost in a landscape of longing – confused, hopeless and wild – thank you for leading me through to the other side of the madness. I don't know how I would have done it without you.

Permissions

The publisher is grateful for permission to use the following:

On p. vi, 'A Scattering' by Christopher Reid. Published by Arete Books, 2009. Copyright © Christopher Reid. Reproduced by permission of the author c/o Rogers, Coleridge & White Ltd., 20 Powis Mews, London W11 1JN.

On p. 39, lyrics from Faith, Words and Music by Justin Vernon, Brandon Burton, Camilla Staveley-Taylor and Francis Farewell Starlite. Copyright © 2019 April Base Publishing, Brought To You By Heavy Duty and BMG Rights Management (UK) Ltd. All Rights for April Base Publishing and Brought To You By Heavy Duty Administered Worldwide by Kobalt Music Publishing Ltd. All Rights for BMG Rights Management (UK) Ltd. Administered by BMG Rights Management (US) LLC. All Rights Reserved Used by Permission. Reprinted by Permission of Hal Leonard Europe Ltd.

On p. 184, lyrics from Mr. Brightside, Words and Music by Brandon Flowers, Dave Keuning, Mark Stoermer and Ronnie Vannucci Copyright © 2004 UNIVERSAL MUSIC PUBLISHING LTD. All Rights in the United States and Canada Controlled and Administered by UNIVERSAL – POLYGRAM INTERNATIONAL PUBLISHING, INC. All Rights Reserved Used by Permission. Reprinted by Permission of Hal Leonard Europe Ltd.